WITCHSHADOW

WITCHSHADOW

Susan Dennard

**TOR
TEEN**

A TOM DOHERTY ASSOCIATES BOOK

New York

WITCHSHADOW

Copyright © 2021 by Susan Dennard

A Tor Teen Book
Published by Tom Doherty Associates
120 Broadway
New York, NY 10271

www.tor-forge.com

Tor® is a registered trademark of Macmillan Publishing Group, LLC.

Library of Congress Cataloging-in-Publication Data

Names: Dennard, Susn, author.
Title: Witchshadow / Susan Dennard.
Description: First edition. | New York : Tor Teen, 2021. |
Series: The Witchlands ; 4 | "A Tom Doherty Associates book"
Identifiers: LCCN 2021010722 (print) | LCCN 2021010723 (ebook) |
ISBN 9780765379344 (hardcover) | ISBN 9781466867352 (ebook)
Subjects: CYAC: Fantasy. | Magic—Fiction. | Witches—Fiction.
Classification: LCC PZ7.D42492 Wit 2021 (print) |
LCC PZ7.D42492 (ebook) | DDC [Fic]—dc23
LC record available at https://lccn.loc.gov/2021010722
LC ebook record available at https://lccn.loc.gov/2021010723

Our books may be purchased in bulk for promotional, educational,
or business use. Please contact your local bookseller or the Macmillan Corporate
and Premium Sales Department at 1-800-221-7945, extension 5442,
or by email at MacmillanSpecialMarkets@macmillan.com.

First Edition: June 2021

Printed in the United States of America

0 9 8 7 6 5 4 3 2 1

FOR CRICKET,

who taught me what motherhood means

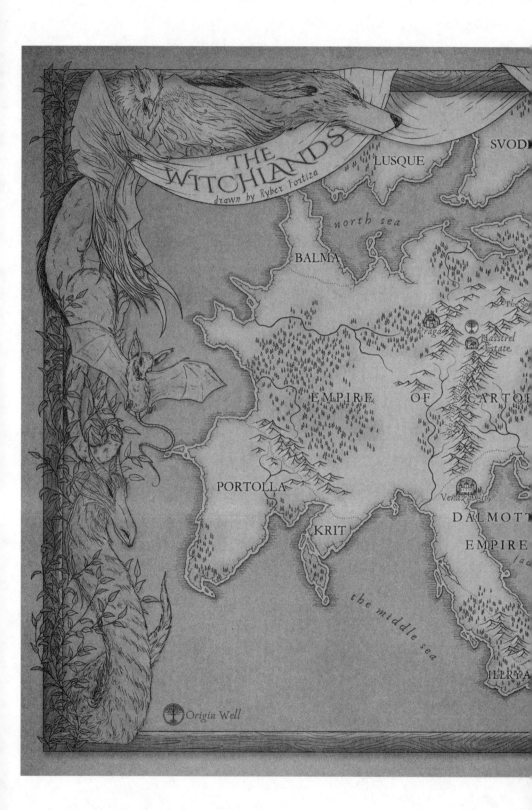

THE
WITCHLANDS
drawn by Ryber Fortiza

SVOD

LUSQUE

north sea

BALMA

The So

Praga

Hasstrel
Estate

EMPIRE   OF   CARTOR

PORTOLLA

Venaza City

DALMOTT

KRIT

EMPIRE

jad

the middle sea

ILLRYA

Origin Well

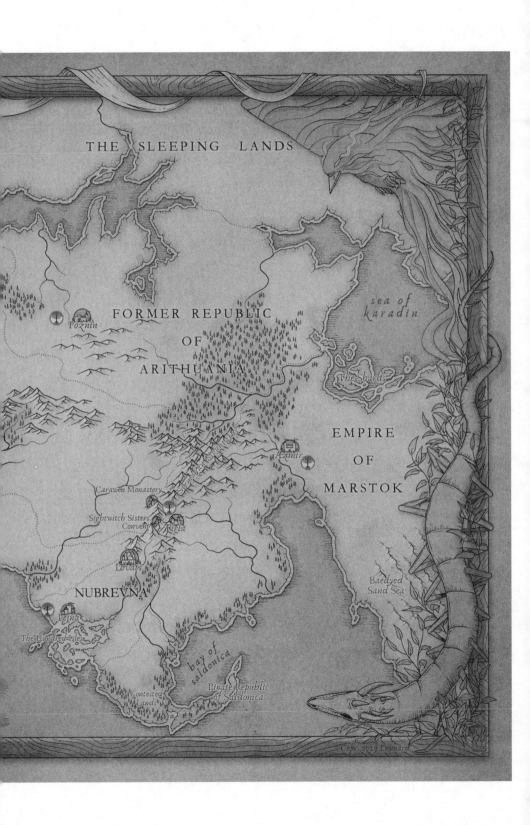

Stones in motion,
Tools cleft in two.
The wyrm fell to the daughter made of moonlight long ago,
He just did not know it yet.
                    —from "Eridysi's Lament"

WITCHSHADOW

For a recap of the Witchlands series,
head here:
SusanDennard.com/recap/

BEGINNINGS

✳

The Rook watches from an oak branch.

His feathers rustle. His beak clacks. It has been a long time since he saw the Sun and the Moon come together.

It has been even longer since he saw them heal a Well.

A hundred people attend, arranged in stiff rows around the wide pond. Some have weapons, most have uniforms, and all have bored scowls. Behind them, long-dormant beech trees stand sentry. Six—always six.

Snow fell in the night, a light dusting that has turned the pine forest to fragile white. But it never touches the Well, nor the mossy flagstones surrounding it, nor the beech trees waiting to come alive.

The people call the Sun "Domna." They call the Moon nothing at all. Both girls wear matching brown shifts that come to their knees, but this is where their likeness ends. The Sun, with her golden hair, is annoyed and does not try to hide it; the Moon, with her black hair, is impassive, all her feelings and thoughts kept tucked away behind lucent nothing.

They remind the Rook of someone he knew long ago. Someone who broke the world just to make it new again.

Both girls are clearly cold. Both shiver and bounce, breaths fogging. A stone overhang lurches above the Well, blocking what little light the true sun gleans at this early hour. The girls are trapped in shadow.

When at last a round man with furs nods for them to begin, they do not hesitate. A single glance passes between them, a hint of a smile on the Sun's face, then, hand in hand, the Sun and Moon dive into the cold, dark Well.

Soon, all that is visible are their legs, flashes of pale skin that wink beneath fresh-churned froth. A flicker of pale hands, a shimmer of toes. Then they vanish entirely, swallowed by the Well.

Several moments pass before a graceful man with hair the color of sunrise begins to prowl along the Well's southern edge. Back and forth, back and forth, always staring into the depths with an intensity no one can match, not even the Rook. The rotund man snaps at him to stop; the graceful man ignores him.

That one has never been good at listening.

Then it happens: a gentle boom, so subtle one might think it a trick of the mind. A heartbeat that has pulsed too long. A tremor in the muscles, not the earth.

But the Rook has seen this before. He has felt it before and watched as ripples tore out across a pond. Perfect, concentric rings to lap against a Well's rim.

The graceful man smiles.

Then a second boom breaks loose—strong enough to shake snow off the trees. Strong enough to rattle in the Rook's hollow bones. Suddenly, none of the people surrounding the Well are bored.

The graceful man cries out, a whoop of joy, and his arms fling wide. Triumphant. He twirls to face the other man. Yet as he turns, his eyes briefly catch on the Rook's. If he is surprised to see the bird, he does not show it.

"It is done," he declares, advancing on the round man. "The Well is healed."

The round man smiles. A slow thing that makes his dark eyes gleam—for as the Rook well knows, there are no creatures in the Witchlands as hungry as men.

"His Majesty will be pleased," the round man begins, but a splash steals the rest of his words. The girls have returned.

The Sun appears first. Initiate. The Moon follows next. Complete.

They both gasp for air, paddling clumsily for the Well's edge. Cold has leached color from their skin, save for a painful pink along their noses. Two uniformed guards await them with thick blankets. The Sun reaches the rim first, and after the guards haul her free, she turns back to help the Moon. Not because there aren't men to aid her too, but because this is who she is. Who they both are: inseparable and true.

And the Rook nods at that. Clacks his beak too, just for good measure. Everything has happened as it ought, and now it is time for him to leave. He has orders to follow and this detour here wasn't one of them.

But the Rook feels that he deserved to see the Sun and Moon united. A reward for all his centuries of devoted focus. After all, there are still pieces of humanity twinkling inside him. Tiny slivers that like chocolate and sweet jams.

And tiny slivers that like rewards for a job well done too.

With a flap of his glossy wings, the Rook bursts off the oak tree. The branch shakes, snow flutters, and soon the discussions of two men accustomed to power fade from the Rook's hearing.

PART I

Puppeteer

ONE

✳

One Month After the Earth Well Healed

She knew she was walking into a trap. She had seen their tracks twenty paces before, just beside that bend in the road, and she had sensed their Threads even sooner.

Maybe, if she had wanted to, she could have avoided them. But she didn't want to. She was hungry. Winter's cusp had left nothing to forage on this side of the Ohrins, and what little she had managed to gather she'd given to her tiny companion, now waiting in a hollowed-out beech with a weasel who wasn't really a weasel.

When she reached fifteen steps from the closest soldier, she stopped and planted her staff into the mud. It was roughly hewn silver fir, taken off a corpse two days before. Silver fir, the hill folk said, was good for warding off nightmares. So far that had not been true.

The closest man's Threads hovered green with concentration. He was poorly hidden behind an alpine rhododendron, and even if his Threads had not given him away, the footprints speckling the road would have. Muddy from yesterday's rain, the road had grooved so deep from travel it was practically a ditch—giving all these men in the forest brush higher ground.

Not that it would help them.

"I know you're there," she called.

As one, bright alarm punched across eight sets of Threads, each poorly hidden.

"And I have nothing of value," she continued. Her voice was rough with hunger and the world had been a sickening spin for days now. If not for their Threads, she would never have been able to focus on them.

Or on the one man, now stalking toward her down the path. A Hell-Bard. She didn't need to see his scarlet uniform to know that. The shadowy twirl at the heart of his Threads gave him away.

"We were warned about you," he declared, pausing at twenty paces. Near enough for her to spot the ruddied nose of a man who drank too much. He smiled. "You don't look like a threat."

"Oh, but I am." She lifted her right hand and flipped it his way. "Do you know what this means?"

He didn't answer, but fresh concern rippled across the hidden soldiers' Threads. Few people bore a filled-in circle for a Witchmark.

"And do you," the Hell-Bard countered, drawing a gold chain from beneath his collar, "know what this means?"

She laughed at that—a dry, starving chuckle. "I guess they didn't tell you, did they?"

His eyes thinned. He took the bait. "Tell me what?"

"They tried to make me like you, Hell-Bard." She let a dramatic beat pass. Then added, "It didn't work."

The Hell-Bard swallowed now, his weight shifting and his Threads flickering like a stormy sky. He would attack soon. So would the other soldiers in the woods. Bushes shifted; branches snapped. These men did not like feeling afraid. They would end her and be done with it.

She sighed. She was tired, she was hungry, but she was not weak.

"You have two choices," she offered them. "I will cleave you or I will kill you. There is still a chance at life if you choose—"

"Nommie filth," the Hell-Bard spat.

And inwardly, she smiled, grateful he'd revealed his true values. It would make this next part so much easier. Or rather, it would make the nightmares so much easier. After all, she had already decided to finish these men; now she simply had a good reason.

The man whispered his blade free. He attacked, charging with sword arm high. Foolish. Easily dodged. Men always did underestimate her.

When he reached her, she swept sideways, planting her heel on the path's inclined side. She launched up, a brief boost of speed and air. Then she twirled past him with staff extended.

It cracked the back of his head, right where spine met skull. Not hard enough to kill, nor hard enough to knock him out. Just enough to drop him to his knees and buy her the time she needed.

She wasn't done with him yet.

As seven more soldiers charged toward her—none of them Hell-Bards, none as well trained—she grabbed the closest man's Threads. Just a simple reach, a simple grasp. They were slippery and electric. Like river eels made of lightning.

She brought them to her mouth and chomped down in a single movement that had become as natural to her as swinging her staff. All she had to do was yank and bite. Yank and bite.

The man began to cleave.

He was not a witch, so no wild winds or vicious flames ripped loose. But he didn't need such powers to cleave. Magic dwelled in everyone in the Witchlands, and now that same magic burned through him. He was a pot boiling over.

He screamed, a sound of such agony it stopped every soldier in their tracks. It did not stop her, though. Instead, she wound her fingers more deeply into his shredded Threads, even as it sent fire through her veins. "Kill them."

So the man did, turning on two of his fellows—vicious, bloodied attacks with teeth and clawed hands—before a third man finally brought him down.

She was ready for that. Waiting for it. This was not her first fight, and it would not be her last. With a yank and a bite she cleaved a second man. Then a third, ignoring the raw power in their Threads that made her fingers shriek. Made power and pain judder into her soul.

The first time she'd done this—cleaved someone and held on—she'd fallen over. The second time, she'd been smart enough to lean against a tree. The third time, she'd had the staff.

Soon, her three Cleaved had burned to empty, blistered husks, framed by the tarry oil that their blood had become. Surrounding them were the brutalized bodies of their fellows.

Steam coiled in the air.

Slowly, her head still throbbing with power, but her fingers finally empty, she approached the only man left alive. He was pinned to the mud, his own gold-hilted blade stabbed deep into his stomach. It had been shoved there by one of her Cleaved.

He would die slowly from that wound, and contrary to what Hell-Bards wanted the world to believe, they were not truly dead men. There *was* still a final precipice from which they could never return.

She came to a stop before him and gazed down. She would take that blade once he was dead; it was too fine to leave behind.

"Nommie bitch," he said.

"That's not polite." She knew what she must look like, towering over him with no expression and a teardrop scar beside her eye. She knew because she had seen that face in her dreams—in *their* dreams. They would not let her forget, no matter how fast she ran.

She knelt on the mud beside the Hell-Bard. Terror wefted through what remained of his Threads. He tried to pull back, but there was nowhere for him to go. He was a dead man in more ways than one. "How?" he rasped. "Did you . . ." He didn't finish, but she knew what he meant.

"You know what I am," she told him. "You just didn't want to believe it."

"Yes," he said on a sigh.

"I did try to warn you." She unsheathed a rusted cleaver at her hip.

"Yes," he repeated, and this time resignation swept over his Threads. A beautiful rose red to match his blood. Which was good. There was no sense in fighting the inevitable. She knew that better than anyone.

"May Moon Mother light your path," she told him in Nomatsi, pressing the blade against his throat. "And may Trickster never find you." She sliced into his flesh.

Blood burbled. His Threads faded. She did not sit and watch—not as she had done before, back when she'd still cared about respecting the dead. Instead, she pushed to her feet and tossed her rusted, bloodied cleaver into the forest. It vanished into the wintry underbrush. Then with one foot on the Hell-Bard's chest, she wrapped her fingers around his sword hilt and yanked the blade free.

A fine weapon, even with all that blood. She would clean it as soon as she had the chance.

She took the man's sheath next, and after fastening it at her hip, she swept a final, disinterested glance around her. At the road, sunken like a frown into the mountain. At the eight corpses with steam clawing off their bodies. So much blood, so much Cleaved oil.

She had told herself at the last fight that she would find a cleaner way to do this. If not for her own eyes, then for whoever had to find the bodies. Perhaps at the next ambush she would finally succeed. Or at the ambush after that—because there would always be another. Just as eventually the Emperor's army would catch up to her from behind, and she would kill, kill, kill.

Her stomach growled, an earthly reminder of why she had come here and why she had wanted to slay all these soldiers in the first place.

Even Puppeteers had to eat.

So after reclaiming her staff, she hauled herself off the muddy road, and Iseult det Midenzi entered the forest in search of food.

TWO

Safiya fon Hasstrel watched her hand, resting above the flames. It should have hurt. It should have burned and smoked and sent her howling.

Instead, she felt nothing. Wherever fire touched her palm, the flesh turned to shadows and the flames flickered through. She could see her skeleton, gray bones wrapped inside the darkness, disrupted only by a faint circle where a new Witchmark stained her skin.

"That's enough, Empress." An armored hand swatted Safi from the candle. "That'll leave scars."

"I know," Safi replied. It was why she couldn't stop doing it.

"Where are your attendants?"

"I sent them away." Safi scrutinized the clot of pale crosshatching on her palm. It grew thicker each time she touched the Firewitched flame. Fascinating. Foul.

"Hell-pits, Safi, you can't keep dismissing them."

Safi. The Hell-Bard rarely forgot Safi's new title. It was that misstep more than anything that sent Safi's gaze to Lev. One of only three people she trusted in this entire wretched palace. This entire wretched land.

The sturdy woman was in full Hell-Bard regalia today, as she had been every day since her appointment as Safi's private guard. Crimson and gold, the chain mail should have shone. The leather should have gleamed.

Instead, the uniform was dull. Drained of dimension and color like everything else in the world. The four-poster bed was no longer scarlet, the thick Hasstrel rugs were no longer blue, and the palace spires outside the wide windows—the city rooftops spreading on and on and on until the white-capped mountains beyond . . . the mountains Iseult had run to with Hell-Bards in pursuit . . .

It was all gray and flat. A painting left too long in the sun.

"You need to get dressed." Lev laid a hand on Safi's shoulder. "His Imperial Majesty is expecting you."

"Good for him."

"Safi."

There it was again: her real name and not the title. This time, Lev offered it as a warning. Her grip dropped and her weight shifted, a subtle clink of armor. "I know you have a fancy title now, but it doesn't make any difference if you're wearing that noose."

Safi almost laughed at those words: *if you're wearing that noose.* Like wearing the gold chain around her neck was an option. Like she could remove it at any time and have her magic once more bound inside her.

"Let the Emperor command me," she declared with false lightness, returning her attention to the candle, Firewitched and always flickering atop a hexagonal golden base.

Fascinating. Foul.

"It is not you," Lev began, "he will command."

As if to demonstrate this—as if the Emperor knew exactly what words Lev had just uttered—the Hell-Bard doubled over with coughing. It took Safi a moment to understand what was happening. A moment to spot the tainted lines swirling over Lev's skin. But as soon as she saw and understood, horror yawned inside her lungs. She lurched at Lev and yanked off her helmet. The Hell-Bard didn't resist.

And there they were: more shadows writhing across her face, wriggling in her eyes. Emperor Henrick fon Cartorra was commanding Lev to deliver Safi, and Lev was failing to obey.

For the first time in fourteen days, heat ignited in Safi's veins. Rage that tasted so thick, so good.

In ten long strides, she reached her bedroom door and burst into the hallway, where five Hell-Bards leaped into formation around her. Lev did not join, so the knights closed the gap where she usually stood. They were accustomed to comrades felled by punishment.

Without any verbal command from Safi, the Hell-Bards aimed for the imperial wing on the western side of the sprawling palace. Through the Gentleladies' Gallery they strode with Safi in their midst, the wood gleaming beneath crystal chandeliers, the various seating areas covered in enough gold to sustain a small nation. *A nation like Nubrevna.* Safi hated this room, not merely because of the waste, but because once upon a time, she had thought all that glittering beautiful.

Now it was just a washed-out reminder of what her world had become.

Gods below, how had everything gone so thrice-damned wrong? How had Safi done so much damage in so little time? She had left Mathew and

Habim in a world of flames a month ago—two men she loved as fathers—and then she had lost Vaness somewhere inside a mountain.

She'd found Merik, only to lose him as well. And then, after two glorious weeks with Iseult, she had lost her too. And for what? Safi had come here to save Uncle Eron from execution, but she was no closer to achieving that than she had been in Marstok.

Everything she'd ever fought for, everything she had ever loved had been scorched away. She was trapped here, inside this palace. Inside herself.

The Hell-Bards' footsteps changed from *clack-clack* to echoing hammers as they crossed into the oldest part of the palace. Then Safi's footsteps changed too, and harsh drafts swept against her.

Everything felt colder here. Larger too, each stone in the wall as tall as she was, each banner stretching long as a sea fox. It reduced her to tiny insignificance—as no doubt the Emperor wanted. And no doubt why he kept his personal quarters here, despite greater comfort in the newer additions.

Safi followed the Hell-Bards through the King's Gallery, then the First Receiving Room, the Second Receiving Room, and, at last, the former empress's sitting room, where Henrick's mother had once entertained. Safi stalked past the door to what should have been her bedroom, and stoutly avoided looking at it.

It was just one more reminder of how everything in her plan had gone horribly wrong.

When at last she turned onto the Guards' Hall that preceded the Emperor's personal rooms, twelve Hell-Bards watched her pass. Their expressions were hidden behind their helms, and Safi's own retinue took up positions between them. One Hell-Bard, however, winked as Safi passed.

Caden fitz Grieg, appointed three weeks ago to personally guard His Imperial Majesty.

Safi did not wink back.

One of the Emperor's many simpering attendants rushed forward, the whip-thin man clearly appalled to see Safi still dressed in her green velvet nightgown. Which just reminded her how much she hated him, how much she hated his master, and how *furious* she was that Henrick had hurt Lev.

"Your Imperial Majesty," the attendant began, hurrying toward her, "the Emperor would like you to dress for court—"

Safi threw him. So easily. Too easily, really. When he was near enough to reach, his palms raised and beseeching, she smacked up both his arms, braced one leg against his hip, and dumped him to the ground.

"Stay down," she ordered, pleased when none of the Hell-Bards intervened. Now that she was one of them, they regularly looked the other way when she did things that were . . . *beneath* her title.

A second attendant, his eyes bulging, yanked open the door into the Emperor's quarters. He did not have time to announce Safi before she strode in.

She had entered Henrick's personal office only once before, prior to having her magic severed away. At that time, the scarlet rugs had shone bright as fresh blood. Now, they were old gashes, left exposed and rotten. Even the bookshelves she had genuinely admired—so many tomes from all over the Witchlands and beyond—now felt oppressive. Too many shades of gray stacked around her.

Behind a broad desk layered thick with papers and ledgers sat the Emperor himself: Henrick fon Cartorra. He was, as Safi was meant to be, dressed for court, in a fine brown velvet suit.

The color did not suit him, and for the hundredth time, Safi was struck by his toad-like visage, his face sagging and mouth too wide. Although, now she understood his looks were carefully cultivated. The waddling and exaggerated underbite, the slouched posture and overindulgence in food, the unkempt nature of his graying brown curls. Even the sallow undertones to his pale skin seemed part of the act. And though he might look like a toad, he had the mind of a taro player—one who knew exactly how to play the tricky Emperor card.

Safi came to a stop before his desk. "If you want me to do something," she declared, standing at her tallest, "then pull *my* noose. Do not hurt the Hell-Bards, do you understand?"

Henrick sniffed, an indulgent sound. "My Empress." He pushed to his feet with a grunt. "I will hurt whomever I please, and despite your wishes, that will never be you."

"Then why put this on me?" She yanked at the chain around her neck. "If you do not plan to use it, why bind me to you at all?"

His lips spread with a smile. "That is simply a guarantee." His one snaggling tooth jutted out above the rest as he shuffled around his desk toward her. "You proved I could not trust you, so I did what I had to do. If you did not want others to suffer at your expense, then you should never have returned to Cartorra. You should have continued running, just as your uncle wanted you to do."

It was a fist to the stomach, a blow meant to wound—and it did. Safi knew her own mistakes had landed her here. She'd come for marriage to save her uncle. Instead, she'd ended up a Hell-Bard like him.

It had been so inevitable, really. Her magic had cursed her from the day she'd been born, but only when she did not have it had she realized how much her curse had meant to her. She had once told Caden that her Truthwitchery was like living beside the ocean. Hundreds of tiny inconsequential truths and lies, told every day by everyone. The ceaseless waves eventually faded into nothing.

Except that they'd never truly been nothing. *Now* she knew what nothing felt like. *Now* she understood eternal silence she could never escape.

As Henrick turned away to begin pacing and lecturing—one of his favorite activities—Safi stopped listening. It had been so long since she had felt anything, and this heat in her chest, this jittering in her heel, felt good. This was who she was, even with the noose to imprison her. She was recklessness and initiation, she was foolhardy plans with no escape routes. And gods, what she was about to do could explode so badly.

Which was exactly what made it so perfect.

When Henrick reached the next turning point in his pacing, when his toad-like form swiveled around to face her, Safi lunged. It was not an attack meant for damage. It had no finesse like she'd executed in the hall, and the Emperor could easily defend against it—for he was far more agile than he portrayed.

But Safi wanted to see if he would react not with force, but with power. Not with physicality, but with instinct.

And he did.

As Safi slammed into him and he rocked back toward his shelves, his right hand flew toward his belt, toward a golden chain wrapped around it. Safi had noticed that chain before; she'd thought it decorative. It must instead be a main chain to control all others, and more alarming—more incredible—were the two uncut rubies tucked beneath it, wrapped in thread—

Stop.

The command lightninged into Safi's skull. So powerful, she could not resist. The word lived in her bones, lived in her soul. It froze her with shadows that could not be disobeyed.

And Safi didn't want to disobey. She'd seen all she needed to see.

So she stopped, dropping to her knees before Henrick, and instantly, the pain—and the command—receded. The shadows cleared. Safi's bones and soul were her own again.

"Do not," Henrick snarled, "make me repeat that." He grabbed her hair and snapped her head upward. His eyes burned with fury; her eyes burned with unwelcome tears. "I will put you in your quarters if I have to. Do you understand, *my Empress?*"

When she didn't answer, he yanked at the chain upon his belt once again . . . and startled cries erupted in the hallway outside.

"Stop," she croaked. Her heart still thumped too fast from his command. Her muscles still felt like ice had shattered within. She wished such agony on no one.

"I will stop"—Henrick pulled her hair tighter—"when you say you understand. Do you?"

She nodded.

"Say it."

"I understand."

He released her. She crumpled to the floor, scalp sore. Body broken. Her mind, though . . .

She lifted her gaze, a sneer settling over her lips. *I hate you, I hate you, I hate you.* "You are poison," she whispered. "Twisted and hateful and poison."

For the briefest flicker of a moment, Henrick's face tightened. His brows pinched, as if Safi had hit some buried nerve, some forgotten shame. And as if, for a mere instant, he was indeed the fragile toad he pretended to be.

But the emotion vanished in a heartbeat, replaced only by thunder and rage. "No, Safiya." He leaned close; spittle flecked her cheek. "I am the Emperor of all Cartorra, and this is what my power looks like."

※

Four Days After the Earth Well Healed

*T*he world at night is more forgiving. Just darkness and hazy shapes. No scars, no stares, no vibrant, waking Threads. Iseult's mind at night is not so kind. She has scarcely slept in over a month. First because she was tracking Safi across the dangerous Contested Lands. Then because a Firewitch she'd cleaved had somehow haunted her mind.

But she has found Safi again, and the Firewitch's ghost is gone. Presumably released into the Aether Well. Yet still, Iseult sits every night on this windowsill, awake while the world sleeps. Alone while the world dreams.

Four days she has been at the fon Hasstrel estate, surrounded by fon Grieg's soldiers and servants. Grieg has taken over Safi's family's lands now that her uncle is imprisoned for treason, and his people bow low to Iseult. Treat her with the same respect they give Safi, the same respect they give Leopold.

Iseult knows the truth, though, for she can read what lies in men's hearts. And they know she can—it's why they fear her. Why they shiver whenever they think she cannot see.

Movement rustles on the bed. Safi's sleeping Threads brighten toward wakefulness. Then a groggy voice splits the cold, shadowy room: "When was the last time you slept, Iz?"

Iseult doesn't answer. She had hoped Safi would not awaken, would not catch her sitting on this stone lip, staring at a cloudy sky and vague mountains upon the horizon.

"I'm the only one," she says eventually, "who can sense if someone comes." This isn't a total lie, and with Safi's magic half gone thanks to her creation of a Truth-lens in Marstok, Safi does not sense any omission.

"But Lev put up wards."

Yes, the Hell-Bard has. Iseult can see them now, strands of golden warmth that curl across the bedroom's crooked door and across the window too. Threads of protection that somehow coil out of the Hell-Bard's noose on her command.

But Threads mean nothing to a Weaverwitch, and it takes Iseult no effort at *all to bypass them. Like sweeping aside a curtain, she walked right through two nights ago without Lev ever noticing.*

Iseult says none of this to Safi. Instead she murmurs, "Go back to sleep, Saf. Tomorrow will be a long day." The Emperor will arrive from Praga, a hundred soldiers in tow and countless servants too.

Safi does not go back to sleep. She sits up in bed, and the faded Hasstrel-blue covers slink off. Her white shift glows in the night, her chin-length flaxen hair matted and askew, her Threads green with curiosity. "Are you nervous about seeing the Emperor?"

"Yes." Also not a lie. "Aren't you?"

"No," Safi says, and she clambers from bed, the wood groaning, to cross the exposed stone floor. If her bare feet freeze, she shows no sign as she curls onto the opposite side of the windowsill.

Cold radiates through the ancient glass. Warmth radiates off Safi. And not for the first time, Iseult wishes she'd lit a fire when she'd awoken. Her fingers and feet are going numb. Her nose too.

"Our plan will work," Safi insists, and her Threads give way to green conviction. She curls her bare toes against Iseult's stockinged ones. "We have done everything exactly as . . ." A pause. A swallow. A flicker of pained Threads. Then: "Exactly as Mathew and Habim taught us."

Iseult's chest tightens. Her nostrils flare. Mathew and Habim. The men who'd raised Safi and Iseult, training them in the art of battle and the art of words and schemes . . . and who'd betrayed Safi only days ago in Azmir.

Iseult bends forward and pats Safi's foot. "They thought they were doing the right thing, you know. We have to believe that."

But Safi isn't having it. Her knees quiver, and her Threads quiver too, with sapphire loss. With tan confusion. Then she hops off the windowsill, a burst of energy and eruption of muscles so she can pace the floor. This is her childhood bedroom, one of the only inhabitable rooms in this crumbling wing of the estate.

As she lists out the pieces of their plan—carefully crafted, meticulously plotted—Iseult's mind wanders back outside to the clouds and the distant mountains, mere shadows against the night. She doesn't like the plan she and Safi have made, but it's the best they have. Eron fon Hasstrel might hang for treason any day now; the only thing keeping him alive is Safi's promise to marry the Emperor.

And marry him she will, for what better way to get close to him than on a wedding night? What better way to claim power than to incapacitate him exactly as he has incapacitated so many, including Safi's uncle? Including the three Hell-Bards who have become her Thread-family?

Safi will imprison an emperor exactly as he has imprisoned so many Hell-Bards, and then she will sit upon the throne, finishing the plan Eron and Mathew and Habim began twenty years ago. Except Safi and Iseult will have done it on their own terms, without bloodshed along the way.

And Iseult will follow Safi every step of the way because that is what a Threadsister must do. Because no one can protect Safi like Thread-family, and because this is all Iseult is ever meant to be: the one who completes what Safi initiates. The one who cuts the purse while Safi distracts.

Yet Iseult's gaze lingers on those mountains. Not so different from the Sirmayans, where the world had been simple. Pure. Silent. Where each day had begun with clarity and focus, no Threads to confuse her. No people to get in the way.

Iseult doesn't want those days back. Of course she doesn't. She has only just been reunited with Safi. She has only just been made whole again. And yet . . .

The mountains call to her. The silence tugs.

No, it is more than silence. Visions are forming in her head that shouldn't be there—that don't belong to her. And there is something outside. Tiny, white, and scampering this way through the night. A streak that Iseult would never have seen if it hadn't started talking to her.

If she hadn't started talking to her.

I am here, the weasel seems to say. I have come for you.

THREE

✳

Iseult found food sooner than she'd expected—sooner than she had even dared hope. The soldiers had commandeered a shepherd's hut not far from the road. Tidy, well stocked, and with a campfire still smoldering.

She quickly scanned the surrounding conifers for Threads, but no human was near. She did, however, discover two shaggy horses beside the hut that she recognized as the local mountain breed. They were thoroughly disinterested in her, while she was *very* interested in them. Such beasts would make her journey through the Ohrins much easier.

"Thank you," she breathed to no god in particular. Trickster, perhaps. Or Wicked Cousin. She'd lost all right to address Moon Mother.

She reached out with her mind, aiming vaguely south. Vaguely downhill. *Come,* she told the weasel. *And make sure you avoid the road.*

A question came in response—more niggling in the back of Iseult's mind than actual words, for the weasel had no voice. She had only impressions and feelings for Iseult to interpret.

Right now, the creature shivered with joy and wanted to know how Iseult's slaughter had played out. Iseult didn't want to remember it, though. Not for the weasel, not for herself. So she closed off her mind and shoved into the hut.

The door slammed backward, hitting something wooden. A cot, Iseult soon discovered as she stepped inside. Gray light fanned over seven bedrolls neatly arranged across the earthen floor. Everything stank of old sweat and older blood. On a rickety table at the hut's center was an iron pot with a ladle poking out the side.

At the sight of it, dizziness washed over Iseult, so strong it almost stole her legs. But she was already moving, already lurching for what she prayed might be inside. She hit the table, dropped her staff, and hauled the iron toward her.

Stew. Within it was *stew.*

With shaking hands, she spooned cold, congealed liquid into her mouth. Stringy with unknown meat, it was the most delicious thing Iseult had ever tasted. She chewed, she swallowed, she slurped in more until it started coming back up again and she had to heave into a nearby bedroll.

Then she wiped her mouth and ate some more. Only when Owl's pale Threads burned into her periphery did she finally stop.

Using her staff to steady herself, she gathered up the soiled bedroll and stumbled outside, where she found the girl just shuffling toward her from the forest's pine shadows. A sleek white weasel scuttled nearby, her black-tipped tail flicking sideways.

Iseult sensed frustration in the weasel's mind, but she offered no response. After all, it wasn't Owl's fault she was tired. The girl had walked for days up a mountain, and just like Iseult, Owl had lost everything and everyone that had mattered to her. First Blueberry had been left behind in the Sirmayans. Then she had lost her magic to the Hell-Bard's heretic's collar. And finally, she had lost all warmth and safety when she and Iseult had been forced to flee Praga two weeks ago.

It had been a night of hell-fires. A night of terror and desperation through a sprawling city where Nomatsis were hated and Hell-Bards hunted here. Iseult and Owl had barely escaped alive. If not for the weasel and the tools she'd given Iseult, they would still be back there. And they would probably be dead.

The heavy wooden collar at Owl's neck clinked with each of her steps. The furs draped across her body—much too large—scraped over the ground. Iseult took Owl's hand, too cold, and guided her toward the hut. "I will start a fire," she said.

"Food?" Owl asked.

"I'll get that too." Then she added, "Fresh food," because she had been selfish and finished the stew by herself.

Owl paused before the hut's entrance, faded Threads tinted with mustard concern. "There is no one inside," Iseult assured her, but Owl was focused sideways, on where the shaggy horses poked their heads around the hut's side.

Before Iseult's eyes, Owl's Threads reached for them, straining and hopeful . . . until they hit an invisible wall an arm's length away because the Hell-Bard's heretic's collar blocked her Earthwitchery. It was not so different from the golden chains the Emperor forced Hell-Bards to wear, except that those permanently cleaved away magic, severed away souls, and bound each Bard to the Emperor. The collar simply blocked a person's magic from use.

As always happened when grief and despair claimed Owl's Threads, tears began to erupt at the edges of her eyes, and Iseult could do nothing but stare. Stony. Silent. Useless.

She wanted to do more than simply hold Owl's hand. She *wanted* to take the child into her arms and hold her. Tell her everything would be all right, that she would keep her safe and warm and fed. But instead, Iseult did nothing because no one had ever done it for her and she did not know how.

Then Owl's Threads flashed with pale pain. "You're hurting me."

Iseult released her, snatching back her hand as if scalded. This was not the first time she had squeezed Owl too tightly, nor the first time her body had betrayed emotions she'd told herself she did not feel.

Stasis, she thought out of habit, even if she'd stopped believing in that word. *Stasis in your fingers and in your toes.*

Iseult pushed into the hut alone. The weasel followed; Owl did not. Iseult wished the child would, though. Just as she wished she could be a better guardian, better protector.

When at last she had managed to feed Owl with porridge and fresh leeks, she left the girl dozing before a small stove in the shepherd's hut and turned to searching supply crates in the woods nearby. She wanted food that would travel well, and to her heavy relief, she found it: a cheese wheel, smoked meats, crab apples, and water bags. She also found the horses' gear: black leather saddles, faded scarlet pads, and saddlebags stamped with the Cartorran double-headed eagle. Inside one of those bags was a map.

Iseult's heart surged. After two weeks traveling by the stars and a weasel's vague impressions, a map and horses could easily triple how much ground she and Owl covered each day.

Once more, she sent her thanks to whichever god had decided to favor her.

After checking on Owl beside the stove, Iseult stretched the map across the hut's table. While she lit a lantern with cold fingers, the weasel explored the calfskin vellum. She sniffed, she chirped, and she stared at the black ink.

Iseult stared too, her mouth gradually opening in a way her mother would never have allowed. She couldn't help it, for this was no ordinary map. Not only did it show roads and passes and villages of the Ohrins, each meticulously drawn, but it showed the location of the Emperor's troops: his Hell-Bards, his soldiers, his guards. All were noted upon the map.

And all were moving.

Iseult had heard of Aetherwitched miniatures used in warfare upon a battle map. Small imitations bound by magic to their life-size counterpart. Where the ship or battalion moved, the miniature moved as well. Iseult had also heard of Wordwitched documents—had seen ones crafted by her mentor Mathew. Such pages allowed communication over long distances and contracts bound by deed. Yet she had never heard of a map where the ink symbols moved.

The weasel dug her dark nose into a red X nestled on the eastern side of the Ohrins. *Look,* she seemed to say in Iseult's mind.

So Iseult looked . . . and then found the X on the legend. *Heretic Target,* it read, referring to witches who'd been caught hiding their magic.

Her stomach bottomed out. While there were other Xs on the map, this X was near a small road. *And here is the stream we crossed this morning.* There were the falls they'd passed after that. And here was their little shepherd's hut.

No wonder the Emperor's soldiers had always seemed to be waiting for Iseult. They knew exactly where she was at all times.

"But how?" she asked, more breath than sound. "How do they know we're here?"

Owl's collar. The answer hit her right as the weasel shot her gaze to the child and hissed. The collars must not merely block magic but also allow Hell-Bards to track them, so it was only a matter of time before more soldiers found Owl and Iseult again.

Fortunately, Iseult could see exactly where and when that would happen, thanks to the map. A battalion of Hell-Bards followed from the west—they'd been following since Praga, and they lagged a full day behind. It was more people than she'd realized, though. Tens of them, some on horseback, most on foot. If they caught up to her, she would not be able to fight them.

The weasel twined against Iseult, her fur soft and posture seductive. *You could leave the girl,* she seemed to say. *Then no one could follow us.*

Iseult swallowed. Scratched her nose. She hated that temptation even billowed inside her. She hated that her mind instantly raced ahead to how much easier everything would be. She traced her fingers over Praga, so far west now. She'd left Safi there. Abandoned her to save her own neck and Owl's. If she weren't slowed by the child, she could return so much sooner.

No. She shook her head, almost frantic. Certainly ashamed. Owl was the only Thread-family she had left. She would never leave her behind.

The weasel seemed to understand, and she gave an almost human shrug—*Suit yourself*—before moving to the map's edge, where she sprawled out and began to groom. Somehow, she made each lick across her paws seem thoroughly disdainful, thoroughly bored.

In moments like this, it was easy to see she had once been human. *Ancient things made new again.*

With a sigh, Iseult dragged her attention east, toward Arithuania. East toward safety. The most direct route would take her and Owl down this mountain and to a long lake, crescent shaped and vast. Once Iseult and Owl crossed that, they would be on the Windswept Plains.

At the northern tip of the lake, an imperial hunting lodge stood filled with the unmistakable symbol for Cartorran soldiers and Hell-Bards. And at the lake's southern tip was a sprawling imperial sulfur mine. Neither route was ideal.

The weasel offered an impatient squeak, and the image of Owl's collar filled Iseult's mind. Because, of course, as long as Owl wore it, the Hell-Bards would keep hunting. All the way to the fallen republic of Arithuania. All the way to its fallen capital of Poznin.

Iseult glared anyway. "You know I can't remove it." The collar could not be sawed, it could not be hammered, it could not be picked, and it could not be magicked. Iseult had tried everything. And unlike Hell-Bard protection wards, where Iseult could see the very Threads of protection at work, she could sense no magic upon the collar.

In fact, if not for the faded appearance of Owl's Threads and the invisible wall they hit whenever she tried to use her Earthwitchery, Iseult would never have even known the device was magical. She would have thought it nothing more than a simple piece of wood.

Iseult spread her fingers between the red X that symbolized Owl to the ridge above the crescent lake. "Twenty leagues," she estimated.

That was two days on horseback to figure out the collar and remove it. Or two days to come up with a better plan.

The weasel chittered, a wickedly gleeful sound. She wanted to travel now and wanted to be the one to wake Owl. Iseult shook her head. "Let her sleep. We have time."

And you? the weasel seemed to ask. *Will you sleep?*

"Yes," Iseult lied, though she knew the weasel didn't believe her. Yet the slithery creature had never had any solutions to offer—the nightmares had never plagued *her*, after all. She had killed for pleasure as a human; she killed for pleasure as an animal. And after a few moments of watching Iseult map the next day's route, the creature slunk outside to enjoy the night.

FOUR

✳

Never had Vivia Nihar seen such extravagance. The Floating Palace of Azmir was a lesson in minimalism compared to the Doge's mansion on the edge of Veñaza City. The glass walls alone must have taken a hundred witch artisans to create, and the gardens—so lush were they that even with Plantwitches to tend and coax, they must have required decades for the assembly.

"Do not look so horrified," Vaness murmured beside Vivia. "The Doge is very proud of his gardens."

Vivia's face twitched. *When you are with others, the Little Fox must become a bear. Now, is your mask on, Vivia?* She patted the edges of her face, but no amount of grasping for her mask had seemed to work today. Or yesterday. Or any day since reaching Veñaza City a week ago.

Out of her depth was a vast understatement. Everything in Dalmotti had been foreign, exhausting, and terrifying. She was the klutz to everyone's grace. The barbarian to everyone's flawless manners. The hardened sailor to everyone's soft wealth.

Right now, her only tether to good manners was Vaness—and Vaness was her only tether to calm as well. As long as she had Vaness to imitate, Vivia could do this.

Keep moving, she told herself, and her feet obeyed. A little bit faster in their pace. A little bit longer in their stride. Jasmine fragranced with sea salt brushed against her, while a breeze kept the city's oppressive humidity away. It billowed through the golden gown draped over Vaness's petite frame. It tugged at the coattails and ruffled collar on Vivia's salmon-red suit.

She might be a queen with no queendom, but curse it all, she was still a captain and she had earned this broadcloth and these silver buttons.

"Through here," offered a spindly servant. He scraped a bow before an open glass door that towered to twice Vivia's height. Light glared, hiding who or what might be within. The hair on Vivia's arms pricked upward;

she stretched her magic wide, combing for the nearest water. *A watering can tucked behind that flowering ash. A small fishpond hidden in the lemon grove.* She could use those if she had to—not that she sensed soldiers or assassins nearby, but how could anyone feel safe with so much wealth around?

"Relax," Vaness murmured.

Vivia did no such thing, but as Vaness strode through the glass door, she did hurry after. Light softened. The room took shape. No soldiers, no assassins. Only the Doge, leader of all Dalmotti. He was a small man, bespectacled and with a tendency toward runny eyes—as if all the flowers outside irritated his nose. Unfortunate, considering the Witchmark on his right hand was a single leaf etched within a square: a Plantwitch.

"Ah, you are here." The Doge looked up from a large desk layered in more papers and books and pens than any person could possibly need. He pushed to his feet, and with unhurried—and unsurprised—movements, he shuffled around his desk.

Vaness paused ten paces away, so Vivia paused as well.

"Your Imperial Majesty." The Doge bowed for Vaness before turning to Vivia. "And Your Highness. You look so much like Queen Jana."

Oh. Vivia's shoulders tensed higher. Her magic keened higher too, and though she couldn't see it, she felt the water in the fishpond riffle and groove. She had not expected the Doge to invoke her mother's name. Nor had she expected the subtle slight. "Your Highness" instead of "Your Majesty."

To this imperial leader, Vivia was no queen. To him, she was still just a princess—one who now drowned in the silence and the heat and the weight of jasmine clogging up her nose. The water riffled faster.

"You know why we have come," Vaness said, cutting through the moment with the ease of sharpened steel. "And we will not waste your time nor ours with useless pleasantries." She waved a hand toward the guards and servants. "Out. All of you."

When none of them obeyed, her nostrils flared. The iron bracelets at her wrists slithered like baby cobras. Yet only when the Doge gave a casual flick of his fingers did the soldiers and attendants finally march into the garden.

The insult was clear, and before the Doge could open his tiny, fluttering mouth, Vivia knew what he would say. "I am afraid the Dalmotti Empire cannot help you." He blinked behind his spectacles; Vaness's bracelets writhed faster. "I have spoken with the Guildmasters, and we are all in agreement: we simply do not possess the resources you require."

Lies, Vivia thought. This palace alone could more than fund what Vivia and Vaness wanted. Why, even two of those blighted glass panels would probably fund it.

"We will continue to house and protect you, of course, though you need not remain on your ship. In fact, I insist you join me in the palace as guests." The Doge smiled, a simpering thing. "Claiming any thrones, however, must wait until the fighting concludes."

"Until the fighting concludes," Vaness repeated, and Vivia could practically hear her internal screams.

Her own screams were at approximately the same pitch. In fact, all her discomfort had washed away beneath the power of those screams, building in her belly. A rage she so rarely felt—much less let loose.

Her fingers stretched against her pant legs. If Vaness could remain calm, then she could too.

"You," Vaness said softly, "are a disappointment, Doge. You turn down our offer and then lack even the decency to explain the truth."

"The truth?" His fingers steepled.

"You could have had an alliance with the Marstoki Empire and Nubrevna." Iron snaked up and down her arms, betraying her feelings even as her face did not. "Such power is not something you will come by on your own—nor something you will be able to forge. Right now, our people are your enemy."

The Doge bristled, and for half a moment, Vivia saw how someone who seemed so mild-mannered might have risen to the top. A flash of heat across his eyes. A stiffening up his spine. "We lose lives in battle every day, Your Imperial Majesty. We cannot spare more lives to try to win back thrones we have no guarantee of winning."

"In battle?" The words loosed from Vivia's tongue before she could stop them—as did the laugh that followed. The fishpond riffled anew. "You call what your navy does 'battle,' Doge? You defend trade ships."

"Against empires and raiders." His spine hardened all the more. "We are attacked daily, and our navy does what it must."

"To *protect trade*." Vivia's head thrust forward. "Don't pretend to care about the war, Doge. You care only for supply chains and gold."

And there was the heat in his eyes again. He yanked off his spectacles. "This empire has no wish to expand its borders, Your *Highness*. We have never tried to grow beyond what we already have—"

"Except for your markets," Vaness cut in. Now her iron belt spiraled too. "And war must be *such* a lucrative time for each of your guilds. I wonder which ones profit the most in times like these? The weaponry guilds? The shipbuilding guilds?"

The Doge sneered, all veneer of welcome shed. "If you think that insulting me will improve your odds of an alliance, you are sorely mistaken. Dalmotti allies itself with winners, and *you* are not winners." He spun on his heel, a gust of robes and cold dismissal, before stalking back to his desk.

And Vivia's magic sparkled, a riptide hungry for freedom. She could shatter this glass in a heartbeat. Show the Doge exactly with whom he toyed.

"Come." Vaness knifed through Vivia's thoughts. Her warm hand lay over Vivia's biceps. "He is not worth our anger." Even as she said this, her fingers dug with barely contained ferocity into Vivia's coat.

"No," Vivia forced out. "No man really is." Then she allowed Vaness to pull her around, and once more, she followed her lead: chin high, stride long, expression hard and unapproachable.

They did not speak again until they were outside the Doge's glass walls and in the garden once more. There, Vaness paused just long enough to flash Vivia a smile—alluring, coy—and then lift her hand. "I changed my mind."

She snapped her fingers. The iron frame around the nearest window melted. Glass shattered to the ground, a great cacophony of spraying shards. So loud, so satisfying.

"Oh my," Vaness drawled. "What a mess that will be to clean."

Vivia smiled.

When at last Vivia and Vaness reached the canal street outside the Doge's palace, the sun had reached its peak. Heat rose from the cobblestones, carrying the morning's rain and the stink of sulfur and fish. Gone were the jasmine and rose; gone were the guards and attendants.

The main gate clamored shut behind them, final and disapproving.

A lone four-horse carriage waited nearby—an extravagance that had cost Vivia and Vaness most of the pitiful funding Vizer Sotar had graciously donated to their cause. They'd thought the price worth it at dawn, when they'd still believed they might turn an empire to their cause.

Now, all Vivia saw was more waste. More failure.

If Vaness felt as defeated as Vivia, she gave no indication while she waited, posture perfect, for the carriage to rattle their way. Soon it was before them, and the nearest door popped wide. Their lone attendant—if he could really be called that—scampered out with a stepping-stool.

That stool had cost an extra ten piestras.

"Majesties," Cam Leeri said, offering a clumsy bow. "Did it go well?"

Vaness gave no answer; Vivia simply sighed.

And Cam winced. The reaction was short-lived, though, as it always seemed to be for the boy. With his dappled brown skin and its golden undertones, as well as his doe-dark eyes and quick smile, he was easily the most optimistic person Vivia had ever met. Sometimes it grated on her, but most of the time, it was refreshing to have someone so determined to see good.

It wasn't until the carriage jolted to a start that Vaness finally spoke. "You know," she said, gazing out the open window, "I understand your brother better now." Wind tousled her hair. "Two months ago, when he lost his temper at the Truce Summit luncheon and blasted his winds, I thought him childish. Now I see the empires are unfeeling, and Nubrevna . . ." Vaness tore her gaze off the canals. Her dark eyes settled on Vivia's. "You have always been at their mercy. At *my* mercy, which I did not give."

"No," Vivia said. "You did not." And there was nothing else to say. Vaness was right. She had shown no mercy for almost twenty years, and now she was tasting the poison she'd once dispensed.

Cam cleared his throat. Outside, traffic and voices and horses filled the day, filled Vivia's ears. But she didn't tear her gaze from the Empress. One month they had been together, yet somehow, she felt she scarcely knew the other woman. Vaness had far fewer masks than Vivia—only one, in fact. Yet that Iron Bitch facade so rarely budged, so rarely revealed.

Even now, after a confession, there was only steel in her eyes.

After finding Vaness in the Lovats under-city, badly injured and surrounded by raiders—and after flooding those raiders and leaving them for the Royal Soil-Bound and Navy to handle—Vivia had fled Lovats on her old ship, the *Iris. Stealing,* her father had called it, and *traitor,* he had called her. He'd even gone so far as to offer a bounty to anyone who brought her back to the city. Two thousand gold martens that he certainly could not afford, but that would certainly entice the hungriest and most desperate of Nubrevnans.

She and Vaness had taken to the sea right away, only a skeleton crew to sail with—but enough loyalty in all of the sailors to fill an armada. After sailing aimlessly for two weeks, they had finally arrived here in Dalmotti, hoping to forge an alliance with the Guildmasters and find some sort of help in their quests to reclaim their thrones.

Vivia hadn't expected them to fail quite so quickly.

She was the first to break the stare with Vaness, and she could feel Cam practically melt with relief beside her. "Leeri," she said, angling toward the boy. He wore the Sotar livery—the same salmon-red broadcloth as Vivia's uniform.

Not that his appearance or hers had helped them any more than this carriage had.

"How quickly until the crew can set sail?"

"Right away, Majesty." His dark eyebrows lifted. His left hand— missing its pinkie—rapped against his knee. "I told them to be ready, just in case."

Just in case. So even the boy had had little faith in their mission. Vivia hated how much her stomach dropped just thinking that. While she had hardly possessed Vaness's certainty, she'd at least had some hope.

No regrets. Keep moving.

As the carriage rolled into the Southern Wharves, the *Iris* came into view. A two-masted half-galley with the sharp, beak-like bow of all Nubrevnan naval ships. A sleek creature with her oars stowed and sails furled, and just seeing her made the knots in Vivia's chest—knots that never fully went away—loosen. The *Iris* had served Vivia for years, first on the rivers of Nubrevna, then briefly at sea . . .

And now upon the Jadansi. The only home she and Vaness had. The extent of their holdings, the breadth of their empires.

The horses and carriage clopped to a halt, and Cam hastily helped his royal charges exit. Vivia didn't need the aid, but she accepted it anyway. Vaness, she noted, did not. The Empress had retreated entirely behind her cold exterior, and if Vivia had to guess, she would speak little for the rest of the day. Perhaps even for the rest of their journey.

Vivia stalked across the gangway. Tar and salt mingled in her nose. The sea's breeze fingered her hair, trailed across her skin. She inhaled deeply. Smiled at the nearest sailor and then the ship's girl after that.

Cam and Vaness followed, but Vivia scarcely noticed. Her eyes were scanning the deck for her first mate . . . *There.* Broad-shouldered and broader-chested, he too wore the warm coral red of his family's livery.

It had become the color of Vivia's cause. The color of her small but loyal crew.

Vizer Erril Sotar hurried toward Vivia. He did not ask how the meeting had gone, and Vivia could see in his dark eyes that he too had not expected any progress. There came the knots again.

"Sotar," she said, aiming for her main quarters. "I want to make way tonight. If we are lucky, we might escape this cursed place before the moon reaches her peak."

"Where will we go?" His voice was a warm baritone. Familiar and kind.

"Away. Far away." It was a nonanswer, but the best she could give. Nubrevna was not an option. Marstok even less so. The only harbor they might safely lay anchor in was the Pirate Republic of Saldonica, and though Vivia had been willing to dabble in piracy in the past—given the right target—she'd also seen Lovats almost destroyed by Red Sails and Baedyeds. Twice.

She had no interest in allying herself with true raiders.

"Then away it is, Captain." Sotar pressed his fist to his chest before striding ahead to open her cabin door. Though Vivia had told him over and over and *over* again that he didn't need to open doors, he still did it. Every time.

And every time, it made the little rip in Vivia's heart stretch wider. It used to be Stix opening that door for her. And Stix taking her commands. But Stix had disappeared a month and a half ago, and though Cam had explained a hundred times—backward and forward and every direction Vivia had demanded—that her former first mate and Threadsister was inside a mountain in the Sirmayans . . . that she'd had memories that were not her own and was now with a Sightwitch named Ryber . . .

None of it had ever made any sense.

Then again, nothing ever made sense anymore. Vivia's brother, Merik, had been declared dead, but then he'd appeared in Lovats quite alive. Her father, whom she'd spent her entire life trying to appease and prove herself to, had betrayed her and claimed the throne she had worked so hard for. And then magic doors had mysteriously opened inside the under-city of Lovats, and raiders had poured through, followed by the Empress of Marstok, dethroned but not broken.

No. Nothing in this world made sense, and come floods or hell-waters, Vivia had to make peace with that. Stix wasn't coming back. Merik wasn't coming back. Her title was gone. This was her life, salmon-suited and rejected at every turn.

She reached the central table of her quarters. Charts were stretched and weighted, while miniature ships had gathered against the table's raised rim. Unmagicked. The expensive Aetherwitched miniatures she'd wasted a tiny fortune on had been lost or destroyed or Noden only knew by Merik.

Vivia waited until Sotar had closed the door into her cabin. Vaness would likely sequester in her quarters belowdecks, where she often hid, and Cam would be organizing the crew to set sail.

"Has the blockade cleared your departure?" Sotar asked. He joined Vivia at the table, watching as she lined up ships outside the Veñaza City harbor upon a chart. Thirty-four warships, letting no one in and no one out without approval from the Doge.

"No," Vivia said. "But our names got us through the blockade. They will get us out."

"Are you certain?" Sotar lifted cool eyebrows, and once more, the similarities to Stix . . .

Vivia's throat clenched tight. She chewed her lip several beats before nodding briskly. "They cannot stop us. We are a queen and an empress, even if they refuse to help us reclaim our thrones."

She grabbed a second set of miniatures, painted rich, iris blue. One she placed in the harbor, west of the blockade.

"Us," she said. Then she plopped down the remaining two. "Our ships."

One she placed in Lovats, useless and destroyed. The other she set near Lejna. "I sent out three ships two months ago under the Fox banner. One was captured in Saldonica." *And sent back to Lovats filled with seafire.* She did not say that part aloud. Sotar knew; Sotar had been there. "One we now sail, and the third . . ." She glanced at Sotar. "I ordered them to hide in the Hundred Isles, and they have been awaiting orders ever since."

Sotar's lips pursed. Contemplative, perhaps. More likely disapproving. He had known of Vivia's attempts at piracy and he had looked the other way. When he spoke again, it was to say simply, "I see, Captain. Shall I tell Cam to fetch the banner then?"

"Not yet." Vivia matched his grim expression. What she had done two months ago, she had done with no pleasure—but she had also jumped in too quickly. As desperate as she'd been for food, for weapons, the bounty had not been worth the price.

Sometimes little foxes were run into holes with nowhere to hide, while other times they had to turn and face the danger before it was too late for themselves, for their cubs, for everything they'd ever loved.

If that moment ever came, *then* Vivia would raise the Fox flag.

"The Nubrevnan iris will do," she told Sotar, referring to the banner now flapping against the mast: a blue iris on a checkered field. "For now, we are the Royal Navy, and I pray that is enough to get us through."

FIVE

✳

Stacia Sotar had endured her fair share of bad smells, but the Pirate Republic of Saldonica was a new winner. It beat all the various spots in Lovats: Hawk's Way where boats dumped trash; the Skulks where too many people had been forced into squalid, single-room homes; and even the Cisterns that were literally filled with the capital's shit.

Saldonica smelled worse.

Maybe because the sailors and raiders and gamblers who made up this makeshift port thought baths were for cowards, or maybe because sulfur seeped up from the swamps all around, leaving even the cleanest person unable to escape the stink of rotten eggs. Or maybe it was because all those smells were compounded when one entered Baile's Slaughter Ring. Built in the ruins of some forgotten fortress, the base of the arena was ancient stone, the rest wooden scaffolding that stretched upward. Eight towers. Thousands of seats, and so very little breeze to sweep away the stench.

Ryber held a bundle of dried lavender beneath her nose. Stix regretted not buying one of her own when they'd set off for the Ring that morning. In her defense, it hadn't smelled *this* badly in the Baedyed district where they were staying. In fact, their little inn was surprisingly immaculate for a port run by pirates.

Except for the rotten eggs, of course.

The wooden bench beneath Stix rattled. A rat scuttled over her boot—the fourteenth of that day—disturbed by the stochastic drumroll of feet as viewers watched the day's winner depart. Once a year, a massive, violent fight filled the ring, drawing people from across the continent. Baile's Slaughter Ring, it was called, with hundreds of prisoners pitted against each other.

Stix was glad she'd missed that event, and she was glad that today's more standard fight featured a willing participant who entered the Ring for coin and glory. Not that it changed the fact that hundreds of prisoners were currently trapped beneath the Ring, waiting for next year's Slaughter and guilty only of working on a ship when raiders had come.

The day's winner, a Stonewitch called the Hammer, pumped his arms in victory as he strode off the dusty Ring floor. One of his arms was made of stone, though he didn't always wear the stone limb outside the Ring. Sometimes he didn't wear it inside either, for whatever the Hammer fought, the Hammer clobbered. He was the Ring's reigning champion, and the money that changed hands over his fights was enough to feed Stix's old crew for a month. Ten of Stix's old crews.

Today, he had destroyed a horde of crocodiles, each as long as a galley and almost as wide too.

Despite her new spectacles, Stix had to squint to watch him depart with any sort of clarity. He aimed for one of the three wooden boxes that led out of the Ring. And though Stix couldn't quite discern the woman waiting for him on the other side of the open door, she knew who it was: the reason she had come here today.

Stix nudged Ryber beside her, and Ryber nodded. She had far keener eyes and a Sightwitch's gift: *Once seen, never forgotten. Once heard, never lost.* "Let's go," Ryber murmured, and as one, she and Stix pushed to their feet. A single plait pulled free from the rest of Ryber's braids—at least the tenth that day, though she tried to keep them pulled back. The heat in Saldonica was just too intense for any human to deal with long hair. Stix kept her own pulled into a low bun.

Ryber's skin was a cooler brown than Stix's, reminding Stix of a burnished silver mirror she'd loved as a child. And although coltish in her figure, Ryber had muscles hidden beneath her loose tunic and breeches. Meanwhile, behind her magically silver eyes, she had the sharpest mind Stix had ever encountered.

They had spent a week in the Pirate Republic trying to find a way into the Ring. Not because Stix or Ryber cared about the fights below (Stix had wagered on one fight with the Hammer, gained a tiny fortune, and never wagered again), but because it was the only way for them to gain access to what rested *beneath* the Ring: ruins from a thousand years ago. Ruins that called to Stix with voices that never seemed to relent. *Come this way, keep coming.* Stix had followed those voices across the Witchlands because it was the only way she knew to make them shut up.

And that was all Stix wanted—silence. No more screaming memories that weren't her own. No more doing as the voices commanded. No more following them like a fish on a line. Once she had done what they desired, seen whatever it was they wanted her to see, then she could leave this rotten Hagfish hole and go home again. Back to Vivia's side, back to where she belonged.

She and Ryber pushed past spectators who groused and swore and shoved at them to move faster. Quit blocking the view. Get out of the thrice-damned way. It set Stix's teeth on edge. Even the rowdiest of Nubrevnans—with whom Stix had spent plenty of evenings at the Cleaved Man—seemed an orderly lot compared to these people.

Stix missed them. She missed Vivia even more.

When they reached the end of the bench, Ryber led the way up a rickety set of stairs to the exclusive seating area. There the Masters of the Ring kept private boxes. Thus far, none of the Masters had been willing to sponsor Stix. She'd used every trick in her Waterwichery arsenal trying to convince them, from creating fog on the spot to freezing water in their mouths. But all they'd done was glower and say, *Too powerful. How're we supposed to design a fight for you when all it takes is a single snap and you've frozen everything?*

Stix had been forced to admit they had a point. There wasn't much sport for someone with total control over water—and the truth was that Stix *was* unbeatable. She had never encountered a waterfall she couldn't scale, a wave she couldn't ride, an opponent she couldn't decimate.

Her father had always told her such natural power made her overconfident, that one day, *You will meet someone you cannot match.* And in the end, he'd been right: the voices had snuck up on Stix, unexpected. Unfathomable.

Now here she was, over a month since they'd arrived, still battling against them. Still losing every day.

The raiders that guarded the highest scaffolding let Stix through at the flicker of a gold coin, and she and Ryber strode quickly down the covered walkway. Banners and curtains trailed at the corner of Stix's vision; the crowd's roars thrummed in her ears, blessedly muffled this high.

The smell was muffled too, thank Noden, with salty ocean wind to lick over the wooden planks.

Soon Stix and Ryber reached the final private box on the walkway, where the final Master of the Ring awaited. The only one Stix had yet to meet. She doled out four gold coins each to the two guards here. Two for letting her in and two for alerting her that the final Master had returned to town. Then the tallest guard called in an alto voice, "Visitors," and prodded Stix and Ryber through the doorway.

Though not as resplendent as some of the other decks Stix had visited, the space was still draped in fine rugs and cushions. Wind kicked over the waist-high railings, flapping at two strips of jagged-edged red cloth. It carried bidding and laughter and roars of anticipation for the next fight—and it carried moisture that sang to Stix's magic. A harmony of humidity, of distant sea spray off the bay, of brackish droplets from the marsh.

On a long chair lay Admiral Kahina Léon.

She sucked at a pipe, smoke rings circling her white-haired head and cool-toned walnut skin. She wore an impeccably pressed coat that reminded Stix of a Nubrevnan naval uniform, except where her own coat in Lovats was navy, Kahina's was rich, starfish red—and Stix suddenly felt like a new recruit, failing to meet muster in her sweat-sticky white blouse and brown breeches.

One more thing she missed from home: her clothes.

Beside Kahina stood the Hammer, his stone arm gone. He looked at Stix and Ryber with no attempt to conceal his annoyance. Up close, Stix's spectacles revealed amber-brown skin and black hair coiled into six long tails like she'd seen on some travelers from a southern stretch on the Fareastern continent.

"I don't throw fights," he said in Dalmotti with a slight accent, and Stix frowned, confused.

Ryber, however, understood his implication immediately. "We aren't here to bribe you." She moved in front of Stix with liquid ease and puffed out her chest with the confidence of a well-seasoned merchant. Her ware, of course, was Stix.

They'd played these parts—trainer and fighter—enough times now that Stix should have been comfortable with them. But unlike Ryber, who could slip as easily into roles as she could new clothes, Stix always felt stiff. She didn't have the Sight; she'd seen very little of the world outside of Nubrevna; even speaking in Dalmotti required concentration because she hadn't practiced it in almost a decade.

"We have come to offer you the fighter of a lifetime." Ryber offered Kahina an Illryan-style bow: fist to forehead, chin dipping low. They'd heard that Kahina, like Ryber, had roots in Illrya. "I present to you, Stix of Nubrevna."

"Sticks of Nubrevna?" Kahina puffed her pipe. "Never heard of her."

"Because this is her debut in the Slaughter Ring." Ryber flashed a smooth smile. Another braid sprang free. "Until now, she has only ever fought in Lovats."

This was true. The extent of Stix's spectator sporting had been done at the Cleaved Man every sevenday.

"She was called the Water Brawler there," Ryber added. "And she's never lost a fight."

Also true.

"And you are the first Master of the Ring we've approached with this opportunity."

Definitely a lie.

Kahina sniffed. "Another Tidewitch. We have plenty of those in the Ring." She shifted away.

Stix stepped forward. "I'm a Waterwitch, actually. A full Waterwitch." To prove her point, she offered her right hand to Kahina and let her title dangle in the air like bait on a hook. Her Witchmark hung there too, a hollow diamond indicating full mastery over all forms of water.

Kahina paused. "A full Waterwitch, you say." Her honey-dark eyes sharpened onto Stix's face. Seconds drifted past.

And Stix slowly felt their roles reverse. She became the bait. She became the target of a fish too large to escape.

Kahina removed her pipe from her mouth. A jade thumb ring winked. "Have we met before? You look . . . familiar."

Ryber, who was usually so poised—so good at mimicking the people she'd once seen and never forgotten—glanced at Stix with open surprise.

"No," Stix said. "We haven't met before."

"Indeed?" Kahina smiled, a sideways thing. "Well, in that case, Lady Fate must favor you today, for I have just the idea for you." She turned her face to the Hammer, though her eyes remained on Stix. "Tell the guards that Kahina wants the Water Brawler in tomorrow's arena."

The Hammer scowled but didn't disobey. He simply stalked into the hall, red cloth over the doorway flapping behind him. Meanwhile Kahina popped her pipe back into her mouth. The bowl sparked, sending smoke to wreathe around her white hair.

A Firewitch, Stix thought as she and Ryber aimed for the exit after the Hammer. *No one ever mentioned Kahina is a Firewitch.*

It was sunset by the time they reached their inn in the Baedyed territory of Saldonica. Streetlights flickered to life, and evening patrols directed crowds as a day's work segued into a night's revelry. The voices pushed against Stix's skull, furious she had left the Ring. *Come this way, keep coming.*

"I know," she groaned at them, clutching her forehead as she staggered out of a hired carriage and toward the tidy inn. Though she didn't lean on Ryber to ascend the stairs, she did regret picking a room on the third floor. It had seemed private at the time; now it seemed impossibly far away. It didn't help when an orange tabby tangled in her legs halfway up the narrow, creaking steps.

"Where did you come from?" Ryber cooed, scooping the cat into her arms. "Are you a stowaway from the Ring? You are, aren't you?" She nuzzled the cat's ear, which was missing a corner, and at Stix's face of mild horror, she shrugged. "I like cats. Plus, they're good luck around here."

This was undeniably true, for as the saying went, *Six-fingered cats will ward off mice*. Not that Stix had ever heard that phrase before her arrival in Saldonica. Now it and the rest of the rhyme were everywhere her bespectacled eyes could land. On small signs inside the inn, carved into walls over tavern booths, etched into rings, or recited by merchants and pirates and innkeeps alike.

> *Three rules has she, our Lady of the Seas.*
> *No whistling when a storm's in sight.*
> *Six-fingered cats will ward off mice.*
> *And always, always stay the night for Baile's Slaughter Ring.*

Nonsensical, though catchy when sung to a tune—and apparently effective at luring gamblers to Saldonica every year for the main fight in the arena.

Once in the room, Ryber deposited the tabby by the door and Stix toppled onto the cot they alternated using. Technically tonight wasn't her night, but she didn't think Ryber would argue. She knew what the voices could do. Her Heart-Thread Kullen had endured something similar.

Initially, when these memories had begun in Stix's brain, carried by souls that apparently lived alongside her own, Ryber had expected it would all make sense immediately. "A few memories," she'd said. "It only took Kullen a few memories before he recalled all his past lives at once."

Good enough, Stix had thought, and she'd waited patiently for her voices to do the same. But after two weeks of them shouting louder at Stix every day, of a ceaseless headache and sleepless nights, Ryber had been forced to admit that Stix's Paladin soul might be different from Kullen's. That maybe the only way to finish releasing her own ghosts was to do as the voices wanted: come this way, keep coming.

So they had gathered up their few belongings at the Sightwitch Sister

Convent, including a new pair of spectacles for Stix, and they'd traveled southeast. First to the Pirate Republic. Then to the Slaughter Ring. And soon, they would enter the heart of it all.

"At least we've gained access to the Ring, right?" Ryber settled onto the edge of the cot.

"Not sure the price was worth it." Stix hauled a pillow over her head. It didn't quiet the voices, but the weight was comforting. When the tabby crawled onto her belly, though, it ruined the effect. She lifted the pillow and glared. "I did not invite you."

"Come here." Ryber gathered up the cat, plucking free a few claws. "It just wants to comfort you. And look! It has six fingers."

"She," Stix said, "has six fingers."

"She?" Ryber peered into the tabby's face.

"Hye," Stix murmured. She slung the pillow over her head again. "The voices tell me she's a she."

"In that case, we should name her Baile." Ryber switched to a syrupy voice that Stix had never heard before. She promptly decided she hated it. Or maybe it was just the words she hated, knowing that Ryber believed Stix to be a Paladin. Knowing that Ryber accepted it all so easily while Stix could barely keep her sanity intact.

She prayed every night to Noden that her mind would stay wholly hers. That it wouldn't fracture into past beings like Kullen's had.

They never spoke about that part—about the fact that Kullen was gone with only an ancient fury to remain.

Stix also prayed every night that Vivia was safe. The news of Serafin's takeover had reached Saldonica two weeks before, and Stix had hated learning she hadn't been there when Vivia had needed her most. What sort of Threadsister was she? What sort of first mate?

It was an open sore inside Stix's chest. Always oozing, always pained. Worse, she couldn't stop poking at it. When she had been at the Sightwitch Sister Convent with Ryber, she'd poked. When they had been on the road, traveling with dreary slowness through the Sirmayans and then the Contested Lands, she'd poked. And now here in Saldonica as she and Ryber tried every day to get into the Ring, she *poked*.

Vivia had to wonder where Stix was, vanished for a month. Stix might have sent Cam to deliver a message about magic doors and raiders, but she had no way of knowing if the boy had ever made it through. No way of knowing if Vivia had even believed him.

By the Hagfishes, Stix wished she'd never left Nubrevna. Hye, remaining would have led her into a different sort of nightmare, with voices screaming at her and memories surfacing. Her mind understood all that had happened. Her heart, though . . .

Oozing, pained, a scab she couldn't stop poking.

It was with Vivia on her mind that Stix dozed off—specifically of Vivia's crown. Stix had only seen it once, tucked away in a tiny, forgotten playroom that was so obscure, no one would ever find it. Vivia had held the golden crown with a strange sort of terror while Stix had eyed it with a strange sort of awe.

That crown belonged on Vivia. It was hers and always had been.

Stix stands surrounded on all sides by thick forest and white-capped peaks. Snow falls, and nearby, a river churns, its dark waters moving beneath a stone bridge.

A man in black furs strides her way. In his hand gleams a silver sword. On his head shines a silver crown, and for the first time, it occurs to Stix that he is a king. That, although she and the others were never meant to rule, he has taken power like an Exalted One.

He points beside Stix, and she realizes with a start that she isn't alone in this grove at the heart of a mountain range. She cannot turn her head though, she can only slide her eyes sideways to where a woman lies on her back, a blade thrust through her belly. Silver pools around her, glowing with power. Magic entwined in her very blood, and where the raw magic moves, fissures gouge into the rock.

Two paces away, on his knees and crying, is a man with scars down half his face. He looks at Stix. "I am sorry."

It is all right, Stix wants to say, for she loves that man, Bastien. Yet no words come; she cannot part her lips to speak.

Bastien doesn't turn when the Rook King arrives. He doesn't turn when the Rook King calls out, "Is your fury quenched? Is your wrath complete?" Nor does he turn when the Rook King unsheathes a saber at his hip.

Only when the king comes to a stop before Bastien, does Bastien finally twist his head. "I will find you," he rasps. "In the next life, I will—"

The king slices off his head. The man's words end. His head flies to the ground, blood spraying and mixing with the silver. Then the Rook King fixes his dark gaze on Stix. "It will all be over soon," he tells her before his blade arcs out and crashes against her own neck.

Only as the sword cracks against stone does she realize why she has been locked in place. Only when it cuts through the rock—three swings it takes him— does she realize she has been encased in granite.

Then blade bites into flesh.

At least, *she thinks before she dies,* the people oppressed by the Exalted Ones have been freed. *At least she and the others accomplished this one small task before they were betrayed and their worlds came to an end.*

SIX

✳

The Emperor's crown was too tight. It squeezed the flesh of Henrick's temples, practically blending into his skin and brown curls. As if his own body had grown around it. Safi had noticed it the first time she'd seen him in Cartorra with Iseult at her side. Then she'd noticed it again during their brief wedding ceremony . . .

And again on every night of these celebrations since.

Safi's golden velvet gown, trimmed in Hasstrel blue and bobbin lace, swept around her in time to her forward steps. Domnas and doms bowed like wheat beneath the winds of power. She waved. She offered wisps of a subtle smile. The burn mark around her thumb glistened in the night's candlelight.

"I am not so awful as you think me," Henrick murmured beside her. He patted her arm where it was hooked into his. A tender move that was pure performance. "You will come to see that in time."

"Of course, my Emperor." Safi continued waving.

Every night since her marriage to Henrick two weeks before, Safi had endured this parade. And every night for two more months, she would continue enduring it. Tonight, however, was different from previous nights, for tonight, Safi burned. Beneath every nod and *yes, my Emperor,* she clung to her rage. No more layers of gray. No more lightless, purposeless life.

She had no real plan yet—just a vague notion that she needed the chain upon Henrick's belt, the one he'd used to stop her attack only a few hours before. And perhaps more importantly, she needed the Threadstones beneath the chain. *Her* Threadstone. *Iseult's* Threadstone. Taken from them before the noosing. With those, she could find her Threadsister again.

Even now, dressed for the evening's festivities, Henrick wore the same belt. Unobtrusive, easy to miss. "Smile," he ordered as he guided Safi onto the raised dais at the end of the room. "The world is watching."

Safi did not want to smile—not for Henrick, not for any man ever again. But she did as she was ordered and bared her teeth for all the room to see. *I hate you all*, she thought before turning her most dashing grin upon the Emperor. *And I will destroy you.*

Henrick nodded, approval in the twitch upon his lips.

After a flippant wave at musicians across the room, a brisk tune began. The nobility, whether they wanted to or not, began to dance while Henrick sat upon his throne and Safi sat upon her own. The thrones were modern additions of scarlet satin that clashed with this ancient stone corner of the palace.

When Safi was a child, she'd found this room immense, terrifying. Now as a prisoner, she found it too small, too crowded, and dreadfully hot. Every member of the Cartorran nobility was crammed in here to celebrate. Again.

That was another thing that had, when she was a child, been so different. Then, Safi had come here to cower behind her uncle Eron, praying throughout that neither Henrick nor his Hell-Bards would realize what magic she kept hidden away.

She'd hated Eron for dragging her to Praga every year so he could pay the Hasstrel tithes. She'd hated him—with shit-roasting *fury*—for disappearing every night to drink himself into oblivion.

But everything had changed in Veñaza City two months ago when Safi had learned he was not, in fact, a drunk. Rather, he had a complex, sweeping plan to bring peace to the Witchlands—until he'd gotten caught before the plan could finish. Now he was somewhere in Cartorra, imprisoned for treason. And incomprehensible as it was, only Safi seemed to care about that fact. To Mathew and Habim, execution of the plan had mattered more than Eron's life.

Well, Safi thought the entire plan was horse piss, and Eron didn't get to die before he'd given her solid answers to the hundreds of questions she'd assembled since Dalmotti. So far, she'd discovered nothing. So far, she'd only gotten her magic stolen and her Threadsister lost far away.

I hate you all, Safi thought again as dancers swished past. Tonight was a quieter affair than the first weeks of dancing and music had been. No public feasting, and rather than a full orchestra rattling the room with heavy traditional marches, an octet of winds and strings was scarcely audible over a hundred voices and stamping feet.

Two of those feet belonged to Dom fon Grieg, who never missed a chance to bow dramatically at Safi when he saw her and inform her that *her lands were still thriving beneath his hand.* Safi smiled at him as he swept past, surprisingly graceful in this modern take on a country dance. *I will destroy you*, she thought, tossing him a wink for good measure.

To her delight, he missed a beat. His partner ran into a neighbor, and several people cried their annoyance—which only made Safi smile all the wider. Oh yes, this anger was *delicious*.

"You will dance tonight," the Emperor said, scattering her thoughts and her smile.

"Your Imperial Majesty?"

"My nephew will ask later, and you will agree."

Safi blinked. As far as she could tell, this was no joke. Henrick's expression had not changed; he looked as foul-tempered and bored as he always did.

Every night since Iseult's departure, Leopold had requested a dance with Safi. Every night, she had refused because she would, with no exaggeration, rather pull out her own toenails than dance with him. Or speak to him ever again.

He had realized what Henrick could do to her, yet he he had done nothing to stop it. Even now, with the Emperor's Hell-Bard forces tracking Iseult by the day, Leopold did nothing to interfere.

All she said, however, was: "I would prefer to remain here, my Emperor."

Henrick sighed and shifted his weight. Like the crown, his throne was too tight. "Leopold asks you every night." He flicked a hand to the floor of dancers below them, where Leopold's strawberry curls glistened and swirled. "The court notices. The court talks. They wonder why you refuse."

Safi's heel tapped beneath her gown. "Please do not make me."

"Oh, but I will." A smug smile stretched Henrick's lips. He toyed with his belt, a blatant warning. "Tonight when he offers, you will accept. No more discussion."

Safi's heel stilled. Her ire flamed higher. "Of course, my Emperor." She flashed a dazzling smile. "I look forward to it."

Leopold must have sensed that his moment had come because he glanced Safi's way midspin. And for once, she did not look away. Instead she arched her eyebrows.

He smiled—a beautiful smile because everything Leopold did was beautiful. Then his spin carried him away.

Moments later, the current dance ended and Leopold materialized before the dais. Dressed in silver velvet, he looked lithe and graceful while also looking more virile and masculine than any other man upon the floor. Safi hoped his Aetherwitched tailor was well paid.

"My Empress." He bowed low, as he had every night. "Would you honor me with a dance?"

He knew she would say yes tonight. Safi could see it in the way his sea-green eyes gleamed. The way his tongue ran over his top teeth in anticipation.

She wished she could knock those teeth out.

"Yes," she said simply. "Let us dance." And with those words, she stood. At once, the court took notice. The voices softened, and all eyes slanted her way.

Curse Henrick for making her do this. Curse Leopold for persistently asking—and curse Leopold for every lie, every trick that had landed her here, imprisoned and separated from her Threadsister.

Leopold offered Safi his hand when she reached the end of the dais, but she glided past him, head high, and claimed a spot on the floor, front and center where her husband could watch. She even flung Henrick a little smirk while she waited. *She* controlled this space; Leopold had to come to her.

He did come to her, right as the strings began thrumming from the shadows, and he offered Safi a curt bow when the dance began. It was not a difficult dance—there were more complex arrangements popular in Cartorra—and Leopold was comfortable with the steps. He moved gracefully because there was no other way he could move. A series of steps and twirls, hops and spins led them in a wide circle around the room. On their second turn past Henrick, hulking upon his throne, Leopold asked, "Why tonight?"

"Because your uncle commanded me."

"I see." A pause while Leopold and Safi briefly parted, briefly looped. Then: "I heard what happened this morning."

Of course he had. Leopold's spies had spies. Like Henrick, he had fooled her into believing he was nothing more than a fop. A well-dressed, well-spoken fop, but a fop all the same. In reality, he was even better at cultivation and performance than his uncle was.

"I will kill you," Safi replied, offering one of her daintiest smiles. "Once I kill Henrick I will kill you."

"Well, as long as you do it in that order," Leopold replied smoothly, "I shall not interfere." Again he paused as they separated. "Any other order," Leopold resumed once they were together again, "and I will not be able to free you."

"Lies," Safi said, and she waited for her magic to confirm. But nothing came back because there was nothing to come back and there never would be for all the rest of her days. Nonetheless, she had absolute certainty as she added, "Everything you say is a lie, Polly."

"Not *everything*." His eyebrows rose. "For example, in your left pocket I have dropped a device you made. A lens that can tell truth from lie."

Safi stumbled a beat; Leopold caught her. Glided her into a flourishing spin.

"How do you know about that?"

"Careful," Leopold murmured. "You look upset."

I am upset, she wanted to snarl. Instead, she laughed. The most twinkling, delighted laugh she could conjure.

"Mathew sent it to me," Leopold replied, as if this somehow explained everything. "And I would have given it to you weeks ago, had you only agreed to dance."

"Lies," she repeated, though this time she was not so sure. "You betrayed me. You betrayed Iseult."

"Check your pocket" was all he said in reply, and moments later, Leopold's footsteps—and Safi's too—slowed in time to the music. As he drew her in for a final parting twist he whispered, "I am on your side, Safiya, and always have been."

The strings and winds softened to silence. Leopold released Safi directly before the throne. Henrick inclined his head at his nephew, and Leopold bowed in return. Before Safi could hurry back to her own throne, though, or even pat her pocket to see if the Truth-lens had indeed been dropped there, a command sliced through her.

Cold, but not bone-gripping. Clear, but not overly loud. *Again*, the Emperor said in her mind. *You will dance again.*

Safi bobbed a curtsy, her teeth grinding, her rage rekindling. Moments later, she turned to the pretty young domna now approaching her and she slid into the next dance.

Four Days After the Earth Well Healed

Furry and lithe, silent and feral, a weasel, dressed in its white winter cloak, scuttles over the forested earth toward Iseult. Clasped in its teeth are pages.

Iseult is too stunned to react. She has left the Hasstrel castle while everyone sleeps. Only Safi knows, and she would never reveal. Still, Iseult must be careful. Fon Grieg has placed guards throughout the Hasstrel lands. He does not trust that Safi's surrender is real, and he certainly doesn't trust the Nomatsi girl at Safi's side. Cahr Awen or no, Iseult is not to be trusted. She is different, she is other, and she has a power linked to the Void.

The weasel reaches Iseult. It drops the papers from its mouth. Worn, dirtied, and flattened, they are pale against the frozen soil. No moonlight beams down, but the stars shine and Iseult has been in the darkness long enough to see. To her left are the knotted roots of a winter-bare oak. To her right, a stretch of evergreen hedges that rustle on an icy breeze.

The pages rustle too as the weasel stares at Iseult and Iseult stares back. There is something in the creature's glinting eyes that is more than mere animal. This is no trained pet sent on an errand; this animal is sentient. And this animal is waiting.

"Who are you?" Iseult asks, though part of her—a deep part, like the veins of ore inside a mountain—already suspects the answer.

Then it comes, like it had in the castle: images to suffuse Iseult's mind and drape over her thoughts.

Poznin. The Wind Well surrounded by six oaks, surrounded by Cleaved.

A tower workshop with rounded walls decorated in dead flowers and bits of dangling felt.

Iseult's face, tired and haggard inside a forgotten ruin in the Contested Lands, where Esme had asked, "Are they owls or are they rooks?"

And lastly, a worn diary from which the weasel rips out pages.

Iseult's breath hisses. Everything inside her has gone cold—colder than the winter against her skin. Cold as the certainty of death and Trickster's endless games. Because it cannot be. It simply cannot be.

Then another image plays through Iseult's mind, and she knows it's true. So very, terrifyingly true.

A knife stabs Esme in the back, thrust by a Northman who used to be her Cleaved. The Prince of Nubrevna has betrayed her. This Northman has betrayed her, and now blood, blood everywhere. Now the world's Threads fading away.

"Esme?" Iseult whispers, and the weasel purrs. "But . . . how?"

The weasel does not answer, but instead slithers over the pages. Paper crackles, and Iseult realizes Esme wants her to look at them.

"It's too dark." *Iseult motions to the empty sky.* "I'll have to take them inside—"

The weasel squeaks, an emphatic no, and stamps across the pages again. Here, *she seems to say.* These can only be read here.

Iseult glances toward the castle. It is nothing more than pale lights between branches from this distance. No Threads approach, and it will be some time before Safi worries. After all, Iseult has taken nightly walks for several days now.

Her bones need movement. Her soul needs silence.

"Yes," *Iseult says at last, and she takes up the top paper. It is torn in places and slightly damp in the center, where tiny tooth marks pucker. After several moments of squinting, she is finally able to detect a diagram: crude figures on one side, a solo figure on the other, lines stretched between them. Words are scribbled in neat handwriting around the picture, but it takes Iseult a moment to recognize Arithuanian—strange Arithuanian, as if written a hundred years ago . . .*

Or a thousand. *Understanding pitches over her; the cold inside her deepens.* "This is Eridysi's diary," *she says, and Esme nods her weasel head.*

Suddenly, the night's darkness means nothing to Iseult. Suddenly, she cannot stop reading. Devouring each word, each illustration, each stroke from a pen wielded a thousand years ago. Here is a description of cleaving. Here a description of releasing Threads so they do not become ghosts to haunt the mind. Here is an explanation of how to hold Severed Threads and control them, and here is an introduction to cleaving from afar.

There's a guide to dream-walking, and even a small snippet about failed attempts at reanimating the dead. They're all observational notes, of course, for although Eridysi had been able to touch some magic, she had not been a Weaverwitch.

But that doesn't matter to Iseult, for the person Eridysi had observed had been the Void Paladin of a thousand years ago. Portia had been her name, and she had been able to cleave and weave and break and bind. She had even made the first Loom, binding people who would eventually become the Hell-Bards.

And she'd forced Eridysi to watch every step of the way, to record every detail. Now all her methods, all her experiments, all her thoughts on the power of the Void—the power that lives inside Iseult—are written out for Iseult to read.

Except that this is only part of the diary. Only a few stolen pages.

"*Where's the rest?*" *Iseult asks when she gets to the final damaged paper. Her nose is going numb; her fingers already are.*

A vision of Poznin appears in Iseult's mind, of Esme's tower, and the meaning is clear. If Iseult wants to learn more, she must go to Poznin. There, she can learn exactly as Esme did. She can lay claim to what the girl-turned-weasel left behind.

"*I . . . can't.*" *It is surprisingly hard for Iseult to say this aloud. Never has she been so close to understanding her own power. Never has she been with someone else who has a magic like hers.*

Had a magic like hers.

"*I have to stay with Safi. But what happened to you, Esme?*" *Iseult extends a tentative hand, and the weasel nuzzles against it. For a moment, she feels far more feral than human.*

Then the images begin anew.

A man shrouded in darkness, tall and lithe with no face and only limbs made of shadow. "It will all be over quickly," he tells Esme in Nomatsi before his shapeless hands close around her. Heat spears through her body. Cold too. She stretches and shrinks, painless yet more pain than she has ever known. But as he'd said, it is all over quickly. Her vision changes; the old world vanishes and a new one begins.

"Find her," he commands. "Find the dark-giver and keep her safe."

Iseult sucks in sharply as the memory fades. "*Who . . .*" *Another gulp of air. She felt that pain as if it had been her own skin rearranged.* "*Who was that?*"

Esme seems to shrug. She doesn't know, and she doesn't care. For all that she was once a young woman—once the Puppeteer—she is now an animal with a tiny brain. Some of her humanity remains, but not everything.

She leans into Iseult's hand, almost feline in her desire for a good back scratch. Study the pages, *she seems to say.* Then we will go to Poznin.

Iseult sighs, steam puffing from her lips, and though she knows she shouldn't, she finds herself grasping the torn pages once more and holding them high for a reread. She does not want to learn. She does not want to sever, sever, twist and sever . . .

But she has to. It is the magic she was given by Moon Mother. The only way she can protect herself, protect Safi. She spent all her life trying to be a Threadwitch, powerless and cast aside. Stumbling every step she took and weighing Safi down. Now Iseult has a magic like Esme's and the descriptions from this diary. She has saved lives with it before; perhaps she can learn how to do so again.

With a second sigh, Iseult settles into a cross-legged seat beside the oak. Esme coils across her lap, and with shadows to cloak them completely, Iseult studies what a Voidwitch did a thousand years ago.

And she studies what it will take to become the next Puppeteer.

SEVEN

✳

Iseult hadn't meant to sleep, but exhaustion would not be denied. It wasn't surprising really, she'd slept so little these past two months.

Fool. Iseult had promised the weasel that she would keep watch tonight; she was lucky no one had appeared while she slept.

The nightmares had come, though. They always did. Except it wasn't the faces of the Cleaved or the killed that haunted her tonight. It was Safi, a week before she'd been wed and had her magic shorn away. Iseult had been so selfishly focused on herself, so selfishly *consumed* by her longing for simpler days and her hatred for the lingering eyes of Cartorra, that she hadn't been ready.

She had failed at her one and only task in this life: protect her Thread-sister because, as she'd been told, *No one can protect Safi like Thread-family.*

"I'm coming," she whispered to the shadows of the hut. Owl slept beside her, Threads faded with sleep, the weasel curled nearby. "I'm coming." Iseult shoved down all the maggots burrowing in her chest and fumbled for a nearby lantern. It guttered, the oil sloshed. Less oil than before she'd fallen asleep. *Fool, fool.*

Iseult pushed to her feet. Owl did not awaken, but the weasel did. She followed Iseult to the table and watched with glittering eyes as Iseult removed a roll of tattered papers from inside her woolen tunic. Torn, water-damaged, and flattened, these eight diary pages had been Iseult's salvation. And her curse. The final stick upon the pyre. The final step away from Moon Mother's light.

Her eyes briefly slid to the black circle on her hand. The ink sucked up all light; a tiny doorway into death. It had hurt when the Witchmark master had tattooed it, but as Henrick had told her and Safi: *The world must know who you are. The world must know that here, in this palace, lives the Cahr Awen.*

Iseult and Safi had complied because they'd thought that giving the

Emperor what he'd expected to see would allow them to cut the purse more easily. How wrong they'd been. How wrong *she'd* been. They had gone to Praga to find Safi's uncle and save him from death as a traitor. Instead, Safi had been turned into a Hell-Bard and Iseult had been forced to flee.

Iseult smoothed down the pages. The weasel had not been elegant when she'd ripped apart Eridysi's journal, and there'd been the wear of travel. Esme had crossed marshes and mountains, farms and forests in search of Iseult.

There was so much missing too. So much Iseult didn't know and could not figure out on her own. Even with the weasel's mental images to guide her, Iseult needed more words, more diagrams, more explanations.

What I need is the full journal. But Poznin was still at least three weeks away. Probably closer to a month, even with horses. Which meant for another month, these eight pages were all Iseult would have to learn by.

"Dream-walking," Iseult said, removing a single page. It was the one skill in these pages that Eridysi had been able to do herself. Iseult had done it before as well, when she'd had her Threadstone and Safi had had hers . . .

But Henrick had taken those stones, just as he had taken everything else from them. And although Eridysi wrote of ways to dream-walk and to find someone *without* a personal item of theirs, Iseult hadn't been able to make it work. She hadn't even been able to enter the Dreaming to search.

Perhaps tonight would be different, though.

Resting her palms upon her thighs, she took several long, relaxing breaths. She let her eyes rest on the lantern's flame, vision unfocusing. *In. Out. In. Out.* Not so different from the way Aeduan had taught her to meditate.

Aeduan. Thinking of him sent her mind spiraling sideways and her pulse rising. She'd lost her silver taler somewhere at the Monastery, which meant Aeduan could not find her. Might never find her again . . .

"No," she hissed. This was always what happened. If her mind didn't veer off toward Aeduan, then it spun toward Safi. Or to Prince Leopold and the layers upon layers of secrets he hid beneath. Or sometimes to Evrane and the strange possession that had controlled her at the Monastery.

With a groan, Iseult pushed away from the table. She needed clarity. She needed a focus item, just as Eridysi explained—something that would give her guidance.

Then it hit her: a new angle she could try. A different approach that hadn't occurred to her before. It was a long shot, but at this point, what more did she have to lose? Besides, Trickster or Wicked Cousin was watching over her today.

Maybe they still had some blessings yet to give.

Iseult stared down at the dead man. He had looked peaceful in his final moments, when resignation had swept in. If not for the blood and entrails, he might've been asleep.

It was midnight; the moon was high and full. *A Threadwitching night,* Iseult's mother would've called it. *When Moon Mother's glow washes away all color, leaving only Threads. Leaving only our work.*

Little good that had done Iseult. She had been no Threadwitch then, when she'd wanted it most, when her mother had wanted it most. And she certainly was no Threadwitch now. Even her Weaverwitchery was no use here. The man was too dead to reanimate (not that Iseult had tried that magic yet), and he lacked the Severed Threads of the Cleaved.

He was nothing more than a cold corpse who had something she wanted.

With a steeling breath, Iseult knelt beside him. Her gloves, stolen from camp, were intended for a larger person, but it was better to be clumsy than risk touching the chain before she was ready.

Touching it not only hurt, but it connected her in ways she didn't understand to Emperor Henrick. She'd discovered that entirely by accident after a Hell-Bard kill one week ago. And since, in theory, all Hell-Bards were bound to Henrick, and Henrick was bound to Safi, then perhaps . . .

Please, Iseult prayed as she slipped her fingers around the gold chain. The corpse's skin was stiff behind it. With a small knife from a thigh holster she'd found at camp, she set to sawing. She sawed and sawed and sawed. She yanked, she twisted, she pulled. But to no avail. The noose was like the wooden heretic's collar: it could not be removed.

Iseult had known this might be a possibility, even if she'd fervently hoped otherwise. And she could not let a squeamish stomach get in her way. Qualms and regrets belonged to the old Iseult. The one who had hidden within scarves and hoods. The one who'd let everyone else decide who she was, who she should be.

That old Iseult had ruined countless lives. Whatever she'd touched had unraveled. Whomever she'd loved had been cleft in two.

But no more. She was the Puppeteer now, and Puppeteers felt no regret. Now Iseult unraveled what *she* wanted. Now *she* chose whom to cleave in two.

Sever, sever, twist and sever.

Yes, the weasel purred in her mind, and for once, Iseult did not push her out.

After replacing the knife at her thigh, Iseult unsheathed her sword. *His* sword. A few cautious swings to line up her aim . . . Then she swung with all her might at his neck.

Shock waves boomed up Iseult's arms, but she managed to sever the spine and get the blade almost out the other side. His head flopped sideways and hung upside down with eyes staring. Only a few strands of muscle and sinew held it on.

"Sorry," she mumbled, though she didn't know why. She'd killed the man, after all, and had not apologized then.

Two more practice swings, then she arced the blade through once more. It slid easily this time. The head finished its gruesome fall beside the Hell-Bard's thighs, and he did not look like he was sleeping now.

Iseult stoutly avoided his dead stare while she hooked her thumb beneath his noose. It slid upward, past the tattered edges of his neck, past the pointed remnant of his spine. Then it was off completely. After scrubbing away blood with her gloves, Iseult tucked the chain into her cloak's pocket and set off for camp.

She did not look back.

Soon enough, she was in the hut once more, before the table and before the diary pages. The weasel glared at her from her spot beside Owl. She'd wanted to join Iseult, but Iseult had made her stay behind to stand watch.

"I have a new plan," Iseult told her as she sank onto the stool. Instantly the weasel's glare melted. She scampered toward the table, shimmied up a wooden leg, and came to a stop beside the lantern. Her excitement was palpable. She was bright and bubbly, as she often had been in her human life.

Or maybe that was Iseult's own excitement. Her heart hammered. Her hands, for some reason, trembled, and heat gathered on her back and in her face. This was going to work. She was certain of it.

The golden noose glittered on the table, winking in the lantern's uneven glow. The hut had grown hot from the stove; Iseult peeled off her outer cloak. *Comfort,* Eridysi's notes said, *is critical. One must be able to relax the body, and relax the mind.*

After draping the chain over her thigh and removing her gloves, Iseult repeated the steps she'd tried before. Breathing in, breathing out. Staring into the lantern's flame, focusing on both the light and Safi's face. Until finally, she placed her hands over her thighs, over the chain. Breathe in, out, in, out . . .

Cold crashed into her. Her lungs compressed. Her whole body sharpened, even as her hand seared. She did not let go. Hell-Bard ice could not stop her. *Safi, Safi, Safi. In. Out. In. Out. Safi, Safi, Safi—*

The world fell away.

It was the Dreaming. Iseult knew that right away—only in the Dreaming was there so much gray, so much empty space with nothing inside. But this was different from what Iseult had experienced before, when she'd first communicated with Esme. Or when she'd met the Rook King in her sleep. There was movement in this great expanse. Pulsing and writhing. She saw it, she felt it, like a riptide bearing down, gentle at first. Then rougher, harder, as each frozen breath passed.

The magic was working.

Safi, Safi, Safi. In. Out. In. Out.

Pressure increased around Iseult. Her ears popped. Her breath fogged. She felt brittle and thin, like she was being stretched out, her very soul pulled taut as a bowstring.

Safi, Safi, Safi. In. Out. In. Out.

That was when the voices began and the figures appeared. One moment, nothing spanned before her; the next, a stampede of shadows rammed into her.

They poked, they grabbed, they dug into her flesh and yanked her hair—all while they whispered in tongues she could not understand. She tried to ignore them at first, even as faces began to form, made of Aether and Threads, sparkling, bright, colorful. Yet also tainted by the shadow of Severed Threads.

The deeper she pressed, the more each face looked human, and the more she tried to scan them as they rushed against her. Because even in all this madness, the logical, detached part of Iseult's brain knew where she was.

This had to be the Hell-Bard Loom. She was *inside* the Hell-Bard Loom, and somewhere amidst these thousands of souls, thousands of ghosts, her Threadsister waited.

A shadow slammed into Iseult, grinning and hungry. It bellowed wordlessly, frozen fingers scraping into her skin. Then another shadow came from behind. From the left, from the right, until she was surrounded. Trapped. She could not move and could not see.

Safi! she screamed, though no sound came out. Only fog that crystallized and disappeared.

The voices filled every piece of her, their hands ripped and shredded. She felt trapped by their anger, and no amount of struggling would let her break free.

This is what drowning feels like, she thought as she was dragged beneath an ocean of forgotten souls who were bound for all eternity to a Hell-Bard Loom. Yet before she could crumble away forever, a figure moved over her. Fully formed, fully alive.

Relief washed through Iseult. This person would help her, just as the Rook King had helped her before. She would not be lost to drowning. She would not crumble yet. But then the person's face coalesced: a pointed chin and long jaw framed by black hair, graying at the temples. His yellow-hued eyes were small, his lashes short, and on his forehead were deep trenches that made him seem forever mildly surprised.

He looked mildly surprised now, turquoise frothing within his bright Threads—but there was pink pleasure in those Threads too.

"Ah," he said, a smile sliding over his face. "I had been wondering when you would finally step inside." Corlant's hand reached for Iseult's face, fingers long and spindly. "It will be easier if we meet in the real world, though, Iseult det Midenzi. I will be waiting."

He shoved. Iseult screamed.

The Dreaming ended.

EIGHT

✳

It was well past midnight before Safi was able to confirm whether the Truth-lens actually rested in her pocket. She had returned to her quarters, her usual Hell-Bards flanking with Lev at the lead. Her muscles burned after hours of endless dancing, her bad ankle ached, and her face had gone stiff from too many smiles.

But those were all distant, cursory sensations. The whole of her being was focused on the Truth-lens.

If the device, which Safi had made in Marstok, was indeed within the folds of her pocket, then she would need to be very careful over the next quarter hour. The Hell-Bards could not see it, for they would know right away what it was—what magic it could do. Her attendants could not find it, for they would certainly tell the spymasters they reported to. And Safi could not openly examine the device in her bedroom, for she was under constant surveillance.

Not the magical kind—her Hell-Bard powers would have sensed that—but rather the human kind with peepholes and listening horns.

Fortunately, although she also loathed him for it, Leopold fon Cartorra was one step ahead. When the Hell-Bards reached Safi's door, one of her attendants (named Svenja) rushed to open it while another (Nika) hurried forward to greet her. Clasped in Nika's hands was fine courtly paper with a red ribbon twined around it.

"For you," Nika said. She spoke with the slightest northern accent, her family hailing from some wealthy estate on the North Sea coast. "It is from His Imperial Highness," she added, and there was no missing the bright spots of color rising on her pale cheeks. They made her lovely face even lovelier.

Well, Safi thought, *she obviously read the message.* After accepting the letter while her Hell-Bards fell into their usual positions in the hall, Safi followed Svenja into the bedroom. Svenja was also an attractive woman, though with a more regal bearing. No smiles or blushes from her. Only business.

"I have chosen the blue nightgown," Svenja began.

But Safi snapped up a staying hand. "I will undress myself." She flashed the letter at both women. "And I would like to read my letter in privacy. I will see you in the morning, yes?"

"Oh, of *course*, Your Imperial Majesty." Nika curtsied buoyantly, her cheeks still aglow. Svenja curtsied more stiffly, with a murmured "Your Imperial Majesty," before hooking Nika's arm in hers and practically tugging the younger woman from the room.

Safi hurried to her desk. She'd had no occasion before to use it—who would she have written to? But the desk itself possessed a privacy screen. *For writing lover's letters*, Svenja had explained, which had made Nika giggle behind her hand, blushing all the while.

A blush not so different from the one Nika had just made, Safi realized as she unfolded the four-panel screen from its slots within the desk. She was surprised to find it didn't match the rest of the room. Even to her gray-shrouded eye, the silver silk clashed with the room's gold, and the elaborately printed flowers seemed too delicate next to all the Hasstrel bats.

It would protect Safi's privacy, though, and that was all that mattered. In moments, she had the ribbon off the letter and the paper smoothed across her desk.

My dearest Safiya,

You know how much I burn for you. Have always burned, since that summer long ago. I realize this is why you have avoided me and refused my offers to dance. But tonight, you have given me such hope. Please, tell me my hope is justified!

Feeling your supple waist beneath my fingers, seeing your eyes–blue, so blue–mere inches from mine, watching your lips move as you smiled or laughed . . . It felt like that summer all over again. Please, please consent to meet me tomorrow, in the Winter Garden, at the tenth chimes. I will ensure that we are alone.

Do you remember that first night together, Safiya? The way you laughed when I led you into that garden in Veñaza City? There was the alcove hidden by jasmine, and I pulled you close, our lips and hands desperate. And do you remember how I lifted you onto—

Safi slammed down the letter. Her eyes bulged, her cheeks scorched, and she rocked back from the privacy screen's protection.

No, it wasn't just her cheeks that were aflame—her whole body was. Not a word in this letter was true, of course, but gods below, the detail! Anyone who read it would surely think Safi and Leopold had shared an extremely passionate teenage affair.

No wonder Nika had looked so delightfully scandalized.

Well done, Polly. Safi now appeared, for any spies who might be peeking in her bedroom, like a woman who'd just read a lascivious letter from her lover. One could not fake a flush like this one, and she was even fanning herself against sweat—because *hell-fires*, the encounter in this letter was so acrobatic, she could scarcely imagine what body parts went where.

Oh, well *done*, Polly. Safi still didn't trust him, and given a chance, she would gladly do him bodily harm. But she couldn't deny this had been a clever ruse. No one in court would bat an eyelash if she and Leopold began an affair—not even the Emperor. Lovers outside of marriage were so common among Cartorran nobility, it was considered strange *not* to have one.

As the old skipping song went, *Robins and magpies on branches above. Money for marriage, and Heart-Threads for love.*

The cleverest element of Leopold's letter, though, was that it had given Safi the perfect reason to send away her attendants *and* a perfect reason to sit at her desk with the privacy screen. Now she could easily withdraw the item burning in her pocket.

While she shifted her dress around her, as if trying to billow in more air, she slipped out the small metal cylinder. And while her left hand tousled her hair, fanned at her face, her right hand slid the cylinder onto the desk beneath the privacy screen.

Safi grinned, and with a great flourish, she plucked quill and paper from beyond the screen. Then she hunched forward as if to scrawl a similarly seductive letter in return.

Instead, she examined the Truth-lens—and it *was* the Truth-lens. Exactly as she'd made it in Marstok. There was the brass casing, taken from a telescope's eyepiece. There were the outer lenses, and she could almost see hints of thread and flashes of quartz within. The only real difference between now and when Safi had crafted it a month ago was that now Safi was a Hell-Bard. Now, when she looked at it, her Hell-Bard senses revealed it to be magical.

She could not explain how she sensed that or why. Magical items were simply a bit more colorful, a bit more dimensional than anything else in her leached world. Witches too, and without any effort, her brain simply *knew* what witchery was before her and how powerful.

Sometimes it felt as if the information came from some vast, collective consciousness. Perhaps directly from the magic that bound all Hell-Bards as one. But when Safi had asked Lev about that, the woman had simply shaken her head and said, *Word of advice, Imperial Majesty: thinking leads to hoping, and nothin' is more futile when you're a Hell-Bard.*

When Safi looked at her Truth-lens now, it gleamed against the desk's glossy wood, and as soon as her fingers touched the brass . . .

Ah, there it was. The certainty trilling down the back of her neck that this was Truth magic—and what a strange, awful feeling that was. To stare at the only remnants of her own magic. Untouchable, unusable. Because, of course, magic didn't work on Hell-Bards. It could not harm them, it could not trick them. Whatever happened when the noose cinched into place, it rendered all magical effects obsolete.

Safi couldn't resist trying, though. She bent her head farther beneath the screen and pressed her eye to the glass.

It was like peering into a kaleidoscope, but with no rhyme or reason to the patterns. She trained it on her right hand, and her Aether Witchmark, only three weeks old, turned a variety of colors thanks to the stones and threads within. No longer a hollow circle, but a jagged, broken ellipse.

She'd never used her invention before. After pouring all of her energy and the false half of her magic into the various parts, Safi had attended Empress Vaness's birthday party—and then that party had ended in tragedy. So, *so* much tragedy that even now, she struggled to fully fathom it all.

Tragedy that could have been prevented. Tragedy *she* had caused.

At that thought, the lens turned white.

Safi snapped back her head, blinking. She shook the lens; quartz rattled. Then, after a quick scrub at her eye, she peered through the device again, this time fixing it on Leopold's letter. *You know how much I burn for you.* Safi dragged her gaze across the colorfully contorted sentence, mouthing each word to herself.

The lens went white again.

And Safi snapped back her head again. Surely the magic wasn't working. *Surely* the change in color was not a sign that something was false. Instinct sent her fingers rubbing at her eyes, though she knew perfectly well her vision was keen.

Ducking under the screen once more, she peered through the lens and whispered, "I am in love with Leopold fon Cartorra."

Oh, how the Truth-lens turned white at those words, and oh, how Safi smiled. The magic *was* working, even if she had no idea why. Perhaps it was simply because the lens was her own creation, hewn from her own witchery.

Either way, it changed everything.

Yes, she might be bound to Emperor Henrick. Yes, her magic might have been sliced away from her, lost for good. But she was no longer powerless, and with the Truth-lens, she had an advantage no one could ever suspect. Least of all Henrick.

Smiling—her first true, *happy* smile in two weeks—Safi finally grabbed for the inkpot and quill. Now that she had her Truth-lens, there was no reason not to meet him. No reason, in fact, not to trust him, since she could catch him in his lies.

> *My dear Polly,*
> *It brings me such joy to remember our summer together, and yes, dancing with you tonight brought it all crashing back. I have resisted being near you, but can no longer ignore how much my heart calls. Or how much my body. Seeing you dance each night was torture.*
> *I will see you tomorrow in the Winter Garden at the tenth chimes. The wait until that moment will be agony.*
>
> *Yours always,*
> *Safiya*

When Iseult awoke, she was shaking from cold. Somehow she had fallen to the shepherd's hut's floor, and now she stared up at a plank ceiling flickering with shadows. Everything hurt. Her head, her eyes, her lungs. Distantly, she felt the weasel scramble on her lap. She heard the creature squeaking with alarm. "Hush," she tried to say, but her throat was burned raw.

No, not burned raw. *Frozen.* She'd screamed so much when the souls had pulled her down. Before *he* had shoved her back into life. Surely that had not been him though. Not in the Dreaming, not in the Hell-Bard Loom. But there was no other explanation. Corlant det Midenzi had found her once more.

Ever since his cursed arrow had failed to kill her in the Midenzi tribe, he had hunted her. He'd sent raiders after her in the Contested Lands; he'd sent Aeduan after her too. And now he'd finally found her in the Hell-Bard Loom of all places.

I will be waiting, he'd said, and Iseult couldn't help but laugh at that. A huffy, broken sound—because he would be waiting for all eternity if he expected her to come to him.

With no grace and limbs that roared in protest, Iseult hauled herself back onto her stool.

"I think," she told the weasel, "I was in the Hell-Bard Loom."

She felt Esme crawl up her leg. Then suddenly the creature was digging her cold nose into Iseult's face. Images erupted in Iseult's mind, not so different from what Iseult had just seen: a gray world filled with darkened souls.

"Yes." Iseult nodded. Her eyes hurt too much to keep them open. "It looked just like that. But how did you navigate it? The Severed spirits overwhelmed me."

This question seemed to puzzle the weasel. She curled around Iseult's neck, clicking in her throat as if saying, *I did not have that problem.*

And Iseult sighed—because of course the weasel hadn't. She had had an entire diary to learn from and years of practice. Iseult had only a handful of pages and two weeks.

"There was someone else there," she went on, finally lifting her head from her hands. "I saw Corlant. The Purist priest you knew by a different name."

At first, the weasel offered no reaction. Silence filled the hut for several moments, and Iseult thought perhaps the creature had forgotten their conversation from a month and a half ago. Then suddenly the creature leaped off Iseult's shoulder and darted for one of the diary pages. With tiny teeth, she chomped down and dragged it to Iseult.

It was a description of making the first Loom—the Hell-Bard Loom Iseult had just fallen into. Incomplete, but with a basic illustration of the Threads binding each Cleaved soul to a person at the center of it all: Portia. She had built the first Loom by cleaving the other Void Paladin, by binding that woman's powerful Threads to stone.

At the Loom in Poznin, Esme had been the person at the center of it all. She had made the Loom by cleaving the very Air Well itself and binding hundreds of souls to her own. She had controlled them, and upon her death, those Cleaved had been left behind.

"You're saying Corlant is at the center of the Hell-Bard Loom?" Iseult shook her head. "That makes no sense. He has no connection to Cartorra or the Hell-Bards, no reason to bind such people to him." Besides, Iseult had seen Henrick dominate his Hell-Bards. *He* was in control. "Corlant must simply be able to dream-walk. Eridysi did it. You did it. The Paladin Portia did it. Perhaps all Voidwitches are able."

The weasel shook her head, unconvinced. Then she nudged Iseult's jaw and a new image formed. One of cleaving, one of Threads.

The message was clear: if Iseult wanted to understand the Hell-Bard Loom and free Safi, then she needed more power. And to get more power, she needed to go to Poznin and claim the rest of Eridysi's diary. Only then could she could march back across Cartorra to rescue Safi, no fear of Hell-Bards. No fear of Henrick or Corlant or *anyone*.

"Yes," Iseult told Esme, scratching her weasel ears. "When we get to Poznin that is exactly what I will do."

NINE

Thirty-four naval ships floated across the Veñaza City harbor. Spindrift and humidity thickened the night, casting everything in a ghostly haze. While Vivia stood at the *Iris*'s tiller, spyglass to her eye, the royal Nubrevnan flag snapped and waved on the mainmast.

"Why are they not moving?" the Empress asked. She stood beside Vivia, having traded in her golden gown for one of Vivia's old naval uniforms, though the navy coat swallowed her and only her iron belt kept her beige breeches high.

Vivia ignored her, lowering her spyglass and beckoning her Voice-witch near. Ginna, a round-faced woman with coloring brown as fresh clay, hurried over. Meanwhile, every sailor on the *Iris* waited poised and ready. Some at oars, some in the rigging, and some simply watching the blockaded horizon from the narrow windows belowdecks. Their shadows stretched over patches of swaying lamplight.

"Find the nearest Dalmotti Voicewitch," Vivia commanded. "Ask them why they do not move aside the blockade for a royal Nubrevnan ship."

"Hye," Ginna murmured, and instantly, her eyes turned glassy and pink. A sign her magic had stretched wide like a fisher's net. Four long breaths trickled by with only the moist wind on Vivia's hair and the rhythmic creak of the *Iris* to fill the weighted silence. Then Ginna's voice dropped to a baritone: "This is Captain Kadossi of the *Lioness*. You are ordered to return to the Southern Wharves, Your Highness."

"Turn back?" Vaness demanded before Vivia could speak. "On whose orders and what grounds?"

Vivia's shoulders tensed upward. This was not the first time Vaness had taken the lead despite Vivia being the captain here.

"By order of the Doge, you must return to the Southern Wharves. Dock your ship and come ashore immediately."

Vaness's lips parted, but Vivia thrust up a flat hand. "Don't," she ordered. "I am captain." Then to Ginna: "What will you do if we disobey?"

"We have orders to stop you by any means necessary."

"Is that a threat?" the Empress spat before Vivia could intervene.

"Merely a warning," the captain replied.

"How dare he," Vaness snarled beneath her breath. She glared at Vivia. "He would not truly shoot us down. We are worth more alive."

"Are we?" Vivia was not so sure. She was also going to throttle the Empress if she interrupted again. "We thought the Doge would aid us. He did not, and I suspect these *warnings* are genuine."

Vaness recoiled. "Are you suggesting we return to the city?"

"No." Vivia found Ginna's unseeing eyes. Then she wet her lips and chose her words carefully. "Tell this captain that we will be passing his blockade, and at any sign of force, we will retaliate to the maximum of our abilities."

The Voicewitch quickly passed along these words, and moments later, her eyes stopped glowing. The pink faded. She was herself again. "He ended the communication," she said, and Vivia nodded. She had expected as much. "The maximum of our abilities?" Vivia asked. "What does that even mean?"

"It means we have one cannon on our main deck stolen from you two months ago." Vivia pointed to the lone iron machine. "And it means you are the Destroyer of Kendura Pass. Take your station, Empress, and get ready to fight."

For half a moment, Vaness's face paled, almost as if in fear. Which of course made no sense, but Vivia had no time to question or repeat her order. There was much to do and a blockade closing in fast. Plus, she was the only Tidewitch on board, and even with three Windwitches to flank her, it was less than her usual forces.

"Leeri!" Vivia barked, flying down the main deck toward the stern. "Give us a beat to sail by, boy, and make it a quick one. Witches, take your positions, and Sotar, you're on the tiller." She sprinted for the ship's end, her magic already rising. These waves belonged to her.

"I want full power in the sails," she ordered as her witches gathered in a row beside her. Then louder, for the rest of her crew: "Battle stations, everyone! We are punching our way through."

She did not wait to see if her crew obeyed. Punishment was now Sotar's domain. Even Vaness was at his mercy, though Vivia prayed to Noden that the Empress did not make trouble.

She needed that Iron Bitch right about now.

At the ship's stern, Vivia grabbed the balustrade. Already the waves licked toward her, hungry and ready. *Command us,* they said. *We are yours.* And Vivia smiled. She was a sea fox, she was a Tidewitch, and the Doge had chosen the wrong queen to anchor down.

"Prepare your winds," she roared at her officers while she called the waves to her. Up, up, a catapult ready to launch. Air gusted around her. Swirling, charged, and powered by three witches as eager and as powerful as she.

Almost as powerful, anyway.

Two heartbeats boomed, wild against her chest, and the wind-drum began. No one sang—this was not a sailing beat. It was a battle beat, and it thrummed in Vivia's very bones. *Boom-da-boom-da-boom.* Faster, faster, while the winds around her churned stronger and the waves below her readied.

"Make way!"

The ship gave a groan to split ears. The *Iris* launched forward, an arrow from its bow, a dog from its kennel, a firepot erupting that flew over the harbor's easy waves—waves that Vivia now commanded. Magic poured through her, swelling out from her fingertips and into every droplet of sea beneath, around, beside. She was a conduit for power, a vessel that nudged the water in ways it already wanted to move.

Yes, it seemed to tell her. *Faster, faster, forward, faster.*

"Warship ahead!" Sotar's deep voice bellowed above the *Iris*'s creaking skeleton and Cam's frantic drumbeat. Over the winds and ceaseless waves. "Cannons are aimed at us!"

Vivia did not respond. She couldn't. She was the water, and it was up to Sotar to heave the tiller and guide the *Iris* where she needed to be. A cannon fired; Vivia heard its distant thunder, heard Sotar bark at Vaness to intervene.

Faster, she commanded the waves. *Faster, faster—*

An explosion blasted behind her. Noise and splinters slashed into her. Vivia slammed against the balustrade. Then she fell overboard entirely. She crashed into the water, headfirst. So fast, she couldn't comprehend what had happened. So fast, she could not gather breath before she plummeted beneath the waves.

But the water welcomed her—it always welcomed her—and without fully realizing what she did, she gathered her tides to her and launched upward again. Toward the sky, out of the sea, then through the air, droplets shedding.

She hit the deck and found a hole splintered through the main deck. Vaness was sprinting toward it, her arms out, her eyes huge and hair wild. A second later, the cannonball roared upward from the hole. Vaness spun, a whirling dance, and the shot launched back toward the *Lioness*.

"It . . . did not . . . break through," she panted, her gaze briefly catching Vivia's. "We will not sink."

Before Vivia could ask why it had hit them in the first place, Vaness was rushing toward the bow and cannon again. All the while, the wind-drum still pulsed *ba-doom-ba-doom* and the Windwitches still heaved their power into the sails.

The *Iris* flew.

More cannons blasted—not just from the *Lioness* but from other ships too. At least five others, now steering this way guided by magic and oars and well-aimed sails. Lights flared across the decks, sailors scurried, and their weapons fired as fast as pistols.

It was too much for Vaness to hold off. It shouldn't have been—she had toppled an entire mountain—yet for some reason, this was proving too much. So Vivia bolted across the deck. No words for Sotar as she sprinted by. He might have been off the seas for almost two decades, but he wielded the tiller with natural ease. His shoulders bulged as he pushed into each movement. His voice boomed over the madness of battle.

Vivia reached Vaness, braced against the balustrade while two sailors shoved fresh shot into the *Iris*'s cannon. They ignited the tip; light flared and hissed, unmagicked but deadly.

Then the cannon let loose, and iron rocketed outward, guided by Vaness's magic. Which was wrong—all wrong. She should not have needed fire. She should have been able to launch those cannons by herself.

The cannonball connected with the *Lioness*'s foremast. It snapped in two before colliding next with the mainmast.

"Hold steady!" Sotar bellowed, and the *Iris* listed sharply to starboard.

Vaness fell. Vivia lurched for her. Caught her right before she went overboard. She was cold to the touch, and when Vivia got her upright again, she found the woman's face pale. Blood trickled from her nose.

"What's wrong?" Vivia scooped an arm beneath her.

"Nothing." Vaness tried to pull free. Tried to reach around and grab at new cannonballs whizzing this way, but Vivia held her back and shoved her at the closest sailor. "Take her," she yelled.

"Get off me," Vaness snarled, and suddenly she was at Vivia's side, glaring death. "Do not interfere with me again, *Majesty*." Then, as if to prove she was fine despite the blood oozing down her chin, she lifted her hands and caught two more iron balls hurling there.

They slung about in midair in sharp, vicious arcs before flying back toward the decks they'd just abandoned and shooting right back into their cannons.

One explosion. Two. The *Lioness* went up in flames. Which meant now was the time to sail. "Don't pass out," Vivia ordered, but the Empress only bared her teeth. They were bloodied too.

There was no time to fret over Vaness though or wonder what was wrong. The *Lioness* was scrambling to stay afloat, and the *Iris* could not miss this chance. *Come,* Vivia thought, calling to the waters. Begging to the waves. *Carry us high and carry us fast.*

All around her, the water seemed to laugh, a buoyant lift in her chest. Of power, of the strength that only water—the most ancient of elements—could provide. It crashed against the hull. Hard enough to steal everyone's legs. Not Vivia's, though. She was ready for it, and as soon as the waves collided against the wood, she sent it charging onward. A steed that no one could stop.

The *Iris* barreled toward the sinking *Lioness*. Wind slammed against Vivia, magicked and natural and thick with spindrift and cannon smoke. Ahead, the warship was a mess of broken wood and blackened fumes. Fires licked across the deck, and sailors sped like rats.

The *Iris* was headed straight for it. Faster, faster, higher, higher. And just as she knew he'd be able to do, Sotar leaned into the tiller at the perfect moment. Right when Vivia could see the Dalmotti captain, clad in gold, at his own tiller and bellowing orders while his ship dropped low.

He had witches—Wind and Tide—but they were focused on keeping their ship afloat. They could no more stop Vivia and her ship than they could stop Noden and the Hagfishes.

Screams flickered over the winds and waves. Eyes widened and soldiers gaped at the Nubrevnans rushing by. Vivia smiled. A real grin, alive and throbbing through her. No one could stop her. No one could stop her ship, the sails taut with wind and the hull carried on waves that reveled in their own speed. *Faster, faster.*

Wood streaked by. The *Lioness* was twice the size of the *Iris*, as was the second warship closing in on the starboard side. But it wouldn't reach the *Iris* before she was past. No amount of magic could move a ship that did not want to be moved.

And the *Iris* wanted to move. All Nubrevnan ships did—it was their secret. Why Nubrevnans had kept their shores safe for so long against the empires. They had sleek vessels whose sails were more like wings and whose planks and sails were crafted with Nubrevnan desperation. Not even the Shipbuilder Guild of Dalmotti could match that.

More cannons fired, but Vaness was ready this time. She caught, she launched, and her aim stayed true. Distantly, Vivia heard the drum still pounding and Sotar still shouting. But she was so deeply bound to the water that the beat was meaningless. The words incomprehensible.

Faster, faster.

On and on, the half-galley rode the waves, and on and on, the magic coursed through her. She might not have the Nihar rage—not truly—but she had this. A power no man could ever dominate.

It wasn't until Sotar stood before her, his hands grabbing at her biceps, that Vivia finally allowed her power to soften. And it wasn't until Vaness was shoving in front of him, her coat and blouse soaked in blood and her eyes aflame, that Vivia finally let her magic dry completely.

"She's going to pass out," Vaness said, and briefly her ire gave way to something Vivia thought might be concern.

Maybe, though. Only maybe.

Vivia's knees gave way. She tumbled forward into the Empress's waiting arms. She did not go under, however. Not yet at least. Instead she clung quite firmly to consciousness and murmured, "Well done, Imperial Majesty." She sucked in a ragged breath. "Well done."

TEN

✳

In the gray hours when moon and sun shared the sky, Iseult nudged Owl awake. The girl pretended not to notice—and Iseult bit back a sigh. Scolding never worked on Owl, and though they had come a long way in their month together without Aeduan, most days, Iseult was the enemy.

Perhaps if she used softer words. Perhaps if she could smile and caress. Perhaps if she offered love and kindness, as Zander had done with Owl in Praga when he'd been her primary guard . . . then *perhaps* Owl would behave.

And perhaps I will grow wings too. Iseult could no more change what she was—what her mother had made her—than Owl could suddenly become an obedient child. Which was why the words that escaped her throat as she toed Owl again were "I can see your Threads, Owl. I know you're awake, and I don't have time to play your games."

The mound of blankets shifted; Owl's Threads flashed with stubbornness. "I want to stay."

Iseult's nose wrinkled up. She would not get angry. *Stasis in your fingers and in your toes.* After all, no one would willingly leave the only true warmth they'd felt in days. Or the only cooked meals.

"It's not safe for us to stay here," she said at last.

"It is," Owl countered. "You'll just kill the bad people anyway."

Something hard clenched in Iseult's belly. She had done her best to hide the killings from Owl, but the child had often refused to look away, just like her namesake, who had kept her eyes open when Trickster had betrayed them all.

Iseult scratched her cheek and shoved the clenching downward to her toes. She didn't kill because she wanted to; she killed to protect Owl. She killed because, with a magic like hers, it was the only path she could ever tread.

Sever, sever, twist and sever.

"What if," Iseult proposed, turning nonchalantly away from the blankets, "I tell a story while we travel. Will you rise for that?"

Owl's Threads perked with interest. She peeled back her blankets to reveal a single eye. "Five stories."

"Two."

"Three, and one has to be the little hedgehog."

"Deal." Iseult's nostrils flared with triumph as Owl threw back her blankets to reveal a triumphant smile of her own—and Iseult realized she had, in fact, lost Owl's game.

"Where is the weasel-girl?" Owl asked, flinging a suspicious glower around the hut.

"Scouting ahead. She will find the safest path for us."

"I don't like her."

"I know." Iseult aimed for the hut's exit, and Owl shuffled behind.

"She is worse than Wicked Cousin."

"Yes. I know that too." Unlike Trickster, who caused trouble because he was bored, the goddess Wicked Cousin caused trouble because she enjoyed pain. Yet it was not Wicked Cousin who betrayed the gods in the end.

"'Evil is not the enemy,'" Iseult quoted as she stepped into the cold dawn. "'For without it, there can be no good. Chaos, however, is unstoppable.'"

"Hmph" was all Owl said in response to that, and she kept silent while Iseult made porridge and saddled the horses (whom Owl had named Lady Sea Fox and Lord Storm Hound). On Lady Sea Fox, she loaded sacks filled with dried meats, a cooking pan, a snare, three blankets, and several water bags. On Lord Storm Hound, she placed herself and Owl. Then they set off into a sunrise still hidden behind winter clouds.

It had been the same every day since they had fled Praga: gray, gray, dreary gray. Sometimes there had been rain. Sometimes snow. But never sunshine, never blue skies.

As bargained, Iseult told Owl the required three stories, including the little hedgehog, and eventually, Owl dozed off. Iseult had to fight the urge to do the same. Lord Storm Hound's gait was soothing and sure, and she'd spent most of the night mapping a route to the large lake. A route without Hell-Bards and Cartorran soldiers along the way.

You'll just kill them anyway.

No. Iseult snapped her head sideways. She could not change who she was. She'd tried for eighteen years, and it had only led to pain and death. It had only failed Safi in the end. At least now *she* chose who felt that pain. At least now *she* chose whose life came to an end.

Threads that break, Threads that die.

Yes, Esme sang, and Iseult almost smiled. One creature in this world understood her. *Where are you?* she asked, and a moment later, the image of a river filled Iseult's mind. No people, no signs of travel. A good place for rest.

Wait for us, she ordered, and the weasel agreed.

Time ambled by. The landscape shifted from muddy evergreen to muddy deciduous, branches bare, before Iseult and Owl caught up to the weasel by a wide river. Beyond the main flow lay tens of old oxbows, forgotten by the waters' changing tread. Pools glittered; the trees whispered. And for the first time in two weeks, as Iseult made a small camp, the clouds parted overhead. Sunshine and blue skies peered down.

Today is good, she thought while handing Owl a crab apple. Then she blinked because she couldn't remember the last time she'd thought such a thing. The last time she'd felt it. Yet here she was, pleased by their pace down the mountain, pleased by the absence of Cartorran soldiers nearby, and pleased by a soothing landscape on a cold but sunny winter's day.

Most of all, she was pleased that she and Owl could enjoy a snack of crab apples and salted deer instead of foraged nuts gone rancid. That they could, for a time, relax without fear of ambush.

The only problem was the lack of a clear path across the river. The horses could not take the stepping-stones, and there was no obvious passage that Iseult could see to the east or west. Esme, when Iseult asked about it, had nothing to offer. She had scouted no farther.

"Then you stay with Owl," Iseult replied. She felt calmer than she had in days. Stronger too. "I'll be the one to scout ahead this time."

For once, the weasel did not argue. She'd been walking all day; she was hungry and tired and deeply annoyed that Iseult had not let her bite Owl's nose. (Owl had, after all, stepped on her tail first.) For once, she seemed content to rest while Owl dozed in a sunbeam.

After grabbing her staff, Iseult set off across the river. The stones, though slick and worn by waves, were spaced far enough apart that she could reach them with easy leaps. Only one required a full running jump, and even that movement felt good.

She couldn't explain it. After last night's foray into the Loom, after encountering Corlant and being pummeled by ghosts, Iseult had expected exhaustion.

Instead, she felt alert, alive, and powerful. Perhaps it was the sunshine, perhaps it was the food, or perhaps it was simply knowing that the end of the Ohrins was only a day and a half away.

On the river's opposite shore, sand stretched flat until the pools began. Scrub grew in patches, some trees too. Mostly it was a low, tickling grass that Iseult found easy to tromp over. Around the pools she went, some no larger than the shepherd's hut from last night, but most as long as a galleon and wide as the river they had once been. Minnows skated within, vanishing each time a wind danced over the waters.

Iseult was in no rush to circle the pools, and it took her some time before she finally reached an area where pine trees once more speared the sky. She paused there, at the forest's edge, to glance back toward their temporary camp. Owl's Threads were still muted with sleep; no other Threads glittered nearby.

Satisfied the child was safe, she strode into the woods. Massive conifers, their trunks large as towers, blocked all sunlight, leaving only a sandy needle carpet to trek across. Some bushes and saplings had taken root, but most of the ground was easy and clear.

Iseult must've truly won the favor of her mysterious god. Never had she had so much luck.

Soon, she heard the gentle lapping of the river again. Closer than expected—and welcome. If the river bent this sharply this soon, then the horses could simply carve around with it and continue on. No need for a crossing.

Each step made Iseult's heart rise a bit higher. Made her pace quicken and bounce. She couldn't explain how she knew, yet somehow, she *knew* once she saw the river, she would be happy. It was as if . . .

As if the Threads that bind were pulling her onward. As if someone she cared about was waiting just ahead.

But that was impossible. Of course it was impossible. Who could be here in the middle of a mountain range? Yet Iseult's body did not seem to care. She wanted to move faster. She wanted to run.

So she did—a three-beat rhythm of feet and staff upon the sand. The river was so close; she had to see it, she had to know.

When she was almost to the forest's edge, she glimpsed the water. The sun beat off its surface, glaring and true, while on the river's opposite side stood a figure in white.

It can't be, she thought even as she knew it was. *He* was who her body had been running to. *He* was who her Threads had reeled her toward.

She cleared the forest, her feet now sprinting, breaths now shallow, and heart caught somewhere in her mouth. Because he was here. The

Bloodwitch named Aeduan was here, standing on the other side of the river.

That white cloak, that pale face and sharp jawline. Iseult would know him anywhere. Her Threads would know his anywhere. *Mhe varujta. Te varuje.*

Eleven Days After the Earth Well Healed

*I*t is the room where Hell-Bards are made. *Safi cannot believe Henrick is show-ing it to her. At first, she thought it was a warning. Now, she thinks it merely a point of pride—and as disturbing as it is, she cannot deny she understands.*

The room is beautiful. Square, marble, with four pillars to support a high, domed ceiling. There is something ancient about it, as if she has stepped into another time. The floors, marble tiles with gold-inlaid eagles, are worn but me-ticulously maintained. The ceiling, streaked in more gold, teases and taunts like fish fins in a pond.

It is the walls, though, that draw the focus. Thousands, perhaps tens of thou-sands of gold chains dangle on invisible hooks. They are still, silent, yet they echo footsteps and voices in a way that makes them seem alive.

Safi half expects to find eyes winking out from them.

Despite the nooses—despite knowing what they mean—there is something soothing about this room. Something unnaturally peaceful, and she wonders if there is a spell. Some Aether-bound magic that erases fear and numbs the soul. Without her full Truthwitchery, though, she senses nothing false.

"This is where chosen Hell-Bards swear fealty," Henrick says. As usual, he wears brown. As usual, he looks squat and graceless and his snaggletooth wig-gles. He and Safi are the only people in the room.

"The noble Hell-Bards," he elaborates. "Or officers in the army who have proven themselves worthy. I bring them here, and they enter my service." He speaks with no arrogance, no performance. Though he is proud of this room—of the power it gives him—he is also respectful of it. He wants Safi to see it, to understand it, because she will be his wife soon.

She hates that she appreciates this gesture. And she hates *that she appre-ciates this room. It is betrayal of the four Hell-Bards who matter most to her: Caden, Zander, Lev, and Eron. She will help them, though. Soon, when the plan is complete, she will help all Hell-Bards.*

"How?" she asks. "How do you . . . enter them into your service?"

Henrick licks his lips. Several seconds trickle past. Then without preamble, he waddles to a stone table at the heart of the room. It is also marble, but with no adornments save for the four iron straps at each corner. Safi swallows at the sight of it. The straps are clearly intended for wrists and ankles, clearly intended to restrain.

"It is simply a matter of placing one of these chains around the person's neck. But there is great pain, hence the iron straps." Again, no pleasure in his voice. Only matter-of-fact honesty that Safi's magic knows is true.

"I will show you one day," Henrick adds. He taps his fingers against the table. "But not today."

Safi's fingers flex against her thigh. She doesn't want to see a noosing ever, but she can hardly say that.

Henrick abandons the table and approaches her, arm extended. He has been a doting betrothed these past five days, and to his credit, he has treated Iseult with the same consideration. Safi almost feels bad about what she and Iseult have planned.

Almost.

"Did my uncle become a Hell-Bard here?" Safi asks before Henrick can reach her.

He pauses and she quickly turns away. Four long steps bring her to a wall of nooses. They flash and wink, and yes, she swears that eyes ought to be there.

Behind her, Henrick says, "Yes. He was. By his choice and by my hand."

"Oh." She sucks in a long breath and runs her fingers over the chains. They chime like tiny bells. "And why did you discharge him?"

She tells herself she only asks this out of curiosity. She tells herself it is not some perverse need to understand the uncle she has always hated. But even a Truthwitch cannot lie to herself. The truth is that she has always wondered why Eron chose his Hell-Bard duties over protecting her parents. She has always wondered what drives a man to hate himself so.

To her surprise, Henrick actually answers her: "Eron disobeyed an order."

Eyebrows lifting, she slides a noose off the wall and twists back to face him. "But can't you force Hell-Bards to do anything you wish?" She dangles the chain his way. "I thought they were bound to you."

"I can and I did." Nothing in Henrick's expression or tone changes. It only makes Safi want to know more.

"What was the order?" she asks.

A pause stretches between them. The Emperor watches Safi; she watches him, her arm still outstretched. The chain still hanging between them.

Then at last he says, "No," before turning away. And as he strides for the door, Safi is left wondering if he meant No had been the order or No he would not answer her. Either way, she has gained no ground. No understanding. Her uncle remains an enigma—and also remains imprisoned.

She does not return the noose to its hook as she hurries after Henrick. Her footsteps bounce the chains. "Where is he?" she asks once she reaches Henrick at the door.

"Patience," he replies.

"You told me I could see him, Your Imperial Majesty. You told me you would not execute him."

"And I meant that." He glances back, the tiniest of smiles upon his lips. "I will not execute him, Safiya."

True, her magic sings, warm and tender. A balm to soothe. Yet Safi does not miss that Henrick has only replied to one of her comments. She doesn't miss that he said nothing about visiting Eron.

But that is all right, she tells herself. For she and Iseult have their plan, and so far, each step has gone accordingly—including today's, which has left a shiny golden noose resting inside her pocket.

When she reaches Henrick's side, she bares her brightest smile. Her most persuasive grin. "Thank you," she tells him, accepting his offered arm. "I am grateful that my uncle will be spared. You are a generous man, my Emperor."

He does not contradict her.

ELEVEN

✳

Snow had fallen in the night, leaving the skies leaden and the ground white—not that any white remained on the paths Safi now followed. They had been carefully cleared away by an army of ever-invisible servants.

A terrible job, working in such temperatures for rich nobility who *might* use the sprawling courtyard gardens at the center of the imperial palace. Safi hoped the servants had thicker layers than she.

Svenja had been right: Safi *should* have worn her heavy cloak. But she had wanted to give the impression of a girl in love, and girls in love tended to favor fashion over practicality. So did men in love, for that matter, and all other genders too. As such, she'd donned a lighter, golden velvet cloak over her forest-green wool.

At least she'd had the sense to wear the ermine muff and matching hat, what little good they did. By the time she reached the Winter Garden, nestled between the evergreen maze and the Royal Greenhouses, her nose had gone numb and her ears were headed that way.

She strode, Hell-Bards in formation around her, through a lush archway designed for some empress almost a century ago. The paths and flowers were meticulously maintained year-round by an army of dedicated Plant-witches, and though there might be snow on the ground, there were also roses in bloom. Daffodils too, and crocuses and dahlias, hyacinth and tulips and hydrangeas with heads large as carriage wheels. There were varieties of flowers Safi had never seen before—much less blossoming in winter.

Like the stone paths, the stone benches had been cleared, and, of course, the flowers themselves had been carefully wiped, so that a thousand colors shone against the surrounding world of white.

Those poor, poor servants.

As Safi passed through a second archway, her eyes snagged on one bench in particular. Shaded by a blossoming lilac, it had lion paws for feet—and Safi knew those feet instantly. Just as she knew that lilac, though it had been smaller ten years before. A sapling newly added.

Henrick had spotted her playing here, her doll dressed in as many furs as she had been. The toy, newly acquired in a rare burst of generosity from Eron, had delighted her with its eyes of Hasstrel blue. Her uncle read on a separate bench nearby, already sipping from his flask though it was not yet noon.

He glimpsed Henrick right as Henrick glimpsed Safi, and in a move that now seemed much too graceful for a drunkard, Eron skated in front of the Emperor before he could address his niece. And Safi used that time to scrabble behind the bench, heart pounding.

"She looks so much like Laia," Henrick murmured. Safi didn't see his face, but she felt a frown bunching there. "Remarkable."

"Yes," Eron drawled, unscrewing his flask. It always squeaked. "Unfortunately, she lacks her mother's wit. Or her refinement. Or"—he paused for a gulp—"her initiative. She is a candle to my sister's bonfire. She ruins everything she touches. But come, my Imperial Majesty. Share a drink with me."

At the time, those words had gouged. Fanged and serrated, each sentence had burrowed deep into Safi's heart. Her eyes had burned; tears had fallen; and she'd scolded the doll again and again for being just a candle. For ruining all she touched.

"Safiya?" Light fingers hit Safi's elbow. Her lungs clenched. She whirled about, arms rising. But it was only Leopold—of course it was only Leopold.

"Are you all right?" Genuine concern darkened his seafoam eyes.

And Safi nodded. "Of course." She forced a smile. "I am perfection. As are you on this fine winter's day." Nothing she said was a lie.

Leopold wore soft silver beneath a cape of glistening mahogany. Unlike most days, he wore no extra ornamentations. No decorative weapons at his waist, no jewels upon his fingers or at his neck. It was as if his outfit was selected to highlight the colors of the garden, and Safi had to wonder, not for the first time in her life, if *he* had chosen his clothes or some well-paid attendant had.

Growing up, she had always assumed the latter, for even as children, he had dressed in a way that flattered while it also impressed. But in the last month, her judgment had changed. He might have given her the Truth-lens and a clever means of examining it, but in the end, he was as duplicitous as his uncle—and far more inclined to laugh while he watched his enemies fall.

"Thank you, my Empress." He flourished a bow. "If it is acceptable to you, I will have the Hell-Bards leave us in solitude."

Of course it was acceptable, but Safi found it hard to believe they were allowed to lose sight of her. As if sensing her thoughts, Leopold added, "Oh yes, my own Bards are in position with spyglasses and crossbows fixed this way." He motioned a lazy hand toward the ramparts that surrounded the outermost edges of the garden complex. "I expect no danger here."

"In that case . . ." Safi turned to Lev. "Please wait for me outside the garden."

A curt bow from Lev, face invisible inside her helm, and as one, the Hell-Bards marched stiffly out of sight.

"Now then." Leopold offered Safi his arm, and once she'd accepted it, he murmured, lips unmoving, "We must pretend to be very much in love. Do you think you can manage?"

Safi bared her sweetest smile. Even cocked her head and cooed, "As I once told Captain fitz Grieg, I can smile at even the ugliest toad and flatter him on his perfectly placed warts. And you, Polly"—she reached up to gently touch his jaw—"are the ugliest of ugly toads."

"Excellent." He cupped his hand over hers before she could withdraw it. He wore no gloves; his fingers were cool against her fur-warmed ones. "We will provide a good show for the spies then."

"Are there many?" Safi batted her lashes.

"Always." His eyes flicked to her lips.

"Should we be worried?"

"No." His eyes moved back to her own. They were a vivid green in the light of the flowers. "My uncle was the one who suggested that we rekindle our passion."

"Rekindle?" Safi asked, pulling her hand free.

Leopold relinquished his hold with a sigh. Then drew her into an easy pace through the garden. "I *might* have told him the eve before your wedding that we had once been lovers."

"And he believed you?"

"He had no reason not to, and I had all the reason in the world to find a way to see you privately—oh, that frown will not do, Safiya." He smiled handsomely at her. His skin seemed to gleam.

And Safi quickly brushed away the frown she hadn't realized she'd been wearing. As startled as she was that Henrick had so easily believed Leopold, she was far more annoyed that Leopold had told such lies in the first place.

"You should have warned me," she said with a twinkling laugh. So false, she could only imagine how white the lens in her pocket must be. "What if Henrick had asked me about it?"

"He would not have believed your denials. You *do* recall what happened after the wedding."

Of course Safi recalled. It was the moment when her whole life had been flipped, shredded, tossed away. And when the person in this whole thrice-damned world who mattered most to Safi had been forced to run.

"No thanks to you," Safi whispered. She couldn't keep the venom from her voice. Leopold must have known what was coming—he had to have *known* what Henrick planned to do to Safi and Iseult. And he had done nothing to stop it, nothing to protect them from the pain of Hell-Bard cold.

"The truth is not what you think it is." Leopold pulled Safi to him. His lips hovered near hers while his eyes bored deep. "I will explain everything to you, and you can use the Truth-lens to confirm I do not lie. But we must go somewhere more private for such a conversation."

His breath fluttered over Safi's skin. She dipped her lips a bit closer. "How can anything be private when spies live everywhere?"

"There are secret ways of moving, even here. Tonight, after the dancing, I will send another letter, and you will come to my quarters."

"I will?" She pulled away. Cold air rushed between them. "And if I refuse?"

"Let us not even consider that thought." He offered a flirtatious grin and resumed their walk.

Except that before he could actually step onward, Safi grabbed his cape and pulled him to her. Her lips hit his a split moment later, and where she had expected surprised stiffness, she got only willing embrace. Leopold's hands instantly moved to her hair, his mouth pressed firmly against hers. He deepened the kiss. She deepened it right back.

At some point, her ermine hat fell off.

This was not, in fact, Safi's first kiss with Leopold. As shy ten-year-old, she had experimented with him in the dustiest corner of the imperial library. It had *not* been a passionate affair, and it had *not* been particularly interesting. They'd both laughed afterward and vowed never to try again.

But Leopold had clearly honed his skills in the last eight years, and Safi had certainly honed her own. Were this not purely for show and if she had not *hated* Leopold with every droplet of her being, she might have enjoyed the kiss. He was an undeniably beautiful man, and she was a woman with needs.

She broke the embrace. "I will come to your quarters," she whispered. Her hands were still around his neck; his lips were swollen and red. "You will have one chance to explain to me why I should trust you, and if you fail that chance, I will hand over the Truth-lens to Henrick and turn you in for a traitor."

Leopold smiled—a brilliant smile that settled deep within his eyes. "I have no doubt you will, Safiya." His hands fell from her hair. "But I promise it will not come to that." He swooped down to retrieve her hat, dusting off the snow and placing it tenderly atop her head. "Let us finish our walk." He offered his arm once more. "And let us hope that kiss was convincing enough for even the most suspicious of my uncle's spies."

It was not Safi's usual Hell-Bards who escorted her from the Winter Garden and into the palace. Instead the Emperor's dedicated eight awaited her, led by Captain Caden fitz Grieg.

"The Emperor has asked that you join him in court," Caden said with a stiff bow. With his split helm covering most of his face, Safi could not read his expression—but she could hear a familiar warmth marking his voice.

She had scarcely seen Caden or Zander since her noosing. Caden had been promoted upon his return to Praga and Henrick kept him close. Zander meanwhile had been assigned outside the palace. He had failed to keep Iseult from claiming Owl when she'd fled, and Safi could only assume some punishment had befallen him for that lapse.

"Captain," Safi said with a smile. "It has been a while." She stepped into a long-legged stride, moving in a way that forced Caden to walk beside her instead of flanking.

She was Empress now, and he could hardly reject her conversation. So while the other Hell-Bards moved accordingly to fill in his empty space, he fell into step beside her. He even went so far as to remove his helm. His brown hair was matted to his head, his freckled face pink with cold.

"Have you heard any news of Iseult?" Safi's stomach yawned at that question, but she had to ask it. Every time she saw him, she *had* to ask.

"No," he said on a sigh. "No Hell-Bards have caught up to her yet."

"Thank the gods," Safi breathed, and her shoulders wilted, her neck relaxed.

Caden, who watched her sideways through hooded eyes, only tensed all the more. "Lev tells me you keep testing the noose."

"So Lev spies on me too."

"It isn't spying," he countered, a bit too sharply. A bit too loud. He cleared his throat. "She . . . cares for you. We all do, Your Imperial

Majesty. Becoming a Hell-Bard doesn't only sever magic. It severs our lives, our minds, our souls. You aren't alone, Safi."

Safi. It was nice to hear her name again, though it was also a reminder of just how alone she truly was. "I am surrounded by no one I can trust, Caden. Except Lev. And I have no idea where in all the Witchlands my Threadsister might be." She chewed her lip. Her words sounded whiny. Pathetic. Yet she couldn't seem to stop them. "I'm forced to do whatever the Emperor desires because if I don't, he hurts you. *All* of you."

Caden's frown deepened. For several moments, he said nothing, as if he was thinking through every sentence, every word, every pause. Ahead, massive doors into the old palace were whispering wide, opened by waiting servants. The Hell-Bards did not break formation as they marched purposefully through, Safi and Caden still tucked within their ranks.

At a broad staircase, however, the Hell-Bards finally slowed to a stop— forcing Safi and Caden to stop as well. Then they separated into lines along the entryway's walls while a new set of Hell-Bards descended the steps, Lev at the fore.

Caden turned to Safi, his posture stiff and military as he popped a bow. "Your Imperial Majesty, remember what I told you." With a stiff flick of his hand, he motioned to his neck, to where his noose rested beneath layers of armor and padding. "You are not the only dead woman here, and we protect our own." Then he lifted his voice—just loud enough for the nearby Hell-Bards to hear. "Toward death with wide eyes," he said, quoting their motto.

As one, they replied, "All clear, all clear."

Gooseflesh crawled down Safi's skin. Her throat swelled. For though she had heard the Hell-Bard motto before, she'd never had it directed at her. She had never had it *include* her.

She was one of them now. A Hell-Bard. *All clear, all clear.*

Safi turned away from Caden then and allowed Lev and the others to clack into formation around her. It was time, once more, to enter the palace and take up her mantle at the Emperor's side.

TWELVE

✳

When Vivia awoke, it was to find the sun rising and the world silent. No drumbeats, no winds, no cannons firing. Just a ship's familiar creaking, wood and ropes and sail all moving in tandem.

Swallowing, she eased upright. She was in her bed, fully clothed, and—

"Finally." Vaness's voice slid across her, and on a stool beside the cot sat the Empress, arms folded. Face and clothes still bloodied. "You have been out a long time. Does this usually happen?"

"No." Vivia frowned and finished rising. She ached, but in an old way. Ancient as the water that had briefly consumed her. It would pass in a few hours. "I'm not sure I've ever tapped into that sort of power before."

Vaness sniffed.

And Vivia had to fight the urge to point out all the blood caked across her imperial chin. Never had she seen the Empress so filthy. Never had she imagined it possible. And most amazing of all, Vaness didn't seem to care.

The Empress stood, a slight wobble to her carriage—she was no sailor—and approached the bed. She stopped only when her thighs hit the edge. Then she glowered down, fury in every piece of her, and though Vivia couldn't see the iron bracelets, she had no doubt they skated and spun.

"Never," Vaness said softly, "do that again."

"Do what?"

"Command me without warning. Command me without consent."

Vivia sighed and leaned back against the cabin wall. She had no headrest because the wood was better used elsewhere; she had no elegant covers either. Cotton suited her just fine.

She ran a hand through her hair, still slightly damp. "You are on my ship, Your Imperial Majesty. I am captain here, which means my word is law. You know that. We've been over that, and you *claimed* you understood."

"That was before you ordered me to run the cannons. Never"—she wagged a finger at Vivia—"do that again."

Vivia didn't answer. A flicker of anger spread up her spine. "We would have died if you hadn't stopped those cannons. We almost *did* die, even with your magic."

"And I should have let that iron go all the way through." She kept her finger stretched long in Vivia's face. "I should have let it crash to the ocean and watched as we all sank and your Hagfishes claimed us—"

Vivia grabbed the finger. Her lips curled back. "All because you want to prove a point?" She swung her legs out of the bed, covers sliding off her. Still she gripped Vaness's finger, even when she stood. Even when the room spun and she glared down at the smaller woman. "You would have damned us all just because you did not want to obey?"

A long breath slid by. Then a second and a third before Vaness finally spoke. "I am not your sailor, I am not your soldier. I am the Empress of Marstok, and I will never fire a cannon again."

She yanked her finger free, and though Vivia could have held on, she saw no reason to. Vaness could win this one. But if the Iron Bitch thought she could be on board without using her magic to fight, then she was sorely mistaken. Every sailor did their part here, even royalty. Especially royalty.

It wasn't until hours later, as Vivia oversaw repairs to the *Iris*'s main deck, that she remembered all the blood. Vaness had almost passed out. In fact, she'd almost lost control entirely . . . So maybe it was not mere insubordination that made her so angry, so vicious.

Maybe it was fear. Maybe something was wrong.

It was nearing midday before the Dalmotti navy caught up. Vivia didn't know why she was surprised. She'd likely sunk their ship, and she'd outrun a Doge's command. Of course they would want retribution.

The question was why he had wanted her and Vaness to remain in Veñaza City at all. Why he had risked battle in the first place just to keep them there. No matter the answer, when the ship's girl shouted, "Warships on the horizon," Vivia knew right away that the chase had begun.

"Witches," she hollered, abandoning the tiller to Sotar again, "it's time to fly. Leeri! Take the drum."

"Where will we go?" Sotar asked, spyglass trained on the horizon.

"Nihar," Vivia replied.

He snapped down the glass. "Your father will have people there—"

"And we won't stay." An unwelcome flush rose to Vivia's cheeks. Stix would never question her. Stix would never pause.

Sotar seemed to realize his mistake, for his expression shuttered. He bowed his head. "Of course, Your Majesty. Do we go to Lejna, then?"

"No." She flung her finger east. "We go to the Lonely Bastard. For now, steer us directly to shore. I will handle the rest." Then she loped down the main deck, aiming for the ship's stern once more. Her Windwitches were lined up, their wind-spectacles on, and Cam was once again at the drum.

"Not too fast a rhythm this time," Vivia called as she clipped past. "We'll need to hold the space steady."

"Is this wise?" came a new voice, and suddenly the Empress of Marstok was in step beside Vivia. Cleaner, though her baggy uniform still bore stains. Perhaps Vivia should find her more clothes.

Incomprehensibly, she was embarrassed she hadn't considered that sooner.

"You overdid yourself only last night, and now you plan to use your magic again?"

"Why, Empress." Vivia bared a sideways smile. "If I didn't know better, I'd say you were worried about me."

Vaness's lips compressed. She regarded Vivia with open disdain.

"But I *do* know better," Vivia finished, reaching the stern. She grabbed hold of the railing. "I won't exert myself. Just an easy tide to get us ahead of those boats and into hiding."

"They will have Tidewitches of their own."

"Hye."

"And twice, if not three times, as many Windwitches."

"Hye." Vivia nodded, and her own lips pursed to match the Empress's. "But they don't have Nubrevnan ships, and they don't have"—she tapped her skull—"Nubrevnan knowledge. My people have evaded the empires for decades. This is nothing new."

Vivia twisted toward the horizon and toward the ships just forming in the distance, four small specks without her glass to magnify. Yet for some reason, the Empress still stood beside her.

Vivia fought the urge to glare. "What is it?" She lifted her hands toward the sea. "Speak now before I loose my magic."

The Empress swallowed. Her throat bobbed, a strangely nervous movement. And a strangely attractive one. Then she bounced a shoulder and said, "Do not kill us all," before whirling away toward the door belowdecks.

Vivia would have smiled at that—a sour thing—if not for her magic. It was pouring through her again. The waves, the water, the lapping, kissing sea. *Command us, command us.*

"Prepare winds," Vivia hollered at her officers. "Make way!"

Winds funneled into the sails, and water lifted beneath the *Iris's* hull. The ship groaned to a start. Due east, straight and true, exactly as Vivia had commanded Sotar. Exactly as she commanded the waves. Gentler than yesterday, in an easy pace that matched the wind-drum, now rising.

At some point, the sailors began to sing. Softly so as not to be heard by any approaching ships, yet loud enough, steady enough to steel Vivia and her witches. To focus their magic, one crew, joined as a single voice.

Just as the Empress had said, the Dalmotti ships had their own witches, and they were fast. Yet no one knew the coast like Nubrevnans, and no one but Nihars knew about the Lonely Bastard. A jagged rock thrusting up from the sea, the Bastard hid a small cove in the cliffside behind. The waters were cruel, the passage narrow, and only the right-size ship with the right-minded witches could ever slip through.

Vivia just had to make sure the *Iris* got there before the warships could see where they went. Otherwise she had no doubt they would simply build a new blockade and keep her and her crew trapped. Or worse, they might try to find somewhere to lay anchor and come ashore.

Faster, Vivia coaxed the waves. *Just a little bit faster.*

"The maidens north of Lovats," sang the crew. "None ever looked so fair! When they catch your eye, you'll fall in love, so everyone beware!"

Winds cycloned. Water kicked. The *Iris* moved faster, and the first glimpses of land came into view, crowned by rocks and exposed reefs. Not that Vivia could see it—her attention was wholly focused below, on the tides thrusting and currents carrying. But she felt the shore. Felt the waters shallow and the waves break over shipwrecks from navies past.

"The maidens north of Lovats are as strong as ten large men!" The singing grew quieter. Strained. And even the winds seemed to weaken.

"Do not slow!" Vivia screamed, briefly turning her gaze to the fore. "Trust me!" Then to prove her point, she wrenched her arms sideways and the waters wrenched the *Iris* too. "To port!" she shrieked at Sotar, who instantly threw his weight into the tiller.

The ship listed, the world dragged while the drum beat on. And the singing bellowed once more: "With minds as sharp as hammered steel, when they fight they always win!"

When the ship was upright again, it was perpendicular to the approaching Dalmottis. Dangerously exposed. Dangerously visible. But ahead, the first of the rocky outcroppings waited. They would dart and hide like a minnow. They just had to reach it before—

"*Cannon fire!*" The ship's girl's voice cut through song, drum, and winds. "*Two incoming!*"

"I have them," Vaness said, somehow as loud as the ship's girl, though she did not shout. Somehow flat and detached, like the iron she controlled.

Vivia turned, briefly startled. She hadn't realized the Empress had returned to the deck or that the woman stood only paces away, braced against the rail and watching the chase unfold.

Now her arms were rising, her face draining of blood as the two shots zoomed in. With a sharp gasp, she stopped both midflight . . .

Then let them fall into the sea. No sending them back. No using them against the enemy. Her arms dropped. She gripped at the rail, and Vivia knew instantly that such a display could not be repeated.

"And you're worried I overdid myself?" Vivia hooked an arm behind the woman. "Get back to your quarters."

Vaness resisted. "Who will stop the cannons?"

"No one, because in just a few moments, we won't need to—"

"*Cannon fire!*"

"Shit." Vivia lurched back to the rail; Vaness stumbled with her, and before Vivia could forcibly stop the Empress, Vaness had her arms high and magic out. Again, she halted the iron shot—three balls this time—but it was slower. Like trying to get a dog to change its course, they dragged to a halt. Then fell, one by one.

Vaness swayed, and again Vivia grabbed her. Rage licked up from her toes. Sharp and fueled by a hot sea. The Empress could barely stay upright. Her eyes were rolling, her posture wilting.

"Take her," Vivia barked, pushing the woman onto a nearby sailor. Likely she'd get an earful later, but better that than a dead empress on her decks.

She didn't wait to see what happened. As she'd said, it was only a little longer before the *Iris* was fully covered. She thrust her magic into the sea, her whole body swelling with power. *Faster,* she practically screamed at it. *Almost there.* The first of the rocky outcroppings hissed past, near enough for her to see the barnacles, near enough for her to see slick patches of algae.

Water sprayed against Vivia. Her waters, warm yet cooling. Powerful yet calm. She let her breath ease out and motioned at the Windwitches to do the same.

The sails slackened, and the sailors silenced. The wind-drum silenced too. The *Iris* was hidden, meaning now was the time for stealth, and tactics like the Foxes of old. "Keep your winds going," Vivia ordered as she strode past the witches. "But lightly. Very lightly. And sailors, pick up the oars. From here until we lay anchor, your strength is our salvation."

Her crew obeyed, launching for their stations along the main deck. With muffled attempts at quiet, they unlocked oars and gathered two by two against them.

Vivia reached the tiller, where Sotar stepped aside, fist to his heart. Respect in his eyes. Hell-waters, he looked like Stix. And hell-waters, Vivia missed her first mate. If Stix were here, then they'd already be at the Lonely Bastard. In fact, Stix would have capsized those blighted boats—or at least frozen the sea long enough to hold them back.

But Stix wasn't here. *And might never be here again.*

With a sharp sawing of her hand, Vivia set the oarsmen to their grueling work. Wood scraped and water splashed. Muscles rippled and breaths panted, but no one slowed, no one spoke. Soon the *Iris* skated atop the choppy sea. They passed gaps in the rocks. Sometimes large enough for them to spot the warships. Sometimes large enough for them to be seen in turn and fired at. But always they were covered before any cannon could make contact.

The Lonely Bastard soon appeared, a wicked knife to pierce the sea. Behind it, hidden from view, was a narrow passage in the seaside cliffs. It had been years since Vivia had come to Nihar—a place that had never welcomed her. That had never felt like home. It had been Merik's domain, not hers.

"Sonja!" Vivia lifted her voice to the crow's nest, where the ship's girl waited. The first words uttered since the oarsmen had begun to row. "Do you see the ships?"

"Hye," the girl called back. "They're almost through the rocks."

And once they were fully through, the *Iris* would be visible. Vivia's plan for hiding would be ruined. But they were so, so close. She wasn't going to miss this chance. Oh, the *Iris* might scrape her hull. Holes might rip through. But if they could reach shore unseen, then the cost would be worth it. It had to be worth it.

"Faster," she barked at her oarsmen. Then to the witches, "Raise winds." And then to the water foaming against the planks, *Carry us.* Timing was key. This was a sharp turn, followed by an even sharper turn after that. Vivia's strength against the tiller and her magic against the waves would be pushed to their limit.

Do not kill us all, Vaness had said, and Vivia almost laughed at that.

No, she *did* laugh. She couldn't help it. The water loved this. Wild, stormy, untamed—the water was reckless decisions and impulsive actions. It was the reason Vivia had earned a reputation for the same fierceness and temper as the rest of the Nihars. People didn't understand that it wasn't her, but the waves. She was just a little fox letting power course through her in the name of what had to be done.

"To port!" she screamed as she pushed all of her being, all of her heart into the tiller and into waves. *To port, to port.* Everything tipped. The sky, so blue, rose up on the port side; the sea loomed in on the right. No oars moved, no sailors moved. Even the world held its breath, each drumbeat seeming twice as long.

Then the ship righted and the world righted too.

"Hold!" Black stone rushed in close. She shoved. With magic, with muscles. That narrow passage ahead—invisible if you didn't know what you were looking for—was tighter than a needle's eye.

"Row!"

The oarsmen obeyed. The *Iris* kicked forward, and Vivia gripped the tiller, gripped the waves.

They reached the gap in the rocks. A wave rocked against them—unexpected. Laughing. And the *Iris* lurched hard to starboard. Stone thundered against wood. Oars snapped and oarsmen dove sideways. But Vivia already had the tiller moving again, already had her own waves fighting back.

The ship veered. Then settled. Then slowed. No more rowing. No more winds. They were in the passage.

They were safe.

THIRTEEN

✳

Iseult stared at Aeduan, shocked. Elated. Aeduan was here, somehow, and standing before her. A mere forty paces away with only lazy waters to separate them. Except that as she took two steps forward, Aeduan's forehead pinched. His gaze swept up and down her. His body tensed with caution.

And a strange, heavy heat tunneled through Iseult's chest. Yes, she had changed since she'd last seen him. She had entered Cartorra a Weaver-witch; she was leaving it a Puppeteer. But surely he would still know her?

"It's . . . me," she called. When he still looked confused, she added, "Iseult."

And then it happened: Threads, clear blue with understanding, swept toward the sky. Iseult gasped. Rocked back a step, and even rubbed her eyes for good measure. Yet the Threads remained.

Which was *wrong*. Aeduan did not have Threads.

"No," Iseult breathed. Then again: "*No.*" For it was not merely colors that dazzled her eyes and magic but shadows and shapes. Only once had Iseult seen such darkness on someone's Threads: on Evrane, the woman who had saved her almost seven years ago. The monk who'd sworn to protect her and Safi.

Evrane had been possessed in ways Iseult still did not understand, and now Aeduan was corrupted too.

"No," she said once more as a slow smile spread over his lips. A full, hungry thing that stretched his face. Foreign, wrong. The Aeduan she knew did not smile. He did not leer.

Later, Iseult would curse her instincts. Later, she would wish—not for the first time—that she had Safi's gut to guide her instead of her own slow logic. For logic was the last thing she needed here. There could be no arranging the puzzle pieces before her; there could be no coherent shape found. And because of that, this Aeduan-who-was-not-Aeduan had the advantage. The extra burst of two seconds that would ultimately decide whether Iseult escaped the fate the Bloodwitch had planned for her . . .

Or became his prey.

He charged into the waters, straight for her. No concern for depth or cold or difficulty. His Threads radiated purple hunger and green focus. He hunted her and nothing would stand in his way.

Those Threads finally forced Iseult to move. Aeduan-who-was-not-Aeduan wanted her, violently, just as Evrane-who-was-not-Evrane had wanted her at the Monastery.

Iseult spun to flee. Her heel slipped on the wet shore. She fell to one knee, but the subsequent pain was distant. Swallowed by a determined, rhythmic splashing from behind.

She used her staff to scrabble upright, and ran for the trees. But what had been an easy race down to the water now seemed viciously steep, viciously long. Her feet wouldn't land properly. Her staff kept getting in the way.

And the splashing, *the splashing*. No normal human could move so fast.

Iseult reached the first snags of barren underbrush and pine-needle earth. There was the trail she'd taken before, obvious from her footprints still fresh in the cold soil. She had no time to try to hide them, no time to find another way.

But as she skidded around a pine trunk, she realized she could no longer hear splashing. Maybe that meant he had stopped. *Please, please, please.*

He had not stopped.

When she risked a glance back, she found he was out of the water and sprinting up the shore. Too fast, too fast. Even though he was not Aeduan, whoever . . . *whatever* possessed his body was using his Bloodwitchery. He would reach her soon.

Which meant she would have to think her way out of this. That was all there was to it. Somehow, as she pumped her arms and tried to move faster, as pine needles sliced her cheeks and roots threatened to steal her legs, Iseult needed a plan.

Think, Iseult, think. Beyond this forest were the crystal pools, and beyond that, the river with rocks for crossing. If she could just get to those stepping-stones, then she could get to Owl and the horses. Surely not even Aeduan-who-was-not-Aeduan could outrun horses.

She reached a bend in the path, and flung a backward look. He was so close, his cloak bright and unmissable through the trees. She would not reach the pools before he caught her.

She wanted to scream. Wanted to end this chase now, call it quits like she used to as a child playing fox and hen. Running without pause always ended in tragedy for her.

So don't run, her brain provided, right as she approached an immense pine, its lowest branches above her and its trunk three times as wide as she. Beyond it, the crystal waters shimmered in cold mountain air.

She knew her opponent and she knew this terrain. Not well, since she'd only just passed through, but she still had an advantage. Which meant it was time to pick her battlefield.

Another backward look. He was still there, though all she could see was his white cloak. She wore brown; she would not be so visible. And her footprints—they mixed with her others from before. It would be impossible to tell if she had stopped or continued on.

Iseult reached the pine, and with a bounding leap to avoid leaving fresh prints, she shot behind its wide trunk. Then she clapped a hand over her mouth and waited. For what seemed an eternity, she heard only her heartbeat galloping through her very skull.

Soon she heard footsteps. He was not as graceful as the real Aeduan, yet like the real Aeduan, he also couldn't seem to smell her blood. One small boon, at least.

He did not slow at the pine, and as he passed it, Iseult circled around. Away from him. All the way behind him . . .

And something about that, about briefly gaining the upper hand—*an Empress card against the Emperor,* as Safi would say—gave Iseult the respite she needed. She could see her next actions, she could imagine the fight about to unfold. She abandoned her staff on the forest floor, unsheathed her new sword, and charged.

Aeduan had paused at the pools, and his back was within easy reach. Iseult arced out her blade. He looked back. His ice-blue eyes met hers, so familiar, so foreign. Then her sword hit his arm. It dug deep. It sliced, but did not sever.

And later, when Iseult cursed her instincts, she would also find herself grateful for this. He *was* Aeduan, somewhere in there. Possessed, usurped, and controlled, but Aeduan all the same—and she wouldn't have wanted to maim him.

Not entirely.

Aeduan attacked with Bloodwitch speed, yet when he grabbed for Iseult, she ducked and moved outside him. When he lifted a knee, she dropped her elbow into his thigh. And when he tried to shift to a hook kick, she caught the leg and yanked it skyward. She knew his body better than whatever controlled him did.

He grappled for her as he toppled back, but it was wild. Useless. He hit the ground.

"I'm sorry," Iseult told the Aeduan she hoped was still in there. Then she raised her sword and stabbed him. Through flesh, through organs, and out the other side, she shoved her sword as deeply as it would go.

And once again, just as it had done to the Hell-Bard from whom she'd claimed it, the sword pinned him to the soft earth below.

Iseult released the hilt. Aeduan gasped and snarled at her. He was stuck—though not forever. Already, she could see the wound trying to heal, instantaneous and unpreventable.

She resumed her sprint. Nothing looked familiar from this angle, and the sun blinded her, shooting into her eyes and glaring on wind-dappled waters. But she couldn't slow. Better to go in the wrong direction and gain distance than lose time searching for the right way.

There. That little sapling. Beyond must be the largest pool, which meant cutting right would bring her to the stepping-stones and camp.

She looked backward. Already, Aeduan was rising—too fast, too fast. She reached the edge of the largest pool and there was the stretch of soggy land that would lead to the river. She could hear its moving waters, and the sun's sharp rays would soon be shaded by mountain. She would reach the river in seconds . . .

But so would not-Aeduan. *How* had he moved so fast? How had he already circled most of the largest pool?

Iseult launched herself off the shore and onto the first stepping-stone. Then another. Another. The splash of the river and her booming heartbeats could not block Aeduan's approach. He was to the river's shore before she was even halfway across the water.

She readied her legs for the next leap. She sprang up and out—

And jerked straight backward.

A scream split her lips. Her neck yanked, her balance collapsed, and cold crashed over her. Water shoved up her nose.

She paddled and flailed and fought to escape the water, but it was not the water she needed to fight. It was Aeduan. He was dragging her upward, scraping her back on rock, and soon he had her stretched across the stone. She sputtered, sucked in air, and tried to rise.

But it was no use. Aeduan now held her bloodied sword at her throat. "Stop."

Iseult wanted to weep at the sound of his voice. Once so familiar, now utterly unknown. Wanted to weep at the way her neck shrieked with pain and her whole body was cold, cold, cold. Most of all, though, she wanted to weep because she had failed. She had been captured by a man who was not Aeduan, while Owl and the weasel waited unsuspecting at camp.

The weasel, she thought. She could send her a message, and maybe the weasel could make Owl understand they had to flee.

Iseult's dream was short-lived. Shattered as quickly as it had formed, for as she lay there with Aeduan's boot digging into her breasts, a voice split over the river's churn: "I have the girl!"

Iseult squinted through wet lashes to where another Carawen monk hunched over a tiny figure, bound and gagged upon the shore.

Iseult had been too late, too slow, too foolish. Evrane had captured Owl, and there was nothing, *nothing* Iseult could do. She had failed one more person. She had cleft one more life in two.

This time, Iseult did not fight her tears.

＊

Twelve Days After the Earth Well Healed

They are in the imperial Tailorwitches' room, Iseult, Safi, and Lev, surrounded by cloth and thread and scissors and needles and more light than any other room in the palace—natural and Firewitched. The three have ejected the witches and tailors who had only just been there. Their Threads drift impatiently in the hallway outside.

Safi glares at herself in a looking glass. "The hips are too loose." She picks at the Hasstrel blue rippling below her waist. The complex gold pattern stitched into the bodice—geometric suns and moons—must have taken days to embroider.

Lev twirls her noose lazily nearby, leaning against a table covered in bolts of silk imported from Dalmotti. For once, the Hell-Bard is not in full armor but in a new dress uniform.

And Iseult is dressed in new clothes too. The gown is far finer than anything she has ever worn before—and more ostentatious. She cannot blend into the shadows with silk the color of sea-foam, and she cannot hide weapons beneath gauzy skirts. She does like the pattern, though, matching Safi's but in silver instead of gold.

The Emperor has given Iseult and Safi every item they could desire. More than everything. They are lavished upon, the Cahr Awen.

"No, this absolutely will not do." Safi's Threads, calm and focused, clash with a fake frustration as she flexes and fists her fingers. She and Iseult are under constant watch. Right now, two sets of Threads hover within the walls, one set in the ceilings, and another four on the balconies across the garden.

The endless observation has made studying the diary impossible for Iseult, and meeting with Esme even more so.

"I will tighten this," Safi declares, twirling away from the mirror.

"You mean the tailors will." Lev points toward the hall.

"No." Safi bobs her head imperiously. "I mean I will."

Lev's Threads flutter with tan confusion. A hint of suspicion too. "Why?"

"Because I'm tired of being poked," Safi snaps. "I'm tired of having people parade me wherever they want me to go. I'm tired of being prodded and nudged and seated on stiff thrones. I'm tired of being watched"—she glares toward the ceiling—"and being told constantly that other people will do things for me. What if I want to do something myself?"

As Safi rants, she flings up her hands and paces. Like before, her behavior doesn't match the easy calm of her Threads. It never does when she's performing.

"Fine, fine," Lev interrupts. She drops advances on Safi. "Hell-flames, I didn't need the lecture."

Safi has the grace to blush. A real one.

"I'll have sewing materials sent to your room," the Hell-Bard adds. "I have to admit, though . . ." She bounces her eyebrows conspiratorially at Iseult. "I'm surprised you know how to sew."

Safi sniffs. Iseult attempts a grin. Then, with a nonchalance she has never been very good at, Iseult says, "Tell me about being a Hell-Bard." She shuffles toward Lev. "Your gold chain looks so like the one that Purists wear."

While she asks this question, Safi leans against a different table. One covered in scraps of silk, and asks: "Don't Purists claim to have made the Hell-Bards or something?" She is much better at this than Iseult is.

Lev rolls her eyes, and in the ceiling and walls, Threads shift to green curiosity. The spies are briefly focused on Lev instead of Safi.

"Yes, yes," Lev answers. "The Purists claim they made us because they think Midne could erase magic. But they have it backwards."

"Midne?" Iseult presses, and she locks eyes with Safi. Now is their moment, and with a quick swipe of Safi's hand, a silk scrap vanishes from the table. It will make a very good pocket later on. Just the right size for holding a delicate golden chain.

"The first Hell-Bard," Lev explains. Then she cracks her knuckles, her Threads twisting with discomfort. She doesn't like talking about this. "But Midne didn't steal magic. She had it stolen from her. Just like . . ." She swallows and doesn't finish the sentence.

Not that she needs to. Just like I did is clearly what she'd been about to say. And Iseult can't help but pity the Bard—pity all of them for what their lives have become. It will be better, she wants to assure Lev. Once Safi and I finish our plan, she'll make sure no ruler ever abuses you again.

"I wonder," says a new voice. Drawling, bored, and accentuated by meteor-bright Threads. Leopold slinks into the room, and Lev drops a low bow. "If Midne did not erase people's magic, then who did? Who made Midne?"

"Your Imperial Highness," Lev murmurs, eyes dropping to the floor.

Leopold ignores her and runs a finger along the nearest table of cloth. A pink velvet ripples beneath his touch, almost a perfect match for his playful Threads.

"There is so much of the past lost to time. So many stories that depend entirely on who is telling them." He glances at Iseult, then Safi. His Threads shiver into cobalt regret.

And Iseult's gut sinks. She knows what's coming next.

"I fear I am here to summon you," Leopold says, and the regret darkens.

But it isn't his fault that Iseult and Safi must face the Witchery Examination Board. They agreed to this when they met Henrick at the Hasstrel castle. Still, doing it feels vastly different from simply imagining.

Safi's fingers settle on Iseult's biceps, her Threads a tender peach. "You can change your mind," she offers.

But Iseult shakes her head. If Safi can wear her magic openly, then so can she. She is half the Cahr Awen; her magic is nothing to be ashamed of.

"Lead the way," she tells Leopold. "We are ready to receive our Witchmarks."

FOURTEEN

✳

Heat billowed against Stix. Wet heat, sticky with sea salt and mosquitos. It would become a dry heat any moment now, when the flame hawk broke its restraints and the battle began. Thank Noden there were no other people here, no prisoners Stix would have to fight. It was just her and that flame hawk.

Of course, at the edges of her mind, she supposed the flame hawk was a prisoner too.

"Three," chanted the crowd, watching the same rope Stix watched. "Two." It was burning fast. The next white mark would be gone in . . .

"One!" The final fibers snapped. The flame hawk screamed its awful scream, and launched at Stix, fire winging wide. While it gained altitude and the crowd of the Slaughter Ring bellowed and bet and washed her in sound, Stix flung out her arms and summoned all the water she could find.

She didn't have to think about it, the magic was simply there, just as it always was and always had been since she'd first discovered it ten years ago. Her father might call her boastful, but when she spoke of power, it was merely truth. If she called, the water answered—and in a place as humid as Saldonica, the air itself was laden with droplets for her to use.

Freeze, she thought, imagining ice. Becoming ice, from her toes to her white eyebrows. She was a winter wasteland, and this water would be too. *Freeze.* Fog formed around her. Thick, heavy fog that frosted the skin and hid Stix from view.

The crowd shrieked their approval.

Overhead, the flame hawk reached its zenith, flipped, and dropped fast. Its fire feathers whistled, its flame throat screeched. Stix sprinted through the fog, her already weak vision reduced to near invisibility. She should have taken the spectacles with her, but the risk of broken glass in her eyes had scared her. A mistake. She'd gotten too used to clear sight.

Heat thundered against her scalp. Light and sound seared in, and the flame hawk arrived. Claws out, gullet wide.

Stix shot sideways, a frantic flinging of her body while her magic scraped for water. Humidity turned to ice again, then those ice droplets thickened into shards.

She hit the ground next to a shredded dog from the previous fight. The stench of roasted innards filled her nostrils. A fraction of a heartbeat later, the flame hawk hit the earth too. The ground undulated; heat rolled across Stix. So dry, so close.

She sent her ice shards flying, already pushing to her feet and grasping for any other water she could find. She needed more than this. She needed a river, a pond, the bay beyond the Ring. She couldn't snuff out eternal fires with only fog.

Stix resumed her sprint. The flame hawk had stopped its screaming, and the heat had faded. It must be on the rise for another attack.

She reached the wooden stall she'd entered by, knowing full well it would be locked now. Knowing full well that the guards would only laugh at her and wave their heated pokers in warning. She had watched enough of these fights to know the rules.

Arms rising as she pounded closer, she felt for a bucket of water that waited beside the door. The crowd blared their disapproval. They thought she was fleeing, and a tiny piece of her wanted to glare. She never backed down from a fight. Not at the Cleaved Man, not at sea, and most certainly not here.

She didn't have to. She was a full Waterwitch. People ran from *her*.

In a vine-thin line of power, the water snaked up from the bucket and sliced through the tiny, barred window at the door. Then it was to her, then it was touching her—and just in time. The flame hawk had almost arrived. It barreled toward Stix, once more drowning everything in its violent heat.

Stix tossed her hands high, fingers shaped like claws, and the water obeyed. It split in two, forming arms like hers, yet with the fingernails hardened to ice. She jabbed out her left arm—quick, distracting—then followed up with a right power strike.

She'd always been proud of that punch. After all, it had earned her the title of *Water Brawler* at the Cleaved Man, and it had won her many a brutal fight.

Her water arced out, pure speed, pure power, and slammed into the flame hawk's head. Where a true arm would stop, Stix's water simply shot onward. A pillar of water to pound the hawk's skull. To wash over it with targeted precision aimed right for the hawk's eyes.

Where Stix turned it into a mask of ice. Suddenly the bird couldn't see, and it toppled like a graceless fledgling to the ground. It slid toward Stix, heat coursing against her. Cotton burned, her hair singed, and her skin blistered. But she launched sideways before any real damage could be done.

The crowd erupted with delight, and Stix couldn't help but revel in that sound. Just as she had at the Cleaved Man, even if her father told her it wasn't seemly for a Sotar. She readied her second water whip for the final knockout . . .

And that was when it happened. Because of *course* that was when it happened: the voices returned and the memories punched into her. Hye, she had come here for those exact memories, those exact voices, but did they have to show up now?

"No," Stix snarled, watching as the world dissolved around her. Listening as the crowd's cheers fell away and the past shoved in. "No, no, *no*."

But the old lifetimes didn't care what Stix wanted. They had been waiting for her to come here, so now they had something to say. And as it always was, they spoke in a language she could not understand. A hundred languages all clashing together.

Stix didn't need words to know they were angry. *Come this way, keep coming,* they seemed to cry. *Come, come, come this way, keep coming.* Light flickered at the edge of her vision, eating her sight like flames eat paper. Like this flame hawk would eat her. But she couldn't see the bird anymore, for the past had arrived and it would not be ignored.

Her Heart-Thread is on fire, flames from an Exalted One named Lovats. Laughter from him too. "Food for my flame hawk. Food for my pet."

Stix's voice breaks as she begs Lovats to release Bastien.

"You should not have turned on us," Lovats says in reply. "You should not have turned on me."

Stix's eyes meet Bastien's eyes. "Blade," he screams through the flames. "Use the . . . blade."

The vision ended. The voices vanished. And Stix found herself on her knees with her face in her hands. She was weeping—but it was not *her*. It was the Old One. The one they adored here, patron saint of change, seasons, and crossroads. The one who lived inside of Stix along with so many other souls.

There was no time when the voices took control. Stix had learned that after the first intense memories had overwhelmed her—that whatever passage of time she might experience did not match the rest of the world. She might slip into a memory and half a day had passed, or she might drift off and it had been only breaths.

Right now, thank Noden, it seemed to be the latter. Stix dragged to her feet and faced the flame hawk again. Ice still covered its face; its body was still prone—though not for long. Smoke coiled into Stix's nose.

She swung. Water loosed like an arrow, long and true. It hit the hawk's feet, then circled and circled before finally cinching in place and freezing. The bird was stuck. The bird was masked. It could not even scream its defeat.

Stacia Sotar, the Water Brawler, had won her first Slaughter Ring.

Immediately after the fight, two guards escorted Stix to Kahina's private box. Ryber was not allowed to join, and though she put on a good performance as a trainer offended by the separation, the guards were intractable.

When Stix arrived, she found Kahina alone, sprawled across her long chair. She seemed thoroughly disinterested as Stix was nudged to a floor cushion several steps away, as if she hadn't invited Stix here at all. As if Stix was just another piece of furniture on her towering private space.

Minutes gusted past, and Stix silently waited. That blighted flame hawk had gotten her good at the end. Her shirt had burned through to her right shoulder, leaving pieces of cotton inside the damaged flesh. She'd gotten a stripe across her jaw too, and her white hair had burned to shriveled shortness around her right ear.

When Kahina still had not acknowledged Stix after several minutes, Stix cleared her throat. And Kahina sighed. The pipe clutched within her teeth snuffed out. She rolled languidly to one side.

"You do not look so good." Kahina swung her legs to the floor. "But what an impressive display. You made short work of my pet."

Pet. The hair on Stix's arms shot high. "The . . . flame hawk is yours?"

"She is." Kahina withdrew her pipe and smiled. It was a predatory grin. A powerful grin.

"You don't treat it very well."

"Is that what you think?" Kahina gave a throaty laugh and clapped her hands against her knees. The jade ring glinted on her thumb. "Do you know who I am, Water Brawler?"

Stix nodded. "Leader of the Red Sails."

"No, no." Kahina pushed to her feet. Without her spectacles on, Stix had to squint to follow Kahina as she strutted for the deck's edge. "Everyone knows I am the admiral. I mean do you know who I *am?*" A glance backward. "Or for that matter, do you know who you are?"

Again, the hair on Stix's arms shot high. A Firewitch with a flame hawk. A Firewitch who took cruel delight in the violence unfolding below. *Food for my flame hawk. Food for my pet.*

"Ah," Kahina murmured. "I see that perhaps you do." She thrust the pipe back into her teeth. With no match nor uttered command, the pipe flared. Fresh smoke plumed, and Stix wanted very much to be gone from this deck. She wanted Ryber's steady silver eyes or that orange tabby's relentlessly happy purr. She wanted the safety of her cot and the pillow, and she wanted Kahina far, far away.

"You do not remember everything yet, do you?" Kahina asked.

Stix did not respond.

"You will soon enough." Kahina shrugged. "That is the way of it when we find one of our old places." She motioned toward the arena while wind sprayed her pipe smoke. "And once you do remember, then all of this will be so much easier."

"All of what?"

"There is something that we must find. Or some*things,* I should say." Kahina leaned against the balustrade, seemingly unconcerned by the wood's dangerous groan or the sheer drop-off below. "But we will make no progress if you do not have all your memories." This thought made her frown, and she pushed off the railing to approach Stix.

Though every muscle in Stix begged to lean away, she held her ground while Kahina dropped to a crouch before her and gripped her chin. Smoke drifted into Stix's eyes. The jade ring shimmered.

"We have work to do, Water Brawler." This close, there was no missing the tiredness on Kahina's face or the lines carved deep around her eyes. "A great deal of it, in fact. So be ready and try not to die in the meantime. It's so *tedious* waiting for the new lives to be reborn." She released Stix, swirling gracefully toward her long chair.

Food for my flame hawk. Food for my pet.

Stix offered no greeting once outside Kahina's deck. She merely gripped Ryber's biceps and in hushed tones said, "We need to talk. Alone."

Ryber nodded, and with an arm to keep Stix steady, she guided Stix down to the limestone bowels of the Ring. The dank halls carved a honeycomb beneath the main arena. Firewitched lanterns mingled with smoky torches, and none of the tunnels were straight or flat. Every ten steps or so, rats skittered in their path. Icy water dripped off the stone ceilings onto their heads, until eventually they reached a fork in the main path.

Instead of cutting right toward the subterranean carriage entrance, Ryber hauled Stix left, toward the prisoners Stix didn't think she could stomach seeing. It was bad enough watching them die in the Ring by lion claws or crocodile fangs, but to have to see them in their cells? To see so many faces and know she could do nothing, that their fates belonged to Kahina and the other Masters of the Ring? Stix feared she might destroy the arena and every raider in it.

Maybe you should, her heart nudged. *Maybe that is what you are here to do.*

But what if it isn't? she countered. *What if I destroy it and then the voices never leave?*

Her heart had no time to argue before Ryber towed Stix into an alcove littered with rat droppings. Hidden it certainly was, but filthy too.

"What happened?" Ryber asked, and Stix shoved aside thoughts of the prisoners. In broad strokes, she sketched out what Kahina had said—as well as the memory she'd seen inside the Ring.

Ryber's face dragged long with horror. "You think she is this Paladin called Lovats?"

"Who else can she be?" Stix attempted a shrug, but her burned shoulder barked in protest.

Not that Ryber noticed. Her attention had already been claimed by a deck of taro cards freshly plucked from her pocket. Some had torn edges, some were creased and frayed. But that didn't matter to Ryber, who handled them with the tenderness of a mother. She drew them for everything—to learn tomorrow's weather, to be ready for today's surprises, and to answer whatever big questions might come her way.

She flipped over three cards. "The Queen of Hawks," Ryber said, handing the first to Stix. "The Queen of Foxes and the Giant." She handed off those two as well, and Stix held the cards toward the dim light from the main hall.

On the Queen of Hawks was a flame hawk fanned orange and yellow across the paper, an iron crown hovering at its heart. The Queen of Foxes was similar, but a sea fox coiled around a golden crown with starfish points—a crown that was eerily similar to Vivia's actual crown. And on the Giant card was a snow capped mountain silhouetted against a starry sky.

"What question did you ask?" Stix returned the cards to Ryber, only to find the other girl massaging her temples.

"I asked who Kahina is, and I was expecting to draw at least one Paladin card. Not . . . *these.*"

"Why not? What do these mean?"

Ryber's hand fell. The usual braid sprang free. "I don't know," she admitted, and Stix fought off a frown. It wasn't Ryber's fault the cards were confusing. It wasn't Ryber's fault they didn't spell out a clear way to avoid Kahina or unlock the answers of the Ring. Stix and Stix alone had to figure it out if she wanted to get home—and that was all she wanted. Silence and home.

And maybe freedom for others too.

"Maybe," Ryber said with a furtive glance toward the hall, "I can pull out the blade and glass once we're back at the inn. We could use the glass on Kahina to see if she really is—"

"No." The word rang out, louder than Stix intended. Colder and harder too. But she couldn't help it. Even hearing those words, *blade and glass,* made her insides shrivel. Worse than when Kahina had gripped her. Worse than during her vision from the Ring.

"You don't have to use the glass, Stix. I'll be the one to look through."

"No," Stix repeated. Then again: "No, no, no. No blade, no glass, Ryber. We're here to deal with my memories, and that's *it.* Whatever Kahina wants, it doesn't matter. She isn't my problem. She isn't yours." Stix spun away and limped into the hallway, moving too fast for Ryber to argue. Too fast for the voices, always lurking behind her eye sockets, to awaken and lay claim.

No blade. No glass. Not her problem.

Stix had found the items inside the Sightwitch mountain. They had called to her, much like the voices did. *Death, death, the final end.* That was what the blade had seemed to sing, while the glass had crooned at her with promises. *Just look through me, and you will get all the answers you need.*

A lie. All Stix had seen when she'd peered through was her own death, borne on rook wings and gleaming beneath a silver crown. It had felt real because it *had* been real. That death had happened to one of these screaming voices inside Stix's head, and now, whenever she closed her eyes too long, whenever she let her mind drift, whenever she slept, the memory was all that she could see.

She had wanted to leave the blighted items behind; Ryber had insisted otherwise. "They are too dangerous," she'd said, and then she had explained to Stix what they were.

The glass allowed a person to find Paladins, to see which humans carried more than a single soul inside them.

And the blade could kill a Paladin, ending their reincarnation—silencing their multiple souls—forever.

As far as Stix was concerned, though, that didn't matter because as far as she was concerned, the tools didn't exist. If Ryber cared about them, then they were Ryber's problem. Which was why, for weeks, Ryber had kept them close, wrapped in a brown salamander cloth she was careful to never let Stix see.

But clearly she was done playing that game, for she raised the subject three more times on their carriage ride back to the inn. Stix ignored her every time.

Death, death, the final end. Death on flapping wings.

FIFTEEN

✳

Once, the monk named Evrane had been gentle with Iseult. She had saved her life on multiple occasions and had even been Iseult's hero—and been *the* reason Iseult wanted to see the Carawen Monastery and become a monk.

Now, Evrane was a monster, possessed by shadowy Threads shaped like birds. And now, her fingers were rough, her eyes cruel.

"What do we have here?" Evrane pulled the stolen noose from Iseult's pocket. She'd already claimed Iseult's thigh knife, a small canteen at Iseult's hip, and the Hell-Bard map from her pocket.

Iseult couldn't answer. Her mouth was stuffed with pieces of her own wet cloak that Aeduan had shoved in after dragging her over the stepping-stones and binding her wrists with leather cord. All the while, Owl had watched from beside Evrane, eyes huge with silent tears.

The weasel was nowhere to be seen.

Evrane lifted the chain toward Aeduan. "This looks like his, no?"

Aeduan glanced over, Threads and expression bored. He'd already finished searching Owl and now he was preparing the horses by tossing away most of Iseult's carefully chosen supplies.

"Yes," he said without interest. "It's what Portia's cursed wear. The ones they call the Hell-Bards."

"So why do you have it, I wonder?" Evrane stared at Iseult, her Threads keen with interest. "This Witchmark upon your hand is new too."

Evrane dropped the noose into her pocket, seemingly unconcerned that Iseult could not answer her interrogation, and resumed her search, probing, groping, scrutinizing, until at last she reached Iseult's neck and pulled back Iseult's collar. A strange gleeful hunger widened in her eyes, smearing her Threads to purple. She expected to find something—was ready for it, even.

But when she stared into Iseult's shirt, surprise brightened her Threads. "She does not have it." She yanked Iseult closer, peering deeper into her tunic. *Please don't see the diary pages,* Iseult prayed.

Somehow, Evrane did not. She released Iseult's collar, and Iseult listed back. "Where is it, girl? Where is the stone?"

Of course, Iseult couldn't answer—and now Evrane's Threads were blood red with frustration. She yanked the wool from Iseult's mouth. Iseult coughed.

"Where is it?" This time when Iseult did not answer, Evrane slapped her. A crack of flesh that sent Iseult's head snapping sideways.

"Enough." Aeduan pushed Evrane aside.

"She is no use without the stone." Evrane tried to grab for Iseult again, but Aeduan deftly blocked her. His Threads, like Evrane's, burned with frustration. His impatience, however, was not directed at Iseult.

"You forget our orders. We are to leave her unharmed."

Evrane laughed, a shrill sound. "Oh?" she mocked. "You bow to one of the betrayers now, do you? You always were the weakest of us."

"It is not weakness," Aeduan clipped back, "but self-preservation. This"—he motioned to Iseult—"is to be my body. You will leave her untouched."

Iseult didn't like the sound of that, *This is to be my body.* But she also dared not ask about it. Not while the two monks stared at each other like dogs in an alley, hackles high. Threads twined between them, clotted and confusing. There was hate, there was love. Trust and mistrust and a hundred other contradictions she could not understand.

For the moment, at least, they weren't looking at her. "Owl," she whispered, canting toward the child. Her mouth was silty from the rag; any moment now, they'd stuff it back in. "Don't be afraid. I will take care of you, all right?"

Owl didn't acknowledge Iseult. Her Threads did not change. And now Evrane was scowling and spinning away. "Fine. You find out where the stone is." She stalked toward the horses, her stride all wrong. Stiff and jerky, as if her clothes did not fit.

Iseult's eyes itched. *Stasis,* she told herself. A useless word that she had given up weeks ago, but sometimes training ran deeper than truth. Especially now that Aeduan was studying her with an ice-blue stare.

Iseult met his gaze. She wasn't sure what she hoped to see, what she hoped would happen, but she found herself speaking in Nomatsi anyway. Saying: "If it's my Threadstone you seek, it is in Praga."

There was no recognition on Aeduan's face. Only whispers of tan confusion and clay frustration in his Threads.

So she repeated in Arithuanian, "If it is my Threadstone you seek, it is in

Praga." She didn't know why she changed languages for him. She didn't know why she was making it easier. It was as if her heart wanted to help him—*had* to help him—even as her brain warned her away. "Emperor Henrick took the stone from me," she went on. "I can only assume he destroyed it."

"Hmmm." Aeduan's lips twitched with an unnatural smile. "Such items, Dark-Giver, are not so easily destroyed."

Dark-Giver. Her skin crawled. Her spine shriveled. *Stasis, Iseult. Stasis in your fingers and in your toes.* "Why do you want it?"

Aeduan ignored her. "Get up." When she made no move to obey, his Threads flashed crimson. He dug his hands into her armpits and lifted her savagely to her feet.

Iseult saw no reason to resist. Her legs had gone numb, and a glacier now leaked through her veins. Nothing made sense. Nothing felt real.

Aeduan turned to Owl next. "Get up." He shifted as if to grab her.

But Iseult touched his sleeve. "She doesn't speak Arithuanian."

A twinge of surprise crossed his face and Threads. He peered down at Owl again, but this time with cold assessment. "That collar blocks her, I suppose. Perhaps a good thing. For us and for her." His gaze returned to Iseult. "Get her up, and get her on a horse. We have far to go before the sun sets."

"So you have taken a lover," Henrick drawled. He sat upon his too-tight throne with his too-tight crown, Safi seated in her own throne beside him. Their daily session at court had not yet begun. "It took you long enough."

Safi choked. Then shook her head. She *must* have misheard. "Forgive me?"

"It took," he repeated impatiently, "you long enough. Everyone was expecting it—though I doubt they were expecting it with my nephew."

Safi wet her lips. Of course Henrick knew of her affair with Leopold. He'd suggested it. Nonetheless, she had not expected him to discuss it so directly. Her fingers tapped against her lap. At the opposite end of the room, supplicants and sycophants lined up. Some were tattered, some were opulent. Henrick would listen to each of them equally.

"Is the imperial prince . . . a problem?" she asked eventually.

"No. Having an affair will give you something to do." Henrick offered a bland sideways smile. "Perhaps if you are physically engaged, you will look less . . ." A sniff, a wave at her face. "Sullen."

Safi's fingers tapped faster. *Do not punch him, do not punch him.* Not that she would leave much damage before he reached that glistening chain at his waist and rained frozen hell upon her.

"Speaking of physical engagement," she said, as elegantly poised as any domna, "I was hoping perhaps I might train with the Hell-Bards. I have heard they practice in the lower levels of the new wing."

Henrick shifted in his throne and stared at Safi. She stared right back, while on the floor, the first Cartorran was rushing forward to speak.

She knew there was great risk in her request. Her noosing was not public knowledge, and training with soldiers was hardly the *thing* empresses did. But ever since Caden had said those words to her in the entryway, *Toward death with wide eyes*, and each Hell-Bard had replied . . .

She couldn't get the notion out of her head that she needed to train with them. How else was she going to understand this chain around her neck? Besides, her muscles would atrophy if she did not use them soon. She was a swordswoman who hadn't touched a sword in weeks.

"A lover," Henrick said quietly, "*and* training with Hell-Bards. If I did not know better, my Empress, I would think you intended to overthrow me. Fortunately . . ." His lip quirked sideways, his tooth jutted out. "I *do* know better."

He stroked the chain on his belt, and cold lanced through Safi. Down her spine, into her abdomen. It took all her self-control not to chatter her teeth or curl into a quaking ball. But he would not cow her. He would not win.

"Yes, my Emperor," she gritted out. "You . . . do know better."

He nodded, seemingly satisfied with her words—and with her pain. Then he released the golden chain and turned his attention to the man now kneeling before him. "Ah, the blacksmith from Haemersmeid. I remember you. Is the dam still hurting your forge?"

They rode for hours. Owl sat with Evrane on Lady Sea Fox; Iseult on Lord Storm Hound with Aeduan. His Threads never veered from concentration. The Aeduan Iseult had saved from death at the Aether Well was gone. And just as shadow birds winged across Evrane's Threads, the same shapes now galloped across his.

Iseult had no idea what they meant.

Aeduan was a stranger now. He did not notice that Iseult shivered against him—still so wet and so cold from the river. He did not notice against the wool scraping the roof of her mouth, or when she choked and her eyes streamed.

Or perhaps he did notice, but did not care.

They followed the river west, Aeduan leading the way until they reached a spot where the water was shallow enough for the horses to cross. Iseult's earlier search had been such a waste. Such a pointless, stupid endeavor by a foolish girl who never seemed to learn. If only she and Owl had never stopped to rest. If only she'd never crossed that river.

If only, if only, if only. She had enough of them to fill an ocean, and not a one could actually help her.

Except she wasn't totally alone. The weasel was still out there somewhere. Iseult had seen no sign of the creature, and each of her attempts to reach the weasel's mind had yielded no results. Which surely was a good thing—it *had* to be a good thing.

Owl's Threads meanwhile had been trapped in white terror, pure and unchanging for hours. Iseult did her best to comfort the child by twisting around to look at Owl, but it was a useless endeavor. Owl would not meet her eyes, and Aeduan always shoved Iseult's head forward again.

To think that only yesterday Iseult had been the Puppeteer, reveling in her own strength. Now she was nothing except a prisoner to people she'd once loved. She would've laughed at that, if wool did not gag her, for this was how it always went: she ruined everything around her. She hurt whomever came near.

When at last the sun was setting, the horses carried them into a small clearing surrounded by old growth. Here, Aeduan called a halt. He pulled down Iseult, rough in a way the true Aeduan never was, and tied her to an ancient ash. Moments later, Owl was bound beside Iseult, and while Evrane and Aeduan built a cooking fire, the child pressed in as closely as she could. Her collar bumped Iseult's hip bone. Shivers racked her tiny body.

Which was why the first thing Iseult said when at last Aeduan removed her gag was "The child needs a blanket." Her voice was rusted, her mouth painfully dry. Still she repeated her words: "The child needs a blanket."

It was the first clear thought she'd had all evening: *Owl is too cold.* And it carried with it the first streaks of anger. She clung to that. "She is freezing and must be warmed."

Aeduan glanced at Owl, his Threads calculating. "Yes," he said at last. Then he grabbed Iseult's biceps and pushed her toward the campfire, where Evrane stirred halfheartedly at an iron pot and watched Iseult from across the flames. "Sit," Aeduan ordered before turning back to untie the child.

"You look worse than when I saw you last." Evrane grinned, a hateful look that did not belong on her face. "And you were quite broken then, surrounded by monks who wished you dead."

Iseult didn't react, even as she stoked the fire in her chest a bit hotter. "Who are you?" she asked as Evrane approached with a bowl of soup.

The woman smiled again, her eyes crinkling this time and her Threads pink with pleasure. "Ask the little one." She waved at Owl, who sank clumsily to a cross-legged seat beside Iseult. "Do you remember us, Saria?" Evrane looked at Owl as she asked this. "Do you remember what you did?"

"Leave her." Aeduan's voice was low but commanding. "She's just a child."

"That is no child." Evrane stepped closer. The bowl steamed in her hand. "How many lifetimes have you had since that day? How many lifetimes have you enjoyed while we lay trapped in darkness?"

"You talk too much." Aeduan nudged Evrane with his boot, and the older woman did not resist. Her expression smug, her Threads satisfied, she offered Iseult the bowl. Iseult tried to accept it, but she was awkward with her wrists bound. Oily liquid sloshed.

And Evrane laughed. A hideous, brain-scratching sound while she returned to her place beside the fire.

Aeduan passed the second bowl to Owl, but the child only looked at Iseult with confusion. She had a bruise on her left cheek. New and purple. More fury swept through Iseult.

"Drink it," she whispered. Then she demonstrated, sipping as best she could. Some leaked down her left cheek. Greasy from whatever fish had been boiled.

"She's lucky," Evrane commented, still watching Owl from across the fire. "If not for that collar, I would have to put her to sleep." Her smug smile slid to Iseult. "The dark-giver knows how much fun that can be."

Aeduan grunted, but if in amusement or annoyance, Iseult could not say. His Threads were once more unreadable, once more masked by avian shadows. Evrane's Threads, however, were easy to interpret. She enjoyed taunting Iseult, just as she had enjoyed keeping her bound by nightmares at the Monastery.

Iseult kept her face blank as she swallowed more stew. She was stasis on the outside. Cold enough to make even her mother proud, while inside, she burned. These usurpers had chosen the wrong targets. They had imprisoned the wrong girl. Iseult was not the weakling of old. She didn't cower, she didn't break.

And she didn't forget.

When she'd finished her food, Aeduan reclaimed her bowl and Owl's. Like Iseult, the child had spilled soup down her cheeks. Iseult moved to wipe Owl's face, but Evrane knocked her arm aside before gripping Owl by the hair. She tipped back Owl's head and moved to stuff the wool gag back in.

Owl screamed.

And just like that, Iseult's outward stasis crumbled. The fire in her chest erupted. The rage of the road, the rage of the Puppeteer. "*Stop.*" She leaped to her feet, hands clawed even as her wrists were bound. She would take Evrane's Threads and she would destroy them. She didn't care whose body this was, didn't care what damage she caused.

Aeduan grabbed her. A rough slinging of his arms around her torso before he wrenched her away from Evrane. Brutal, hard, but Iseult could be brutal and hard too. She turned her claws on his face, her fingernails on his flesh. But he was stronger than she, and in mere heartbeats, he had her pinned to a tree.

The tree she'd been tied to before, while at the campfire Owl wept, her tiny body dry-heaving against the wool. Evrane laughed and laughed.

"She's choking." Iseult grabbed at Aeduan's chest. She didn't fight him this time, didn't resist the arm he pressed into her throat. Instead she simply begged. "*Please*, the child can't breathe. Help her."

"She's fine," Evrane spat, and she dragged Owl toward the ash tree. In moments, she had the girl tied up again. Still, Owl choked and cried.

Meanwhile, Aeduan simply watched. Simply waited. Only when the other monk was seated at the fire again did he show any reaction or make any move. Without releasing his hold on Iseult, he bent sideways and tugged at the wool in Owl's mouth. He didn't remove the gag entirely, but he pulled it far enough forward that Owl's chest and throat relaxed.

"Thank you." The words squeaked from Iseult's throat, cracked and quiet—and in Nomatsi. She still burned inside, but it was a weaker flame. A dying flame. She settled into Aeduan's grasp. Her head lolled against the tree, bark rough against her scalp. "Thank you," she repeated.

For half a moment, Aeduan stilled against her. As if he understood her words. Suddenly, Iseult was not tired at all. She was taut as a Heart-Thread, her vision shrinking to pinpricks upon his blue eyes.

"Aeduan." She stood taller against his grip. "*Te varuje, Aeduan. Te varuje.*"

Pale consternation rushed up his Threads. He frowned.

"*Te varuje,*" she said again, urgency in her voice and in her posture as she tried to lean toward him. "I told you that at the Monastery, and I know you remember. I know you're in there—"

He shoved her. Hard enough to break off her words. Hard enough to send stars across her vision. Then suddenly the wool was back in her mouth. Too fast for her to evade, too rough for her to resist.

Iseult choked as Owl had. Her eyes watered, her nose burned, and silt grated down her throat. She could do nothing but try to breathe and keep her supper from coming back up—all while Aeduan refastened her to the ash.

"I told you," he said when he was done, her bindings so tight she could already feel the blood leaving her extremities, "I do not speak that language." Then he turned as sharply as Evrane had and joined the other monk at the fire.

SIXTEEN

✳

He did not know why he had listened to the one called Iseult. He did not know why he had helped the child by loosening the wool in her mouth. After all, pity was an emotion he had abandoned long ago, and mercy he had lost even before that. There was no space for such weakness when one was all that stood between the world and chaos.

Though chaos had still won in the end.

He had no name—or rather, none that he remembered. It had been lost in the dark water of a thousand years, and history had successfully erased it. When he had come into this new world, others had called him Monk Aeduan, so Monk Aeduan he had become.

Yes, the first Aeduan still wrestled inside of him, swimming toward the surface. But that man would never survive. He would tire eventually, then fade away.

As the new Aeduan sat beside the campfire, he watched the girl called Iseult. Even bound to a tree and helpless, he could see there was fight in her posture, fury in her heart. She only ever had gentle words for the No'Amatsi child, though.

It reminded him of someone else. Someone from before the world had ended. The one they'd all loved, even as they'd betrayed her.

This is not her, he told himself. *This is just a girl whose body you will one day claim.*

He had to wonder if Corlant saw the resemblance too. If perhaps that was why the man was so obsessed with her, for the priest's fascination certainly went beyond mere familial interest.

But no. Corlant was obsessed with Iseult because she was half of the Cahr Awen. She and the other girl were the only people who could end the way Corlant lived . . . and the way Aeduan lived too.

"You are awfully calm," said the older woman who was now called Evrane. She sat across from Aeduan. The fire morphed her face until she looked almost as she had all those years ago. "Without the Threadstone, she is useless to us."

"There is no reason to panic." He gazed steadily at her, inhaling the strange angles and curves of her blood. He had gotten used to this body's magic. It was powerful, it was useful.

And strangely, he found Evrane's scent soothing. *Crisp spring water and salt-lined cliffs.* It belonged to the first soul who had worn that body—it was too pure, too tame to be the Old One's.

"No reason to panic?" She snorted. "It took him centuries to make those stones."

"And we have waited a millennium. He will not give up so easily."

"I hope so." Her voice came out softer than usual. A sure sign she was worried, perhaps even frightened. "As long as they exist, we are at risk."

Who is the weakest now? he wondered, though he preserved his silence. She was too quick to anger, too slow to cool off. Even a thousand years in darkness had not robbed her of that.

So Aeduan drank his soup. It was disgusting. Easily one of the worst meals he had ever eaten. He might not remember his name, but he remembered good food. Cinnamon-spiced lamb and white-ginger veal. Wine from the south and beer from the north. More fruits and flavors than most people would ever encounter in a lifetime, he had feasted on daily.

He would feast on it again, once all of this was over. Once the Lament had come to pass and five had turned on one. Then this new world would be right again, the chaos finally contained.

Several long moments passed before Evrane spoke again. As he swallowed, Evrane pushed to her feet. "I will sleep first," she declared, turning away. "Wake me when the Sleeping Giant hits her peak."

"Yes," Aeduan murmured, glad to be left alone. "When the Giant hits her peak, I will wake you."

Evrane did not walk away, though, and after several seconds, she said: "He was waiting for me. When I came out of the Well, he was there."

"Corlant?" Aeduan set the bowl, half-empty, upon his knees.

"No." She frowned. "*Him.* The Rook King."

Aeduan's vision sharpened. He had not thought the Rook King still alive. "He remembers who he is?"

"Yes."

"Then you should have killed him."

Evrane glared. "I would have, but I was weak. I had only just awoken.

Besides, he would have simply been reborn again." Her gaze flittered toward their prisoners. "Like Saria, like Midne."

And like we should have been. Aeduan's nostrils flared. Evrane was right, of course: there was only one way to kill a Paladin, and simple death was not it. Still, a Rook King newly reincarnated was better than one at peak power.

"What does he look like?" he asked. The Rook King of a thousand years ago, the Rook King who had killed Aeduan with his magicked blade, had been tall and dark. He'd worn thick furs and a silver crown—plain, simple, cold as the mountains on which he'd dwelled.

"I didn't see his face," Evrane admitted.

"Then how do you know it was the Rook King and not someone else?"

"Because he had that bird with him." She shuddered—and Aeduan hated that he wanted to shudder too. He had never liked that bird. Death on glossy wings.

"On whose side is he? Does he serve the Exalted Ones or the Six?"

"I do not know." Her eyes swiveled to Aeduan's, two pools of black in the shadows. "He could have killed me, though, and he did not. He simply told me it was good to have me back again . . ." A pause. A twitch of a grim smile. Then: "And he asked me if I'd slept well."

Of course he did. A thousand years the Rook King had lived. One life after the next. No danger, no Threads, no vengeful Old Ones to get in his way. Now he mocked Evrane. He mocked them all.

If Aeduan ever encountered him—if this new iteration of the Rook King had the audacity to ever cross Aeduan's path—then Aeduan would end him. A blade in the heart, exactly as the Rook King had done to him. Then when the Paladin soul was reborn, he would track down that new body and kill it too. Over and over again, for a thousand years. Over and over again, for the rest of time.

He gulped back the remnants of his soup, scarcely noticing the taste, the oiliness, the temperature too cold. Then he stared into the darkness with unseeing eyes and imagined pain on glossy black wings.

The end of the night could not come soon enough. Safi had danced until she could dance no more, and though Henrick had not touched his chain of command again, cold had lingered. An aching too, like illness coming on.

Hell-gates, but she had never hated the Emperor more.

An attendant opened the door for Safi as soon as she and her Hell-

Bards appeared in Leopold's dedicated hall. He lived in the oldest part of the palace—even older than where Henrick resided. So old, it looked halfway to ruins despite the lush carpets and flickering sconces. As a girl, Safi had never understood why Leopold chose to live here, and she did not understand it now. There was no power to be played here as there was in Henrick's quarters, and the crumbling black stones sucked up all warmth, all light.

In fact, the tower in which he lived was more fortress than living quarters. No dressing chamber, no sitting room, no space for guards or attendants to comfortably spend the night. Yet Leopold had chosen this rounded stretch of granite as his home for as long as Safi had known him.

The only advantage, Safi supposed as the door into Leopold's room swung wide, was that no one ever traveled this way. It was secluded from the rest of the palace, and the number of hallways needed to reach it—not all of them even indoors—was an inconvenience no one ever willingly made.

Two steps in and she realized there was another advantage: the stone walls were too thick to allow for spying. The entrance into the room alone was a solid three paces deep, all of it contiguous black granite. Presumably every wall in the room was the same. There could be no hollow spaces here, no peepholes, no listening horns. Aside from the fireplace on the left and a single window on the right, the room was completely impermeable.

"Safiya," Leopold said with a smile, rising from an armchair before a blazing fire. He opened his arms to her, and she hurried forward as if all she wanted was to be wrapped in his embrace.

Even after the door shut behind her, she allowed him to pull her tightly to him. He wore a blue dressing robe over what she assumed must be his nightwear, and he smelled fresh, as if he'd just bathed.

Safi pretended to melt into him, looping her arms around his waist and resting her head on his shoulder. "Can anyone see us?" she murmured.

"Yes." He spoke at a normal volume. "There are a handful of spies with glasses trained on my window. No one can *hear* us, though. And as soon as I draw my curtains, they will not see us either."

Safi lifted her face toward his and offered what she hoped was a suitably *in-love* smile. "Then close it please because I have no desire to continue holding you."

A bark of laughter, and Leopold withdrew. While Safi settled herself in the armchair he had just abandoned—there was no other chair—Leopold closed the curtains. They were thick velvet brocade, blood red like everything else in the room: the four-poster bed and its coverings, the rugs woven with golden double-headed eagles, and even the tapestries draped over most of the stone. It was almost overbearing in its masculinity, yet somehow thoroughly devoid of any personal touch. Safi could only assume that, like everything else about the prince, this space was cultivated and groomed, while Leopold's true self stayed tucked away.

As Leopold strode back toward the fire, Safi withdrew her Truth-lens and pressed it to her eye. A shattered image of the prince crossed into view, and though she could not see him clearly, she could sense he leaned against the fireplace's enormous oaken mantel.

"We are safe to speak?" she asked. "About *real* things?"

"Indeed," he replied, and the lens made no change. "I am sure you have a thousand questions—"

"Why did you betray us?"

"Ah," he exhaled, posture tensing. "You waste no time in getting to the point. However, before I answer . . ."

Safi dipped the lens and watched him lift both arms and declare, "Lower." As one, every wall sconce dimmed. "Lower, lower," he repeated, and they dimmed more and more until at last, they were snuffed out entirely and the only light came from the fire's continued radiance.

He offered a shadowy smile. "More romantic, would you not agree? Now all that's left is to latch my door, and we may proceed." After doing as he'd said—with three latches on his door, and two of them Aetherwitched with lock-spells—he strode to the armchair and reached for something at Safi's back.

She twisted about and realized two black scarves were draped behind her. She'd thought them decorative, but now Leopold was wrapping one around his shoulders and offering her the second. "Where we are going gets cold," he explained. "This will help with the chill."

"Where we're going?" She accepted the scarf and stood. "Is there some secret way out of here?"

Leopold smiled slyly. "Guessed it in one." He strode past the fireplace to an iron sconce on the other side. With a fist, he knocked the stones three times. Air whooshed outward, gusting against Safi, and her Hell-Bard senses ignited.

Magic, her skin whispered. *Glamour!* And before her eyes an entire stretch of wall disappeared. A single heartbeat later, an archway revealed stairs spiraling downward out of sight.

Leopold's smile widened, and with a mischievous cant to his eyebrows, he beckoned for Safi to follow as he set off into the darkness. The staircase was as ancient as the rest of this wing.

"What is this place?" Safi asked, her voice a mere whisper.

"Forgotten," Leopold replied. His hand trailed along the wall as the last remnants of firelight faded. "Put your hand on my shoulder. I'll lead us the rest of the way."

Safi obeyed, putting one hand on his left shoulder and the other on the wall as he'd done. The stone was frozen to the touch, slightly damp, and surprisingly smooth. Whoever had created this passage had not used chisels, but magic. Every few steps, her fingers brushed over grooves in the rock. Carvings, she thought, though she could not discern what.

"I discovered this as a boy," Leopold explained eventually. Safi had no concept of how far they had traveled, but she suspected they were now belowground. "This tower was nothing more than exposed ruins then, and Uncle would let me camp out sometimes. He even let me go alone, though I am certain he had a hundred guards spying on me nearby."

Safi frowned into the darkness. She couldn't imagine Henrick indulging anyone, much less a young child.

"One night, as I was pretending to be a great Paladin with flaming sword, I accidentally tapped that wall three times. And . . . well . . ." She felt his shoulders bounce softly, as if he laughed. "You saw what happens—oh, watch this step. It's a bit taller than the rest."

Leopold slowed slightly, and sure enough, when Safi's slippered foot hit the ledge, she *did* have to reach farther to hit the next.

"I realized I had found something incredible, Safiya, and I also knew I was being watched. So rather than explore that night, I tapped the wall again and waited. Then, on my birthday a month later, I asked Uncle Henrick to restore the tower's roof so that I might live there."

"I remember," Safi murmured. "Your tenth birthday."

"Exactly. And Uncle allowed me to lead the witches restoring it, which in turn allowed me to make sure no one discovered my secret passage. Even at ten," Leopold added, his tone turning wry, "I knew how special such a passage might be. And indeed, Safiya, it was . . . it *is* more special than anything I could have imagined. We are almost there now. Can you see the light?"

Safi blinked. She had been so focused on getting her feet in front of her and keeping her balance, she hadn't noticed the subtle changes in the darkness. Or the subtle changes in the air, a welcome warmth building against her skin.

Three more sharp spirals, and suddenly heat and light billowed fully against her. The space opened up; a cave spanned before her—as well as a three-foot drop-off. Leopold gracefully padded to the floor and turned back to offer Safi his hand.

She didn't accept it. She simply leaped to the unhewn floor and hurried past. Awe expanded in her rib cage; excitement raced through her veins. Even with her vision sapped and life drained, there was no mistaking this place for anything *but* otherworldly.

The cave stretched far ahead and out of sight, its high ceiling naturally rounded like a dome. Firewitched torches cast the walls in a glittering golden glow, and the soft mist that hovered over everything seemed lit from within. Safi had never seen spirit swifts, but something about the shimmery fog made her think of them.

She sensed Leopold following behind, but he said nothing as she wandered onward. A subtle sense of sulfur permeated the air, growing stronger with each step. The warmth increased too, balmy, relaxing. *Hot springs*, she decided. The palace was heated by them, and one such spring must bubble nearby.

After several minutes of traversing the cavern, Safi reached thick chunks of stone that looked randomly placed at first glance, yet upon closer examination were in fact buttressing a weak ceiling. And like the tunnel in the tower, they were undoubtedly made by magic.

Safi paused at one and dragged her fingers over a series of carvings. They felt identical to the ones she'd sensed in the tower. "An owl," she said after studying the first symbol. "And . . . a crow?"

"A rook," Leopold corrected, and when Safi glanced his way, he shrugged. "After I discovered this place, I spent years trying to determine what it was and who had built it. Come." He set off deeper into the cave.

"And what did you find?" She skipped into step beside him.

"I found a Paladin once called the Rook King. The same one I believe Iseult told you about. He lived in the Sirmayans a thousand years ago, in the Monastery where Iseult met his ghost. The woman he loved, however, lived here." For once, as Leopold spoke, no affectation coated his words. No careful pauses, no musically placed inflections. He simply described what he had uncovered.

On anyone else, it would have sounded perfectly normal. On him, it sounded hollow. It sounded sad.

"She was also a Paladin," Leopold explained. He had to speak more loudly now; water flowed ahead. "Their love was forbidden, and so they built this secret place where they could meet. One of many such places, actually." As he said this, the cave turned slightly—and the churn of running waters doubled in volume.

Then a frothing hot spring appeared. Its waters had been arranged into a series of cascading, rectangular pools for swimming while a dozen columns framed the space, all connected by long benches.

"A bath," Safi said.

"Romantic, no?" Leopold glanced at her, expression unreadable. "And also quite unknown. I placed alarm-stones all around this cave shortly after I discovered it, and not once, in all my years of coming here, has a single stone been tripped off." Spreading his arms wide, he stalked forward. "We are very safe, Safiya fon Hasstrel, and very alone."

He twirled about to face her, swooping a dramatic bow. Gone was the flat Leopold; returned was the charming prince—and returned was Safi's wariness. *Very safe and very alone.* She did not like the way that sounded.

She kept her chest high and shoulders back as she strode to the nearest bench, where she withdrew her Truth-lens and once more trained it on Leopold.

"Why did you betray us?"

"And we return to the heart of the matter." Movement flickered across the lens's colorful glass, and when Safi opened her other eye, she saw Leopold had joined her at the bench. After draping his own scarf down, he sat.

Safi remained standing.

"I did not betray you to my uncle." Leopold lounged lazily, bracing both hands behind him and stretching out his legs. With his dressing robe, he looked like some wealthy gentleman come to enjoy the steam.

Safi shuttered her one eye again and stared only through the lens. So far, the colors remained true.

"Not on purpose, at least. If Henrick had known I worked with you, Safiya, then I would have been executed."

Safi's toes curled in her slippers while heat curled in her chest. "And that would have been so bad?" She lowered the lens. "You protected your own skin, Polly, and now *I* have no magic while Iseult is leagues away and hunted by Hell-Bards."

"Yes," he admitted, and he did not even try to look apologetic. "Iseult is indeed leagues away, and your magic has *indeed* been severed from you. But you have that." He tipped his head toward the Truth-lens. "And you have this. *We* have this." He flipped a hand toward the bath. "Which is entirely thanks to me."

Safi's molars ground in her ears. She yanked the lens to her eye once more—while his words still hung in the air and the magic still might respond. But the colors remained; everything he'd said was true.

She huffed a low snarl and kicked into a prowling pace alongside the bath's foggy edge. "I can't deny the value of the Truth-lens, but this?" She sawed a hand at the columns. "What good does this do us? Do *me*?"

"Why, Safiya." Leopold sat taller, his legs uncrossing. "I thought you would have figured it out by now: this cave connects to the outside world. Just as there is a secret way in, there is a secret way out. With *this*"—he parted his hands—"you can leave."

"Leave?" She rounded on Leopold. "And what of the noose?" She fished it out from beneath her collar. "If I leave, then Henrick will simply call me right back."

"Yes." Leopold steepled his hands. "That is certainly the greatest challenge facing us, but I don't believe all hope is lost. Not yet, anyway." He reached for the Truth-lens, clutched tightly in Safi's right hand. When she did not release it, he let his hand fall back to his side.

"That lens contains your magic, meaning whatever power was carved away from you, some yet remains."

"Oh." Safi stared down at the brass-bound lens upon her palm. Mist beaded against it. While she had considered that the device held half her magic, she had not considered that it might mean she was only half a Hell-Bard. "So you think . . . I can get my magic back?"

"*That*," Leopold answered, "I do not know." He patted the space beside him on the bench. "But if we could somehow gain access to Hell-Bard Keep, I think we might be able to find answers. Unfortunately, they guard their premises and do not welcome outsiders."

"But Polly." Safi sank onto the bench and grinned. A real, *true* grin. "Surely your spies have told you by now that I will train tomorrow with the Hell-Bards. His Imperial Majesty gave me his permission just tonight."

"Indeed." Leopold matched her smile.

"Indeed," she replied. Then she popped the Truth-lens back upon her eye. "Now tell me everything you know about Iseult and where you think she might be."

SEVENTEEN

✳

All was silent within the cove. After the madness of the escape—after the waves crashing and the ship groaning, after the splash of oars and surge of magic—the cove felt too calm, too still.

No one moved and no one spoke for an eternity. The day's sun lifted higher and higher while the sailors watched Vivia, still at the tiller, and while Vivia watched the snaking passage behind the *Iris*.

But no one came down it, and no Windwitches suddenly appeared. Vivia's plan had worked. For now. And the instant she twisted toward her crew, everyone seemed to collectively exhale. A great loosening of spines, a great drooping of shoulders.

Sotar was the first to speak. "Stow oars," he called, just loud enough to be heard. Though it was unlikely a shout would carry out of the cove while the tide carried in, there was no telling what lay nearby. Or who, for this was Nubrevna, and Vivia was not welcome here—not as queen, at least.

After unfurling her spyglass, Vivia scanned her gaze over the gravel beach and cliffs that surrounded the *Iris*. Everything looked as she remembered it, and in some ways, that was a comfort. The world here remained dead, outside of time. The same wasteland she'd always told herself she wanted no part of. This was where Merik had grown up, free on the Nihar estate several miles inland, while Vivia had been trained, groomed, molded into the queen her father wanted her to be.

Or the queen she'd thought he'd wanted. As Noden would have it, he'd only ever wanted a sycophantic pawn. Someone to tend him and flatter him. To obey him and mimic him. *Share the glory, share the blame,* he'd always said, but it had been a lie. *Give up the glory, take all the blame* was the truth Vivia now saw.

It was also where Merik's ship, the *Jana*, had been blown apart by Baedyed seafire. Everyone had thought he'd died; only Vivia and Cam knew he still lived. Remnants of the *Jana* lingered in the cove: charred wood, shredded sail cloth, and old caulking.

"Your Majesty."

Vivia lowered her glass and found Cam beside her. He smiled his sunny smile as he popped a bow. "I delivered food to the captain's cabin—and the Empress too."

Of course she's in there, Vivia thought with a sigh. She could no more escape Vaness than she could the Hagfishes. "Thank you, Leeri." Vivia clapped him on the shoulder; his smile widened. Then she strode for her cabin, adjusting her cuffs, her collar, her salt-crusted hair as she went.

She found the Empress standing at a window when she marched in. Vaness's cheeks were no longer pale, her posture no longer weakened, but there was a dullness to her eyes.

"You," she declared as soon as she saw Vivia, "must be cleaved. What you just did . . ." She shook her head. Her hair, damp against her skin, swished with sea-spray curls. "We could have died."

"But we didn't." Vivia shut the door behind her. "Would you like to eat?" She motioned to cheese and old bread that Cam had laid upon the table. A solid snack for a ravenous Tidewitch.

Vaness shook her head—and Vivia desperately wished she hadn't. She was half starved, but the thought of eating alone while Vaness watched on . . . It felt awkward. Filthy. Brutish next to Vaness's tiny, ever-graceful frame.

Noden curse her. She'd come in here expecting a fight. Not whatever this was with Vaness leaning against a window, her forehead pressed against the glass.

Vivia's stomach growled. She swiped up a chunk of hard goat's cheese. *No regrets, keep moving.* Yet before she could stuff it back like the beast she was, Vaness asked: "Why are there so many dead birds?"

Vivia froze. This was most certainly not what she'd expected. "The dead birds," she answered carefully, "are because the water is poison."

An audible swallow. "That was twenty years ago."

"And the imperial witches were thorough."

"You mean *my* witches were thorough."

Vivia didn't argue with this. Instead, she moved to another window on Vaness's other side. "The empires have always crushed what they could not control. We were the last nation to resist, so they . . . *you* allied together to ruin us."

"We failed, though." Vaness withdrew from the window. Her eyes fastened onto Vivia's.

"Did you, though?" Vivia stared right back. "Look at this cove, Empress. Dead birds, dead fish, no trees for miles. People can't live here, so they live in Lovats, which . . ." She swiveled her head to rest it against the frame. "Lovats cannot sustain. Because after you'd ensured we could not live on our lands, you impoverished us through trade."

A soft sigh. "We did, and I cannot even pretend otherwise."

"Is that an apology?"

"Would you accept if it were?"

"No," Vivia admitted. She had spent her whole life hating the empires. Hating Vaness and every leader like her. A hate nurtured by the constant death, constant hunger, constant need surrounding her. That she and Vaness were allies now—that there were even aspects of the Empress she liked—couldn't erase what waited outside the window.

She shoved the cheese into her mouth. Hard, strong. Then she chewed and chewed, her gaze shifting to the barren shore.

Vaness also returned her attention to the window, and for several moments, the only sound to interrupt this graveyard was the high tide whispering and lapping against the hull. And Vivia's smacking mouth. She should have grabbed the water.

"I am sick, you know," Vaness said eventually. "It is a disease of the blood. One I have always had. In Marstok, I had healers attend me, and I regularly bathed in the Fire Well. But it has been a month now since I was able to heal."

Vivia swallowed her cheese. Then wiped her mouth with the back of her hand. "Why didn't you tell me sooner?"

"Because no one but my healers and my Adders have ever known. It was a weakness I could not let free. A weakness I've hidden since childhood."

"Yet now you've shared."

Vaness opened her hands. "Now I've shared. Which places my future—once again—squarely in your hands."

It did, and Vivia of a year ago would have reveled in that. Vivia of two months ago too. She would have rushed to tell her father, and they would have schemed how best to use such information.

But Vivia of two months ago also would never have allied with the Empress to get back their crowns, because Vivia of two months ago was still the Queen-in-Waiting, catering to her father's every whim. Certain he only ever held Nubrevna's interests in his heart.

She had been miserable. Broken. Mind-controlled by a man who had only ever loved himself.

"I have . . . attacks," Vivia said eventually. Then, before Vaness could see the flush rising to her cheeks, she fled from the window to the table. "They sit in my chest, like storm clouds through which I cannot breathe. Sometimes, they are mild and I gasp my way through. Sometimes, they are so bad, I cannot move. No one knows about them, though, because like you, I have hidden them since I was a child." *Even from myself.*

It was the first time Vivia had ever looked this truth in the face or given it a name. *Attacks.* She had thought such a confession would be more freeing. She had thought such acknowledgment would be more soothing. Instead, she wished she'd kept her mouth shut and never looked inside. She and Vaness were bitches in the alley again, but this time, Vivia had left her neck fully exposed. All Vaness had to do was bite.

Vivia felt eyes boring into her.

She was pleased her hand didn't shake as she poured a glass of water. "Now you have my secret." *Don't bite, don't bite.* "And I have yours. Our futures are once more shared and equal, just as they have been for this past month."

"And just as," Vaness murmured, "they always have been."

She spoke so softly, Vivia almost thought she'd misheard, and when she frowned at the Empress, Vaness did not repeat. Instead she motioned to the door and said, "I will be in my quarters if you need me."

Vivia didn't watch her go.

Vivia breathed in the sea air, savoring the way it filled her lungs. Savoring the way the coast looked alive, healthy. Moonlight glared on the dark waves, calm now with the tide out. For all she knew, so long as she kept staring in this direction, there was no poison. No dead, barren land.

"I don't see anyone," Cam murmured. He had a spyglass to his eye—a fine bronze thing Sotar had given him and that he polished daily. "I think they're gone."

"Hye," Vivia agreed. Like Cam, she was sprawled on her belly. The pale earth scraped against her white clothes. The Lonely Bastard loomed to the west. The cove waited half a mile behind.

Vivia pushed to her knees, then sank to her haunches. There was no one on the ocean. No one to see her or Cam. It should have been a relief, but instead, Vivia's nerves twanged higher by the breath. Why hunt her ship across a sea only to abandon chase once the *Iris* vanished? And why hunt her at all? No Voicewitch messages had come in. No threats or explanations.

Cam clanked shut his spyglass and shoved into his own seated position, cross-legged beside Vivia, hands over his knees. He had a floppiness to his movements that was both graceful and puppy like. "I found Merik near here, you know."

Vivia stiffened.

"I tended him back to health in a hut nearby, then we went to the capital. He hated you."

"Ah," she breathed, and for some reason, her stomach hollowed out. She wished Cam hadn't said that. She wished she hadn't heard the words so directly: *He hated you.* It didn't matter that she had always hated him right back, and it didn't matter that the last time she'd seen Merik they had parted on solid terms. Not loving, not even good, but solid.

What mattered was that he had hated her, and she'd deserved it.

She picked up a rock, palm-size and dry as sun-bleached bone. It was rough against her fingertips. "Why are you telling me this, Cam?"

"Because he was wrong."

Vivia dug her thumb into the rock. A corner crumbled.

"Merik wanted to lead Nubrevna, and I think he will make a good king. One day. But you make a good queen now, and wherever you lead us, I'll stand beside you."

Vivia crushed the rock in her hand. It fractured to sand and she watched it fall from her palm. A moonlit trickle of earth that had once held life.

After several moments with only wind and sea to fill the silence, Cam clambered to his feet and offered Vivia a hand.

She didn't take it. "Head back to the *Iris*," she told him. "I'll join you there soon."

His hand dropped. He bowed. "Hye, Majesty." And soon, his footsteps sifted into the night. He returned shortly, though, a soft crunch upon the earth. Vivia assumed he'd lost his bearings. And after rising and dusting off her breeches, she turned to face the boy.

But it was not Cam who came prowling out of the white trees before her. It was a lean man with a scar across his face and skin weathered to dark, seamed brown. "Hello, Princess." Master Huntsman Yoris waved, revealing only three fingers upon his left hand. "It has been a long time."

Four more people emerged from the ghost forest: two women and two men, each dressed in the same yellowish-white shade as the land. And each with a crossbow aimed at Vivia's head.

EIGHTEEN

✳

Iseult looked for an escape. All night and into the dawn, she studied Aeduan's and Evrane's Threads and waited for moments when one of them
was off guard. She scanned the trees for anything she might use as distraction. And she called and called to the weasel.

Pointless. The weasel held her silence. The Threads held no answers,
and anytime Aeduan's attention wandered, Evrane's did not. Or it was
reversed, with Evrane's eyes meandering into the woods while Aeduan
observed Iseult like a wolf. The one time both monks were distracted—by
a strange, scuffling sound in the forest—Iseult couldn't wriggle free from
her bindings upon the ash tree.

"Can you sense what that was?" Aeduan asked after yanking the gag
from Iseult's mouth. His voice was all wrong, wrong, wrong. The morning's
cold had turned his nose red.

"No," Iseult croaked between coughs. "I cannot . . . sense animal Threads,
if they even have them."

"All life has Threads."

"You don't."

He tensed before her, Threads sputtering with surprise.

"The real you," she added. "The Bloodwitch whose body you stole."

He sniffed, the sound almost lost to a breeze biting through the trees.
Then: "Interesting. I did not know such a thing was possible."

"Portia once told me it might be," Evrane inserted. She stood before
Owl, and at her voice, Owl huddled deep beneath a blanket. Iseult's own
blanket had fallen off in the night. "She said for those born directly in the
Sleeper's glow, their Threads never form. Something like that."

Portia again. The woman from the diary pages. Iseult ought to ask about
her—press for how these usurpers knew such a name—but that was when
the rustling resumed in the forest. A snapping branch. A pattering like a
hundred feet. And Threads. Faint but unmistakably silver.

Now Iseult was the one to tense. Aeduan noticed. "What is it?"

She didn't answer; instead she squinted into the barren hardwoods and green pines. Twice she had seen Threads of such pure silver: Once on sea foxes in the Jadansi Sea. Second on Blueberry, Owl's mountain bat. And as much as she wished those Threads might be Blueberry, they were too quiet. Too stealthy.

"What is it?" Aeduan repeated.

"Something hunts us," she said, glad they spoke in Arithuanian so Owl wouldn't understand. "We should leave."

Alarm brightened Aeduan's Threads—and Evrane's too. But neither monk argued. They simply unbound Iseult and Owl and hurried them onto Lady Sea Fox and Lord Storm Hound. They'd already loaded up camp, and neither Iseult nor Owl resisted as they were forced into the same pairings as yesterday.

Eventually the silver Threads faded. Eventually the sun rose. And eventually signs of humanity laid claim to the forest. A well-trod road, cleared fields for grazing, and finally fieldstone huts with thatched roofs. A family's farm, one of thousands like it spread throughout the Ohrin Mountains. Sheep called from within fences as Lady Sea Fox and Lord Storm Hound passed. A lone dog barked his alarm, ears high and gray fur thick upon his back.

Soon, Iseult heard the villagers. Shouts as if soldiers corralled. Cries as if families resisted. Then came the Threads—later than they should've come, muted and slow. Fear and rage, violence and obedience.

Corlant. He was here. It was the only explanation for so many pallid Threads: a Cursewitch's power and corrupted touch.

The cries of the village. Owl's Threads blanked out, and Iseult's fingers tightened into fists. White, white, always white. One day, Iseult would make sure the child never felt fear again.

An empty promise. One more failure to add to her growing list. She could no more help Owl than she could help herself. *Please, weasel. Please come.*

The commotion brimmed louder, bouncing off stone walls. Threads tangled and clotted at the center of the village, and as the horses rounded a corner, chaos unfolded before Iseult's eyes: an open square turned to mud by hooves and shepherd boots. Sixteen people kneeling, backs bent and Threads saturated by uniform terror. Two children weeping. And twelve women and men with blades out and Purist robes billowing on a winter wind.

At the center of the yard, where an ancient well slouched, stood Corlant. *He's so tall,* Iseult thought distantly as the horses continued their approach.

She'd forgotten how much he towered over everyone, hair oily and eye-brows perpetually high. With furs atop his shoulders, he looked broader. Commanding, even, as he smiled at the sight of Iseult.

"Your timing is perfect," he called. He flung open his arms like a per-former.

And Iseult blinked. She'd only ever heard him speak Nomatsi, yet now he spoke Arithuanian—no accent, no stumbling.

"Get them off the horses," he commanded. Aeduan dismounted and dragged down Iseult too. She hit the earth with a knee-snapping jolt, no balance with her wrists still tied, before Aeduan pushed her toward the well.

Owl whimpered.

"Gag her," Corlant ordered once Iseult was before him. "It is her fangs we must watch out for." His Threads sharpened with anticipation. He knew what Iseult's true magic was. Somehow he *knew* she needed her mouth, needed her teeth in order to cleave.

He smiled as Aeduan grabbed the back of Iseult's head and thrust in the old filthy wool. She tried to avoid the Bloodwitch, but he was stronger. The cloth filled her mouth, her eyes burned, and she gagged ineffectually against bile rising in her throat.

Owl's tiny sobs joined with the other children's.

"You will enjoy this," Corlant murmured to Iseult, closing the space between them. *So tall.* He ran a single finger down her jaw, and though she screamed stasis within, her body could not obey. Iseult recoiled, and Corlant laughed. Then, with that same finger, he beckoned to the nearest Purist.

"The Herdwitch," he said. "Bring him to me." The Purist grabbed for a man at the edge of the kneeling family. The man yelped. His Threads ignited with fear while beside him a woman reached for him. "No, please no—"

A second Purist kicked her, square in the back. She splayed out on the mud, a cry scraping from her throat. Iseult moved, muscles reacting with-out thought. She would attack that Purist, attack Corlant—

Aeduan moved faster. He yanked her back, arm sliding over her throat. He squeezed. Her vision crossed. "Stay."

Iseult nodded. She had no choice. And though she wanted to screw her eyes shut as Owl did, she forced them to stay open. She forced herself to witness Corlant's powers in action.

The first Purist hauled the Herdwitch to Corlant. Sheep bleated fran-tically; in the distance, a dog howled.

"Blessed are the pure," Corlant told the man as he drew him close and placed his palm upon the man's forehead. "May you become as clean as Midne, as pure as the world when it was born." With his free hand, he grabbed at the air above the man's head, at Threads pale with terror.

Iseult could do nothing but gaze on, her belly sinking like a stone. Her breaths coming in shallow gasps.

She might have seen Corlant's magic at the Midenzi settlement—seen how his presence faded Threads like rain erases paint—but she'd never encountered his magic used openly. She'd never watched as he slashed away the very power that made this Herdwitch who he was.

As Corlant's long fingers curled around the man's Threads, they grew fainter, fainter. The man's body limper and more slumped.

"Don't," begged the woman. She did not rise from the mud. "Please, please leave him—"

A streak of gray bolted into the yard. Snarling, barking, the dog from before surged around the Purists and aimed straight for Corlant.

"No," the Herdwitch mumbled, a desperate, broken sound. Then the last of his Herdwitch Threads swelled into Corlant, like a vine coiling around a tree. Corlant laughed, and as the dog reached him, teeth bared and legs ready to leap, Corlant snapped a single hand toward the dog.

The dog stopped in its tracks. Its fur settled, its teeth vanished behind suddenly loose jowls. A whine wisped from its throat.

"No," the Herdwitch mumbled again, his legs buckling beneath him. But he could not stop Corlant any more than he could stop his fall. Corlant swiped his hand toward the well, and the dog obeyed. Six loping paces before it reached the stone rim. A single vertical leap and it dropped over. It dropped in.

Half a heartbeat later, its body hit dry ground with a yelp and snap of bones. An empty well, a pointless death. Owl's wails filled the midmorning sky.

The Hell-Bard training "space" was a misleading term. It was, in fact, a vast complex beneath the newest wings of the palace. Three levels beneath the earth, the cold of the Stonewitch-carved caverns washed over Safi. The heat from the springs—and Leopold's secret bath—did not reach here.

At dawn, Lev guided Safi into the long main room where Hell-Bards circled at a brisk jog. Several spread apart to allow Safi into their ranks. Her lungs seared within a single lap of two hundred steps. By four hundred steps, the burn had moved to her stomach. To her thighs. But she welcomed it—sank into the sensation of pushing through pain and running like she hadn't run in days.

She wondered if Uncle Eron had ever trained here. She wondered what he had been like before he became a drunk. She had never known that person. For her, his very Aether was made of bitterness and alcohol.

Eight hundred steps, and Safi was sprinting.

One thousand steps, and the other Hell-Bards had stopped running and had paired off for other training. The sounds of clanging metal, thumping arrows, and flesh pounding into flesh soon echoed off stone walls. Sweat, steel, tallow—the smells blurred together in Safi's nose, familiar and palliative.

She didn't join them in their training. Instead, she kept running. Three weeks of being in Praga, but she was no closer to her uncle than she had been in Azmir. It had seemed such a simple plan: bring down an emperor, then hand over his crown to an heir better suited. But nothing had gone as expected, and now Safi was trapped and useless and alone.

With Iseult countless miles away.

And with a favored owed to a raider admiral. Safi wasn't sure where that thought came from, but she didn't like it. It was one more thing she'd done wrong, and she had the blister around her thumb to prove it.

Safi sprinted faster, faster, until nausea charged up from her stomach. Until black floated across her vision and her breaths were so shallow that they eventually stopped billowing at all.

Then and only then did she stagger to a stop and drop her hands to her knees. Wheezing, she stared at the sand-covered ground. Her golden noose dipped out from her shirt. Once it would have been her Threadstone dangling there.

She would get that back, though. Somehow. Just as she would find Iseult and she would find her uncle.

Safi had asked Leopold the night before if he knew where Eron was. His denial had been an honest one. Yet, despite talking for hours and despite never catching Leopold in any lies, Safi had returned to her bedroom with the nagging sense that there was more to what he'd said. That he'd somehow hidden lies from her by wrapping them in pretty truths.

She had no one else to help her, though. The Hell-Bards were as bound to Henrick as she was. So for now, to Leopold she must turn.

"Heretic."

Caden's voice filtered through Safi's breaths, and when she hauled up her thousand-pound head, she found him slouching nearby. Comfortably. Patiently, even. In one hand he held a practice sword; in the other, a real one.

"Fight me." He offered Safi the true blade, its steel glinting in the cellar's cold light.

And Safi couldn't help it: she smiled. "I believe the title you meant to say was *Your Imperial Majesty.*" She took the sword, pleased to find it well balanced in her hand.

"No," Caden countered with a slight smile. "I said exactly what I intended." He charged.

Safi twirled sideways. His attack swung wide, but he quickly altered course, curving in for a follow-up. His wooden sword hit Safi's steel. *Chop, parry, thrust, riposte.* Safi's muscles sang with each movement. Her blood thrilled. All the sweat from running that had cooled across her skin was now hot and slick again.

"I need to know," she said between grunts, between attacks, "how to get . . . into Hell-Bard Keep." Nothing in Safi's movements was graceful, but sometimes a person just needed to *pummel* things. She was also a month out of practice.

"Is that why you came to train?" Caden's lips quirked as he easily outmaneuvered each of her swings. "And here I thought you missed me."

She laughed and swung again. "I missed beating you up."

"And I've missed being beat up, Safi."

"It's *Your Imperial Majesty* now." She ducked a swipe, catching it with her blade.

"Not down here," he countered. "Down here, you're one of us. We're all heretics, all Hell-Bards." To prove this point, he swooped his practice blade against her next attack, flipping the wooden blade of his sword around her wrist and yanking.

Safi dropped her sword. Steel clanged to the ground. If his blade had been real, her hand would have fallen too. But his blade *wasn't* real, and she wasn't done with this fight. With all her strength, she pushed into Caden. His elbows crumpled in, the wooden sword pressed flat against him, and with her free hand, Safi grabbed his chin.

She moved forward, ready to brace behind him just as she had done to Henrick's attendant only two days before. Except Caden was trained, so when her hip cocked against his, he slung an arm around her shoulders . . .

And brought her down too.

She landed on her stomach. Caden landed on his back, and for several seconds, neither of them spoke. Neither of them moved. Safi just stared into the sand and tried to get her lungs and skull working again. Her wrist hurt. Her weak ankle too.

"If," she panted out eventually, "I'm a Hell-Bard now, then why won't you tell me how to get into the Keep?" She swiveled her head and found Caden watching her. Sweat glistened on his red face; the scar on his chin stood out white and long.

And not for the first time, Safi was struck by how thrice-damned handsome he was. *No wonder he tricked you so easily in Veñaza City.* He had been the Chiseled Cheater then. Now, he was Caden fitz Grieg—and now, Safi knew she could trust him through hell-fires and back.

"Why do you need to get into the Keep?" His chest moved in time to his shallow breaths. "Trust me when I say the Keep is not a place you want to go. It's not a place I or any other Hell-Bard wants to go. It is . . ." He hesitated, as if searching for the right word. "*Bad.*"

"Bad," she repeated. That descriptor could mean so many things.

"If you're hoping to find a way out of this curse, you won't find it there, Safi. All of us"—he spun a tired hand—"have hoped for that same thing. And we've only ever found disappointment."

But I'm not like you, she wanted to volley back. *You don't have a Truthlens, Caden, and you aren't half the Cahr Awen.* Safi wasn't that person anymore, though—the one who always had to retort. Who always needed the last, fiery word. These Hell-Bards had tried and failed to earn freedom; she would not disrespect their trials by claiming her own chances were any better.

Instead, she said: "I have to try, Caden. I have to see the heart of it all with my own eyes. And perhaps . . . perhaps there will be some clue there about my uncle."

Caden's expression softened at those words. "I see." With a grunt, he pushed to his feet and offered Safi a hand.

She took it. But once he had her upright, he didn't release her. Instead he tugged her close. "There is a way to get you there, Safi. A quick way that even Henrick cannot deny. But you aren't going to like it." His face was mere inches from hers, their fingers still intertwined.

"Anything," she breathed, leaning in more closely. "Caden, I'll do *anything.*"

His eyes held hers for two heartbeats before he nodded. "Good enough. Just remember you said that when you're cursing my name in two seconds.

"What do you mean?" she began, but Caden was already pulling back, already drawing a knife from his belt.

He stabbed her in the thigh.

NINETEEN

✳

This was what Iseult knew about her terrain: she was in the Ohrins in a shepherding complex with countless miles of forest surrounding her. And this was what Iseult knew about her opponent: Corlant could enter the Hell-Bard Loom. He could take magic from others and use it. And for some reason, he had hunted Iseult across the entire continent.

He stared at her now, seated at a table not so different from the table Iseult had studied on the night before in a hut not so different from the one the Hell-Bards had commandeered. She wondered if that hut had belonged to these poor shepherds too. She wondered if, now that Corlant had taken the Herdwitch's magic, he would let the family go free.

Currently, they were shut in a cellar below the largest building. Their sheep had gone silent.

Behind Iseult, Owl lay curled on her side atop a bunked sleeping cot. Every few seconds, blue grief waterfalled over her Threads. The only color, the only sign she had not fallen into herself forever. Otherwise, all was white, all was numb.

Aeduan and Evrane stood guard outside the hut.

"What do you want from me?" Iseult asked in Arithuanian. The first words uttered since Aeduan had dragged her in here and removed her gag. *And released her fangs.* Not that she dared use them with so many enemies about and hostages all too easily killed.

Corlant steepled his fingers. The grooves on his forehead trenched inward as his Threads flickered with surprise. "I would have expected your mother to explain when she hid you away. But perhaps not." He lowered his hands to the wood. The fingers spread wide, knobby-knuckled and long. "I am not your enemy, Iseult. We are in fact on the same side."

"I don't steal people's magic."

"Oh, but you do. And you have done it before. A Firewitch, if I recall correctly."

Iseult's breath slashed in. How had he known? She *had* taken that raider's power. Not on purpose, but when she'd cleaved him, the ghost of his soul had stayed trapped against her own. But *how* could Corlant know?

Stasis, stasis. Corlant would not see her feel.

"I'm not like you." She pointed to Owl. "I don't kidnap children. I don't kill dogs or terrorize families. I don't turn tribes against someone or shoot them with cursed arrows."

"The arrow was an accident," he said, and to Iseult's surprise, regret swaddled his Threads. "I didn't know what you were then. What you are."

"And what am I?"

"Powerful." His hand slipped into a pocket of his robe, and after fidgeting out a worn tome, he slid it onto the table.

Iseult's pulse quickened. Her mouth watered.

"I see you recognize the diary." He smiled. "And I see you want it. Oh, I do not see Threads—not in the way you do, with emotions to shade and define—but hunger . . . It is a feeling I know well." He nudged the diary closer to Iseult, so she could clearly read Eridysi's handwriting scribbled on the spine. The front cover did not match the rest. It was newer, stiffer leather.

"I will give this to you, Iseult." Corlant's Threads morphed with sly pink. "If you give me the two rubies your mother stole from me."

The Threadstones again. Iseult's hand moved to her collarbone, to the empty expanse there. "I don't have them."

"Yes, yes." Corlant's fingers tapped across the table. "The one called Aeduan told me you left them in Praga. Unlike him, though, I am not so foolish as to believe you."

Iseult snorted. "Then I wish you luck finding them." She patted her collarbone again, this time emphatically. "The Emperor of Cartorra took them off Safi and me, so if you want them, you'll have to go all the way to Praga to get them."

"Hmmm." Corlant eyed Iseult, gaze resting first on her collar. Then on her face. "You must not know what they are, or you would never have left them behind."

Iseult lowered her hand. "And what are they?"

"Valuable." He pushed to his feet, table and chair creaking. "And if we must go to Praga to get them, then that is what we will do."

He turned as if to leave; lilac hope trickled over Owl's Threads. But Iseult couldn't let him walk away. "Wait." She shot up. Corlant paused. "The Loom. I saw you in the Hell-Bard Loom. How?"

There it was again: the smile. The delight to suffuse his Threads. He lifted his chain—the chain he'd worn as long as she'd known him, golden and plain. It glinted in the fragile light. "I was the first she ever claimed, Iseult. And this chain was the first she ever made. But you can learn all about that in here." He scooped up the diary.

"Not if you don't let me have it." She watched him stuff it back into his pocket.

"Oh, but we have a deal. When the Threadstones are in my possession again, then this"—he patted his pocket—"will be yours." He left the cabin, his Threads grassy green with contemplation.

And a darker, pine green too: the lingering magic claimed from a Herd-witch.

"Gag them," he ordered once he was outside. "Gag them, tie them to the bed, and let no one in without my approval."

Safi was in agony. She'd had injuries before—a shattered ankle, a broken nose, burns and scrapes and stitches aplenty. A knife stab in the thigh was a new one.

And not being able to use magical healing was *also* new and also rutting horrible.

After the initial shock of a hole in her leg gushing blood, fire had set in. She'd been unable to walk, even with the bindings Caden had quickly and efficiently wrapped around her.

"I will kill you," she told him over and over again.

"No you won't," he replied each time.

After that, the journey through the palace had passed in a haze. Caden had carried Safi up from the bowels of the training area, across several blustery courtyards pink with sunrise, and finally into the palace stables. She was vaguely aware of Hell-Bards marching around them. Of Lev ordering attendants to inform His Imperial Majesty of the injury. Of a carriage being summoned and grooms rushing out with horses for the Hell-Bard.

A training injury, Caden kept telling them. *Alert His Imperial Majesty. The Empress was hurt in training.*

Then Safi was dumped into the carriage, and Lev and Caden were scrambling onto a seat beside her. Rather than help her sit up or check on her injury, though, Caden barked, "Wards," and he and Lev clasped hands.

Their heads bowed low, and through the pain, Safi sensed power gathering. A swell of static. A magic her Hell-Bard senses instantly identified as *our own.* It took only moments before the wards were done. Then Caden and Lev released each other.

Caden knocked on the carriage's front wall. The horses clopped into motion, and with a gurgle of fresh flames, Safi fell against her leather-bound bench. Each quake in the carriage sent eyeball-crushing pain throughout her.

"Why," she ground out, "does it hurt so thrice-damned much?"

"Because that's what knives do." Lev removed her helm and offered a tight-lipped frown. "I was wondering when you'd set your mind on the Keep—and I was hoping you never would."

"I warned her," Caden defended, "but she insisted."

"We all do." Lev wagged her head. "We all do. Except this time, I would wager the Emperor himself will come deal with the damage."

"She's right." Caden turned to Safi. She struggled to keep a lock on his face. "You won't have much time at the Keep, and that"—he waved at her leg—"is only the beginning."

"Beginning of *what*?" Safi tried to sit up, but Caden swatted her back down. She glared at him, though it quickly turned into an eye-rolling moan. "Is this carriage hitting *every* hole in the street?"

"Every one," he replied.

Lev snorted. "When we get to the Keep, Safi, you'll be taken right away to the special healing wing. Hell-Bards can't be treated by magic, but there are . . . well, there are *other* ways of keeping us alive."

Caden nodded. "And as the Empress, you'll get a private room. You'll need to wait until Henrick arrives before you make any sort of move, though. He will need to see you in the room being treated. Then you can ask him to leave for privacy's sake. Hopefully, he agrees."

"Shoulda stabbed her near her lady parts," Lev muttered. "That would have kept him from coming in."

Safi turned her next glare on Lev. "What do I do once he leaves the room?"

"I presume you want to see the Loom?" Caden asked. "It's what all Hell-Bards want . . . no, *need* to see. The device we're all bound to. The reason we can never escape."

"*Yes*," Safi snapped. "Obviously I want to see this Loom." For some reason, that word *Loom* sounded familiar. Iseult had told her of looms— that much she remembered. But what they did or why Iseult had studied them . . . Nothing came to mind.

Perhaps because her entire existence was consumed by the hell-flaming agony of her thigh.

"Zander," Lev inserted. "He's at the Keep, and he'll help us."

"But you'll need healing first." Caden's eyes flicked to Safi's wound.

His face scrunched up apologetically. "I might have, uh, stabbed a bit too deeply."

"*Might* have?"

"Yeah, but if you'd gone any easier," Lev countered, "then Henrick could've argued that a regular healer would've done the trick. Sorry, Safi." Lev winced at her. "But to get into the Keep, an injury's gotta be bad."

Safi's eyelids briefly shut. *You agreed to this, you fool. You agreed to this.* Actually, she'd specifically asked for it. "How much longer?"

Lev peeked behind a curtain. Then quite noticeably did not answer the question. "While Zander gets her to the Loom, what are me and you gonna do?" The question was addressed to Caden. "Pull another Kristazhoffen?"

He shook his head. "A big distraction won't work here. As soon as Henrick knows what's happened, he will use his power over Hell-Bards to track her."

Lev blanched. "You don't mean . . . You *can't* mean . . ."

"What choice does she have?" Caden glanced at Safi. "While she and Zander are sneaking off to the Loom, you and I will pull an Isnie."

"What's an Isnie?" Safi asked—or rather, moaned—at the same moment Lev said, "Oh, that's risky, Captain." But she had a smile on her face as she spoke. Then she turned her attention to Safi and said, "Let me tell you about the time that me, Zander, and Caden here got stuck on an island called Isnie in the middle of the North Sea."

As Lev settled into the story, Safi knew she was being handled. *Distracted* from whatever horrible future had made all the blood drain from Lev's face and made Caden ask, *What choice does she have?* But her leg hurt too much to interrupt the tale, and her whole body hurt too much to demand answers. Caden's roughshod bindings were already soaked through, and there was a very real chance she would pass out at any moment.

Not a chance, she realized as shadows swept in, *but the reality.*

✳

Fourteen Days After the Earth Well Healed

*H*ave I ever told you the story of how the hedgehog came back to life?" *Iseult gazes down at Owl, who shakes her head with such energy, her heretic's collar clanks.*

Five days she has been wearing it, and today is the first day she seems accustomed. They have made it to midmorning without a tantrum, without tears—not that Iseult would blame Owl if she started sobbing. The collar was the only way the child could enter Praga without her life consigned to the Hell-Bards. A magic like hers is "too dangerous to be kept free."

Of course, Iseult wasn't surprised when Owl refused and fought and tried to flee. Yet somehow Leopold coaxed her into compliance in the end, though he spoke no Nomatsi.

"Well," Iseult says, slipping down to the woolen rug beside the child, "it happened long ago, when the gods still walked among us." As she settles into the tale—a silly tale that ends in a song—Owl listens with rapt eyes and rapt Threads.

Her Hell-Bard protector, Zander, stands with his spine erect beside the bedroom door. He cannot speak Nomatsi; Owl cannot speak Cartorran; yet the two of them have a connection that transcends words. It is fascinating to watch, how their Threads have entangled. How thickly the sunset bond of family has already grown.

He is the one who put the collar on Owl five days ago. He cried afterward, when he thought no one was watching.

Iseult keeps her tale short this morning. Not merely because she is crushing her gown by sitting cross-legged, but also because she has somewhere to be. Somewhere that makes her stomach freeze and heart ice over.

She has said stasis a thousand times today, but to no avail.

"Save the bones," she sings, reciting the words Trickster had once sung, "save the bones!"

"Lost without them," Owl joins, "have no home! Wrapped in twine to keep them grounded. Trapped in time and moonlight crown'd them."

"And with those words," Iseult finishes, "the soil twitched and the hedgehog's little nose poked up from the dirt."

"Alive!" Owl claps, her Threads flush with pleasure. She has regressed again—as she is prone to do. Her size suggests she must be six years old, but frequently she behaves like a child half that . . . or like a woman five times grown.

The collar, it seems, has trapped her in the younger state.

"Alive," Iseult agrees. "Trickster's spell was successful, and after that, the witch and her hedgehog friend went on many grand adventures for all the rest of their days." Those words are not how Nomatsi tales end, but Iseult likes the Cartorran turn of phrase. She likes the idea of grand adventures with Safi at her side.

Owl is still clapping when a single knock sounds at the door and Leopold fon Cartorra strides in. As usual, he looks effortlessly perfect. His black brocade enhances the width of his shoulders, sharpens the tapering of his waist. He has even added a small cap that sits jauntily on one side of his head. On anyone else, it would look ridiculous.

On Leopold the Fourth, it looks dashing.

Owl rises and runs excitedly toward Leopold. "She says you are dressed very nicely," Iseult translates as Leopold meets her. The child strokes his black cape with green curiosity. Like most things in the palace, such finery is new to her. Even her room, which is threadbare compared to Safi's and Iseult's, draws comments from her daily.

"It is not a color I would choose," Leopold admits, and he offers Iseult his hands to help her rise. Even his gloves are black. "But it is imposing, and on a wedding day, it is good to look serious . . ." His eyes rake up and down Iseult's new gown. Approval shimmers in his Threads.

Approval and something else. Something lilac that Iseult wishes she could not see.

"I will be back in a few hours," she tells Owl in Nomatsi. Then to Zander in Cartorran: "Keep her safe."

The gentle Hell-Bard smiles, his Threads suffused with warmth. "I always do."

"Yes," Iseult agrees, and she attempts a smile of her own. But it is tight upon her lips. Forced, false, frightening. Ever since she has reached Praga, she has tried to be like other people, wearing emotions on her face. Making expressions that reflect what people think she ought to feel.

But more often than not, she gets it wrong. And judging by Leopold's wince, she is currently failing. Again. So she abandons the smile and hopes the heat rising up her neck is invisible.

She wishes she could simply spend her days alone with Safi. Or better yet, with Safi and the weasel on a road to Poznin. She hasn't studied the diary pages in so long, and Poznin calls to her like a beacon in the night.

Leopold offers his arm, but before Iseult accepts, she grabs a burgundy cloak off the worn armchair in the corner. A matching scarf too, for outside of Owl's room and her own, she dares not show her unnaturally pale skin, her unnaturally golden eyes.

Being the Cahr Awen earns her gifts, but it does not earn her respect.

Once her arm is tucked into Leopold's—he is always so warm to the touch— they enter the passage outside. This is a newer corner of the palace built for the servants. Everything is simple wood and narrow halls.

"You look lovely," Leopold murmurs as they march toward a distant stairwell. Hell-Bards stomp before and behind. "Such colors suit you." There is that lilac shade in his Threads again. Desire on anyone else. On Leopold, it is an enigma.

And Iseult is grateful for her scarf, now wound about her head, for there is no doubt that her flush is quite visible. "No need to waste your charm on me, Leopold."

"You say 'charm' as if it is a bad thing." They have reached the stairs. Hell-Bard boots clomp and clatter.

"What is charm other than lies coated in sugar?" Iseult must lift her voice to be heard. The steps creak.

"It is truth coated in sugar." Somehow Leopold makes himself heard without shouting. And he grins his winning grin. "It tastes so delicious, you do not realize you are being fed something you did not want to hear."

"You think I don't want to hear that I am lovely?" The stairs end, giving way to a covered walkway.

"I think," Leopold says, his grin turning sly and Threads turning darker, "that you do not want to find yourself lovely. It raises too many possibilities."

Iseult scowls—a real scowl that she does not have to emulate. "What is that supposed to mean?"

"For a woman always outside peering in, possibilities are confusing."

"You are confusing."

He laughs, but it is fake. He knows he has hit some truth Iseult avoids. He knows his words and his Threads discomfit her. And not for the first time, she wishes she had the easy rapport he and Safi share. Ever since their arrival in Praga, Leopold has become a Trickster version of himself. He plays with words and dons too many masks for Iseult to keep track of. Safi has no trouble navigating them; Iseult wishes he would just be himself.

Then again, she finds conversation with anyone difficult here, and though she does her best to emulate Safi, she always, always fails.

She will never be like her Threadsister. She will always be trapped in shadows.

Fortunately, Leopold offers no more flattery, hollow or otherwise, that Iseult must wade through, and soon they have reached a carriage that will transport them to the opposite end of the palace—and to the next step in the girls' careful plan.

TWENTY

✳

Safi awoke when the carriage stopped. Or maybe it was Caden's arms moving under her that startled her back into consciousness. Either way, there was pain.

"I'm going . . . to be sick," she slurred as he scooped her up and out of the carriage.

"Please don't," he replied. His face swam over her. She tried to hold on to his neck, but for some reason, her arms weren't in the mood to cooperate.

Distantly, she heard horse hooves and stamping feet. Bellowed orders and Hell-Bard chain mail. And distantly, she noticed the Keep spanning before her. Safi had seen it from afar as a child. It was not a tall fortress, with its cross-shaped alignment and wide battlements, but it didn't need to be tall to dominate. Made from a dark granite unlike anything else in the city, it absorbed all light, all warmth.

One of her greatest fears as a child had been that she would be caught for a Truthwitch and brought here. Now, she had not only come here willingly, but she'd gotten stabbed on purpose just so she could get in.

That thought made her laugh.

Or maybe it wasn't a laugh, but a sob. *Bat tits*, make it stop hurting.

"We're almost there," Caden said.

"Liar," Safi mumbled against his shoulder. Even in her half-delirious state, she could see they were only just entering a shadowy hall. Archways into new halls sliced off in different directions, but Caden's course aimed onward, ever onward down a seemingly endless stretch of exposed stone.

It reminded her of Leopold's tower.

The farther Caden stepped through the Keep, Hell-Bards marching severely around them, the more cold crept into Safi's body. It made no sense to her knife-addled brain—how she could be ablaze, yet frozen to her bones. And what little color remained in this world was being sucked dry. Soon, there would be no color left at all. Just shadows and light and frost inside the flames.

Eventually they reached an open area framed by balconies and stairs. It was strangely beautiful: a graceful circle with three curving stairwells that rose to different floors and branching hallways. At the center of the high-ceilinged room stood a statue of a shrouded woman staring down at her chained hands.

"Who is that?" Safi tried to ask as Caden and her escorts marched for the nearest set of stairs, but either he didn't hear her or he couldn't understand the jumble leaving her mouth. He simply said, "We're almost there. Hang on."

Lev heard, though, and Lev replied: "Midne. The first of us."

That name meant nothing to Safi, and the cold was spindling more deeply inside her. The world turning grayer and shallower and more alone.

More alone? What an odd thought. She was surrounded by people and held by a man who'd saved her many times before.

Caden carried her to the third floor, and if he was flagging—Safi was hardly a small person—he did not show it. His stride stayed as true as that of the other Hell-Bards around them until at last, they entered a new area of the Keep and his stride finally halted.

Safi wasn't sure why she considered it a *new* area, since nothing here looked any different from where they'd been. Black granite, a hall of doors, and no decorations to disrupt the shadows. Yet the energy felt different—more voices, more light, and more fires crackling in hearths she could not see. Then Safi's guards spread apart and a woman appeared.

Like all Hell-Bards, she wore scarlet, but instead of armor, a floor-length robe over high-necked black wool adorned her petite frame. Her amber skin was aged, her nose pronounced, and her black hair streaked with gray.

"The Empress," Safi heard Lev explain. "She took a knife to the leg during training."

"On purpose?" the healer asked, motioning for Caden to follow. "Actually, don't answer that. I gather Emperor Henrick will be here soon?"

"We expect so," Caden replied as he ducked Safi through a low door and down several steps into a wide, boiling room. The other Hell-Bards stayed outside, taking up their usual guardian positions, while Lev disappeared entirely.

At the healer's direction, Caden eased Safi onto a high cot. Instantly, the woman pushed him aside, and with firm hands she forced Safi to stretch upon the hard mattress. "You've lost a lot of blood, but you won't die yet. Although." She pursed her lips and met Safi's eyes. "You aren't going to enjoy the healing."

Safi rolled back her head and groaned. Ever since the training grounds, it had been one *you won't like this* after another. "Just get on with it, please."

The woman complied, starting with the linens wrapped around Safi's thigh. Safi's eyes crossed; black crowded over her vision.

"We need you to send the Emperor away," Caden told the healer. "Once he arrives and confirms the Empress is being treated, we need him to leave."

"I see," the healer said, and to Safi's surprise, she made no argument and asked for no explanations. "In that case, it might be best if you left, Captain. We cannot pretend to need privacy if you remain at her side."

"Good enough." Caden's face swam into view over Safi's. "Zander will come for you, all right? And Lev and I will handle the Emperor."

Before Safi could acknowledge his words, or for that matter, even work through what they might mean, Caden withdrew. "Toward death with wide eyes."

And the healer replied, "All clear, all clear."

The door clicked shut moments later.

"Am I correct to guess," the healer asked, a pair of shears now in hand, "that you've never been healed as a Hell-Bard?"

Safi forced a nod.

"Then I will warn you it is not like other healing." She cut into Safi's pant leg. Quick, sure strokes that let warm air caress her skin. "And it will get worse before it gets better."

Before Safi could ask what that meant—or order the woman to just *cursed well get on with it*—the healer placed her hands on Safi's wound.

And Safi's whole world expanded.

There was no other word to describe what Safi felt. One moment, she was inside her own mind, closed off and contained. The next moment, all boundaries were gone. There was no Safi, there was no brain. No body with a stab wound bleeding out, and no healer with hands upon her thigh. Safi was bigger than that, her consciousness stretched into something she could not comprehend, much less explain.

At first, the change carried with it relief. No more pain. No more chill, no more flames. There was only release and welcome loss of self. But the relief was short-lived. Infinitesimal compared to the agony that roared in. Gradual, gradual, then so fast her entire existence felt ripped apart. A firepot going off. A thousand *thousand* firepots going off. And inside each was wintry pain like she'd never imagined, never known could exist.

The collective pain of every Hell-Bard in the Witchlands and every Hell-Bard who had ever lived.

It was not merely the physical pain of life without magic either, cold and vicious and eternal, but the emotional trauma of having it cut away. Safi became their loss, their isolation, their empty, blundering lives through a world forever gray. All the pain she'd felt in the last two weeks was magnified on a scale no body was meant to feel, no brain was meant to maintain.

She thought surely this must be the end of her life.

At some point, she sensed that she was screaming. Great shrieks that shredded her throat and ripped apart her lungs. She couldn't say how she knew—she'd lost all contact with her body. Yet somehow she *did* know, just as she knew that she and the healer were no longer alone.

Henrick had come; Henrick was watching her.

Eventually he left. Safi's screams, however, did not.

On and on, they tore free, bigger than she was. A voice for all the others, the thousands upon thousands of others, who were bound as she was in the darkest corners of hell. She lost all touch with time or reality while she was trapped, expanded, one with all Hell-Bards. But eventually, the horror did pass. Eventually, as the healer had promised, it *did* get better. And when she finally returned to herself once more—so small, so comfortable, so safe—she found herself soaked in sweat.

The stench of vomit keened in her nose; the side of her face, she realized, was coated. Gone, though, was the pain. Her thigh felt as if it had never been stabbed, and when she flexed her toes, no throbbing racked through her.

"There isn't much time," the healer whispered. She dug her arms beneath Safi's shoulders and helped her rise. "The Emperor has been taken to another wing, where your screams would not reach, but eventually, he will return to check on your progress."

Safi blinked and tried to rub at the sickness, sticky and damp, upon her face. "Wait," the healer said, turning toward a washbasin nearby. While she dunked a towel within, Safi examined her leg.

A thick scar puckered on top of her thigh, faded and smooth. If not for the bloodstains on Safi's cut pants, she would have thought the injury years old.

The healer shoved a damp towel into her hand, when Zander slipped inside the room.

Safi paused her rough cleaning to smile weakly at him. She hadn't seen the massive Hell-Bard since before her noosing, and her friend looked as he always had—though bags now darkened his eyes. And like the healer, he also wore no armor, but rather a simple scarlet-and-gold uniform.

He hurried toward her. "You'll have to clean as we go." He spoke low. "And you'll also have to . . ." He trailed off. Then tapped meaningfully at his noose.

Safi recoiled. "I'll have to what?"

"Remove it," the healer hissed, impatient. "Did they not tell you?"

Safi shook her head. She thought she might be sick again. Removing the noose was certain death. The Hell-Bard's doom, they called it, and she had seen it consume Caden before. He had cleaved before her very eyes— slower than a true Cleaved, but still fast enough to incapacitate and kill.

"With the Loom nearby," Zander explained, pulling the towel from Safi's hands, "we can exist without our nooses. It hurts, but the shadows are slow. They will not kill you before we get to the Loom and return."

"Take it off." Safi tasted those words, coated in stomach acid. She had just experienced the worst pain of her life. How could she possibly endure more? "Can't I just go with you before Henrick returns?"

Zander and the healer shook their heads. "He might sense your movement," Zander explained, and the healer added, "As long as the noose stays here, though, he will have no reason to be concerned."

Safi exhaled slowly. She had wanted to see the Loom. She had *needed* to see it because as Leopold had said: she still had a piece of her magic. Maybe coming face-to-face with the device that imprisoned her would offer some clues as to how she might break free.

"All right." She swung her legs to the floor, and with Zander's help, she stood. Her leg gave her no trouble. She felt strong and whole and new. Then, before she could change her mind or even consider what she was doing, Safi reached up to her noose . . . and paused.

She'd never removed it before. Never even considered how one might try. But it was as if the magic recognized what she wanted. As soon as her fingers touched the gold, the chain split in two.

And there was the cold again, clawing in fast.

"Come," she said before frost stole her voice. "Take me to the Hell-Bard Loom."

If Safi had felt drained and gray before, it was nothing compared to now. All color vanished, all sounds echoed and warped as if coming at her from a thousand leagues away. She lost any sense of touch.

There was darkness and there was light. There was cold and there was more cold. The healer had draped one of her robes over Safi's tattered, battered training clothes. It was thick, it ought to be warm, yet all Safi felt was ice upon her skin.

Zander seemed to expect this and he kept a firm guiding hand the entire way. As they retraced steps out of the healer's wing and into the main area with the statue, as they hurried down the stairs onto the first floor and then veered right down a new hallway. Each step away from the healer's room made Safi's heart thump faster. There was no pain—not yet—but an overwhelming sense of panic.

Several times, her feet slowed. She twisted as if to flee. Each time, though, Zander was ready. "The Loom," he reminded her, hauling her onward. "We will be there soon."

"Liar," she ground out when he said it for the third time. "You and Caden are both . . . liars."

This earned her a wincing, if genuine, smile.

Then they were to a new stairwell, this one spiraling off the hallway and descending into the depths of the earth. A draft billowed up; shadows too. Even if Safi hadn't had Zander to lead her that way, she would have known instantly that the Loom waited at the bottom of those stairs.

On the first landing, Safi heard screams. Tortured screams like the ones she'd made only moments before when healing.

Like she'd made when she'd become a Hell-Bard.

A tight-lipped glance at Zander showed him nodding. "New Hell-Bards," he said, and no further explanation was necessary.

On the next landing, the cries of pain were softer, subdued, tired. "Heretics."

On the third landing, the stairs stopped and hoarfrost lay thick across the granite. It laced over the flagstones and through a crooked door. The stone changed from light to dark, though what color precisely, Safi could not say. Shadows and pale flame were all she could discern.

Her teeth chattered; her muscles ached; but she did not slow as Zander hurried her through the slashing entrance. Beyond was a tunnel, not so different from what Safi had explored with Leopold only the night before. Even the ancient sconces looked the same.

Each step brought more cold, more darkness. Her heart hurt in a way she did not know a heart could hurt. As if she were losing her magic all over again. As if the very core of her identity was being sucked away.

When she made the mistake of glancing down at her hands, she saw small black lines rippling beneath the surface. She was not cleaving yet—she was not turning into the husk made of shadows that Caden had become in Saldonica—but she would be. Soon.

After several turns in the tunnel, the ground dipped sharply. Steep steps had been carved into the stone, and Zander helped Safi descend. Without depth perception, without color, it was almost impossible to see where each foot needed to go. Zander's touch, frozen and numbed though it was, was the only thing that kept her upright.

They were close now. She could feel it, like a new calling, a new tug. Now, instead of the noose yanking at her to run back, the Loom was yanking her to run forward.

When at last she and Zander reached the Loom, Safi's footsteps were mere thudding shambles beneath her. She leaned heavily on Zander, and sensed more than saw that they had entered a large cavern with a vast empty bowl spanning before her, as if some god had planned to add a lake here but then forgotten.

What Safi *did* see was the actual Loom. "Gods below," she rasped, gaping at it while Zander held her upright.

"Yes," he replied.

"The shadows." Safi squinted at the undulating mass before her. It reminded her of an anthill she'd seen as a child. It had been filled with so many ants that the ground itself had appeared to move.

"Souls," Zander explained. "Each shadow is a Hell-Bard's soul."

So mine is in there, Safi thought. *And yours too.* Aloud, she said, "Brace me, please." And then she felt his arms slide around her. She could not feel his warmth, could not feel his breath or see his face, but there was a comfort in knowing he was there.

With fumbling, frozen hands, Safi withdrew her Truth-lens, tucked in an inside pocket of her training clothes. Zander's gentle fingers helped lift the lens to her eye. Then suddenly she *could* see. A flicker of silver. A flash of orange. A spinning, writhing trail of blue. *Threads,* she realized. Iseult had described them so many times over the years, Safi had no doubt she was watching them now. Yet she had never realized how vibrant they were. How rich and real and beautiful.

Overwhelming too. She couldn't conceive how her Threadsister had gone through life seeing such shades and movement all the time. No relief, no escape. It explained why Iseult had detached herself simply to exist.

Safi pored over the Loom, so many souls, so many colors, so many lives. She wondered if she could find herself. She wondered if she could find . . .

"Uncle," she whispered, her voice a thousand miles away. "Where are you?" The Loom gave her no answer; the souls within kept dancing. "Help me . . . get closer," she told Zander, already reaching for the drop-off into the Loom. He did as ordered, even though he too must be overcome by cold and shadow.

Each step brought more colors, more movement. Safi almost thought she could hear whispers, though they did not reach her ears. Instead, they vibrated inside her.

"Empress," Zander said—his voice even more distant than her own. "We must hurry. The shadows are worsening."

She knew it was true. She could feel herself unraveling and her soul reaching for the freedom of the Loom—although it was not really freedom at all.

"Uncle," she repeated, louder. More forceful. "Where are you, Uncle?" Then again, "*Uncle, show yourself to me.*" Nothing happened. The ghosts of Hell-Bard souls did not acknowledge her, did not slow.

And gods, she was cold. It submerged her. Drowned her. She really did not have much time remaining.

"Please, Uncle. Wherever you are, I've come to save you. It's me, Safiya. *Please.*" Still nothing, and now she sensed—as if beneath layers upon layers of snow—that Zander was tugging her away.

"We have to go," he said, and suddenly, Safi was rising up, her feet vanishing beneath her. *He is lifting me,* she realized, though she could not wrap her arms around him or even grip his collar to hold on. Her muscles were no longer her own. She was dissolving into the Loom.

The Loom streaked sideways. The Threads within glittered away . . . But not before Safi saw it. Saw *him.*

"Wait," she said, still holding the Truth-lens to her eye. A cluster of Threads raced toward her. Zooming larger and larger by the heartbeat. Until they were right in front of her. Shimmery white. *Uncle Eron,* Safi knew. And ah, he was an Aetherwitch healer. All these years and she'd never realized it. She'd never known that he—like her—had had his magic cleaved away. And that he—like her—had been bound to the Aether Well.

Whispers drilled into her skull. They were not true words, yet somehow, she understood. The impressions, the feelings, the images all showed her exactly where Eron currently was. Somewhere with fog and heat and waters that boiled on banks of yellow. Where sulfur tainted the air, and dampness soaked through everything.

He was sick. Very sick.

I'm coming, she told him in that same nonlanguage his soul had used with hers. Then she lowered her Truth-lens and forced out the command, "Go."

TWENTY-ONE

✳

They had Cam.

It was the only reason Vivia did not fight: they had Cam, and there was a knife at his throat.

"You would hurt a boy to get to me," she said, voice surprisingly steady, as if she'd pulled on Vaness's iron mask. "That is a new depth of craven, Yoris."

The Master Huntsman gave a croaking laugh. "I would use anyone if they're a traitor to the throne. Even you." He ran his tongue over his teeth, gaze roving up and down Vivia. "Well, 'traitor' is the nicest word they're calling you these days."

Vivia smiled, a cold thing that did not bare teeth and did not reach her eyes. She had never liked the Nihar family's Master Huntsman. He hated anyone who was not Nubrevnan, anyone who was not male. "Hoping to get that reward?" she asked. "I heard it was up to two thousand martens now, though I promise he'll never pay."

Another croaking laugh and Yoris limped her way. He'd always claimed his scars came from a fight with a sea fox, but Vivia had always found the idea laughable. People did not survive fights with sea foxes.

They also did not survive fights with her, and her magic itched to be set free. She ached to use the waves battering against the cliff, but with that knife against Cam's throat—she couldn't risk it.

"Rewards are trivial," Yoris said once he'd stopped before her. "What I'm hoping for is to please my king. Now if you'd be so kind as to give me your hands."

Vivia's mouth twitched, but she obeyed. Not that the ropes Yoris bound around her wrists would stop her magic—which he seemed to realize, for once they were knotted with painful tightness, he said, "Now here's how this will go, Princess. You are gonna walk in the middle of our line. Your boy here will be just behind, a knife at his back and crossbows aimed at both of you. If there's any sign of trouble, we'll drug you. I've got a nice sleeping dart ready. Do you understand?"

"You can try that." Her eyes locked on his. "But I have a ship filled with a loyal crew and loyal witches. You won't get far."

"You mean *had* a ship." Yoris winked. His scar gleamed. "They've been dealt with, just like we're dealing with you, and no one will be coming to your aid."

Vivia did not react. Somehow, though the water shouted at her to be used and though her stomach had fallen all the way to her toes, she let nothing reach her face. "Did you kill them?"

Yoris grinned. "Only the ones who wouldn't bend. Now walk." He pointed toward the forest with his three-fingered hand. "And remember that crossbow aimed at your head."

Vivia walked. Not because she wanted to but because she saw no other choice. Every escape she imagined ended in bloodshed. Every attack she plotted ended with Cam dead upon the bone earth. So she did as she'd been ordered, and she walked. All through the night, with Cam just behind her. Mile after mile, with her blood simmering into rage. *No regrets, keep moving,* she told herself, but the usual refrain did nothing. She was furious in a way that made her eyes cross and her heart thud against her ribs. Yoris would pay for this. Dalmotti would pay.

They hiked for hours, the world silent save for the sea's breeze and rhythmic waves, until they were too far inland to hear even that. Yoris was the first to finally speak, his voice rough despite a guzzle of water from a flask at his hip—water he did not share. "You aren't going to offer me anything, Highness? Try to top your father's reward or convince me that he's the traitor?"

"No." Vivia's voice was rough too, and hell-waters, she would have killed for a drink. "We both know it would only be a waste of my breath. You've made up your mind about me, and well . . . everything I thought about you has been proven true."

"He *is* the traitor, though," Cam said, softly at first. Then a bit louder. "Serafin *is* the traitor. The crown belongs to Vivia, not the King Regent."

"Is that so?" Yoris slowed to a stop, forcing everyone to halt as well. They were beside a low ditch through which water once ran. Now it was only a scar upon the yellow earth. "Forgive me if I don't believe the boy whose loyalty changes like the tide—oh yes, did you think I wouldn't remember you? I recognize you from Merik's crew, even if you had ship's-boy braids then."

"It ain't like that," Cam began, but Vivia shook her head.

"Don't bother fighting him, Cam. His mind is made up, and we can't change it."

Yoris sneered. First at Vivia, then at Cam. His scars scrunched into wicked lines. "Seems to me an innocent person would want to defend her name."

"Seems to me you've spent too long in this dead world to know much about people." Vivia matched his sneer. "Or much about what happens in the capital. Where's my crew?"

His face briefly smoothed with surprise. Then somehow he scowled even more deeply, even more disdainfully. "You'll see them soon enough, Highness. The ones that're still alive."

Oh, she would make him pay. If he'd truly hurt anyone, he would lose more than just his fingers. "How soon?" she ground out.

"When we reach the Gift."

"The Gift?"

"Noden's Gift," Cam said before Yoris could open his mouth. "The place I told you about with the ship—"

Yoris grabbed him by the collar. Shockingly fast, shockingly deft. "You told people about the Gift? You told the traitor about the Gift?"

Vivia charged the old man. She had no water at her disposal, but she had muscles and she had rage. Yet no sooner had she gotten her bound arms around his neck and prepared herself for a choke hold, than four blades swished free. And four crossbows took aim.

Vivia froze, her arm still pressed into Yoris's windpipe—and his hands fastened on Cam's collar. Cam—whose skin had paled, leaving the dappled spots as white as the moon above—had closed his eyes.

"Release me," Yoris growled.

"Not until you release him."

"You can't win this fight, Princess."

"I can if my only aim is to take you down."

A pause. The four hooded hunters kept their weapons drawn and ready. Yoris meanwhile seemed to chew over Vivia's words. She could practically hear him thinking. Then he laughed. A rowdy sound that clashed through the forest and bounced off dead trees.

"Lower your weapons," he ordered, loosing Cam. The boy rocked back two steps. His own four-fingered hand moved to his throat, to his collar.

And Vivia finally eased her arm from Yoris's neck—though not before murmuring, "If you hurt him, I will break you, Yoris, and then you will understand why my father is so afraid of me."

Yoris said nothing as he pulled away from Vivia, and he made no objection when she moved to Cam or examined the boy all over. "Are you all right?"

Cam nodded, a spark in his eyes that hadn't been there before. "My loyalty ain't fickle," he whispered.

And Vivia forced a tiny smile. "I know, Cam." She squeezed his shoulder. "I know."

Then she turned back to Yoris and motioned for him to once more lead the way.

They walked on. Until blisters had formed on Vivia's toes and her throat was so dry, she couldn't swallow without pain. They walked on until the sun began to rise and the Origin Well of Nubrevna finally came into view. It looked exactly as Vivia remembered, silhouetted against a pink sky: a high hill in the land with two pointed peaks on either side. *A fox*, she'd always thought. *Like me.*

Her heart creaked open ever so slightly at that thought. At her mother's voice murmuring, *Little Fox, this water knows us. This water chose us.* She'd come to the Well with her mother only once, not long before Jana's death. Not long before everything had changed, and Merik had been sent south while Vivia had been kept in the capital with a thousand reminders of her mother.

Oh, her father might have stowed away everything that Jana had loved—art and threadbare rugs and all the books she'd held most dear. But he hadn't been able to erase the hallways where she'd walked with Vivia. The garden where she'd read aloud tales of little foxes and their foes. The windows against which she'd placed her head and cried in shattered silence when she'd thought no one was watching.

And Serafin hadn't been able to erase the memories. Jana's soft voice, Jana's soft smile, Jana's soft hand on Vivia's brow. Every night, she had come into Vivia's room and whispered *I love you, I love you, Little Fox, more than life itself.*

Vivia suddenly found it hard to breathe. Her chest was swelling and heat was sweeping up from her toes. Soon the bludgeoning would begin. Soon her heart would be too crushed to breathe.

"No slowing," Yoris barked at her, and Vivia battled the urge to scream at him. Her fingers flexed straight against her thighs. She focused on her lungs, begging them to billow. Begging her heart to move. *Become a bear, Vivia. Become a bear.* She wished Stix were there. She wished everything had gone as she'd hoped in Dalmotti and that the Doge hadn't chased her across a sea.

She wished her mother were there. *I love you, Little Fox, more than life itself.*

Vivia had hurt her crew, she'd hurt Cam, she'd hurt the Empress of Marstok—and for what? So she could be marched across her father's lands and reminded of how much he hadn't wanted her in the end. How the only person who *had* wanted her was dead and gone and lost beneath Noden's waves.

Vivia was going to explode. This weight punching her chest was going to crush her, and then Yoris would win. Dalmotti would win. Because of course she could fix nothing. When had she ever fixed anything? She'd fled Lovats a traitor. She'd fled Dalmotti a criminal. *No regrets, keep moving. No regrets, keep moving.*

"Come on," Yoris barked, and Vivia realized that she had stopped walking. That her gaze had become so fixed on the Well, on the fox's ears, that her knees had locked and she might pass out. She felt Cam's eyes burning into her, but she dared not look at the boy. Dared not look at anyone or anything. This would pass. The attacks always passed. Her heart always eventually regained its shape, and her lungs always eventually resumed their work.

She forced her feet to move after Yoris, faster. Faster. Until she was practically on his heels and pushing him into a half jog down a switchbacking trail to the green valley below, a place filled with life that should have thrilled her. That *would* thrill her once this attack finally slowed.

And it did slow eventually. The buzz of cicadas, the pink light on thick trees, the humidity building in the air . . . Each step deeper into the valley cleared away more of Vivia's storm clouds. Lightened the load on her chest. Released the vise around her heart. And at some point—she could not say when—the tears began. Not sobs nor weeping, but a moisture in her eyes that she didn't feel until it was sliding down her cheeks.

Life in Nihar. Life in Nubrevna. All because of the Origin Well.

Yoris glanced back only once at Vivia, but if he noticed her tears, he said nothing. And if he cared that her pace had pushed him into a wild clip, he didn't show it. He just motioned to his hunters and grumbled, "Don't lower your weapons until we've got her contained." Then his gaze sharpened onto Vivia. "And don't try to use your magic, or the boy will learn what pain means. Understand?"

Vivia nodded. Because she did understand and because right now, she was no threat. The insects and the dawn birds were too loud. The pull of an approaching river was too strong. The life and health and power of the nearby Well overwhelmed her.

It was as if, after thirteen years, she had finally come home.

Noden's Gift was not what Vivia had expected, despite Cam having described it to her several weeks before. She'd imagined ramshackle, beaten-down buildings like the Skulks in Lovats. She'd expected hollow eyes and begging hands.

Instead, she'd passed tiny farms and tinier stone huts, all of them bustling with life. Chickens that needed feeding, sheep that needed grazing, and even cows that needed milking. Noden's Gift was a village—a true village clustered beside a river that traced through the forest toward the Well.

Here, where the river's path was narrow and the earth hard, there were small rapids and chops. Ferns clustered against the shore, thick and tendriling on a morning breeze.

Vivia had never seen ferns in Nihar. Just as she'd never seen water that anyone dared fish, yet already pole fishers clustered along the banks. Meanwhile net fishers carried small boats to a landing beside a crude bridge. If any of them thought it odd that Yoris marched prisoners past, they gave no indication beyond a few curious glances.

Vivia smiled at them. Even nodded, and a few nodded back. She didn't think they recognized her, and she certainly didn't know them, but she felt . . . something. A kinship that made no sense. A familiarity that had no actual grounding.

Perhaps it was the river. Perhaps it was her magic. A whole night and morning of walking with no access to tides, and now these fresh, wild waters. They were skipping, trilling, calling for her to use them.

She ignored. The risk to Cam was too great, even with fishers watching. Plus, her crew must be so near. The Empress must be so near. Vivia had to see that they were safe—had to know where they were before she made any aggressive move.

They reached the center of the village, and Vivia almost laughed at the sight of a Dalmotti trade galleon, upside down and converted into a building. Again, it was so much more than what she'd imagined. For one, it seemed enormous with the hull exposed and curving upward. For two, it had been finely maintained: no old barnacles in sight, no storm damage, no grime.

Yoris and his hunters kept it spotless, and Vivia had to admit she was impressed at his ability to not only run a militia, but to have won such loyalty from them.

Yoris strutted into a gap that cut through the ship's center. On one side was the quarterdeck. On the other, a new structure had been wedged beneath the forecastle to hold the ship flat. He aimed for the new structure, where an archway had been cut into pine planks and double doors opened wide.

They led to a jail dug into the ground. Crammed into the mud walls and six wooden paddocks was Vivia's crew. Some sat against the walls, eyes closed, but most stood. Most huddled. Most whispered.

Until they heard Yoris arrive—and spotted Vivia behind him. Then they rushed to the wooden walls bars. "Captain," they murmured. Or, "Thank Noden." Or, "Thank the saints." Several even spat curses at Yoris as he hobbled by.

And there it was again: that elation in Vivia's chest. That strange, illogical certainty that this was right. That *here* was right, even as she was being marched along in ropes.

She said nothing to her crew. Gave them nods—Sonja, Ginna, and there was Sotar too. All of them grave, even as their eyes shone at the sight of her. *I will get us out of here,* she thought at each face. *I will fix this, I swear.*

At the end of the dug-out hall, where lantern light scarcely reached and roots poked down from the ceiling, Yoris paused before a final cell. The smallest of them all.

"The royal chambers," he said, and his hunters, still marching behind Cam, gave obligatory chuckles. "You'll be the third royal in here, Princess." He pulled a key from his belt and with flourishing, ridiculous movements, he unlatched the door and opened it wide. "We had a Cartorran prince here two months ago. Now you and that Marstoki bitch. Enjoy."

He kicked Vivia; she toppled through the door into darkness. Her knees hit soil. The door thwacked shut behind her, and five sets of laughter drifted away.

Vivia did not move for several minutes. She breathed musky, cold air and waited for panic to lay claim. She listened as they put Cam in a different cell. And she kept listening as voices reached her from other cells. Promises to kill Yoris. Promises to break free. Apologies for failure.

As much as she wanted to answer, as much as she wanted to offer a pretty speech to bolster morale and show them how sorry she was, now was not the time.

Breathe in. Breathe out. *No regrets, keep moving.*

She pushed to her feet. Her eyes opened. And that was when she finally spotted Vaness stretched across the mud. Vivia lunged for her and groped for the Empress's neck. There was her pulse, weak but present. She was ice to the touch, though, and she did not respond to Vivia's fingers or a whispered "Wake up, Vaness. Wake up."

Then Vivia found the marks upon her neck, near the spine. Three fat punctures, the scabs fresh. The Empress had been drugged, just as Yoris had threatened he would do. It must have been the only way to neutralize her magic.

"Noden drown me," Vivia whispered to the mud. She slid to a seat beside the Empress. Then she repeated to no one, "Noden drown me." For there was no water down here for her to use.

And because, for the first time since Yoris had captured her, she felt genuine fear unwinding inside her. Icy and heavy, a little fox lost. A little fox run into her hole with nowhere else to hide.

TWENTY-TWO

✳

Safi sensed Zander was running. She felt the Loom moving away, stretching her out like a hide drying upon the rack. Cold splintered in, and with it came pain. Shadows too that coursed within her, poking and pulling and ripping her to shreds.

She thought she might be screaming. She was certain she must be moaning. Somehow, that one sensation—of air pushing over vocal cords—still cut through the weight of dying.

She did not have much time, and there was nothing she could do about it. She was a corpse unspooling in Zander's arms. Her life and what remained of her soul were entirely in his hands.

She could not sense when Zander reached the healer's room again, nor when he dropped her on the cot or even when the noose was replaced around her neck and her own hands were forced upward to fuse the separate pieces together.

One moment, she was death. The next, she was life. Whole again, with a firm mattress beneath her. But she was seizing. Great convulsions of every muscle she possessed, from toes to thighs to biceps to tongue. The cold and the shadows were gone—only echoes remained, memories that could never be erased, permanent marks upon her bones.

"What is happening to her?" Henrick's voice punched into her awareness. Furious and frothing. "You were meant to heal her."

"We are, Your Imperial Majesty," came from Zander. And from the healer, "There were complications—" The healer's voice broke off, replaced by a choke. A cough. A low, garbled groan.

"*Stop*." Safi did not know how she got that word out when everything within her rattled and something was stuck between her teeth. But she did squeeze it out, just as she also turned her head long enough to look at Henrick's squat form wavering before her. "*Stop*."

A familiar smirk spread over his lips, recognizable even when his face blurred and buzzed. "So you *are* healed."

Safi did not answer and could not nod. Her muscles still shook against Zander's grip—and against the grip of the healer, who was once more holding her.

"A few more moments," the healer said, her voice an octave lower than it had been before. "Sometimes the power of the Loom confuses the body. Soon her brain will realize it is still within her body and the convulsions will stop."

"I have never seen that before," Henrick said, clearly disbelieving. But then Safi's seizing did ease and finally stop.

For several blissful moments, there was only her heart booming against her rib cage. Her lungs billowing and true. She tasted blood and leather; she must have bitten her tongue and now a belt was clenched between her teeth—a belt Zander removed from her mouth.

"Thank you," the healer told him at the same moment Henrick pushed him aside.

Face flushed and shiny, Henrick bore down. "Did you hope to escape me? Did you think death would be your way out?"

"No." She couldn't keep the snorted amusement off that word. He clearly thought she'd stabbed herself. "I am merely out . . . of practice, my Emperor."

"And you will stay that way." Spit hit her cheek. Then he pulled away and arms moved beneath her. The healer's and Zander's, for they were much too mild to be Henrick's. "Get her to the carriage," Henrick barked, already striding for a door that Caden was hastily opening. "We leave immediately."

Caden's gaze briefly met Safi's before he fell into formation behind the Emperor, and at her curt nod, his face relaxed. She could practically hear him thinking, *Good enough.*

"Can you walk?" Zander asked as the healer helped Safi to her feet. Everything hurt. She was one giant bruise.

But she was alive and she had gained new information. It wasn't organized or sensical yet, but it was a start. Surely Leopold would be able to figure out exactly where Eron was.

"I'll help her," Lev said, moving in to brace an arm behind Safi's back while Safi smiled tightly at the healer. Yet before Lev could walk Safi toward the door, Safi grabbed for both the healer and Zander. They had helped her, no questions asked. They had risked punishment, and the healer had briefly endured Henrick's wrath. All so Safi could get a look at a device that—as far as they knew—held no answers and only pain.

She wasn't entirely sure she had the right to invoke the Hell-Bard words, but she didn't know a better way to show them how much their help had meant to her. So as her fingers gripped their hands, a brief squeeze of human contact, she murmured, "Toward death with wide eyes."

"All clear, all clear," they replied, and Safi didn't think she imagined the appreciation on their faces.

"Thank you," she added before releasing them. Then she leaned into Lev and let the Hell-Bard half carry, half drag her back through the Keep and once more into the world of the living.

The return journey to the imperial palace felt longer than the trip to reach Hell-Bard Keep had. Perhaps because Safi was conscious, or perhaps because the entire day had been sucked away by her time at the Keep . . . Or most likely because her companion was Emperor Henrick, and he was quite displeased.

She had never seen this part of Praga before—the slums. Lev's childhood home. Buildings leaned and sagged, while people clustered along the narrow streets to watch the Emperor's procession clatter past. No one begged, no one cheered, no one tried to get close to the Hell-Bards surrounding the carriage. They simply watched, faces of all ages, all genders, all colors, unified by their gaunt skeletons, hollowed-out eyes, and clothes that did nothing to protect against the night's cold.

If Merik Nihar could see this . . .

"You host lavish feasts and dancing every night yet people starve in your slums?" Safi sank back from the window to find Henrick watching her. A calculating look with subtle undertones of ire—though most of his rage had, to her surprise, dissipated once they'd left the Keep. He was a man skilled at finding his calm.

"Pomp and celebration matter as much as food." Henrick spoke gruffly, though not cruelly. "Particularly in times of war."

Safi motioned to the window. "Tell that to them."

"I will," he replied. "When I join my people to deliver the biweekly wagon of rations, I will make sure your words are conveyed."

Biweekly wagon. Safi frowned.

And Henrick smiled. "This empire, Safiya, can feed its poor and host celebrations that raise morale. We are strong enough and wealthy enough to do both."

Safi's frown only deepened. *Cartorra has its flaws*, Caden had once told her, *but it also has safety. Food too, as well as wealth, roads, and education.*

"In time," Henrick continued, "you will understand the importance of a good performance. Particularly if this war continues." His smile faded. "While you were screaming your lungs raw, my Hell-Bards updated me on the Raider King's forces."

Safi's frown disappeared. She turned a sharp eye on the Emperor. He so rarely mentioned the various war efforts that Cartorra had staked across the Witchlands, and she had no inkling why he might be addressing the war now. She had expected to enter this carriage and be yelled at, cursed at, punished. Instead he was *chatting*. "And what are those forces, my Emperor?"

Henrick sighed, a long exhale that deflated him. He looked overwhelmed, he looked old, and for some reason that Safi did not understand, he seemed to have shed his masks. In fact, she had no doubt that if she could train her Truth-lens on him, the colors within would not change. Even his crown was absent today, though a forehead crease remained from its golden grip.

This was the real Henrick fon Cartorra, leader of the largest empire in the Witchlands, and he was tired.

It reminded Safi of a different imperial leader in a different empire, and against her will, something soft settled around her lungs. Something almost like pity that she desperately wished would go away.

"Do not concern yourself," he said eventually.

"What if I wish to concern myself? What if I wish to know the state of this empire I'm meant to lead?"

"Hmmm." His eyes thinned, and something she thought might be respect mingled in them. He did not answer her question, though. Instead, he changed subjects so completely, Safi's mind could not keep up.

"If you are using methods of preventing pregnancy, you may stop."

Safi recoiled against her bench. "My . . . Emperor?" Outside, the slums were fading, replaced by slaughterhouses and the stench of blood.

"If," Henrick repeated, a bout of usual testiness returning, "you are using methods to prevent pregnancy, stop. There is no reason to avoid it, assuming my nephew is your only lover."

Safi had no idea what to say to that. *Yes, he is my only lover?* Or, *I am using methods?* Or, *Why would you want me to stop?* Fortunately, she was saved from asking anything by Henrick's repeated sigh.

And before her eyes, he aged another ten years. The pockmarks on his cheek turned stark and red against his pallid skin. He scratched tiredly at his jaw. "I have spent two decades grooming Leopold to be the perfect emperor, and for all his seeming shallowness . . . Well, you of all people must know who he really is."

Safi's eyebrows lifted.

"My nephew will be an even better emperor than I, and as I have told you before, I have no interest in replacing him. *He*, however, will need an heir. As it currently stands, he is the last in the Cartorran line."

"And you . . . want me to produce that heir?" Safi could not believe she was having this conversation. While she'd known Henrick had no desire to produce children with her, she hadn't guessed he'd want her to have them with Leopold.

It was strange. It was uncomfortable.

Henrick opened his hands. They trembled in time to the carriage's bumps and sways. "When I am gone, you will marry Leopold. You love each other, do you not? We are not all so lucky, you know, so why wait to produce his heir?"

Gooseflesh pricked down Safi's arms. *Why, indeed?* When Henrick had first claimed her as his betrothed at the Truce Summit ball in Veñaza City, Safi had assumed it was because—like everyone else in the Witchlands—he wanted her Truthwitchery. Even when his soldiers had hunted her, even when his Hell-Bards had eventually caught up to her, Safi had believed Henrick wanted her magic.

Then he had erased her magic two weeks ago, making it clear that her Truthwitchery mattered none.

And *now* he was making it clear that he wanted her to remain on the throne even after he was gone. He wanted her as Leopold's wife and the mother of imperial heirs.

"Why," she asked softly, "did you marry me, my Emperor?"

Henrick scratched again at his jaw. Outside, the city turned to beige-and-pink stone. They had crossed into the wealthier merchants' district. It would not be long before the carriage reached the imperial palace.

"If," Safi pressed, "you want me to make heirs with Leopold, then I need to understand why. If you expect me to marry him after you are gone, then I need to understand *why*."

Still, Henrick said nothing—and now Safi could see the first towers of the palace spiring above the city. They would arrive in minutes.

"My magic marked me the day I was born," she rushed on. "I have spent my whole life running, and for what? In the end, I was caught and I was used. Yet you took me with no intention of claiming my magic. I want to know why. Why *me*."

Henrick offered no external reaction, but he was clearly listening. So Safi powered on with her impulsive plea. "I have learned in the last few days that there is freedom in a life without magic—and in freedom, my Emperor, there is power."

"It is power you seek then?"

"I am certainly tired of being powerless." She lifted her chin; it was not a lie. "You married me in chains, but if you want me to rule beside you—and continue to rule with Leopold after you are gone—then I need to know why. If it is not my magic you desire, then what is it?"

He wet his lips, leaving them shiny, and drew in a breath as if to speak. Even his throat wobbled, the words clearly building. But then came the groan of iron and the shuttering of light. They had entered the palace gatehouse; their drive was at its end.

Henrick's breath exhaled, his throat stilled, and Safi knew immediately that her moment had passed. Her chance to learn more was squandered.

The carriage rolled to a stop. The door opened. A footman rushed a stepping-box into place.

"Get cleaned up," Henrick drawled as he squeezed his body outside. "We are late for dinner, and your near death does not excuse you from attending tonight's celebrations."

"Yes, my Emperor," Safi said while inwardly she shrieked and raged. So close, she'd been *so* thrice-damned close, and who knew if another chance would come.

And though she knew that spies might be watching—and that Hell-Bards certainly were—she didn't fight the glare folding over her face as the Emperor strode away. *Curse him, curse him, curse him.*

※

Fourteen Days After the Earth Well Healed

afi never thought she would get married.

And she certainly never thought she would become an empress.

Only ten years ago, she had hidden behind her uncle in this very room and prayed that no Hell-Bard would notice her. That the Emperor would be satisfied with her uncle Eron's tithes so she could leave right away.

Now she stands beside that emperor and wonders how he does not get a headache with his crown so tight.

Her gown is too thin for this weather and this stone wing of the palace. The blue silk clings uncomfortably thanks to the wool cloak that Henrick had told her to remove. She had obeyed; sparks had flown.

Somewhere to her left in the room's darkest corner, Iseult watches. She stands alone save for four Hell-Bards, hoping the rest of the court does not notice her. But they notice her—they always notice her. She is Nomatsi in a world of Cartorrans.

And she is half of the Cahr Awen.

Safi rests her hand over her Threadstone. "Are you all right?" *she whispers, too soft for anyone to hear. But the words reach Iseult across their rubies.*

And Iseult replies: Yes. *A word that blooms in Safi's mind even though no truth hums in her lungs.* Are you all right?

I don't want to do this, *Safi admits, still whispering silently.*

Then don't.

Uncle will die if I don't, Iz. Besides, I doubt Henrick will let me leave now, twenty paces from our wedding.

Iseult seems to wince, a tightening of grief across their bond. I'm sorry. I should have come up with a better plan.

Hush. Don't make me come over there and smack you. *Safi glares toward the corner, and though she can't see Iseult, she senses a smile.*

I'll be here the entire time, Safi.

And Safi nods. I know, Iz. You always are.

Before she can say anything more, Henrick hooks his arm into hers. "Smile," *he commands, and Safi smiles. Her hand falls from her collarbone. Her spine straightens.*

Henrick is shorter than she. Wider too, and despite wearing a color other than brown for once, he still looks like a toad at midsummer. Green, it would seem, is no more flattering on his frame.

Each of his steps waddles, and Safi does her best to match his stride. She has only ever attended one wedding, when she was much younger, and it had not been between nobility, but between farmers on the Hasstrel estate.

Strange. She had forgotten that memory until now. It was so long ago. Back when Uncle Eron had still smiled . . .

Strange. She had forgotten that Uncle Eron ever smiled.

It is Eron who had brought her here. And it is Eron she will find before this day ends, if everything goes as planned—and if the plot is as well mapped as she thinks it is.

Like the farmers of all those years ago, the crowd in the room parts to let Safi and Henrick pass. Instead of an inn's common room, though, it is the Emperor's throne room. And instead of lively music lilting out, there is only silence. A heavy silence weighted by breaths and winter fabric and eyes, eyes everywhere.

They reach a dais at the room's end upon which two thrones stand. One is newly added today, its crimson fabric brighter, fresher. After ascending the short steps, Henrick turns to face the crowd, towing Safi with him.

And then, like the farmers, he says the words that will bind Safi to him. "I, Henrick the Third, Emperor of Cartorra, take you, Safiya fon Hasstrel, as my spouse. By law and by land, we are tied. What I possess, you receive. What you possess, I claim. Until our days are done and our bodies dust, we are bound."

True. Safi's magic trills in her ribs even as cold sweeps down her body. This dress is much, much too thin. Her hand curls against Henrick's arm.

Then she realizes all eyes are on her. They are waiting for her to say the same, waiting for the ceremony to complete. But for some reason, when she tries to lift her voice and say the words she has practiced, nothing will come.

Eyes blink—so many eyes—and people shift. They shimmy. They share glances of confusion, and Safi can practically hear them thinking, Why does she not speak?

But she can't. All she can do is smile, and even that is growing strained. Once she says these words she will be married. What is hers will be the Emperor's. Her body, her being. Until our days are done and our bodies dust, we are bound.

She had never thought she would marry, yet suddenly it is all she wants. But to marry for love, for friendship, for Thread-family. Not for business, as is the Cartorran way. Not to trick an emperor into handing over her uncle . . .

Safi's eyes find Iseult's in the crowd. Her Threadsister has pulled back her scarf. Her golden eyes gleam, her black hair shines. There is iron in that gaze. And a certainty that, no matter what Safi does next, Iseult will be beside her. Initiate, complete until their days are done and their bodies are dust.

And Safi's smile relaxes at that thought. For of course she can do this. It is part of the plan, and by the Twelve, she will follow it.

"I, Safiya, Domna of Hasstrel, take you, Henrick fon Cartorra, as my spouse." She raises her face, draws back her shoulders. "By law and by land, we are tied. What I possess, you receive. What you possess, I claim. Until our days are done and our bodies are dust, we are bound."

The room looses a collective exhale. Even Henrick's chest shrinks. Then, just as the room of common folk from all those years ago had done, the doms and domnas declare, "By law and by land, you are tied. We witness, we abide."

The words rumble in the stones. Quiver in Safi's bones, and she smiles even wider, her eyes still on Iseult—who is nodding her approval. Who is drawing up her scarf once more.

The next step in their plan is complete. Now it is on to the final one.

TWENTY-THREE

※

The Hammer came for Stix at midday. She wasn't expecting him at their inn—wasn't even sure how he'd found them, but when he told her it was time to fight again, she was all too happy to obey. Maybe this time, she'd get the vision she needed. Maybe *this* time, the voices would finally finish speaking and go away.

A fine carriage drove them to the Ring, and despite Ryber's best efforts to chat with the Hammer, all he did was glower and grunt at each of her questions. He clearly saw Stix as competition; he clearly thought she'd come to replace him.

The stink of sulfur pitched higher as they ambled over swamplands toward the Ring, while the voices pitched lower. *Come this way, keep coming.* Once Stix was inside the Ring and once more facing the wooden entry stall, they silenced completely. She felt like she could breathe, could think, could *be*.

And in that blessed quiet, her magic notched to saturation. Somehow, a lake's worth of water waited for her inside the arena. Ryber took Stix's spectacles, and the world returned to the blurry-edged smear it had always been. If there was that much water near, then they would only be in the way.

A bell rang. The crowds outside screamed—a sound that sent Stix's heart soaring. Winning nights at the Cleaved Man had been fun; winning the Slaughter Ring was, she couldn't deny, exhilarating.

The door to the Ring swung outward, and thick, brown water spanned the length of the arena. Afternoon sun glinted off its still surface.

"Get to the other side!" A boot hit Stix's spine. She fell headfirst into the enormous pool, and water crashed over her. Her breath pushed from her lungs and nose, and she let herself fall for several eternal moments. Her power lanced out—a vast sweep of sensory awareness to gain her bearings. Reaching, connecting, controlling.

The water was deep, as if they'd removed not only the dirt that used to be here, but several stories' worth of it. It was also filthy, brackish, muddy, and pumped in straight from the marsh.

Most important of all, the water was not empty. Three massive creatures tangled and writhed on the silty substrate floor, each trying to move fastest. Each trying to get ahead and swim toward Stix with their lithe, serpentine bodies covered in silvery fur.

Sea foxes.

Stix summoned a wave to launch her upward, and the water complied. She broke the surface, flying high, water shaking off her.

Ice. She froze the water's surface, and her body slammed onto it. The bellowing crowd thrummed through her. It seemed to swell and boom in time to her heart, in time to her magic.

She gathered her feet, eyes squinting for the door she had to reach in order to end this round in the Ring. Not that she was ready to leave just yet. "I'm here," she called, opening her arms to the stone ruins. "Show me what you want me to see."

The voices got no chance to answer before the ice vanished beneath her. Stix dumped back into the water and teeth zoomed in.

Fine, she thought as she sank fast. If ice wasn't allowed, then she would attack instead.

She blasted out her waters, slamming away the nearest fox before its teeth could connect. A second blast, a third before she twisted like a diver and aimed herself straight down. Her ears swelled against her skull. She felt the substrate approaching, a stretch of flat nothing that she could not control, but that water had seeped into.

Above her, the sea foxes were changing course. They'd be circling back soon.

Stix's hands touched silt. Her eyes shuttered. *Back,* she commanded the water. *Away.* Then she repeated, *Back away.*

It took the water longer than usual to obey her—not because it did not want to, but because it was so vast. So many minuscule droplets that had to separate from their siblings. *Back away.* They pulled, they stretched, they disconnected one by one, starting at the pool's surface and spiraling down.

A whirlpool formed, spinning faster as each moment passed. Spinning closer to Stix too. *Back away. Back away.* The first kicks of air reached Stix. Her body flipped and spun, and she squeezed her eyes even tighter. *Back away, back away.*

Then it was done. She was fully exposed; the water had parted; a column of air surrounded Stix.

She opened her eyes. Gray light beamed in, and with it came the crowd's roars—the foxes' too. They had been thwarted. Two howled from within the water, a piercing yip that shivered through the sand beneath her feet.

The third thrust its head into the empty column and bayed. A tragic, ferocious sound.

Stix grinned at it. Her chest heaved. She was soaked through, salt coated her tongue, and her muscles quivered with power. She couldn't hold this column forever, but Noden, it felt good. No one was as powerful as she. And now, to reach the other side of the Ring, all she had to do was walk.

"Water Brawler, Water Brawler!"

She lifted her foot. Then her other. Right, left, right, left, a muddy slog that tried to hold her down. "I'm here," she told the voices. "I came this way and kept coming." She lost track of the foxes, circling around the column with predatory rage. She lost track of the crowd, screeching and stamping and clapping their glee.

"Where are you?" she asked again and again. "Talk to me, please. *Show me why the hell-waters I'm here.*" But the memories never came, and when Stix was halfway across the Ring, the first body fell into the pool.

Stix's heart broke in two.

She should have seen it coming, of course—it was the one thing she had desperately prayed would not happen, so therefore Lady Fate would have to make it so: a prisoner sacrificed to the Ring.

The person was still alive when they toppled into the pool, and Stix felt the person sinking. They were weighted by stone, prey for the sea foxes. Bait to draw Stix away. And bait she was going to take because she would never leave another human to die.

With a strangled scream at Noden and his Hagfishes, Stix let her column vanish. Instantly, the water stopped pushing. Instantly, the water slung toward its siblings in a joyous reunion that tidal-waved over Stix. Crushed her, beat her, shoved her back into a swim.

The sea foxes didn't notice. They were charging for the weighted prisoner, now struggling upon the pool's floor. Stix loosed more water, cannonballs of power to pummel the foxes. But she was too slow and the foxes too fast. She felt their jaws snap into bone, felt blood unravel through the water, strands of heat that sang with an ended life.

"No." The word escaped Stix's throat on a bubble of air. *No, no.* Currents keened against her, thrashed by foxes writhing and twirling as they fed. *No, no.*

The sea foxes had almost finished their feast when two more bodies plunked into the water behind her. She sensed the splashes and the displacement of water that spoke of two more lives sinking too fast. Stix would not fail them.

She kicked off the Ring floor, sucking power to her. She needed air—oh Noden, she needed air, but there was no time. She would have to make what little still seared in her lungs suffice.

She raced across the pond, fast as a shark. Faster even, and behind her, the foxes gave pursuit. They'd finished their meal; they were always, always hungry for more.

She reached the first person, and as she'd sensed, they were roped to a stone far too heavy for her to move. They flapped and bent and strained like a worm on a hook, and when Stix grabbed their shoulders—shoulders she could not see—they only fought harder.

I'm trying to help you! she wanted to scream, but she had no breath left and no sound beneath the waves.

She needed to cut these ropes, and she needed to do it fast.

She froze a strip of water in her right hand. An ice knife, complete with handle and edge for slicing. *Sharp, sharp,* she told the water. *Cut, cut.* In seconds, the rope snapped. The person was free—and the foxes had arrived.

Stix slung out her knife, and as it hurtled toward the nearest fox, she froze a hundred more. *Freeze, freeze. Cut, cut.*

The foxes screamed, a piercing burst of sound as every ice blade made contact. As Stix carried herself and the prisoner away. They sped through the water, and though the world was dark, worse shadows were creeping in. Stix needed air. She was going to have to surface. Unless . . .

Back away, she commanded the closest water—the water that haloed her head. *Back away.*

A small funnel formed, and the water parted. It sucked strength from Stix because, like before, the water did not want to separate. But Stix let it have her strength in exchange for blessed, beautiful air.

Her lungs billowed, two gulps as she escalated toward the second prisoner. Her head stopped spinning; her lungs stopped screeching. Then she was to the other person, and she let the waters crush over her face once more. Again, she produced an ice knife, and again, she carved away until the second prisoner was also free.

Now she had two people to protect, and three sea foxes pummeling this way. But the exit must be near. The stall she needed to reach to end this fight and claim victory.

Stix grabbed hold of the prisoners, her fingers digging under their arms, then she used every piece of power that still remained inside of her to shoot for the sky. Up, up, they flew through the water until they broke the surface.

And up, up the foxes flew too. Three sets of fangs, of fur, of bloodied entrails from a prisoner lost. They were clever in their ascent. Cleverer than Stix had been, belying a sentience she hadn't realized they possessed.

One rushed beneath her. One swam behind. And one moved between Stix and the exit.

She and the prisoners were trapped. Rain fell against her face while she treaded water. Clean and new and surprising—she hadn't noticed the storm clouds rolling in.

The sea fox below Stix was readying for an attack: diving low where it could then build momentum toward the surface. Even if Stix could build an ice wall between her and the monster, such raw animal power would ultimately win. These creatures were too huge, too ancient to be contained, even by the Water Brawler.

So of course *that* was the moment the voices decided to come. So sudden, so clear, Stix didn't have time to be surprised. They simply sang, *No whistling when a storm's in sight. No whistling when a storm's in sight*, and the water and the Ring burst away.

"I can stand by no longer," Stix says. "The people can stand by no longer. We have to end the Exalted Ones' reign." She pins her eyes on Eridysi, as does everyone else in the room. Bastien, Midne, Rhian, Saria, and the Rook King's damnable bird.

Eridysi, a willowy woman with pale hair and paler skin who spends more time lost in her head than she does speaking or even acknowledging that the Six are in her workshop, curls in on herself. "I am working as fast as I can."

Stix believes her; her workshop, never tidy on a good day, has descended into utter chaos with heaps of paper or books or, lately, dusty stones.

"Work faster," Bastien growls, and Stix cuts him a sharp look. He only glares in return from behind his mask. He is the least patient of all of the Six and has been urging Eridysi to hurry for weeks now.

"What is it you lack?" Saria asks in her quiet, still way. She is becoming more distant each day, more statue than human. Stix understands. She herself has become more and more mercurial like the tides. It is the only way to endure what the Exalted Ones make each of them be: to sink more deeply into the magic Sirmaya gave them.

"There is nothing you can do," Dysi says. "I must solve this myself." She shuffles her gold-backed cards absently. "I will solve this myself. When next you come, I will have an answer. I swear on the Sleeping Giant." Her silver eyes meet Stix's, then each of the other Six in turn. Even the Rook, who squawks and ruffles his feathers.

"Good," Stix says, lifting a warning hand at Bastien. He has become as harsh as the cyclones on the Windswept Plains, and Stix finds him harder and harder to manage. He loves her just as she loves him, but love is not a cure for what he has endured from the Exalted One called Lovats. Nor is revenge a cure, though Bastien won't listen when she tells him that.

"We will leave first," she tells the Six and Eridysi. "And we will see you in a sevenday." Then she hooks her arm in Bastien's and tows him toward the door.

A familiar orange tabby follows.

Like yesterday's fight with the hawk, when the waves and the Ring and the barrage of the crowd punctured into Stix again, almost no time had passed. The sea foxes were coming for her; it was time to move.

Or time to whistle as the voices so clearly wanted her to do. Stix wet her lips, licking away salt and mud. Then she exhaled a weak burble of air while her heart thumped and her magic held the prisoners afloat.

The sea fox was still charging up from the depths. The crowd was now chanting—some had even started to boo. Why wasn't the Water Brawler moving, they wanted to know? Why wasn't she fighting back? "Ditch the bodies! Toss 'em down!"

Stix whistled again. Long. Clear. And loud enough for the crowd to notice.

They silenced instantly, and Stix had no doubt that if she could see their faces instead of just blurred streaks of skin, she would find a thousand wide eyes. A thousand horrified frowns. Superstition ran deep here, and Lady Baile's poem was not to be crossed.

Stix whistled a third time, and it was the only sound to fill the Slaughter Ring. It carried over the rain, over lapping waves, and over the sea foxes still racing this way. But just as the crowds had heard the whistles, the sea foxes had heard them too—the one between Stix and the exit paused. Its face, silver-furred and sentient, eased into calm interest like a dog awaiting a command.

One of its massive eyes was damaged and milky.

Stix whistled one last time, and the fox listened. It dove beneath the murky water toward the other sea foxes, to intercept, to fight, to stop because the whistle had commanded and it lived to obey. Stix used the moment to kick her magic forward again in a gentle current that propelled her and the prisoners toward the other stall. She was tired; she needed to conserve her energy just in case the fox changed its mind.

No, not its mind, but her mind. Like with the orange tabby, Stix just knew.

She reached the wooden box with ease. And with silence, for the audience still did not speak. Did not even seem to breathe.

It was not until she reached the wooden exit, her waves lifting her up so she could grab at the latch, that someone finally reacted. It was a single voice, throaty and amused. "Well done, Water Brawler," Kahina called. "I knew you had it in you."

Stix had always considered herself cool-tempered. The higher the pressure, the better she kept her head. She had been through brawls and battles and now Ring fights to prove it. Captain Stacia Sotar did not get stressed, she did not get angry.

Right now though, as she stalked out of the wooden stall into the Ring's winding limestone halls, as water shed off her in great, slapping drops, Stix was a riptide of rage. When Ryber offered her the spectacles, she yanked them too hard; the metal warped; she didn't care and shoved them on anyway. When Ryber fell into step beside Stix, asking if she needed healing, Stix only grunted and glared.

She reached the highest scaffolding in a blur of fury that thrummed in her blood, sparkling like her magic at its strongest. She only had to snarl once at the guards, and they got out of her way. Ryber, however, had to wait behind again. Which was perhaps for the best, Stix thought vaguely, since she was on the cusp of violence.

She found Kahina's deck unchanged, though a six-fingered gray cat slept in a ball upon a pile of cushions near the door. The rain had already stopped, leaving a wind-stalled heat thick with swamp stink. The Admiral leaned against her balustrade, scanning the Ring with a gold spyglass speckled in red gemstones.

"You killed that prisoner," Stix said to Kahina's back.

"Did I?" Kahina's drawl oozed over the wooden space. "Or did you kill them because you were too slow?"

Stix's lips curled back. "You set up the fight today, so it is your soul that bears the weight of that death."

"If you think that upsets me"—Kahina closed the spyglass with a *clack-clack-clack*—"then I fear you will be disappointed, my dear. I have killed more men than I can count, and though you may not remember it, so have you."

"I'm not who you think I am, and I'm not your *dear*."

Kahina sniffed. "Such disdain for an ally."

Stix sniffed right back. "You are not my ally."

"Of course I am." Kahina traded her spyglass for her pipe, resting on a nearby stool. "I know who you are, just as you know who I am. And this?" She twirled the pipe around the Ring. "Is not where you belong, as much as you might enjoy it here."

"Enjoy it? You think I enjoyed swimming for my life while sea foxes hunted? You think I enjoyed having a flame hawk sear off half my hair?" Stix knew she was taking Kahina's bait, but she didn't care. She had just faced off with three sea foxes; Kahina didn't frighten her. "If we're going to speak plainly, Admiral, then let us speak plainly: I'm here to answer the voices in my head. I don't care about you or your games or your silly riddles. I want answers, and then I want to leave again."

"Games?" Kahina's eyebrows sprang high. "Riddles? You think I toy with you?"

"Of course you do."

"Of course I do not." For the first time since Stix's arrival, something like anger reached Kahina's face. A strike of stone on flint to flare within her pupils. "The past dwells inside us, Water Brawler, and it can only be set free when we see the places from before. This"—she opened her arms—"used to be yours."

"Not mine." Stix mimicked Kahina's movement. "Theirs. These voices are not me."

"But of course they are." Kahina's face creased with mocking pity. "And you are in for such disappointment if you continue to cling to that belief."

No, Stix wanted to retort, *you are*. But she quashed the words in her throat. This conversation was already slinging out of her control. She had intended to come here and tell Kahina to leave the prisoners alone. Then she'd intended to tell Kahina to leave *her* alone so she could finish what she'd come here to do: Stix wanted out of this cursed pirate hole. She wanted to be back in Nubrevna, back with Vivia. And she didn't want any more deaths on her conscience before she got there.

Kahina slid her pipe between her teeth. The bowl sparked, smoke plumed, and the edge of a smile fluttered on her lips. She saw herself as the winner of this argument, and it made the storm brew once more in Stix's blood. In her fingers, aching to curl into fists. This must be how Vivia felt every time she faced the High Council in Nubrevna: like the only sensical one in a room full of fools.

"I," Stix said, lowering her voice in a lethal imitation of Vivia, "am not like you, Admiral. I am my own person, and soon these voices will go away. And you?" She motioned between them. "Are not my ally and never will be." She turned on her booted heel then, water from the Ring sloughing off her as she aimed for the doorway.

The cat's ears perked at her approach.

"Enough," Kahina snapped, and though all of Stix's instincts shouted at her to keep going, she let her feet slow beside the gray cat. It opened a single green eye. "We are running out of time. We have been waiting too many years for you to find us—your memories have come late—and now the end approaches. We must find the tools, Water Brawler, and we must restore them."

"Tools?" Stix asked innocently. She swiveled her head toward Kahina. "What tools?"

Kahina scowled. "You know damned well what I mean. I can see it on your face, even if you hide behind those spectacles. The blade, the glass. The tools from a thousand years ago that disappeared after our world collapsed and that we must find again before a new collapse sets in."

"So . . . you want them." Stix spoke this as a statement, not a question, and the gray cat popped open both eyes. Meanwhile Kahina cocked her head to one side, studying Stix with a raptorial stare.

It was not the frustrated scrutiny from earlier, nor even the pitying one. This was the stare of someone reassessing what they'd thought was a known quantity. Stix could practically see the knives sharpening behind her eyes. "You know where they are," Kahina said quietly.

"I don't."

"Of course you do." Kahina flipped up her hand and flames ignited around her fingers. "Tell me where you found them."

Where I found them, Stix thought. *Not where they are.* And just like that, she saw a solution—a bargaining weight that tipped the scales in her favor. Kahina was a Master of the Ring; her power was vast. She could fling prisoners into the arena as easily as she emptied her pipe bowl. Which meant she could also . . .

"Free the prisoners, and I'll tell you where I found the blade and glass."

Kahina's pipe ignited. "I could free a few."

"All of them."

Kahina scoffed. Then, after several seconds when Stix offered nothing else, she gave an outright laugh. "You cannot be serious. I can do many things, Water Brawler, but freeing every prisoner from the Ring is not one of them. Many people own them."

"Then buy them."

Kahina's left eye twitched, a movement Stix would never have noticed without her spectacles. Behind her, the Ring's chaos continued unabated, while beside Stix, the cat stretched onto its feet. Moments misted past. Stix refused to break eye contact with Kahina.

Vivia would have been proud.

"All right," Kahina said eventually. Her smirk loosened into a smile, as if this entire arrangement had been her idea and now she were the one with all the bargaining power. "Give me a day, and I will acquire all prisoners. Do we have a deal?"

"Only once you agree to *free* them."

"Yes, yes." She swatted the air. "I will give them to you, and you may free them. Now do we have a deal?"

Stix matched Kahina's smile, while at her shins, the gray cat nuzzled and purred. "Yes," she replied. "We have a deal."

"Excellent." Kahina tapped her jade ring. "Now tell me: where did you find the blade and glass?"

TWENTY-FOUR

✳

Iseult did not sleep. She couldn't have even if she'd wanted to—not while Owl shivered on the bunk beside her. Not with Eridysi's diary so near. Her goal for two weeks, the one item she needed to face Hell-Bards with, was only paces away.

For hours now, Iseult had mulled Corlant's words. His easy declaration that he was the first Portia had ever claimed confounded her. Yes, Lev had described the first Hell-Bard and the saint that Purists worshipped as Midne, a woman who'd lived a thousand years ago. And yes, there were people who could live a thousand years, born and reborn. The same soul passing into different bodies . . .

Paladin. A word relegated to myth. Some called them knights, some called them witches, and most called them nothing at all because they had been forgotten so long. But could Corlant possibly be such a person?

For the thousandth time Iseult wished the weasel were near. *Where are you?* she thought. *Please, come to us. Please help.* But the weasel did not reply.

Midnight bloomed outside. Another Threadwitching night with the moon bright and inescapable through the cabin's lone window. At least, in all her hours of wakefulness, Iseult had managed to almost remove the wool in her mouth. It had taken constant jaw wiggling, constant pressure from her tongue, and repeated shifting of her soft palate—like she was clearing a yawn—but all the effort, all the ache building in her face had paid off.

Just a little more pushing, a little more straining . . . *There.* She spat it to the ground. Triumph wefted through her muscles.

She glanced across the room, at the pale, sleeping Threads that twirled above another cot: Corlant. While on the floor near his feet slept Aeduan and Evrane. Outside, two Purists stood guard, though their attention was weak and one was half asleep.

"Owl," Iseult tried to whisper. All that came out was a filmy croak. She smacked her lips and swallowed. Then: "Owl."

This time, her voice cooperated. And this time, Owl's eyes shot to hers. Surprise rippled across her Threads. She couldn't speak, her own mouth still full, but at least she was now listening—and at least her white terror had briefly misted away.

"Are you hurt?" Iseult asked.

Owl nodded, a stiff movement, before craning her neck toward her arms and wrists.

Iseult winced. "I know. The bindings hurt me too." At first, it had felt like needles. Then wasps. Then fire. Until eventually she had lost all feeling in her left arm. Her right arm would soon follow. "You should try to sleep, Owl. If you can. I won't let anything happen to you."

Owl did not look impressed by this. Worse, white was once more spreading across her Threads. The same dangerous panic, spreading too fast.

But Iseult couldn't do what she'd done before to calm the child. She could not give Owl a stone to focus on, an anchor to ground her in this world. It was a tactic she'd learned from Evrane of all people, and a move Iseult had first tried beside a bridge north of Tirla, beneath a moon not so different from the one outside.

Right now, all Iseult had were her words. They would have to be enough.

"Long ago," she said softly, invoking the first words of every Nomatsi story, "when the gods walked among us . . ."

There was a goddess named Owl. She was Moon Mother's youngest sister, and everyone knew she was Moon Mother's favorite.

Each night, they roamed the forests together. Owl would take her animal form and patrol the trees and life within, while Moon Mother passed from tribe to tribe, village to village, checking on her people and ensuring they were safe.

Moon Mother did not know why, but she was afraid. Ever since she had guided the Nomatsis through the Sleeping Lands centuries before, fear had been building inside her—fear that something would happen to the people she loved so dearly.

Years of nightly searching, though, had turned up nothing of concern. Oh, the other gods had their problems. Wicked Cousin Weasel had a cruel streak, and Little Brother Trickster was always making trouble simply because he could. Meanwhile Middle Sister Swallow lost her temper too often, and Old Uncle of the Tides regularly forgot his duties because he always fell asleep. But Moon Mother did not worry about them. They were her Thread-family, and she trusted them as if their souls were hers.

One night, while Moon Mother and Owl were on their nightly patrols, Owl found herself in a forested valley—one she knew well, where mountain bats hunted and humans dared not tread. There she found a badger, dead for days and out of place upon the detritus floor. Instantly, Owl knew it was Trickster up to one of his games.

You see, one of his favorite pranks was to inhabit the corpses of the forest. He would hide within them and wait for one of his Thread-siblings or Thread-cousins to walk by . . . Then he would leap free and lock them in chains. Sometimes he left his family for hours like that; once, he left Middle Sister Swallow for an entire year.

He had never been so foolish as to play this trick on Owl, though, for with her connection to the forest and all living things, she could always see right through his disguises.

And she saw right through him on that night too.

Normally, she would have turned away, but for once, she felt mischievous. So she pretended not to notice Trickster hiding in the badger's body. She changed into her human form and wandered past him, humming into the autumn night.

As she knew would happen when she reached him, his soul leaped from the badger and returned to its human form. But when he tried to chain Owl, she chained him instead. And though he begged for her to set him free, she simply kissed him on his forehead and took flight as her animal self once more.

And thus it was that Trickster was bound for a full ten years, and no chaos disrupted the Witchlands. And thus it was that Moon Mother found her fear receded—though at the time, she did not understand why.

And, perhaps most important of all, thus it was that Little Sister Owl became known as the cleverest of the gods. She was the only one to ever best Trickster, you see, and some say that is why he fell in love with her—although that is another story for another night.

Iseult sucked in a breath. She couldn't believe she'd made it to the end of the tale without her voice breaking or anyone waking up. She was thirsty; her throat hurt and her jaw ached. But at least Owl's Threads had softened. Gone was the terror, gone was the white. Now, there was a grassy curiosity . . . and a darker determination.

She was not looking at Iseult, though, but at Aeduan and Evrane.

"What is it?" Iseult asked, earning a glare—as if Owl said, *I am gagged, remember?*

And Iseult almost smiled at that expression. *That* was the Owl she wanted to see. "Try to sleep," she said. "I know it's uncomfortable, but we don't know what tomorrow will bring, and we must stay strong."

Again, Owl glared, but this time her Threads were laced with a different sort of impatience. She stared pointedly at Aeduan and Evrane before dragging her hazel eyes back to Iseult's. Twice she did this . . .

But whatever she wanted Iseult to see, Iseult wasn't finding. "I'm sorry." She shook her head. "You'll have to tell me what's bothering you when they remove the gag . . ." Iseult trailed off. Movement had caught her eye—a shape crawling across the floorboards. A trick of the night's shadows, except now Owl was grunting behind her gag and straining against her bonds.

Then an image formed in Iseult's mind. An image of Owl and Iseult roped to the cots. *The weasel.*

Iseult's chest swelled. Her eyes swelled too as tears, hot and sandy, pushed at them from behind. But she made no sound, no movement. She simply watched as the weasel slunk around the stove past Corlant, past Aeduan . . . She paused at Evrane and sniffed.

"No," Iseult whispered. "Leave her." Beside her, Owl had gone completely still, completely silent. Her eyes bulged, her Threads stained yellow with worry.

"*Leave her,*" Iseult whispered again, shouting the command directly into the weasel's mind.

The animal ignored her and with movements slow as tar, she began tampering with something on Evrane's belt. Every pop of the fire sent Iseult's heart into her mouth. Every flicker in Evrane's Threads made her brace for a fight.

But the woman never awoke, and after an eternity of patience, the weasel finally had whatever it was she wanted. Then she was streaking away from the monk toward Iseult and Owl.

When she finally reached them, Iseult saw what the weasel had clutched in her tiny jaws: the Hell-Bard map.

Wicked Cousin, indeed, Iseult thought.

"Can you chew through these cords?" Iseult shook her wrists against their bindings. But the weasel ignored her, and with painfully slow movements, she unfurled the map and dug in her nose. Iseult squinted and strained. In the night, all the lines and dots morphed together.

The weasel chattered her teeth and shoved in her nose again—and this time, Iseult was able to make out what the map revealed.

Dots. Tens of them, right beside a familiar red X. The Hell-Bards from

Praga had almost arrived, and for once, Iseult welcomed them. They would be her distracting right hand.

"How far?" Iseult asked, and the weasel replied with a vision of sheep pens.

They were almost outside then, which meant Iseult needed to move. *Now.*

The weasel sensed this and leaped up Iseult's body. She chewed through the cords at Iseult's wrist before scampering to Owl. Blood roared into Iseult's deadened limbs while she clumsily swooped up the map. Seconds later, Owl was free too. "We must be quiet," Iseult whispered before pulling the gag from Owl's mouth.

Instantly the girl began coughing. She couldn't help it—the sudden pale horror in her Threads made that clear. She also couldn't stop it, even when Iseult clapped a rough hand across her mouth.

It was too late anyway. Across the room, Corlant's Threads were changing. Melting out of sleep, quickly, quickly.

Two heartbeats later, he awoke.

Iseult kept her hand over Owl's mouth, watching as Corlant slid into full awareness. "Hide," she ordered the weasel while shoving Owl back onto the cot as if she'd never been unbound. Then she arranged her own limbs exactly as they had been.

Her arms throbbed. Her heart drummed. But she kept her body still as Corlant dragged himself off his cot . . . then across the room. His Threads brightened with each step. He hugged his robe against the cabin's cold.

His eyes, shining in the shadows, lit on the gags strewn across the floor. He chuckled; orchid pleasure sprayed across his Threads. "Clever," he murmured, snagging the dirty wool. "But useless." He moved first for Iseult, long fingers extended. Aiming for her forehead, exactly as he'd touched the Herdwitch before. A warning and a reminder of what he could do.

His cold palm touched Iseult's skin. Her body screamed, but she didn't pull away. She didn't move at all. As long as he thought her hands still bound, she had the advantage.

His free hand reached for her chin.

She kneed him in the groin. With all her strength, all her rage. Then her fingers launched for his eyes. *In at the edges, out toward the ears.*

Corlant had no time to scream or even double over before she had her thumbs behind his eyeballs. Hot, squishy—a move she'd learned but never used. *In at the edges, out toward the ears.* She yanked. Corlant screamed.

But it was too late for him to stop Iseult. She had dug deep into the blood vessels and pulled with all her might.

The right eye came loose, popping free with a squelch Iseult felt more than heard over Corlant's rising roars. The left eye resisted—so she left it there. Now was the time to run. Before Aeduan or Evrane could fully understand what was happening. Before the Purists outside, now rushing in, could reach her. And before, most dangerous of all, Corlant could try to use his magic.

As Corlant toppled toward the bunk, Owl scrabbled to the floor. "Follow the weasel," Iseult ordered while she grabbed for Corlant's pocket and the diary within. He could not fight back. His Threads seared with anger-tinged pain, and his hands clutched at his face.

His dangling eye glistened in the pale light.

Iseult found the diary, tore it out, and dove toward the door after Owl. The Purists barely registered her, for the Hell-Bards had arrived. Shouts and clashing weapons tore out. Threads churned and violence darkened each set. Nobody noticed Iseult or Owl hurrying by in the shadows.

Horses, the weasel seemed to say, sharing an image of Lord Storm Hound with his bindings already chewed free. He was by the well, a mere twenty paces away and cast in moonlight.

With her free hand, Iseult gripped Owl and sprinted toward that moonlight. Once to the shaggy steed, she hefted Owl onto the saddle, shoved the diary into her small arms, and finally hauled herself up behind. The weasel was already halfway up Iseult's body, already looped around Iseult's neck by the time she dug her heels into Lord Storm Hound's body.

Corlant's screams blistered around her, amplified by shouts from Purists and Hell-Bards. He would hunt Iseult, as would Aeduan and Evrane. In fact, she sensed the Bloodwitch approaching, his muscles fueled by magic. But he was too late. Iseult and Owl were already pressed flat against Lord Storm Hound, and the horse was already cantering wildly toward the trees.

TWENTY-FIVE

✳

White terror had reclaimed Owl's Threads. All-consuming, and Iseult had no doubt that if she could see her own Threads, they would look the same. They were lambs hunted by a wolf; only fear drove them now.

At least they had the weasel to help, and with each crashing fall of Lord Storm Hound's sturdy hooves, she sent images of where to go.

At the hornbeam, go under.

At the linden, go left.

A game trail between two oaks: follow until the patch of mud.

Iseult lost all sense of time as they rode. Only Owl's Threads, bright as the moon above, wavered against her. But Aeduan—or the soul that now wore his body—was faster with his Bloodwitchery to propel his muscles and guide the hunt. He might not be able to smell Iseult, but he could certainly smell Owl. Soon he had caught up. Soon Iseult sensed him in her periphery, Threads green and hunting and tainted by shadow birds.

A dried-out streambed ahead. Abandon the horse at the pine.

Iseult spotted the pine. "Must we leave the horse?" She felt safer elevated and carried on legs faster than her own. But then she spotted the stream: its drop-off was far too steep for the horse. Iseult yanked in his reins and in seconds, she was on the forest floor and tugging Owl down.

"I'm sorry," she told Lord Storm Hound. Then she smacked his rump. He pounded off into the trees—where hopefully Aeduan would follow the horse, however briefly, instead of his witchery.

As Iseult hurried Owl toward the empty stream, another set of Threads skated into her awareness: silvery, muted, prowling this way.

She panicked. Her footing faltered. She fell; Owl fell, and unlike Iseult, Owl did not know how to land to prevent damage. She caught herself with her hands, and a sickening snap hit Iseult's ears. Pain lanced up Owl's Threads, an iron heart surrounded by white. She did not cry out, though. Did not react at all, and Iseult had no choice but to pull her to her feet and into a limping run once more.

Distantly, Iseult sensed Aeduan's corrupted Threads reach the stream's drop-off. Distantly, she heard his boots land gracefully upon the softer soil, but she dared not look back or slow. She simply kicked her legs higher and yanked at Owl all the more. The silver Threads were not yet near—and they seemed in no rush to approach—but whatever wore them was far more dangerous than Aeduan.

Of that, Iseult was certain.

Only when Aeduan was right behind her, only when his bruise-purple anticipation filled her awareness, did she finally react. Iseult shoved Owl in front of her and screamed, "*Run!*"

Aeduan's hand clamped onto Iseult's right shoulder, a grip to break stones. But she was ready for him. With her left hand, she clasped his fingers so he could not release her. Then she turned sharply. Her right fist connected with his ribs. Her right knee connected with his groin. He doubled over, and she used this brief weakness to wedge her elbow on top of his.

Iseult kept turning. So fast and so hard, his arm abandoned its socket. A tearing crack filled the woods. Aeduan had no choice but to drop to his knees. Steel pain and crimson fury claimed his Threads. Brightest of all, though, was the turquoise surprise.

He had not expected this, and unlike the real Aeduan, he did not know how to get out of it.

Iseult moved until she was directly behind him and grabbed his head. One hand she placed on his crown, one hand she placed on his jaw. She snapped his neck.

And like the eye gouge, she'd never actually done this move before. She wasn't prepared for how easily his spine broke. Pain, dark as thunderclouds, laid claim to the entirety of his Threads. He toppled forward and collapsed to the earth.

For several wild, breathless moments, the world was silent. Iseult's lungs were locked; her booming heart was a distant, forgotten thing. Even the silver Threads vanished from her awareness as she stared at Aeduan. As Owl stared at Aeduan. As the weasel stared at Aeduan, his body facedown on the dried stream and his back shuddering with broken breaths.

Then his Threads began to shrink, and Iseult clapped a hand to her mouth. She'd killed him. Oh goddess, she'd *killed* him.

"Aeduan." She sank to his side. With a grunt of strength, she gripped his shoulder and rolled him over. Now his Threads were almost completely gone. Now his chest scarcely moved. Why wasn't he healing?

"Aeduan, please wake up. I'm sorry, I'm sorry." Nothing happened. The last of his Threads scattered away. "No, no, no." She dug her fingers into his cheeks. "Wake up, wake up. Please, I'm so sorry—"

His eyes opened. Ice blue and clear.

Iseult gasped. Recoiled. Then understood. For of course Aeduan's Threads were gone. Not from death, but from life. The true Aeduan had returned.

Te varuje.

A laugh curled up from her stomach. Hysterical and overloud. She leaned in. "It's you. I can't believe it. You're here."

"No."

Iseult stilled.

"Go." Aeduan swallowed; his eyes—now swirling with red as he healed—held hers. Steady in the way that only the true Aeduan could ever be. "He . . . returns."

"Who?" she asked. "Who returns? Who possesses you and Evrane?"

He did not answer right away. He couldn't. His face was tightening, his eyes closing. Not with pain but with concentration. "The Old One," he squeezed out. "From the Well."

Now Threads were wavering to life. Weak bursts of birds as the one who controlled Aeduan broke through.

Aeduan's eyes snapped wide again. Such beautiful eyes, Iseult had once thought. The shade of pure understanding.

"Run," he rasped, holding her gaze. "Iseult, *run.*"

She did not run. Too many points were connecting in her brain, gumming up her muscles. Slowing her in the way that logic always did. *The Aether Well. The Old Ones. Paladins forgotten and gone.*

A scream shattered the night. Near and desperate, it broke off in an instant. Not human, but equine. *Lord Storm Hound.* Iseult pushed to her feet, vision briefly darkening and the moonlit forest briefly wavering. Someone had gotten the horse. Or some*thing* had, for there were the silver Threads, muted but closer. Muted but hunting.

With no grace and all brute strength, Iseult grabbed Aeduan's shoulder and flipped him onto his stomach once more. He did not react. His eyes were closed, his face pinched with focus while someone else's Threads fought to rip through.

And still he healed. She could hear his body mending itself, new bone growing by the heartbeat. She could also hear a rustling in the trees, as if the wind whispered this way. A cold, killing wind with Threads of immortal hunger.

Iseult tore off Aeduan's Carawen cloak. Then she unsheathed Aeduan's sword. In moments she had his salamander cloak slashed in half. The bottom strip, she tied around her own shoulders—dirty, but warm. Then the main cloak, she draped over Owl.

The child did not resist. Wherever her mind currently was, it was not within the stream. She didn't even sense the approaching creature. She was pain, pain, horror, and loss.

"Come," Iseult said, wrapping her hand around Owl's good one. "It's time for us to run again."

The Bloodwitch named Aeduan fought against the water.

Fathoms below the surface with no air to fill his lungs, no light to fill his eyes, he kicked and reached and strained against the weight that held him down.

He was not drowning, but he also did not breathe.

He *had* breathed, though. Briefly, when he had seen the face made of moonlight and shadows only a foot away from his. Iseult's hair had flown on the breeze, her knees had trembled against his ribs, and he'd thought he had somehow returned to the past. To that day beside the lighthouse, when she had broken his spine and stabbed him in the heart.

But this was not that day, and the waves that washed against him were not from the warm Jadansi. These were dark waves with talons that held fast to his ankles, his hips, his lungs. And he knew they would never let him free. Not until they found a different body to hold on to. Not until they claimed *hers*.

He was glad she hadn't found the silver taler still tied around his neck.

TWENTY-SIX

✳

Safi did as Henrick had ordered and returned to her quarters, where she allowed Svenja and Nika to clean her. It required some fancy handwork to sneak the Truth-lens from her shredded training gear, but she managed to tuck it into her court gown before either attendant had noticed.

Then she went to dinner as if nothing had happened that day. As if she hadn't trained with Hell-Bards, as if she hadn't been stabbed, and as if she hadn't gone to the Keep and studied the Loom.

Safi's mind was alight, though. Throughout the tedious conversations about court gossip and sycophantic compliments flung Henrick's way, she considered all she'd learned. All she still needed to find. She had a lead on where Uncle Eron was being held, and she knew that Henrick wanted her for more than just her magic. In fact, he didn't simply *want* her. Safi seemed to be a requirement if Leopold's rule were to ever one day proceed.

Safi kept her face alert, her eyes wide throughout the tedious courses. She had told Henrick she wanted power, and she would do all she could to prove that to him. If only so he would open up again. If only so he would believe her earlier lies.

It was as an older domna chatted several seats away that Safi noticed the woman's necklace. A hideous thing, the chain dangling loosely around her neck while large butterfly bangles hung down. Glittery and golden, gemstones winked upon the butterflies' wings, reminding Safi of the colors in the Truth-lens.

She sat taller in her seat, an idea unfurling. Slowly, slowly, she teased it apart. If she could do what she was imagining—if she could create something not so different from what the domna wore—then it would make her search for answers so much easier.

When at last Henrick finished his dessert and Safi was sent away to change for the night's dancing, she had to fight the urge to sprint through the imperial halls. Her fingers itched to work.

"I want alone time," she told Svenja and Nika the instant she entered her room. "I have a letter to write." Safi offered a shy smile, and as she'd hoped, Nika giggled. Svenja sighed. Neither woman argued.

As soon as Safi was coiffed and dressed in evening finery, they left her at her desk with the privacy screen high. And as soon as Safi heard her door shut, she pulled out her Truth-lens and hastily got to work.

She had no tools beyond a goose-quill pen, which she quickly realized was useless. Fortunately, the outer casing of the device was easily separated. The inner workings—the quartz stones, the threads—were more delicate, but she was patient and did not rush.

Magic tickled her fingers as she worked. *Her* magic.

The twenty-second chimes rang, a tolling of bells throughout the city along with smaller, clockwork chimes in the palace. Then, somehow, the twenty-third chimes were ringing, and Safi could no longer delay her arrival at the dancing.

But that was all right because she was almost done.

Then she *was* done, and she sat back in her chair with a satisfied smile. She grabbed the blotting salts and pretended to sprinkle them over her desk, beneath the privacy shade. A dramatic *whoof* of exhaled air, and her work was complete.

A knock at her door. "A moment," she trilled before tucking her new, rearranged Truth-lens into the folds of her dancing gown. By the time her door opened and Lev poked in her head, ready to escort Safi to dancing, there was nothing in sight except a piece of paper she was carefully folding.

"Seal this," she ordered Lev as she glided toward the door, "and deliver it to His Imperial Highness."

"Of course," Lev said with a bow. Then she, Safi, and the rest of her assigned Hell-Bards fell into their usual stride across the palace.

Safi would not say she enjoyed her evening, but it was the closest she'd come to pleasure in a long time. She was the empress Henrick wished her to be, and soon, Safi would know what she wanted to know and have what she needed to have. Her new Truth-lens *necklace* had worked better than she'd dared hope. Whenever a lie had been uttered near her, magic had hummed against her chest.

And gods, so many lies during the dancing. So many flatterers, so many fools.

It was several hours past midnight by the time Safi reached Leopold's ancient tower. Like before, attendants guided her in with wilting bows.

Unlike before, though, Leopold still wore his evening clothes: evergreen and silver that made him glow like some forgotten forest prince from one of the old stories Mathew used to tell.

Safi also wore her same gown, a rich mustard and maroon.

After a heated embrace that—despite herself—made Safi's head spin and heart pound, Leopold closed the curtains, dimmed the lights, and locked his bedroom door. Three taps upon the wall, the stones opened wide, and he and Safi once more descended.

They did not speak until the darkness was past and the stairs had ended. Even then, all Leopold said was "Does your thigh hurt?"

"No."

Then he chuckled—though not at her. He was clearly amused by the circumstances, and no doubt guessed that her emergency trip to Hell-Bard Keep had been carefully arranged. Several more minutes passed in silence, with only the growing fog and their soft, slippered steps to fill Safi's ears.

"No one seems to have heard of your escapade," Leopold offered eventually, lifting his voice over the building churn of the baths. "I do not know how my uncle kept it secret, but he did." Leopold glanced back, his eyes merry. "What, pray tell, happened, Safiya?"

Her lips twitched, and in broad strokes, she painted the picture of her day for him, beginning with the training session and Caden's knife and ending with the carriage ride back to the palace. At some point in her story, Leopold stopped walking. He stared at her with hard intensity through the fog, and when she had finished, he said—so quietly she almost missed it—"You saw where Eron was, then."

"I did."

"A place like this?" He opened his arms.

"But with yellow shores and waters that boil."

"The Solfatarra." He ran a thoughtful thumb over his lower lip and resumed his march. "Henrick has a hunting lodge there, where Hell-Bards are stationed throughout the year because, unknown to anyone but a select few, there are dungeons beneath it. It is where the worst criminals are sent. The acid in the air slowly—*painfully*—kills them."

Safi's chest tightened. "Did it never occur to you that my uncle might be there?"

"Of course it did." Leopold glared. "But my spies found only empty cells when I sent them." Ahead, the fog and noise thickened. Three more long steps, and they rounded the final bend to the baths. The pillared pools stretched before them, unchanged from last night. Unchanged, Safi supposed, for a millennium.

As before, Leopold aimed for a bench—however, this time, he did not sit. Instead, he was the one to pace while Safi draped herself down.

"I will send more spies to look for Eron. Escape, however . . ." He shook his head, gaze fixed on the wet ground before his feet. "There is little I can do to actually remove him. Henrick will know if Eron leaves. But if he is sick, as you say, then perhaps some relief can be—"

"I will be going after him myself."

Leopold stopped. "I beg your pardon?"

"You heard me perfectly fine, Polly." She set her jaw. "*I* will be going after him myself. Just as soon as I have . . . something." She did not elaborate what that "something" was, but Leopold didn't seem to notice. He was fixated on her first words.

"And how do you propose going after him, Safiya?" He sniffed. "Unless I am quite mistaken, even today at Hell-Bard Keep, you could not escape the Loom's pull for more than several minutes."

"Ah, so you haven't noticed then, have you?" Triumph wreathed around her muscles. Purred into her toes. With two hands, she drew down the high neck of her dancing gown.

Leopold's jaw slackened. "How?" he breathed. Then more forcefully, advancing on her, "Where is the noose?"

"I stowed it in your quarters," she said matter-of-factly before opening the collar further to reveal quartz and thread and brass, all strung together and resting against the top of her breasts.

It took Leopold several moments to understand what he was looking at. Then suddenly, his head tipped back and he howled at the cavern's ceiling. A laugh to rattle stones. "Brilliant," he crowed. "Thrice-damned *brilliant*, Safiya." He rushed the final steps to her and stared at the trappings across her chest. "The Truth-lens, yes? Half of your magic was bound to it, so when you became a Hell-Bard, only half of your magic was torn away." His sea-green eyes met hers, laughter bright within them. "Does it hurt?"

"A little," she admitted—because it *did*. A low scratching of cold shivered inside her. It made her want to run. To move. To do anything at all that might distract her from it. "But," she added truthfully, "it's not a pain I can't sustain. As long as I have it on, I still have half my soul with me."

He chewed his bottom lip. "If you leave, though, you will be going much farther than a few hundred paces. The Solfatarra is on the other side of the Ohrins."

"I know." She lifted a single eyebrow. "Which is why I thought we ought to go into the city tonight. See just how far I can travel before the pain becomes too much. *If* the pain becomes too much."

"Indeed," he murmured, a throaty quality to the word. He did not smile, but there was genuine delight in his voice and in his eyes.

He offered her his hands, and once she had them clasped, he helped her rise. "Follow me, Safiya fon Cartorra. I know exactly where we will go."

The secret passage of owls and rooks stretched for at least a mile, some of it in darkness lit only by the single torch that Leopold carried—and all of it damp. Every few minutes as they walked, Leopold asked, "How do you feel?"

And every few minutes, Safi answered, "Fine. It's annoying, but it doesn't hurt." She spoke the truth each time—and thank the gods for it. She had feared, when she removed the noose in his quarters and stuffed it in his armchair, that every step away would be agony. Instead, this perpetual shivering deep in her bones had not worsened.

The tunnel finally stopped at a wide set of stairs. At the top, a cedar chest waited. Leopold bowed over it and removed two loose, hooded cloaks of dreary, easily missed brown. After draping one over Safi and pulling her hood low, he slipped into the second. Then he lifted an alarm-stone and held it up for them both to see.

It did not flicker. It did not light.

"No one outside," he said before replacing it, and several moments later, he took Safi's hand into his and pulled her to the stairs' end. A simple stone wall waited. Three taps with his fist, just like in the tower, and the wall disappeared.

A cold breeze and moonlight swept in—as did the muddy scent of water and the gentle lap of waves. It was the River Praga, which carved through the city, and the wall opened right onto it. Reeds drifted lazily nearby. Sounds of a sleeping city wafted down, as if a street were above, and Safi could just make out a stone wall on the river's opposite bank.

That fact alone—that she could *see* depth and color and moonlight— sent a thrill winking down her spine.

She was free. For now, for tonight, she was free.

"We are near the Sarian Bridge," Leopold explained. "And we will be getting wet." He motioned to small rivulets swirling toward his feet through the open wall. "Since it is very hard to explain to one's attendants why one's dancing shoes are muddy, can you go barefoot?"

Safi nodded. A grim smile compressed her lips. *Shoes should be a luxury,* Habim had taught her. *Not a requirement.*

That lesson had served her well over the past two months. Her mentor and his Heart-Thread might have tumbled through hell-gates that Safi couldn't comprehend, but she couldn't deny how much they had taught her. How *very* much she owed them.

And they had sent her the Truth-lens. That had to count for something.

Safi eased off her shoes, dropped them into the chest beside Leopold's, and after hefting up her skirts and cloak, she followed the prince into the water. He moved with silent ease through the reeds, like a heron who'd traveled this way many times. Safi felt clumsy and loud in comparison, each footstep splashing and squelching and rolling through her.

The water reached only to her upper calves, but the silt was unstable. It sucked her in. Fortunately, they were cast in shadow from the Sarian Bridge. When she glanced back, only once, she found the hole in the wall was gone. Slimy flagstone stretched as far as she could see, curving with the river and vanishing from sight.

By the time Leopold reached a small shelf onto which they could haul themselves, Safi had lost all feeling in her toes and ankles. The water was beyond frigid, and somehow withdrawing her feet to clamber onto the stone ledge only made her that much colder.

Leopold didn't slow, though, so Safi pushed herself onward until they reached a rusted ladder leading to the street. Leopold ascended first, and Safi followed with a great deal less grace.

Weak streetlamps glared down, revealing the merchants' shops Safi and Henrick had passed earlier that day. At this hour, no lights burned within, no shoppers milled about. Two guards patrolled, but they had their armored backs to Safi and Leopold, who now hurried for a nearby alley.

Once they were cloaked in shadows again, Leopold whispered, "How do you feel?"

"Fine," Safi said, and it was true. She still sensed no significant increase in the shivers at her heart; they remained easy to ignore as long as she kept moving.

"Then we continue on." Leopold took Safi's hand into his own before leading her more deeply into darkness. His fingers were warm and deceptively soft. *He must keep his calluses filed down,* Safi realized, for she had seen Leopold training when they were young. He had been quick with a sword then, and she had no doubt he was quicker now.

I have spent twenty years grooming Leopold to be the perfect leader, Henrick had told Safi earlier. At the time, she'd assumed Henrick meant all the skills needed to run an empire—warfare, diplomacy, bureaucracy, and politics. Now, she wondered if perhaps it also included the art of performance.

Henrick was not the toad he seemed; Leopold was not the dandy.

They traveled several miles before finally approaching one of the city's outer walls, beyond which were suburbs and settlements that had sprung up over the centuries and continued to spring up today.

"How do you feel?" Leopold asked, peering up at the towering gatehouse. Lights flickered within the slitted windows, and soldiers stood watch at the gaping archway. They paid no mind to Leopold or Safi or anyone else hurrying by. Buoyant voices bounced off stone, suggesting alehouses and brothels on the crooked streets nearby.

Safi had never visited this part of the city. It was not so run-down as the slums, but it had certainly seen better days.

"I feel . . . good," Safi said, and to her surprise, the words were true, true, *true.* Yes, her muscles juddered and her toes were still blocks of ice. And yes, the Loom's magic called to her, miles upon miles away. But this was her first taste of freedom in a month, her first trip outside the palace without guards or Hell-Bards or a chain around her neck, and her first glimpse of colors, even if nighttime dulled their edges.

"If I did not have unfinished business at the palace," she continued, "I would leave the city right now."

A murmur of acknowledgment from Leopold. He still held her hand. "You cannot go alone, though, Safiya."

Her brows drew together. "But there is no one who can go with me, Polly."

"Oh, but there is." He tipped back his head until she could see his face beneath the hood. Skeletal in the shadows, but with bright, otherworldly green eyes. "I will go with you."

Safi did not react. She simply gazed at him, grasping for any change in the Truth-lens. But it did not frizz with lies.

"How could you join me?" she asked. "I thought you could not risk openly helping me or execution would await you."

"No," he admitted, tugging Safi back toward the river. Several blocks later, the second chimes clanged, and Leopold finally continued: "It is a delicate balance. My loyalties to Cartorra are true. My loyalties to the

Cahr Awen as well. Until now, I have walked that line as best I could, for I *am* my uncle's heir. I *do* take my future role seriously. More than seriously. It is all I have been raised for, all I have ever wanted."

He hesitated. His footsteps briefly slowed. Then he resumed his pace, faster now, and his grip on Safi tightened.

"However, circumstances have changed." He glanced briefly at her, his hood rustling. She could not see his face. "What is at stake has *changed*."

Safi's eyes narrowed. "My uncle? I realize you're working with him on this scheme to end all wars and heal the Origin Wells, but how does knowing where he is change anything? You didn't interfere when Henrick took my magic. You didn't interfere when Iseult was chased away. And you don't interfere *now* when Hell-Bards hunt her down."

"Ah, but that's just it, you see. Everything is different." He lifted her hand and gazed down at her fingers for several seconds. Then his second hand grabbed hold too, and Safi knew—before he could speak, before he could fully enclose her hand in both of his—she *knew* what he was going to say next.

He pulled her to him and held her hands to his chest. "I know where Iseult is, Safiya. She is near the Solfatarra and your uncle. And I fear she is in great danger."

Fourteen Days After the Earth Well Healed

Iseult never thought she would see her best friend marry.

And she certainly never thought she would see her best friend become an empress. They fled Dalmotti to avoid this; now they run headlong for it. At least this time they are following their own plan. Initiate, complete. A heist only they know of, only they can pull off.

Iseult stands on a private balcony, high above the crowded room as the first night of festivities begins below. It is a private place, meant for servants to observe their masters without interference. Invisible creatures that provide for every whim—or did, when that was the fashion centuries ago. Now it is a sign of status to have one's servants in plain sight.

Which has left this balcony empty and perfect for the claiming.

Safi and Henrick will soon parade through the great hall. So dramatic, so public. Nothing like the braiding ceremony for Nomatsis. Then again, Cartorrans do not marry for love. There's even a song about it. Something with robins and magpies.

When Iseult left the wedding earlier, surrounded by her usual escort of Hell-Bards, her last glimpse had been of the Emperor in pond-scum green. He had kept his face carefully neutral, carefully bored, throughout the ritual . . .

But his Threads had given him away, just as his Threads betray him now while he strides into the room with Safi at his side. She has changed into stunning gold, pure sunlight that makes her skin glow and smile radiant.

He still wears pond-scum green, and he moves with all the grace of the toad he seems to mimic. His Threads are alert, anxious, as if he waits for something. Safi's are the same, though hers twine with brighter anxiety, and brief twinges of terror too.

"It will be all right," Iseult whispers, her hand on her Threadstone. She knows Safi cannot hear—one of her hands is in Henrick's, the other occupied by waving. Without her fingers also on the stone, Iseult's words will fall on no one.

Still, Iseult likes to think the sentiment crosses their rubies. That some burst of strength now shivers into Safi's bones.

Safi and the Emperor reach the dais. Safi curtsies, and the nobility clap—some with delight and enthusiasm, most with confused politeness. It is a churning pool of contradictory Threads. They know she is a Truthwitch; they know she is half of the Cahr Awen; they know she was betrothed to Henrick two months ago in Veñaza City.

What they don't know is why Safi has returned. Why, after fleeing, she is still allowed to marry their emperor instead of living in chains.

Threads tickle Iseult's senses, stronger by the heartbeat. Brilliant Threads with a crackling core. She turns as Leopold steps onto her balcony. He has changed into dancing slippers and fitted silver velvet. Silver always suits him best, and he knows it.

"Dark-Giver," he says with a bow.

And Iseult frowns. A real frown she does not have to fake. Perhaps, given a few more weeks of practice, she will wear emotions easily. Then again, if all goes according to plan, after tonight it will no longer matter if she is expressive or not.

"You mock me."

"No." Leopold lifts his face, eyes and Threads twinkling. "I revere you."

"Empty words." She turns back to the crowd. Back to the dais where Safi and Henrick now sit upon their thrones.

"What makes you think they are empty?" Leopold leans on the balustrade beside her.

"You are a prince."

"And?"

"You have been trained since birth to tell people what they want to hear."

He chuckles. His Threads flare pink. "I would think that you, of all people, would sense my sincerity."

Iseult's lips sink deeper. "I am not a Truthwitch."

"No." He taps his lips, gaze sliding to meet hers. In this warm, Firewitched light, his eyes are the same shade as her gown: seafoam green. "You are much more dangerous, Iseult. You see emotions."

"And Safi sees truth."

Leopold twirls his hands, conceding. "But how often do people make choices based on truth? Based on facts or what their logic tells them?" His mouth twists with a smile. "Not nearly as often as they should. People start wars based on what they feel."

Iseult holds her silence. Leopold is in one of his trickier moods—they come more and more often these days. He prods her with words, testing just how much he can say before she rises. It is her least favorite version of him.

Stasis, she tells herself. *Do not react.*

But he is not done yet. *"You are far more powerful than she."* He motions vaguely toward the thrones. *"Yet she is the one they all desire."*

Stasis, stasis, stasis. "Do you say this to hurt me? Is your intent to cause me pain?"

"No." He frowns. Red frustration shimmers across his Threads. "I simply . . . You must realize you are more powerful. Yet you have been relegated to a servants' balcony while she—"

"I chose this servants' balcony." Somehow, her voice is smooth as snow. "I wish to observe the dancing, Leopold, but I have no wish for the stares."

"And that is exactly it." He spins about so his back is against the railing, elbows braced. "You are the witch in the shadows, Iseult, while Safi lives in the light."

Iseult's nostrils flare, and though she hates herself for it—and hates Leopold too—she cannot deny that he's right. She has always been the one who hides while Safi displays. The one who must drape her hair in scarves and keep her eyes downcast, lest anyone see their shade. And she has always had her heritage to damn her, while Safi has had her title to protect her.

But Iseult doesn't blame Safi for this. She has never blamed Safi for this.

She squares her body toward Leopold's. "You wish to drive a wedge between us. Admit it."

For half a moment, his lips part. The frustration winks brighter. Then he sighs, and his shoulders sink. "Forgive me. That is the last thing I wish to do."

"Then why say such things?"

"Because I merely think . . . no, I *know* that in your shoes, I would not be so kind." He runs a hand through his hair. It tousles the curls. "Forgive me," he repeats, and he offers her a hand.

Iseult stares at it. Long, pale fingers. "What is that for?"

"The dancing is about to begin."

"I do not dance."

"By choice or by force?"

"By choice," she is about to say. But then she bites her tongue. He is poking again, but this time, the question stymies her. Because of course it is not by choice that she has never danced. Gretchya would not let her—a Threadwitch would never dance!—and in Veñaza City, Nomatsis were not welcome.

Dancing was only ever for Safi, never for Iseult.

Leopold's lips quirk. His hand still waits between them, while below, music thrums. A heavy sound draped in strings with a somber beat to twirl by.

"I do not know the steps," Iseult says at last.

And Leopold's smile widens. "You do not need to." Then he takes her hand in his, and she does not resist. His skin is soft and warm. The touch of a prince.

The balcony is small, the space shaded. But the music carries, vibrating the stones as if the orchestra were only paces away. Leopold leads gently, and Iseult tries to follow. To match. But it's like learning to fight all over again; her mind sees what needs doing, but her body refuses to follow.

It does not help that Leopold's Threads blaze brighter. It does not help that the lilac shimmers have returned, a latticework to encase everything that makes him who he is. They burn so brightly, Iseult almost has to squint against them.

"Your Threads," she says when—yet again—she stumbles on a half beat, "are very bright."

His eyebrows bounce high. "Is that a good thing?"

"Sure," she replies.

And he laughs at that. A pleasing sound, a real sound that replaces the lilac with amaranthine delight. And Iseult realizes, with a tiny hitch in her chest, that he might be right: she can see feelings, and what a power that is indeed.

For half a moment, Iseult's spine unfurls. Her lungs expand. She is glad the Leopold she knows and likes has returned, and she pretends that she and Leopold are truly alone with no Hell-Bard Threads tucked into the narrow hall outside. No Threads of elated Cartorrans to wave like the ocean below.

It is the opposite of reaching for her magic. It is shrinking. It is forgetting. It is stasis. And it is dancing.

She and Leopold spin and slide, dip and sweep. The moves repeat every twelve beats, and Iseult quickly starts to remember them. Each step becomes easier than the last. Each worldly reminder more distant. Until at last, the final refrain of the dance susurrates against her skin. Leopold stops his dancing, and she finds herself facing him, her hands still clasped.

"Forgive me for my earlier comments," he says, and there is an urgency on his face and in his Threads. There is something darker too: a deep, frozen blue. "You are the last person I wish to hurt, my . . . friend."

Friend. It is such an odd word to fall from his tongue, and yet there is undeniable need scraping across his Threads.

Then she understands. "You are lonely."

He tenses almost imperceptibly. "One man's loneliness is another man's freedom."

"Not yours, though."

His lips part, and though he does not move, cold seems to swoop between them. After several moments, he pulls away. "Let a man have his secrets."

But Iseult will not. For once, he has worn honesty with her and she refuses to let that pass. When he moves to the balustrade, she follows. "You are am-lejatu, Leopold."

"I am?" He arches a wry eyebrow, his usual mask sliding into place. "And pray tell, what does that mean?"

"It means 'the life-sleeper.'" Iseult rests her elbows beside his. He watches the people below, and she watches him. "It is one who goes through this life, never fully awake. Never fully connected. The Nomatsis believe it is a fate worse than death."

He sniffs. "And you think I am a 'life-sleeper.'"

"Well, you certainly aren't living awake."

His Threads flash darker; blue unspools, and Iseult knows she has found the spot that even he does not study too closely. She keeps her secrets behind her left lung; he keeps his buried even deeper.

"You have no Thread-family," she continues. "I see it, you know."

He bristles. "And here I believed you were my friend."

"I am," she admits. "We have been through too much together for us to be anything else. But friends are not Thread-family, Leopold. One is knowing someone well. Laughing together and sharing interests. The other is risking your life for them—and knowing they will risk theirs for you. You must know that when storm and wildfire come, they will stay beside you."

"And here," he repeats, "I believed that was you." He reveals nothing on his face or in his posture. He is the epitome of stasis, and even Gretchya would have been impressed. His Threads, though, reveal everything. They bleed with blue. They drip and ooze as if tears fall—more tears than a single body could ever contain.

A thousand years' worth of loneliness.

And Iseult realizes she has hurt him. Deeply. She also cannot lie to him. She sees no Threads of family on his soul; she sees only emptiness and solitude.

A new song begins below. Leopold watches the tapestry of dancers in silence, and Iseult watches too. Only when it ends does Leopold finally straighten and declare, "I am going down, if you wish to join."

Iseult shakes her head. "No."

"Hmmm," he replies, and his green eyes meet hers for half a breath before he stalks away, off the balcony and out of sight. His Threads, however, linger in Iseult's awareness long after. Confused, lonely, angry that someone in this world now knows the one thing he hides away.

The one truth at the heart of all his masks.

He is not gone long before another set of known Threads arrive, a shadowy core roiling inside pale urgency. Then Caden's voice skates in from the hallway—overloud as if he wants Iseult to hear.

"There has been a change of plans," he calls. "His Imperial Majesty will be going into the city once the dancing ends. Be ready."

And just like that, all of Iseult's and Safi's preparations turn to ash.

TWENTY-SEVEN

✳

You did what?" A muscle feathered in Ryber's jaw. She and Stix were back in their carriage, the usual orange tabby nestled at their feet, while outside a darkening swamp lugged by. Even with the carriage curtains swept wide, there was no finding a breeze. Only this thick, motionless humidity.

"I told Kahina where I found the—"

"I heard you." Ryber pinched the bridge of her nose. "I meant, how could you do that? If Kahina really is this Paladin called Lovats—and honestly, is there any doubt at this point?—then she is the last person in the Witchlands who should know how to enter the Sightwitch mountain."

"But the blade and glass aren't there. You have them."

"For now. But what about when she figures out we've moved them?" Ryber's hand dropped. "You just told her how to access a thousand years' worth of guarded secrets. Goddess, what if she finds Eridysi's workshop, Stix? Or she gets into the Crypts? Or . . . " Horror bulged in her eyes. "What if she finds the tombs? My sisters are frozen there. *Kullen* is frozen there."

For the first time since leaving Kahina, the triumphant surge in Stix's chest faltered. She had thought herself so clever for telling Kahina where she had *found* the tools, instead of where they were. After all, that meant she had lost nothing, while hundreds of prisoners had gained freedom.

"She won't find the Crypts or tombs," Stix murmured, but Ryber only wagged her head.

"You can't know that. And again, what will happen when Kahina finds out you've tricked her? Need I remind you of what those tools can do? Why they were created in the first place?"

"No," Stix mumbled.

Ryber reminded her anyway. "Eridysi made them to kill the Exalted Ones after they ruined the Witchlands with their tyranny. That broken looking glass will show Paladins for what they are, and that blade will kill them. It will kill you, Stix. *Forever.*"

"I know." Stix's mumble turned to a growl. "I've seen my own death a hundred times, remember?"

"But that wasn't a real death." Ryber fumbled her diary off her belt and thrust it toward Stix. Humidity-muffled moonlight beamed over it. "If you would just read this, you'd understand what I'm talking about. You'd understand why Kahina can't have Eridysi's tools—"

"I *do* understand," Stix snapped. "And I have no plans to tell her where they are." She dug a knuckle into her forehead; her crooked spectacles shifted down her nose. She didn't want to fight with Ryber because it wasn't Ryber she was actually frustrated with. It was herself—*had* she made a mistake?—and it was the voices gathering once more at the base of her skull. *Why are you leaving?* they wanted to know. *Come back this way, keep coming!*

She wasn't sure how much longer she could endure this swollen pressure always buzzing. And she certainly couldn't watch another person die in the Ring.

She had done the right thing to free them. Of *course* it was the right thing.

As if sensing Stix's misery, the orange tabby piled onto her lap. Ryber must have sensed too, for when she spoke again, her tone had softened. "Kahina isn't stupid, Stix. She has lived countless lifetimes, just like you."

"Not like me," Stix countered, but her heart wasn't in the argument. She was tired of the Ring, tired of Kahina, tired of the blade and the glass, and above all else, tired of this Paladin soul she'd never asked for.

As the carriage thumped through a deep divot in the softened road, moonlight speared into the carriage. It bounced off the cat's green eyes, which glimmered like Kahina's ring. Instinctively, Stix rubbed her thumb.

Pain spiked through her.

She flinched, startled by the intensity of it, by the lightning flaring up her arm and down her spine. She jerked her hand into the dim light, only to find a raw, blistering line striped around her thumb.

The cat stopped her purring. Ryber gasped, and Stix gulped over a sudden tangle in her throat. The voices, for once, were silent—as if they too were stunned by what Stix saw. As if they too had grown cold with horror.

"What is that?" Ryber asked. For some reason, she was whispering.

And for some reason, Stix was whispering too when she answered, "I don't know, Ryber. I really don't know." Except that in the most remote corners of her brain, a place fully usurped by voices, there *was* a quiet memory of a green ring, the person who'd worn it, and the pain that came from breaking a bargain bound in jade.

Vivia awoke with the sense that something was off. She'd forgotten where she was. Why, how. Then came the scent of sandy earth and plant exhales. Thick, alive, a smell she'd never known she missed until it reached her again.

This was Nihar, a place that had been dead for so long. *The* place where her father had been raised, and then Merik after him. She'd always wished it had been her to come here, even if she never admitted that to anyone but herself—and only then during these dark, solo moments of the night.

Katydids choired aboveground, outside of this prison where Vivia's crew waited for her to do something. To lead. If only she knew what steps to take, if only someone were here to tell her.

What a great queen she was.

She pushed off the earthen floor and fumbled for Vaness nearby. The lanterns had been extinguished outside the cells—all save one—yet no amount of squinting was making Vaness's unconscious form appear.

She isn't here. It took Vivia several moments to realize this. Too many moments to realize the floor beside her was empty, and the rest of the cell too.

Horror battered through her. She scrambled to her feet, ready to shout for guards and demand answers. Yet as soon as she pounded her fist against the door, it creaked open. Lantern light slid in, and Vivia gaped, brain too stunned to understand. Muscles too stunned to move. Her door was open, Vaness was gone, and . . .

Footsteps. Soft, lethal, moving away.

Vivia pushed into the hall right as a figure exited through the door at the end, thick and bulky as if someone was draped across their back. *Vaness.* Before Vivia could shout for the Empress or kick into a run, a second figure materialized from the same door, a curved knife flickering in his left hand. In his right, winds swirled. Vivia felt more than saw those winds— just as she knew immediately that this man had come for her.

Dalmotti must have sent him. She recognized those rounded knives, just as she recognized the two rapiers hanging at his hips. He and the other man were Assassin Guild. Excellent at what they did: murder, stealing, kidnapping.

A ball of winds loosed; Vivia dove sideways; wind scraped against her shoulder, hard enough to bend bones. Sharp enough to flay skin.

Sailors stirred in other cells. Cam's voice pierced out, "Majesty!"

Vivia lunged for the man in black, but her shoulder hurt. The bones resisted, and he easily dodged before loosing a second blast of winds, sharp and targeted, like knives made for each organ. One at her heart, one at her stomach, and two for her eyeballs.

Vivia barely flung up her arms to protect her eyes and heart. She twisted sideways to prevent a deadly blow to her belly. Still, the winds did damage, hitting her forearms, her side. Heat ignited. Blood and pain, briefly blinding in the intensity.

She screamed. Not because of the injuries but because she could not fight this Windwitch alone. She needed her sailors, now pounding against their wooden doors. She needed Yoris and his soldiers—anyone who might show up before this Windwitch drew in his winds for a third attack.

Still hollering, Vivia propelled herself for the exit, snagging the lantern as she ran. It wasn't a targeted throw or a graceful one, but it was the distraction she needed. The glass connected with the man's shoulder, and she reached the stairs.

She took two uneven steps at a time, bellowing as she ran. "*Intruders! Intruders!*" Then she reached the ground floor and burst out beneath the ship. "*Intruders!*" Lights flickered inside the galleon and footsteps thumped out. She didn't wait for help, but instead skittered left. Toward the river and where another figure was now vanishing into the night.

She didn't consider her own escape as she sprinted for the river. She thought only of Vaness, unconscious and claimed. Vivia would get her back. No matter what it took, she would *get her back.*

The river's waters called to her, powerful. Soothing. Ready to be tapped and used and violent in her name. Each inhale brought more power, more water. Each step sent the wind-shorn pain receding further and the magic suffusing in. It filled her, as it always did, and held her in the moment so that she was nothing more than water, tides, and time.

She spotted Vaness's abductor within seconds. He had reached the low dock where fishers cast their boats, and he was pushing off in a skiff. No oars, only magic.

He was a Tidewitch too, and he wasn't waiting for his companion. No need, Vivia supposed, since the companion could fly.

She reached the dock, her footsteps thwacking a hollow beat. It drew the Tidewitch's attention. His dark eyes glittered in the moonlight—as did his teeth, offered in a smile.

He launched water her way: four whips as deadly as the wind-knives had been.

Vivia ducked behind a chum barrel. Her magic flung wide. She could fight a Tidewitch, but she was losing blood from her abdomen. *Hold me,* she told the water. *Help me.* And the water obeyed.

It leaped up from the river, a shield that absorbed the assassin's water, while Vivia, on her hands and knees, crawled to the dock's edge. She needed a boat, a canoe, a raft—anything that would allow her to chase after that Tidewitch and Vaness.

But there was nothing. Which meant Vivia was going to have to swim. *Noden protect me,* she begged. Then to the water: *Carry me safely.* She toppled in.

The water welcomed her, as it always did, cooled by night, silted by years along these sharp banks. She could see nothing, could hear nothing, but oh, Vivia could feel so much.

The water came all the way from the mountains and carried all the way to the sea, fed by countless tributaries and dividing into countless streams. Creatures lived in the soft bottom, in the crumbly shores—creatures wise enough to burrow deep and hide as Vivia called her power to her.

Her blood ribboned out, one with the water. An offering to appease something more ancient than her little fox mind could conceive. She surged forward as easily as a tarpon and with a thousand times more focus, more ferocity. Dalmotti would not claim Vaness. Dalmotti would not win.

She picked up speed, her course as true as the river's. Ahead was another current, another magicked force disrupting the water's flow. He was a strong Tidewitch—there was no missing it. Vivia felt his magic brush against her, remnants of command that the water still recalled. He was a witch who forced his will upon the element; Vivia was a witch who let the element decide and lead. It was easier that way, and the power so much more vast.

Stix had taught her that, all those years ago on the shores of a lake when they were supposed to be studying history lessons.

Vivia gained speed, the water thrilling at her request. Pushing her onward as if she were made of the same eternal matter. Where the river bent, she curved. Where the waters deepened, she surfaced to gulp in air.

Then she was close enough to feel the Tidewitch's power. It sizzled through the water, sizzled through Vivia's senses. The water did not want to be controlled, yet it couldn't fight a witchery such as his.

He noticed her approach. Water thundered toward her, sudden rapids to pummel her down. But she was ready. She rolled, she ducked, and finally, she surfaced. Her water, loyal and true, punching beneath her.

Air eddied against her. Her vision cleared and her lungs gasped. Blood and water streamed off her. There was the boat, there was Vaness unconscious upon its floor, and there was the Tidewitch.

His hood had fallen back, revealing a mustache and smooth skin. He was young; he was skilled. He kicked more water her way, whips like he'd used at the shore. Too slow, though. Vivia had reached his deck.

Sinking to a crouch, she caught his whips. The water did not want to be dominated, so she set it free. Go, she told it, and it obeyed in its own way: a funnel that sprayed wide and briefly blocked all sight, all sound.

Vivia couldn't see the Tidewitch, and he couldn't see her. She used that moment to burst forward. Water shed off her. Blood speckled the wood, speckled Vaness slumped nearby.

She slammed into the Tidewitch. He was ready for her, though, his feet braced and knives—real knives of real steel—in hand. He sliced, he swung, and Vivia let him. Because he had miscalculated one thing. He had assumed she would resist those blades. He had assumed she would evade.

She didn't. She let the left one slide into her shoulder and the right one slide into her thigh. It hurt. Hagfishes claim her, it hurt. But she was so far removed from her body, so deeply bound to the water, that she could fight on.

Or fight on long enough to end this exactly as the water wanted it to end.

Her body pounded into his. A low tackle that had her arms, bleeding and weakened, flying around his torso. Too much momentum for him to stop, too much clumsy force for him to have expected. He was an assassin, not a brawler—and this was another trick she would have to thank Stix for.

His balance tipped out beneath him. He and Vivia fell overboard. He with Vivia's arms still wrapped around him, and she with two knives still shredding against her bone.

Down, down, she swam. Like a crocodile carrying its prey, like the Hagfishes bearing the souls of the dead to Noden's court. The water was not deep here, but it was deep enough for darkness to reign, and the current at the bottom to slow to near stillness.

Come! the water cried. Come and stay!

Yes, Vivia told it, and she released the young man. He lashed with his own power, tried to mark this river as his own. But these waters were too headstrong to be controlled. They preferred Vivia's requests to his commands, and so her requests won. Ropes of current pulled him down. Chains of water held him there. Vivia felt him sink, sink, then hold fast within the silt. Her blood caressed him as she awkwardly turned her body toward the surface.

Carry me, she told the higher currents. Her strength was fading fast, and she still had one very important thing to do. One final request for the magic that lived inside her, around her, around the man now drowning in an ancient bottom below.

The water would release him eventually. Though if that happened before his last breaths faded into nothing . . .

Vivia had no energy, no mind left to care. There was only the boat approaching fast, and a Well that could fix the mess that her body had become. Vivia reached the boat, and a wave dumped her to its floor. Vaness stirred nearby.

"Vivia?" she seemed to say, though perhaps Vivia imagined that. The Empress never called her by her name.

"Hold . . . on," Vivia told her, dragging herself around to face the tiny craft's bow. Then she lifted her arms and asked the current to go.

It agreed, and soon, she and the Empress of Marstok were speeding toward the sea. Alone save for the stars and the forest, alive and unconcerned by the chaos that had come this way. The crickets still chirped. A raven chuckled. And soon enough, a roar built in Vivia's ears, in her bones. It was not the roar of the ocean, rhythmic and reliable. This was a steady, endless crash from a waterfall toppling down.

A waterfall that had not moved in centuries and had been dead the last time Vivia had come here.

Please, she asked it as the river bent and the first white churn of rapids came into view. *Please carry us to the Well.* Her blood was draining too fast, and pain encroaching even faster.

But she couldn't focus on anything that was not the water, not the falls. She *had* to reach the top. She *had* to reach the Well.

Then the water was carrying them, reversing course to allow this boat to rise and ascend and reach for a double-pointed plateau high above. It wobbled, it pushed. Vivia wanted it to lift, so lift it did.

Almost there. Vivia sensed the waterfall's lip even if she could not see it. Even if her body was fading fast, the fire too much. The blood loss too much.

"Stay awake," Vaness said from somewhere far away. "Please, Vivia, stay awake."

Vivia. She'd said her name again and it pierced through the pain. Through even the water's domineering will, trying to tip the boat in any direction it could. *Vivia.*

They reached the top of the falls. The boat pendulumed up, up, over a lip of man-assembled stone, then finally into the Origin Well, where it splashed down, bouncing, bobbing, listing, and spinning. Vivia couldn't hold on any longer. *Take me,* she told the water, and she let its warm, pure touch embrace her. Then haul her overboard and down.

TWENTY-EIGHT

*

The walk back to the palace was a smear of cobblestones and cold, filthy feet. Of night revelers and bored guards. Other than a few pointed questions to Leopold—*How do you know Iseult is in danger? How do you know where she is?*—Safi strode in silence.

It would seem Leopold's spies had discovered a Wordwitched map used by Hell-Bards, and it would *seem* that the young Nomatsi girl named Owl was marked upon it. "If Owl is near the Solfatarra, we can assume Iseult is too—and Hell-Bards are right behind them."

"But how can they be inside the Solfatarra?" Safi asked once they were ensconced inside the torchlit tunnel again. She and Leopold had grabbed their slippers from the chest, deposited their cloaks, and then continued onward in bare feet toward the baths.

"I do not know." Leopold's cheeks ticced slightly in the torchlight. "Pray they change course before they reach the lake and find all routes cut off."

"Damn it all," Safi snarled. "We *need* one of those Hell-Bard maps. Can your spies get one?" Each of her steps was long. Several times, she even kicked into a half jog—and Leopold kept pace with her. Yes, Hell-Bard shadows still splintered her bones, but they were a cursory annoyance. A weak pain compared to the bright, flaring light of *Iseult at the Solfatarra. Iseult surrounded by Hell-Bards.*

"Maybe." Leopold's skin shone from the moisture in the air. "But if they cannot get one, then *we* cannot risk asking a Hell-Bard. You must remember that they can, at any time, be controlled and punished."

Safi's pace stuttered. She had not considered this. In her usual self-centered conceit, she had completely forgotten that as soon as she vanished from the palace, Henrick would turn his wrath on the people he could hurt in her stead.

The first people Henrick would punish would be Safi's own guards—her *lead* guard, Lev. Then he would turn to anyone else who'd ever con-tacted with her. Caden. Zander. The healer at the Keep.

Her feet stopped beneath her. Mist coiled, while ahead, the first pillars of the bath shimmered in wan light.

Leopold's pinched expression told Safi he understood. "As long as we tell them nothing," he said gently, "then Henrick's torture will yield nothing. He will stop as soon as he realizes that."

Safi didn't agree. Henrick might be an adept leader and a strong emperor—she couldn't deny that—but he also did whatever he needed to maintain power. She had felt it, she had seen it.

She had also felt and seen his temper. It would infuriate him enough to have Safi escape his clutches, but how would he react when he realized his prize nephew and only heir was gone too? Deep beneath all those masks, Safi suspected, Henrick cared for Leopold. Perhaps even loved him.

"This is bigger than the Hell-Bards." Leopold opened his arms, a wide, fluid movement. "You and Iseult are *bigger* than the Hell-Bards or Cartorra or any wrath Henrick might unfurl. All that matters is uniting the Cahr Awen, Safiya. All that matters is getting you to the final Well."

Safi's eyes narrowed. Something in his words did not ring true; something he said made the Truth-lens scratch across her skin.

"If uniting us is all that matters," she asked slowly, "then why did you let Iseult leave?" She had already asked this question; he had already given answers. Yet now, those answers seemed inadequate. False, even. And *now* she had enough of her magic to prove it.

She advanced on Leopold and thrust her face close to his. He was a graceful, beautiful man, but not a tall one. Safi's nose almost touched his. "You let Iseult go. *Why*, Polly?"

He drew in a long breath, but did not back away. Did not avert his eyes. "I told you—" he began.

"Tell me again."

"I could not risk being caught."

"*Why?*"

A slight twitch on his cheeks. He preserved his silence.

"If you expect me to travel with you across Cartorra, Polly, then I need to trust you. So far, you have helped me—I won't deny that. But nothing you've done has given me reason to believe anything you say. You are manipulative, you play games, you were trained by Henrick to be *just like him.*"

Still, Leopold said nothing. As the heartbeats passed, a coldness settled over him. His jaw hardened, his eyes turned flinty.

"Make me trust you, Polly. *Please.* Or I swear I will leave without you."

His nostrils flared. He spoke at last: "I will not and cannot deny anything you've said, Safiya, but may I remind you of a few pertinent details?" He dipped his head closer. His voice dropped low. "I am the reason the Bloodwitch monk did not catch up to you in Nubrevna. I am the reason Iseult escaped Tirla alive. I am the reason she escaped the Monastery and reached Cartorra—reached *you*. And *I*, Safiya, am the reason you have that Truth-lens draped across your neck.

"Did all events unfold according to my plans? No. I did not foresee the internal war at the Carawen Monastery. I did not anticipate Henrick's decision to imprison your uncle, I did not expect Henrick to noose you, and I certainly did not think *you* would be so foolish as to attempt noosing him. But when I say that everything I do is for you and Iseult, I am not lying. You know that I am not."

With stiff, angry movements, he hooked a finger beneath Safi's collar and withdrew her Truth-lens. The brass casing scraped across her chest.

"This tells you I speak the truth, does it not?"

"It tells me you do not lie." Safi's words were as quiet as his had been—and just as razor-sharp. Fourteen years she had known Leopold, yet this was the first time she'd ever truly *seen* him. He was lethal, he was cold, and he was accustomed to having his way.

"I do not lie." He released the necklace, though his hand continued to hover near her throat. "And I do not lie when I say that I will transport you to the Solfatarra. *Safely*, even if it means I must give up my own life along the way."

Safi held his eyes for several long moments. She did not breathe; nor did he. The quartz and threads across her collarbone still did not hiss *lie* to her—and she was, as he must know, out of options. She needed to leave the palace, she needed to reach the Solfatarra, and it would be infinitely safer, infinitely easier if she had Leopold at her side.

"I have trusted you this far," she said at last. "And I will continue trusting you to the end."

He finally lowered his hand. "Good." His lips bounced with a barely perceptible smile. "We will leave tomorrow night, then. Be ready and say nothing to the Hell-Bards." He didn't wait for Safi to acknowledge this command before he turned away from her and resumed his forward stride.

It wasn't until hours later, however, when Safi was in her own room once more and nestling into bed, that she realized Leopold had never actually answered her question. He had given her a list of reasons to trust him, but he'd never actually said *why* he had let Iseult go.

Oh, he was clever.

He had tricked her magic very handily indeed, and she had swallowed every word like a good child taking her medicine.

She would have to be careful once they were on the road. *Very safe, very alone.*

Iseult and Owl traveled for hours, following the weasel wherever she led. A steady pace, occasionally slowed so Owl could catch her breath or Iseult could check the Hell-Bard map. But they always quickly resumed as silver Threads came near.

Though never so near that Iseult or Owl had to sprint. Never so near that Iseult could sense what the creature actually *was*. It always remained just on the edge of her sensory awareness and moved only when she and Owl did. For some reason, that made it far more terrifying. Clearly it was sentient, clearly it was calculating.

While Iseult and Owl half walked, half jogged, Iseult told more stories. *Long ago, when the gods walked among us,* she always began breathlessly, before moving on to whatever tale she could remember best. Sometimes they were Nomatsi, sometimes Cartorran adventures that Safi had shared, about ghosts and ancestors and secret royalty stolen by kings. Iseult liked those stories best. She could almost pretend it was Safi sharing them. Safi hurrying by her side.

And those stories became Iseult's grounding stone as much as they were Owl's.

But as midmorning light began to suffuse the towering forest, the second sunny day in weeks, Iseult could no longer ignore two important truths. First, the unknown monster still trailed. And second, she and Owl could not continue this journey forever. Owl grew clumsier by the minute, the pain in her Threads seeping brighter, brighter, until all that remained was a thunderous, pulsing gray.

"We are almost to safety," Iseult told her after checking her Hell-Bard map for the thousandth time. The crescent lake was only a mile away, and surely, *surely* they could find some way across. Some way that the silver-Threaded creature could not follow. "It's like when Moon Mother and Little Sister got trapped in the storm. Do you remember that story, Owl?"

A muffled yes. A flare of interest in the child's Threads.

"Can you tell it to me?" Iseult folded the map back into her cloak's pocket.

"Long ago," Owl said quietly, "when the gods walked among us, Moon Mother and her little sister got trapped in one of Swallow's storms."

"Oh no," Iseult murmured, glancing behind them and reaching, reaching for the weave of the world. For the silver Threads they could never outrun. *There.* Several hundred paces away and to the right. "And how did the goddesses get free, Owl?"

"Little Sister turned into a bird that could fight against the raging winds, and she went to find Trickster."

"Why Trickster?" Iseult pulled Owl faster.

"Because Trickster could travel without a body, and Little Sister Owl thought that he could enter the storm and save Moon Mother that way."

"And did he?"

Owl hesitated. Umber confusion twined through her Threads. "I . . . don't remember."

"Ah." Iseult pulled the girl toward a clearing framed by alders. So far, her game was working; Owl had forgotten her pain. "Trickster *did* go into the storm, remember? He turned into his soul form and found Moon Mother, clinging to a stone altar on the Windswept Plains."

"He promised to take her with him," Owl picked up, a flash of excitement in her Threads—and on her face as she, unbidden, walked faster. "But only if she agreed to marry him."

"Exactly." Iseult forced a tight smile. The silver Threads had picked up speed too. "Trickster said, *I will save you from this storm if you agree to marry me. I love you, you see.* But Moon Mother only shook her head sadly, even as winds and rains raged around her. *You love no one but yourself,* she told him. *And you will always be alone.*"

Owl frowned as Iseult said those words, and for a brief moment, it was as if the collar were not there. Her Threads burned bright as a bonfire laced with silver. They pulsed, outward and upward. A firepot ripping loose.

Then the moment passed. The Threads shrank; the color dulled to its usual dampened shades.

Iseult said nothing. She simply held her breath and listened to the forest's wintry silence. Felt for the silvery Threads, which were definitely coming faster now, and gaining ground too. But the lake was so near. That *had* to be Iseult's and Owl's salvation.

They had just moved past the alders when the landscape abruptly changed. Like reaching the edge of a farm during fallow season, one moment there was growth, the next there was nothing but fog.

As soon as Owl saw it, her excitement over the story shriveled away. She dug in her heels. "Bad." She bared her teeth, hugged her swollen wrist to her chest, and when the weasel snarled at her to move, Owl snarled right back.

"No," Iseult said, panic creeping into her voice. The Threads were closing in, and now was not the time for Owl to be difficult. "Look, Owl. It's just water." Iseult rushed toward the fog. Its edges roiled and moved like foam on the lip of a tide. She thrust in her hand.

And two breaths later came the pain. Harsh, insistent, fiery. Iseult stumbled backward.

"Bad," Owl cried at her. "I told you, bad, bad, *bad*."

Iseult's hand felt like she'd dumped it into boiling water, and already, blisters puckered. *Acid,* she realized. Then fast on that thought's heels came another: the lake must be inside this fog, and it was no ordinary lake.

It was the Solfatarra, famed across Cartorra for its waters filled with heat and acid. At one end was a hot spring, where the waters were pure enough to enter. At the other was a sulfur mine. Both had been marked upon the map, but Iseult had been too dense to put it all together. What a fool she was. Always a stupid, stupid *fool.*

Worse, more Threads now sped into her awareness, corrupted by avian shadows and headed this way.

Aeduan would reach Iseult and Owl even faster than the silver Threads.

An image burst into Iseult's mind from the weasel. *A small gap in the fog. A wishbone-shaped stick shoved into the mud.*

Iseult gasped. A Nomatsi trail was right here, and for once Iseult knew exactly what to do. Even better, Aeduan would not. The old Aeduan hadn't been able to read such trails; this new one should fare no better.

He wouldn't understand this innocently placed vine Iseult now saw meant a trail waited ahead. He wouldn't recognize that stick ahead pointed toward a near-invisible gap in the fog. He would have to rely entirely on his Bloodwitchery to follow instead of whatever other tracking tools he'd used to get here—and with Owl completely covered in salamander fibers, *surely* Iseult and Owl could gain ground.

The weasel cut left to where a small slip of clear air was winding into the fog. Easily mistaken for a trick of the wind.

Iseult quickly covered Owl's face with the salamander hood's fire-flap and to made sure all the girl's limbs were covered too. Then she wrapped her own face in the remaining strip of salamander fibers, and together, she and Owl dove into the world of the Solfatarra.

Fog rushed around them, tendrils reaching and gusts rolling. Several times, acid blew into Iseult's face, forcing her to shut her eyes. Forcing her to wait and pray and suck in breaths. But the moments always passed; their forward progress always resumed.

Unfortunately, although Aeduan's Threads had slowed, the silver Threads still hunted too—always, always.

"Hurry," Iseult said, voice muffled by cloth and fog. "We must go faster." She freed her right hand—it was already scalded anyway—and grabbed Owl's shoulder.

Then she pulled and pushed and prayed to whatever god might listen.

And once again, her prayers were somehow answered. Forty paces later, they reached a craggy, yellow shore with two narrow canoes thrust upon it. Rickety vessels, but still intact despite the acid in the air, the acid in the waters.

Iseult hurried Owl to the stronger of the two vessels, and after bodily lifting the girl and dropping her inside, she raced to the other boat.

With a grunt and bolts of pain—acid in her eyes, acid on her hands—Iseult thrust the boat into the water. It bobbed away from shore, slower than she would have liked, but she could hardly splash out to help it now.

Right as she returned to the other boat, footsteps crunched on damp stones. She did not look back. Aeduan must have found a gap in the fog. Too quickly, too easily. Iseult grunted and heaved at the second boat, even kicking out two paces into the water. Acid splashed her bare hands and ate into her boots. Then she was far enough from shore to vault.

The weasel squeaked and tried to avoid acid; Owl huddled inside her cloak; and Iseult scooped a lone oar off the boat's bottom. She rowed and rowed and rowed. Acid sprayed with each swinging of the oar, but she could not slow. Could not worry if she hit Owl or the weasel or herself. Acid billowed against her face. Her eyes streamed, and she feared she'd lost the Nomatsi road. That she'd be stuck rowing this canoe forever.

Then the canoe scraped bottom, and it was time to run again. With no concern for Owl's injury, Iseult hefted the girl into her arms and staggered out of the canoe. She could see nothing in the fog, and her eyes scorched so badly she could hardly keep them open.

Owl began to cry.

But then the image of another branch in the earth filled Iseult's mind. She snapped her eyes wide, ignoring the pain, ignoring the fog—and there it was. Right beside her foot. A kinked piece of wood that pointed to another clear trail through the Solfatarra.

She set down Owl and pushed the child forward. This time, though, she did not run. This part of the trail required patience and respect. One wrong move, and they would spring claw-toothed bear traps. Or perhaps hidden crossbows.

Behind her, Threads closed in. Aeduan had found the other boat, and now he rowed with Bloodwitch-fueled speed.

The beach ended at a wall of yellow-and-white stone. Owl cried out, dismay swallowing her Threads.

"No," Iseult said, pushing the girl forward. "Now we climb." The ladder was almost invisible in the fog, its white-and-yellow rungs blending into the stone.

Iseult dropped to a crouch beside the child. "Get on my back," she ordered, stoutly ignoring how close Aeduan was. He had reached the shore. *Thwang!* A crossbow released, mere paces to Iseult's left. Pain flowered up Aeduan's Threads; he slowed but did not stop. Even as more traps fired, he still shambled on.

Owl wrapped her arms around Iseult's neck and her legs around Iseult's waist. Then the weasel crawled straight up Iseult's body and coiled onto Owl's shoulder. For once, thank the goddess, Owl did not protest.

And like that—with so much life to weigh her down—Iseult climbed the ladder. She lost all sense of location, all sense of height. Rough wood bit into her scalded hands. Her eyes streamed and raged. And her breath, already muffled by salamander and acid, was constricted even more by Owl's desperate grip around her neck.

A shout ripped out, followed by Threads of shock and pain—and shadows too. Aeduan must have hit a claw-toothed bear trap. He was near enough, though, for Iseult to see the birds in his Threads, winging past Iseult's eyes, mottling her vision. Spurring her faster despite her muscles' shrieking. Her throat felt crushed. Her back ready to break. Then, when she truly did not know how she could climb another rung, the fog ended.

It was like the edge from before—one moment, pain and clouds and death in all directions. Then suddenly, a clear sky and the cliff's end only fifteen rungs away.

A sob left Iseult's throat, and even Owl seemed to take heart. Her Threads briefly flashed with blue relief.

However, Wicked Cousin and Trickster were not done yet with Iseult. As she pushed herself even faster, straining to reach the ladder's end, a face appeared over the cliff's edge. A young woman with a fringe of black hair and moon-pale skin. In her hand was a bow, aimed directly at Iseult. "No closer!" she barked in Nomatsi. "Or we will shoot."

Iseult did not obey. "Please!" she shouted, continuing to climb, unable to stop with Aeduan so near. "I am Iseult det Midenzi. *Please!* We need your help!"

For another two muscle-burning rungs, there was no reply. However, Threads all along the cliff—Threads Iseult was only just now sensing—shifted into alarm. Only then did Iseult realize the woman above her had no Threads, or at least none that she could see.

And only when she reached the end of the ladder and hands had grabbed hold of her did Iseult finally see who had called down to her. It was, of all the people in the universe, the one girl Iseult would have preferred never to see again. The one girl she had spent her entire childhood hating and avoiding.

Her mother's favorite apprentice: Alma det Midenzi.

TWENTY-NINE

✳

Alma.

There were thousands of people Iseult would have been less surprised to see. She felt sick. Like the world was closing in and she might retch at any moment. She was certainly on all fours, her stomach rebelling. Owl had curled into a ball several paces away, shivering. Her Threads doused again in shock.

"Get them water," Alma said, no inflection, only command. Threadwitches couldn't see other Threadwitches' Threads, so her emotions might have been anything. Rage, annoyance, shock, horror—Alma was so adept at stasis that Iseult had no way of knowing.

"Hunted," Iseult croaked, finding Alma's beautiful heart-shaped face beside her, with its ice-white skin and frozen undertones. "A Carawen monk . . . hunts us."

Alma nodded, as if she'd already known this. "He will be dealt with by our—"

"No." The word cracked out, interrupting in a way no Threadwitch would ever do. "He cannot be stopped easily. He is . . ." Iseult had to swallow. Gulp back the water now shoved into her hand. "He is a Bloodwitch. He will heal from anything you do."

Again, no reaction from Alma, even as the two women with her showed surprise in their Threads and on their faces.

It was incredible really. Alma had to know it was the same Bloodwitch who'd first hunted Iseult in Dalmotti—it was too rare a magic to be someone new. Yet she wore only perfect, unflappable calm as she declared, "We do not plan to harm him. Only capture him."

"There's . . . more." Iseult wiped water off her mouth. "A creature with silver Threads—I don't know what it is, but it has been following us for a day."

"Silver Threads?" Alma's voice betrayed skepticism even as her face did not. Then she turned to the cliff and pressed a brass spyglass to her eye. "I see nothing. It would seem only the monk followed you through."

In that moment, despite Iseult's heart still clattering too fast, despite her skin still searing with the memory of acid fog, and despite the fact that she seemed miraculously safe, the brightest sensation inside her was a foul, gray-tinged heat. It consumed her. Congealed in her belly.

Two months ago, she wouldn't have recognized it. She'd have had to assess and analyze and tease through emotions she wasn't supposed to have. Now, though, Iseult knew. Here was loathing, here was anger, and here was shame all tangled together in a knotted, clotted weave.

And as she sat there, watching Alma's perfect figure stare with perfect calm into the Solfatarra, an image formed in Iseult's mind. *Fat from a borgsha pot.*

Iseult stiffened. That was not her own thought, but the weasel's. The creature was nearby. *So easy to read,* she'd once said when she'd still been human. *All your fears gather at the surface, and I can skim them off like fat from a borgsha pot.*

Teeth clenched, Iseult schooled her face as best she could. She grabbed the shame and the loathing and the rage, and she muscled them down until they were locked in that tiny little corner behind her left lung.

Then, feeling slightly cool, slightly calm, Iseult sent Esme a thought of her own: *Stay hidden or they will kill you.* She hoped to frighten the weasel, or at least jolt her into silence. But her command only earned more borgsha, more fat, and the sense of cackling, gloating glee. As if she were truly Wicked Cousin. As if Iseult had fallen neatly into her trap.

And maybe she had. After all, the weasel had known exactly where she was leading Iseult and Owl, and she'd known exactly who waited at the end.

"He has been caught," Alma declared, fixing her golden-green eyes—beautifully wide set above her high cheekbones—on Iseult. "Is there anyone else we should be looking for?"

"Maybe. Yes."

"Then we will post more guards."

We. Iseult didn't have to speculate who that *we* might be. There was only one person Alma could ever mean.

The last time Iseult had seen her mother, Gretchya, had been two months before in Dalmotti beneath a willow tree's draping branches. Gretchya had tended an arrow wound in Iseult's biceps and declared that she and Alma would be traveling to Saldonica to join a tribe called Korelli. She had claimed she'd always planned to invite Iseult—that they wouldn't have left without warning—but Iseult hadn't believed her then.

And now she saw her instincts had been correct: this was not Saldonica, and this was not the Korelli tribe. The hunters wore thick wool and thicker furs, a style distinctive to eastern Nomatsi tribes. And Alma wore velvet pantaloons beneath her black Threadwitch gown, while a black scarf encased her neck and a vest of thick bear fur covered her torso. Nomatsis from the southwest wore neither fur nor hide; they believed it an insult to Little Sister.

Shame on Gretchya, Iseult supposed, for teaching her daughter too well. Now Iseult had caught her in all her lies—though it gave her no pleasure to be right. Only more loathing that she couldn't keep tucked away. It bled out from behind her left lung, feasting like some parasite upon her chest.

"Can you walk?" Alma asked, still watching Iseult. Scrutinizing her as if she could read her thoughts.

Iseult set her jaw. "Of course." She pushed to her feet and helped Owl rise. Then they hurried after Alma, already striding into a new stretch of forest, the Solfatarra's bite vanishing behind.

It felt as if they walked for miles before Alma finally led them into a Nomatsi encampment. There was no sign of the camp from afar—no smoke to plume. No noises to split the forest. Only old walls thrust up amidst the trees, crumbling ruins from a forgotten past.

As Iseult and Owl trailed around a curved stretch of wall that might have once been a tower, magic dusted Iseult's skin. It pulled the breath from her lungs, plucked the hairs on her arms. *Glamour,* she realized, even as the individual Threads of the spell shifted and fell away, revealing a new world.

It was at once so familiar and at once so strange. The round tents spaced evenly throughout the wide clearing were the inspiration behind the round structures in the Midenzi settlement, yet in place of roofs and walls, there were animal hides stretched over wooden scaffolding. Cooking fires were spaced throughout the camp, but they'd been recently doused, the embers covered with thick blankets. The only sound was the snuffling of horses hidden behind tents and ruin walls—which was where the people were too, their Threads animate. Alert. *Ready.*

They had been waiting for an attack, Iseult realized with a twitch of her nose. She must have triggered some warning system along the trail. But when, what, *where?* And for that matter, how was this tribe so well equipped? Alarm-spells were expensive, while the cost of a glamour-spell was unfathomable.

It was one more question to add to the thousands of others dragging Iseult down.

Soon Alma had reached a taller hut at the camp's center with a woolen blanket over the entrance—black, the color of all Threads combined, and sewn into the edges were the marks of a Threadwitch. A straight magenta line for the Threads that bind. Swirling sage green for the Threads that build. And a dashed gray line for the Threads that break.

Iseult's footsteps slowed. The heat in her chest had crawled down her legs, making them leaden and stiff. *Stasis, Iseult. Stasis in your fingers and in your toes.* She hated that she needed those words. Hated that they surfaced right now. But the truth was that she couldn't face her mother without them. Gretchya would never accept who Iseult had become.

Alma swept aside the blanket and waited for Iseult to enter. Iseult wished the other girl would look away. For that matter, Iseult wished Alma were anywhere in the Witchlands but here. *If only, if only, if only.*

Iseult thrust into the darkness. She saw nothing but lanterns flickering at the edges of her vision. Firewitched. Recognizable by the absence of smoke. Then she heard a voice. *The* voice that sometimes whispered in her dreams or scolded in her nightmares.

"Iseult," said Gretchya det Midenzi, no surprise in her tone. No surprise on the pallid face slowly emerging from the shadows. Beside her, at the heart of the tent, were the customary fire, a communal bowl of stew, and four low stools.

"Why have you come?" Gretchya asked. Her gaze traveled the length of Iseult, and it took all of Iseult's self-control not to curl in on herself.

Stasis. She notched her chin higher.

"Why have you come?" Gretchya repeated. Not, *Are you hurt, my only daughter?* Or, *How is this possible that you are here?* or even, *Who is this injured child with you?*

Instead, Gretchya asked a question that somehow, despite the lack of inflection, still held enough accusation to fill a galleon. *Why have you come?* Gone was the woman beside the willow tree, who had seemed, if only for a few moments, to have real emotions.

"I did not come here by choice," Iseult responded, her own tone just as flat. Her own expression just as cool. Her tongue was *not* fattening behind her teeth. Her throat was *not* clenching shut at the sight of her mother's emotionless eyes. "We were . . . hunted. By a Carawen monk."

She had to speak slowly, but she was proud when no stutter marked her words. *Control your tongue. Control your mind. A Threadwitch never stammers.*

"And this child"—Iseult pulled Owl gently in front of her—"needs a healer. Her wrist is hurt. Sprained, I believe."

Gretchya blinked as if only just noticing Owl. It was the closest thing to emotion that crossed her face; Iseult didn't know what it meant. "What is your name?" Gretchya asked.

To Iseult's shock and to her . . . her something else—something *hot* that wrinkled down her spine—Owl answered: "Dirdra det Allaeli."

Now it was Iseult's turn to blink. A month and a half she had been with this child, and only now was she learning her true name. Only now was Iseult's *mother* so deftly plucking it out of her.

Iseult had no time to dwell on this information, nor time to assess what this new heat might mean, for now her mother was sharing a look with Alma, as if that name meant something. And Iseult felt as if she were falling in the river from two days ago, but instead of ice to dunk her, it was flames. Because Iseult knew the look that passed between Gretchya and Alma. Gods curse her, she knew it well because she'd spent years watching them make it. But only to each other. Never to her.

Her fingers flexed taut at her side, her breaths grew shallow. And there, in the pit of her belly, was the anger again. *Yes,* she coaxed it. *Grow. Expand.* She had no trouble keeping her expression immobile when kindling burned inside. Even her nose, which usually twitched and gave her away, was as still as the stones surrounding the firepit.

"Iseult told us others hunt her." Alma folded her hands behind her back—perfect, perfect—and Gretchya's attention sharpened onto Iseult once more. "Who?"

"Corlant," Iseult replied.

At once, all Threads in the tent flashed with slate fear. All bodies stiffened, even Alma, even Gretchya.

And Iseult couldn't help but delight in those reactions. "There are Hell-Bards too," she said. "Because of Owl . . . *Dirdra's* collar. They have hunted us for days." To prove her point, she withdrew the map. "This shows where they are. None are near for now."

At Gretchya's nod, Alma took the map and unfolded it toward the nearest lantern. "This is valuable." She glanced up. "How did you get it?"

Iseult didn't answer, and fortunately, she was saved from having to by Gretchya. "It does not matter if the Hell-Bards are far away. Corlant approaches, and so we must leave." She snapped her fingers at the hunters. "Alert the tribe. We must move immediately." She waited until the women were out of the tent before squaring her body to Iseult. Like before, her gaze roamed up and down.

And like before, Iseult's parasite reemerged. "Three weeks we have lived here safely, Iseult. Then you shred our careful weave in a single morning."

The heat spindled wider, mixed with a new heat: a Puppeteer's heat. With *outrage*. After all, it wasn't as if Iseult had come here on purpose. It wasn't as if she'd known her mother and these Nomatsis were living in the middle of an acid lake.

But she got no chance to respond before her mother turned away. "Alma," she said, "take Iseult and Dirdra to the healer. If you need me, I will be dealing with the prisoner." Then without another word or even another glance for Iseult, Gretchya left the tent.

The reunion was complete. Iseult was dismissed.

※

Fourteen Days After the Earth Well Healed

afi watches the dancers. Rich gemstone colors stream and streak, thin silks and satins intended only for dancing. Worn once, never worn again. A waste that Merik Nihar would have scowled at.

But Safi cannot scowl—not when so many might see. She sits on this new throne and watches, a tiny smile to grace her lips. A genuine smile for she has a secret, and tonight that secret will come thundering outward.

Her newly sewn pocket scratches against her right breast, where the square-cut bodice dips low. Poorly added, but sufficient.

"You look disgusted," Henrick says. He shifts in his throne, the wood protesting.

And Safi realizes that perhaps her expression isn't as poised as she thinks, but she has always been good at quickly conjured lies. She is the right hand after all, always there to distract. To display.

"There is a war on," she replies, dipping her head toward the dancers. "Yet to look at them, you wouldn't know that Azmir burns or raiders come this way."

Henrick grunts, and several seconds drum past with only strings and footsteps to fill them. "You must understand, my Empress, that there is no war here. To these people, it is a distant thing fought by others—and I work hard to keep it that way."

"So you lie to them?"

"No." His forehead pinches, the skin reddened by the tightness of his crown. "The nobility are not stupid, and the common folk even less so. But as you will quickly learn, people take emotional cues from their leaders. If we are calm, then they are too."

It seems too simple, and yet . . . Safi understands. Vaness's iron demeanor keeps Marstok unified for years, even when not everyone loves or agrees with her. Meanwhile, tenants and farmers on the Hasstrel estate look to Eron for guidance and find only a broken man who drank too much.

It was all Safi had ever found in him as well . . . or so she'd thought until two months ago.

"You understand," Henrick says, and Safi nods.

She also understands that she has severely underestimated the Emperor. His eyes, fixed on her face, are not the vacant eyes of a toad. They are sharp and fathomless, and were Safi to meet him across a taro table, she would not agree to play.

True, true, true.

Suddenly, her new pocket feels aflame. Suddenly, sweat prickles out along her spine. "There are many raiders at the border?" asks, grasping any topic she can to deflect focus off herself.

"Many. And they are not just in the east, but have fortified in Poznin. I will show you on the maps tomorrow."

Safi bows her head as a thank-you, but when she lifts it again, Henrick still stares.

He knows, *she thinks.* He knows and he will act. *She offers a smile even as her toes curl in her slippers and muscles tense beneath her gown. She will not go down without a fight.*

Then his gaze finally breaks, dropping to her Threadstone, visible at her collar alongside the steel chain Vaness made her wear.

"An empress needs better jewelry," he declares, and he angles his body back toward the dancers.

Safi has to fight to keep her lungs from loosing, her shoulders from drooping. Sweat now slides down her back against the throne, and though she knows it looks strange, she drapes a hand over her Threadstone.

As soon as her fingers touch the ruby, warm from her skin, Iseult's voice booms into her mind. HE PLANS TO LEAVE, SAFI. PLEASE LISTEN. THERE WILL BE NO WEDDING NIGHT. WHERE ARE YOU, SAFI? HE PLANS TO—

"I'm here." *She whispers the words on a sigh, dipping her head sideways as if tired. As if taking in the view of dancers. But her fingers tighten on the Threadstone, and she mouths,* "Explain."

Henrick has no plans for a wedding night, *Iseult says.* He has no plans to consummate anything and he will leave the palace after the dancing.

Safi's stomach drops low. She wants to ask how Iseult knows this, but she dares not speak too much, even silently. Too many people watch her, including the Emperor himself. He glances at her sideways, and she smiles in return.

Iseult seems to understand the question anyway, for she adds, Caden told my guards to expect shift changes tonight because the Emperor is going into town.

Safi's heel taps, and though she keeps her smile pasted on, her mind is shrieking every swear word she's ever known. If the Emperor does not have a wedding night with her, then she cannot execute the final step in their plan. She needs to be alone with him, unguarded. As exposed as a person can possibly be.

"We need a new plan," she whispers, pretending to yawn and covering her mouth with her free hand. Before she can actually suggest one, though—or wait for Iseult to—Henrick reaches out and rests a hand on her throne's armrest.

"It is time to go," he says, and Safi realizes with a jolt in her knees that the music has ended. The dancers have stopped.

She's out of time, and she does not try to hide her sudden terror. She can feel that her face has drained of blood.

"Already?" she squeaks out.

And his perpetual frown eases into something almost kind. "You need not worry." He pats the armrest. "I have no intention of bringing you to my bed. A barbaric custom."

Please do! she screams inwardly. Please take me to your bed!

Aloud, she simply says, "You . . . do not want an heir?"

"I have one." Henrick runs his tongue over his teeth. Then: "He is well suited to succeed me and even better trained, so consider yourself free from my bed for the rest of your life."

No, no, no. This cannot be happening. All of Safi's and Iseult's plans are collapsing, for if Henrick will never take Safi to his bed . . .

That is the end of everything. This pocket at her chest and the golden item within are useless.

And there is nothing Safi can do to argue. If she presses the point, it will seem suspicious. Beyond suspicious—downright traitorous. Henrick knows she had no desire to marry him. She ran halfway across a continent to avoid it. If she suddenly insists on sharing his bed, those sharp, taro-playing eyes will understand in an instant that she is up to something.

All Safi can do is nod and push to her feet as Henrick pushes to his own. I am relieved, she tries to say with her posture. With her face. I have just been offered freedom and it is all I have ever wanted.

Yet each step off the dais feels a thousand years long. Each sweep of her skirts across the floor like slogging through mud. She has no time to come up with a plan, and no way to effectively communicate with Iseult. One hand is rested on Henrick's arm, and the other waves while she smiles. Always the smiling.

Ten paces become twenty become sixty, and the arched doorway from the room swallows her. In the hall beyond, Hell-Bards instantly arrange around them with Caden at the fore. Newly promoted and gleaming in his dress regalia.

Safi feels him try to connect eyes with her, but she dares not look. She must think, think, think like Iseult. If Henrick is going into Praga, he will likely take a carriage. That means he will go right at the gardens while Safi goes left to reach her quarters.

She has perhaps two hundred paces to make a plan.

Or to make her move.

And there is no other choice, is there? It's now or it's never. She can bide her time and hope for another opportunity—another moment of half solitude as they'd shared in the marble room filled with golden chains. But what if such a moment never comes?

Gods below, why can't Iseult be beside her right now? Safi is going to ruin this. She knows she's going to ruin this, and yet she sees no other course before her. Uncle Eron's life depends on her. Iseult's too, and little Owl's tucked away in the servants' wing.

All the Hell-Bards as well. She is Empress now, and she is the only one who can make a difference for so many people.

She will have to act fast. She will have to use every tool in her arsenal. The garden path will be dark, lit only by atmospheric lanterns, and presumably Henrick will pause briefly to take his leave of Safi. That will have to be her moment. She will have to make it count.

They reach the door that leads to the gardens. Footmen heave it wide, silent and unseen. Cold air billows in—welcome against all the sweat gathering on Safi's skin. Her heart thuds against her eardrums. The world is fast sharpening, as it always does during a heist. Ten steps and they are in the covered walkway. Evergreen ivy glistens in Firewitched light. Beyond, snow trickles down. So gentle, so at odds with what Safi is about to do.

Henrick slows to a stop to release her, and Safi slows beside him. "I will expect you at court tomorrow," he begins. "We begin at the tenth chimes—"

Safi kisses him. Directly on the lips and before he can pull away. Her free hand is already in her bodice, already in the secret pocket. She has the fingers of a thief, a nimbleness honed for almost a decade.

Before Henrick can react to her lips, she has the noose from her pocket. Then she snakes her arms around his neck and tries to deepen the kiss. Distantly, she is aware of how thick his lips are—and wet too. And distantly, she's aware of surprising muscles under his shoulders and along his back.

Then her hands are behind his neck and the noose is fastening into place.

Except that it's not.

Nothing happens when she tries to press the chain closed. It remains open, unattached, a useless piece of gold.

And now Henrick is shoving her off of him. His eyes bug, his mouth sputters. He grabs her arms and forces her back. "What the hell-gates," he begins . . . until he realizes what is clasped in Safi's fingers. She is too slow to drop the chain, and now he is watching it slip from her grasp.

It lands on his chest, then slinks down his stomach, a golden snake across muddy velvet.

For several seconds, neither Safi nor Henrick moves. The Hell-Bards all have their backs turned discreetly away; they have not seen. *I should kill him,* she thinks. *Before he kills me. But she is, again, too slow.*

Or perhaps Henrick is too fast. With shocking ease and skill, he swoops beneath her outstretched arms and tackles her to the ground. He is viciously strong, and Safi stands no chance.

Her skull cracks on flagstones. Her vision shadows, and everything suddenly moves a thousand miles away. The Hell-Bard armor clanks her way, and Caden's voice barks, "Protect the Emperor!"

And the Emperor himself bears down on Safi with snaggletooth and spitting tongue. "What a disappointment," he snarls, forearm digging into her throat. "You could have been a great leader, but now there is only one path for you."

He rolls off of her as two Hell-Bards lurch in. Her hearing is muffled, her eyesight uneven. She knows, in a far-off sort of way, that she has made a very dangerous mistake. That she has ruined not only her own life but the lives of all those people depending on her.

"Tell Paskella I will not be coming tonight," Henrick commands once Safi is on her feet. He will not even look at her. "And then take my Empress to the Hell-Bard chamber. It is time she learned what true obedience feels like."

THIRTY

There was no time inside the Well. There was only now. There was only all eternity, stretched and unknowable.

Vivia recognized the feeling as soon as it curled over her. It was her favorite feeling—the only thing to truly calm her during an attack. The only time she ever felt truly, truly safe. Except . . .

As she sank to the jagged bottom of the Well, as she watched her blood swirl and spread, she realized this water wasn't calming. It wasn't welcoming. In fact, it felt nothing like the waters of the lake beneath Lovats—her safe place, her secret place. There, fox fire spread across a cavern ceiling, and the presence, the life, the weight of the Well was a comfort. It was as sad as she. It was as lonely as she. And it was always glad to have her there.

Here, six cypress trees were just visible above the water, wavy shadows around the Well's edge. And here, the waters were not glad to have her. *Intruder,* they seemed to say. *Thief, usurper, false queen.*

She wanted to swim for the surface and break free from this strange, burgeoning rage. But she was too weak. She couldn't swim, much less rise.

And she *was* healing, even if the waters resented it and the Well wished it could withhold. *Not you,* it seemed to say. *Anyone but you.* It could not stop the healing, though, and as eternity drifted past, the flames inside Vivia receded. The blood stopped leaving her. Until soon enough, the only pain came from her lungs—desperate for air—and from her mind, still filled with the sense of disgust, disdain, disruption.

Once Vivia could swim again, she did. She frog-legged and spread her arms. She pushed and pushed, no help from the water, until the surface wavered in. She broke free. Air washed against her, spread through her lungs. She gulped and gasped and for several thudding heartbeats, she did nothing but tread water and breathe.

Then she sensed movement, heard splashing, and when she turned about, she found Vaness in the water too. "You are . . . healed?" the Empress asked.

Vivia nodded. Her throat and lungs still hurt too much for words.

"That is good." Vaness offered a tight smile, her limbs splashing to hold her afloat. "I was about to dive under to find you."

Still Vivia said nothing—now, though, it was not because she couldn't. The Well healed constantly; it had already soothed away the sharpness of her lungs overstrained.

No, she held her silence because she didn't know what to say. She had gone racing after Vaness—had killed and almost been killed—to protect an empress she would have gladly left to die two months ago.

Vaness seemed to follow the same thoughts as Vivia. Her cheeks pinkened. Her gaze darted toward the horizon and the sea, where night still reigned. "You saved my life. The assassin was Dalmotti, no?"

Vivia nodded. The waters were warming around her, the Well's strange anger receding. As if it had forgotten her. As if perhaps she'd imagined the entire thing.

"Why?" Vaness's hands reached up to rub water from her eyes, her legs paddling to keep her in place. "Why did the Doge refuse to help us then hunt us across the sea?"

"I don't know." Vivia's voice croaked out, though not from exhaustion. She felt anything but tired now, with the Well's healing touch to course through her.

And with Vaness so near.

Something ached low in Vivia's belly. *The Well*, she told herself, even as she couldn't take her eyes off Vaness's face. Her hair was coiled and wet against her head, while her arms and shoulders, shapely and defined, were somehow far more appealing with white cotton clinging to them than they ever had been in her most revealing gowns.

Vivia wanted to swim closer. Her fingers wanted to wipe that stray hair from Vaness's cheek.

No. She exhaled sharply. This was just the Well's magic. This was just the exhilaration of life when death had been so near. She turned away from Vaness, water splashing, and paddled for shore. A strong stroke while the gently roiling waters of the Well rumbled against her.

Vaness followed—of course she did—but Vivia dared not look back as she hauled herself onto the ramp out of the water. As she shook her arms and legs, and sprayed water in all directions.

And she didn't look back when she walked to the nearest cypress, its trunk hidden within a latticework of green. She braced a hand on the feathered leaves. They scraped her palm as she lifted her leg to wring out her pants. Ineffective. Pointless even, but she needed something to do.

Water dripped and splattered behind Vivia. She could feel the Empress exiting the Well, even if she could not see her. A lantern emanating light. A flame hawk billowing heat.

She kept her attention locked on her pants, on the squeezing and wringing. "How do you feel?" Vivia's voice came out rough and strained. "Did the Well help your . . . illness?"

"I feel good." Vaness's voice held its usual clarity, but there was something else there. Something that made the imaginary light, the heat off of her seem ten times stronger.

Vivia squeezed even harder at her shirt, stained in blood.

"This Well is different from the Fire Well." Vaness's bare feet padded over the flagstones. "A different . . . energy. But it heals, and that is what I needed. That is what *you* needed." She came to a stop several paces away, and Vivia tried to hide behind her arm braced against the tree.

But it was no use. She could still see the Empress in her periphery. Sodden and gorgeous and all wrong, wrong, wrong. Vivia dropped her hand, and with stout avoidance of Vaness's dark eyes and thick, wet lashes, she aimed for the horizon. For the ocean and an empty expanse where maybe she could breathe.

Vaness only followed, though, oblivious to Vivia's building panic.

Or perhaps wishing to push it, wishing to enhance it, for Vivia had scarcely made it five steps before the Empress caught up to her, and her delicate hand had grabbed hold of Vivia's wrist.

It was a fire so different from the fire of the knife. Before the Empress could speak, though, eyes caught on the sea. She was close enough to the plateau's edge to see more than moonlight sparkling on the horizon. Now she saw near shore, where reefs and rocks kept most ships at bay.

They had not stopped the Dalmottis. Their warships floated close enough for Vivia to see sailors. Close enough for her to see individual flags slapping across the masts.

Twelve of them, and each manned with cannons aimed toward the shore.

The Empress spotted it too, and with only a wordless glance passing between them, they spun together and ran. Away from the sea, away from the warships, away from whatever strangeness the Well had brought out between them.

At the foot of the Origin Well, a jungle awaited. Thick with ferns and pines, overpowering in its sound: cicadas, birds, glowing insects Vivia didn't recognize. For several moments, as she and Vaness staggered off the steep stairs that led to the Well, she had no idea where to go. She couldn't hear the ocean, couldn't hear the falls, and all around her was damp forest brightening with dawn's first glow. What had once been a path was now overrun by stinging nettle.

And those several moments of confusion made all the difference. Right as she'd decided which way to run—which way was Noden's Gift because the river, near and singing, slithered from that way—Yoris and his hunters coalesced from the trees. Tens of them, camouflaged and silent. Vivia might never have seen them if Yoris hadn't stridden directly toward her, slashing at nettle with his cutlass and face gleaming with the humidity. There was just enough sunrise to see his scowl.

"A valiant effort, Princess." He came to a stop fifteen paces away. "But ultimately a failure."

Vivia blinked at him. She had no idea what nonsense he was spewing, and her attempt to count the hunters was failing. They blended too well into the jungle, and each time she reached twenty-three, she lost count again. There was no missing their crossbows, though. Or their drawn blades.

Not that those would be any trouble for Vaness, whose bracelets coiled and whose blood—like Vivia's—now skipped with the power of a healing Well.

"Come peacefully," Yoris said, "and my people won't use their weapons."

Vivia scoffed. She didn't mean to, but the laugh simply burst out from her. "You think we're trying to escape? We were attacked by Dalmotti assassins, you old fool. And no thanks to your guards, we managed to stop them."

"Oh, we know about the assassins." Yoris beckoned to some unseen hunter in the trees.

Leaves rustled, and ferns parted. Then two hunters stalked out, and clasped between them was a familiar Windwitch in black. His head hung limp against his chest. Every few moments, he mumbled something and drool slid down his chin. Eddies of harmless wind swirled around him.

Drugged, Vivia realized—the same drug they'd used on Vaness, pre-sumably. But to make it worse, the man was wounded. It was almost in-visible in the shadows, with his clothing pure black, but the wetness of his breaths gave it away. And once he was fifteen paces away, dawn light glittered over a bloody hole in his shoulder.

Vivia had no pity for the man who'd tried to kill her, but the inhuman-ity of forcing him to walk and endure that wound untended was too far. "He needs a healer." She glared at Yoris. "Soon."

"And he will get one, when he returns to his ship."

"His . . . ship," Vivia repeated, and at those words, ice sifted through her. It settled in her belly and sank to her toes. "So you know of the ships beyond the Well."

Yoris smiled.

"And," Vaness murmured, her first word since the huntsman's arrival, "you *let* the assassins have us, no? I suppose the Doge has a better offer for you than your own king?"

His smile faltered. His eyes thinned. "I am loyal to my king and vizer, Marstoki *filth*." Spittle sprayed with that word. "But yes—his offer is a good one. We give you to them, and they leave without attack. It is hard to refuse something that saves lives."

The ice in Vivia's bones laced outward. She felt sick. She felt cold. She felt very small and very alone. For Yoris would not act without com-mand. He was a dog reliant on his master to know what to think, feel, do. He must have sent word to the capital as soon as he had Vivia in his paws. Then sent word again when these assassins had arrived with their offer. And if Vivia had to guess, the Doge was offering more than simply sparing Noden's Gift. There must be gold involved.

Or weapons. Her father could never resist weapons.

Of course it would come to this. Vivia didn't know why she'd ever ex-pected otherwise. Of *course* all her years of scraping and fighting and gush-ing praise upon a fragile, spiteful man had come to this.

"And to think I thought family mattered," she said to no one. She wasn't even sure the words escaped, or if they were entirely in her head. "All that ever mattered was the crown."

"He would not dare," Vaness said.

"And yet he did." Vivia lifted a single shoulder, her eyes finding Yoris's in the shadows.

And the old man nodded. "He did." Then he circled his arm once, finger pointing to the sky, and his hunters emerged from the forest. Their intent was clear: it was time to reclaim the hostages.

"Now if you will release your magics and surrender," Yoris said, lifting his own blade high, "then we can finish this trade. You two will go with the Dalmottis, and then the Dalmottis will sail away."

Neither Vivia nor Vaness moved. For several breaths, the only sound was the forest, humming through Vivia's veins.

"Think of all the lives we will lose, Princess." Yoris shifted his weight, face wrinkling with impatience. "Those ships will make short work of Noden's Gift, unless you surrender."

Vivia ignored him and turned her gaze on the assassin. "Why does the Doge want us? Why did he send you here?"

The man held his groggy silence. His blood had gathered on the pale earth, and if the hunters released him, Vivia feared he would collapse and be gone for good.

A hand slid onto her shoulder. The Empress moved near. "Their crossbows all have iron." She spoke in Lusquan—a language Vivia had not used or practiced in almost a decade. So strange was it, so unexpected, that it took her several moments to unravel Vaness's words.

"And their blades are made of steel. I could end every one of them in a heartbeat, Your Majesty."

"I . . . do not want bloodshed."

A tightening across Vaness's face, still damp from the Well. "Then I will shackle them."

Vivia nodded ever so slightly. *That* she could live with.

"Simply give me the signal—"

"Enough chatter," Yoris barked. "Come with us now and protect Noden's Gift. It is the least a good princess would do."

"Oh yes," Vivia replied. She straightened, letting her magic rise within her. The river was far, but the Well had enhanced her. She could reach it. She could use it. "Perhaps it *is* what a good princess would do, Yoris." She smiled at him. "But I am not a princess, you see? I'm a queen."

She lifted her arms toward the sky, and in perfect sync, Vaness lifted hers.

Arrows loosed, though not toward Vivia or Vaness. They sprang wildly from their bows, melting as they moved while cutlasses flattened and flung. The hunters yelped. Some tried to run, some tried to charge. But it was no use. A fully healed Vaness was unstoppable—and a fully healed Vivia was too.

In seconds, the hunters were pinned to trees, to the earth, to each other while water gushed in, a spout of power that cocooned Vivia and Vaness in an impenetrable curtain. No one could see them nor stop them.

And this time, as they spun to flee, they grabbed each other's hands and threw themselves into the first glimpse of sunrise.

THIRTY-ONE

✳

seult would not be dismissed so easily. After ensuring Owl was willing to follow Alma to the healer, she shot off after Gretchya—already fifty paces away. The two hunters who flanked Gretchya allowed Iseult to get near, and when Iseult barked, "Give us space," they actually obeyed.

Gretchya of course did not slow her loping pace across the tribe. Already, people collapsed tents, their Threads taut, bright with anxiety.

Your fault, Iseult's brain declared. *They have to run because of you.*

"Why are you here, Mother?" She hurried into step beside Gretchya. It was easier to fling out accusations than face the ones flinging in. "What happened to going to Saldonica?"

"Corlant happened." Gretchya did not slow, did not even look Iseult's way. "He caught us before we could leave Dalmotti."

"Oh." It was an easy answer. One Iseult had not considered. "But then why are you here? In the Solfatarra?"

"For the same reason you are. To escape Corlant. To escape his magic."

"Oh," Iseult repeated, and this time, everything settled into place like an anchor on the seafloor. *Firewitched lanterns in the tents. Alarm-spells on the trail. Glamours over the camp.*

"Everyone here is a witch. This isn't a true tribe at all, is it? You fled Corlant and have been hiding here."

"Yes." Gretchya gestured curtly to a group of Nomatsis collapsing a tent beside the ancient remains of a wall. They moved methodically, disassembling a skeletal wood interior with the silent rhythm of experience. Not only were their Threads briefly bound by the united focus of their task, but now that Iseult was looking—*truly* looking—she couldn't miss the hints of power. Faint yellow Threads for a Windwitch, orange Threads for Fire, and even the verdant green of a Plantwitch.

"It is not merely the Purists who have come to hate witches, Iseult. Corlant has drawn many Nomatsis to his cause, and they willingly hand over their family, their friends so that Corlant may, as he calls it, free them.

"A month ago, he began erasing Nomatsi magic. One by one, he took witches into his tent. And one by one, they came out, no longer bound to the elements that they had lived their whole lives by. Then, almost two weeks ago, he went away—and I was ready. I gathered as many Nomatsi witches and their families as I could, and I led them here."

Ah. Iseult's breath whispered out. So her mother was a champion of the people. Iseult should be impressed, she supposed. Perhaps even proud. Instead, all she felt was the festering in her chest.

"Where were you before? How did you know this place was here?"

"We were in the Windswept Plains. Corlant works with the Raider King, and the King sent Corlant west. When Alma and I and all the other witches escaped, we found this place by accident. It was safe and contained, so we remained."

Ah, Iseult thought again, and the festering expanded. It bubbled up her throat. All this time she'd thought her mother and Alma were in Saldonica; all this time, they'd been resisting Corlant in secret.

"So you are a hero then, Mother?" Iseult hated how petulant she sounded. How . . . how jealous. She was the Cahr Awen, yet here she was whining that Gretchya had become a hero. Or maybe that wasn't it at all. Maybe she simply wished she'd been a part of it. That it had been *her* at Gretchya's side instead of Alma.

How foolish. Iseult really should be used to that old ache by now.

Gretchya halted so abruptly that Iseult stalked two steps onward before noticing. She rounded back. "I am not a hero, Iseult. I did what had to be done."

"As did I by coming here."

"I saved these people. You condemned them." Gretchya's gaze skated past Iseult, soaking up the camp around them. The hurrying people, the soft voices, the Threads shot with fear but bound by a single purpose: escape.

Nearby, the false Aeduan's Threads flared. Wings hurtled skyward.

Gretchya's attention refastened on Iseult, green, sharp, and so familiar. "Did Corlant hurt you?"

Iseult reared back. This was not a question she'd expected, nor the faint flicker behind Gretchya's eyes. "No," she replied. "Though he tried."

A nod. Then Gretchya stared pointedly at Iseult's right hand. "And that?"

"Th-they . . . marked me in Cartorra." No, no—not the stammer. Not right now.

"Why Void instead of Aether?" Gretchya asked, even though Iseult could see in her eyes that she already knew.

The lie fell off her tongue anyway: "They mark all Nomatsis this way."

Something new flickered in Gretchya's eyes. A tightening along the lids, a pinching in the brow. Almost sadness, almost disappointment, except gone so fast, Iseult couldn't be sure.

Her mother didn't contradict her, but her next words made it clear she believed nothing Iseult said. "So it is true, then. The rumors of a new Puppeteer."

Iseult swallowed. Heat swept up her chest and face, and the urge to deny—to drop out more lies as easily as Safi or Mathew—expanded in her lungs. It had been so long since she'd felt this small or unwanted.

Iseult had done everything she could to mold herself into what her mother had expected her to be. But Gretchya had given up on her then, and she was giving up on her now. To her, Iseult would only ever be the daughter who had failed. The Threadwitch who could not make Threadstones, who could not weave herself into the tribe and one day take over as leader. She was an embarrassment to be hidden, a mistake to be forgotten.

A cold wind pulled at Gretchya's hair. "How many people have you killed, Iseult?"

A heartbeat pause. A heartbeat more of that instinct to deny. Then it was gone, and Iseult answered truthfully, "Many." Though she couldn't help but add: "They w-were going to kill me."

"And now you have led such people here."

"Not on purpose."

"But the damage is done all the same."

And just like that, Iseult was boiling in gray heat again. Her chest felt crushed, her tongue rolled flat.

Stasis, Iseult. A true Threadwitch shows nothing, feels nothing.

Her breath wavered.

Stasis, Iseult. In your fingers and in your toes.

Her eyes shuttered.

Stasis, Iseult. Do not shame me. Do not shame Moon Mother.

Iseult had never wanted to shame Moon Mother, she had never wanted to shame Gretchya. Not then, not now, not ever. It was inescapable, though, for she couldn't be the block of stone her mother wanted.

Yet she also couldn't be the effusive, expressive human everyone else expected. Only Safi had ever understood that, only Safi had ever really cared.

Sensing Iseult had no reply, Gretchya turned away.

"Wait."

Gretchya paused.

"D-do not hurt him, Mother. The Bloodwitch, I mean."

"I will not, Iseult, because Threadwitches do not cause pain. That is only for the Void. Only for people like you."

Aeduan knew the Threadwitch before him. Not well, but he had seen her at Corlant's side in the caravan out of the east. Her blood smelled of lavender and lullabies, of cold earth and colder gemstones. He had always believed her an odd companion for the priest, but a willing one.

Now, as he stared at her in the light of a brazier's glow, he realized he'd read her wrong. How else to explain this makeshift camp in the middle of a world of fog? He did not know if he should be impressed or annoyed.

Annoyed most likely, since he was now bound by chains to a column at the tent's center. He had tried to break free as soon as the two women who'd captured him had fastened his shackles and left, but his efforts had proven useless. More than wood kept this column staked within the earth.

"Why do you hunt Iseult?" the Threadwitch asked in thickly accented Arithuanian, her voice detached. Intractable. Iseult watched from a nearby shadow, and Aeduan's eyes cut to her as he said, "You know why. Just as you know you cannot escape him. He will find you here, exactly as he has always found you before."

If the words bothered the Threadwitch, she gave no indication. She merely stared up her nose at the monk. It was a distinctive nose, snubbed and small. Iseult's looked nothing like it.

"How many people follow you?" Gretchya asked, and Aeduan shrugged languidly. "I do not know."

"How far behind is Corlant?"

Again, he shrugged. Again, he murmured: "I do not know." But then he dipped his head toward Iseult and grinned. "She did real damage to him, so I doubt he will catch up anytime soon."

The younger woman shifted her weight. Then shoved out of the shadow. "What is the creature that hunts me?" she demanded.

And Aeduan lifted his eyebrows.

"With silver Threads." She strode closer, impatience in her movements though not upon her face. "Some monster. Ancient and huge."

He laughed. Just a scoff at first, but then a full chuckle. "You tell too many stories."

She blinked, her face betraying open surprise. It lasted only a heartbeat before she pursed her lips into nothingness. "How did you follow Owl and me?"

"I smelled you."

"Liar. You can't smell my blood."

"I can." He couldn't. "You reek of despair and loneliness."

The mother tensed, a mere fraction of movement. Then she snapped with atypical force: "If you do not offer us answers, then you are no use to us. When the tribe moves on, you will remain bound in chains. Corlant will not find you. No one will."

He laughed again, this time lolling his head like a wolf might bay at the moon. They would not leave him here. Iseult would not leave him here, for the dark-giver loved the man who'd worn this body before, and she still— foolishly—believed he was in here. Humans were always desperate like that. *Hope dies last,* as the Old Ones used to say.

Gretchya twisted away from Aeduan, and in the language Iseult always used, she barked something at the guards. Then she strode away, each step surprisingly long for a woman as petite as she.

Iseult did not follow. Instead, she waited until her mother was gone from the tent before approaching Aeduan. He bared a grin as she cleared the gap between them. She was so near, her nose mere inches from his. "You are no match for me, Old One."

Aeduan's grin fell. He hadn't realized she knew what he was.

"I went into death and brought him back, you see. The real Bloodwitch. The real Aeduan." With gentle fingers she reached for his face . . . only to pause several inches away.

And for some reason that made no sense, the air between them thickened. Like static heat swelling before a summer storm. He wanted her to back away. He wanted her to keep coming.

"I know he still lives inside you," she went on. Her fingers were not beautiful fingers, not shapely or fine. They were callused and too slender, with knuckles that felt too wide. He couldn't look away from them.

"I saw him in the forest. I even see him now." Her fingers inched closer. He did not move, he did not breathe. Then she dragged them sideways, floating just above his lips. Unbidden, his breath shuddered out.

"You know that I tell stories—something you can only know if you speak Nomatsi. Something you can only know if the real Aeduan still listens within." Her hand fell, and before he could understand what she intended to do, she leaned in close. Lips to his ears, breath along his neck. "*Mhe varujta, Aeduan. Te librahje ma-in, mhe varujta.*"

She drew back, her golden eyes briefly settling on Aeduan's face. Her lips briefly twitching with a smile. Then with fingers he hadn't prepared for, she dug out the silver taler hanging at his collarbone and snapped the leather thong to which it was attached. "I'll take this back now," she said.

Moments later, she was gone.

There were times when the real Aeduan could reach the surface and break through the being that controlled him.

One moment, he was nothing but darkness. No sense of self, no up or down, no existence at all. Then suddenly, he would awaken—on the move, as if a rope yanked him fast, a ship retrieving its anchor.

Or a Heart-Thread retrieving its other half.

He heard her in those moments. So near to him, even if he could not see. He would recognize her voice anywhere, smooth as a scythe and twice as sharp. Perhaps if he just swam harder, just *fought* harder against the claws that pulled him down . . .

There it was. For a fraction of a moment, he had cleared the surface. Light had swept in, carrying her golden eyes, her pursed lips, and the teardrop scar upon her cheekbone.

She was smiling, a hateful smile he'd seen before and hoped never to see again. A smile directed inward. A smile to break men's souls.

Then Aeduan was dragged under once more. Prey to be consumed at the bottom of the sea, his skin eaten off and bones picked clean. But that was all right. He could heal from that—and he *would* heal, because she would not let him die. She had saved him before, in the Aether Well deep in the Sirmayans, and she would save him again as long as their souls were bound.

Aether Well. The word licked through Aeduan's mind as the shadows closed in around him. *Something happened at the Aether Well.* He couldn't recall what or how, but suddenly he was certain: the Aether Well was where all of this had begun.

If only he could remember. If only he could break through and tell her . . .

But he couldn't and he didn't. At least not before the claws and the darkness grabbed hold and dragged him to the depths once more.

THIRTY-TWO

✳

Safi strode confidently toward the Emperor's quarters, down a hall she had hoped never to traverse again. The attendant she'd toppled several days before did not scurry up to meet her, but instead sent his comparably terrified partner.

"You cannot see the Emperor right now," the man said, bowing so low his head almost touched his knees. "He is detained."

"Yes," Safi drawled. "He is currently rutting with his mistress Paskella. I *know*, and I don't particularly care." She motioned vaguely toward the door. "I will wait in his study until he is done."

The first attendant choked. "He does not like for guests to wait."

"And I am not a guest. I am his wife." Safi took a single step forward, and both attendants dove into her path.

"We really must insist, Your Imperial Majesty. No one is allowed in there—"

"I will throw you again," Safi said to the first attendant. "And I will break both your kneecaps while you're down."

Though the man did not step aside, his eyes bugged sufficiently and neither he nor his fellow interfered when Safi marched for the door. Golden light shimmered ahead. Hell-Bard wards—which Caden had warned her about when they had figured out this new plan. The wards would keep out all unwanted intruders and, more importantly, keep *in* any unwanted sounds.

They would not, however, block Hell-Bards, and as Safi pushed the doors wide, a mist of power rustled over her. Comforting, calming, warm. She had not learned how to make these wards since, as Lev had said earlier, she had avoided the usual route of noosing and training. She suspected, though, as the magic slid over her skin, that it was linked to the Loom. To the colors and Threads she'd seen there. To the way Hell-Bards could draw on the life-force of one another to heal from mortal wounds.

Safi glanced back as the doors shut behind her and winked at the attendants. Then the hall was hidden; she was alone in the Emperor's study. As always happened during a heist, Safi's heartbeat sharpened in her chest. Her vision funneled down to only what she needed, only what mattered. She had been raised for moments like this one.

After crossing to a chair before Henrick's desk, Safi peeled off the chain. Cold instantly scudded through her. Fingernails made of shadow. But like the night before, it was easy to ignore. Especially when the colors of the room suddenly brightened.

Ah *yes*, this was the version of herself she loved most. The one built for action. The one who initiated, the one who moved. All that was missing was Iseult.

I'm coming for you.

She tucked the noose out of sight in the chair's cushion, then cut across the room to the Emperor's dressing room. Each step brought new noises into her ears, and by the time she gripped the knob and gently turned it, she could almost discern individual sounds.

Sounds she had hoped she would never have to hear, that made everything inside her curdle and cringe. Henrick, it would seem, was . . . *enthusiastic.*

The door opened silently. The noises beyond the dressing room increased, and Safi's wince deepened. This was, without a doubt, the most perfect opportunity to swap the golden chain and Threadstones—Caden had guided her well. But it was also disgusting, and she wondered if it was possible to cauterize one's brain.

Darkness shrouded Henrick's dressing room, but light from the study revealed shelves and cabinets and a suit hanging on a life-size wooden frame. Safi hurried toward it, hoping it was his suit from that day. That his belt would be draped around it . . .

It was not, and a quick scan around the room revealed no belt, no chain, no Threadstones. Safi was going to have to enter the bedchamber.

After carefully shutting the study door and creeping through the utter black to reach the bedroom door, Safi paused. She listened. The noises from within had shifted to feminine, which, although more palatable, were still more than Safi wanted to hear.

Perhaps even more uncomfortable was the fact that nothing in the Truth-lens hummed *false*. The woman on the other side of this door—his mistress Paskella—was genuinely enjoying herself with the Emperor. She was fully absorbed in her pleasure, and Safi hoped that meant Henrick was too.

With the lightest of fingers and slowest of movements, Safi turned the knob and squeezed back the door. An inch. Then two. Then three—enough to give her a full view of the space beyond.

It was not so different from Leopold's chamber: four-poster bed, fireplace (unlit), a single armchair. Heavy black velvet and glistening red brocades gleamed in the dim light of Firewitched sconces turned low. On the bed, two figures moved with great energy and surprising athleticism. They were, as Safi had hoped, wholly invested in each other. *Where are their clothes?* Safi thought, biting her lip. Henrick and his mistress must have undressed somewhere. The belt *had* to be near.

Then Safi spotted a haphazard heap beside the fireplace and pushed into the room, her eyes never leaving the thick curtains around the bed that hid Henrick and his mistress. Safi's brain would at least be spared *that* imagery.

She kept her posture low and her footsteps quick until she reached the armchair. Then she dropped to her knees and studied the heap. It was indeed the discarded garments of the Emperor, and after rummaging through the pile she found Henrick's belt.

She pulled it to her, head briefly hanging back. Success tasted so good. Even better than she remembered. Within seconds, she had the golden chain off and replaced by the one she'd obtained today in Praga. They were not identical, but a cursory glance wouldn't reveal the differences. Besides, the Emperor in his hubris would never expect her to steal his chain.

It took Safi longer to pry the Threadstones loose. Henrick had had them stamped into the leather, and she lacked decent tools to wedge the rubies free. Eventually, though, with enough prying and pulling, the two Thread-bound rocks popped loose.

And oh, how Safi smiled then.

She shoved both stones into her pocket along with the golden Hell-Bard chain, and withdrew two new uncut rubies. These were a much closer match to the originals than the chain was. Safi had touched her own Threadstone so many times, she'd known exactly what she was looking for while she, Svenja, and Nika had gone from shop to shop.

She'd also had the foresight to bring a small tub of paste with her. After verifying that Henrick and his mistress were not yet done with their revelry, Safi unscrewed the tiny tub, slathered out several dollops of pale cream onto the leather, then shoved the new rubies in. She waited several seconds, blowing lightly, before wiping away excess adhesive.

Lev had said it would take a full minute—at least—for this paste to dry. She'd also said, once that happened, the stones would not be coming loose anytime soon.

Unfortunately, a minute was more than Safi had. As soon as she'd finished wiping, a great scream filled the room. Then a second, in a two-part harmony that made Safi's stomach revolt. She hoped this woman was compensated for her time. *Well* compensated.

The crescendo ended, and silence descended. A net to cage in Safi. She went very still behind the armchair. Each of her breaths rasped overloud. If either Henrick or his mistress looked this way, they would see her shadow between the armchair's legs.

She dared not peek at them. She just sat there, waiting for the paste to dry while two people enjoyed a postcoital haze.

Please don't get up. Please don't get up.

They didn't get up. Instead, the sheets started rustling, and Safi suspected the two had settled in for a cuddle.

Inwardly, she screamed.

"Thirty-five years," the woman said, "and it is still everything I want." She had a deep voice, rough with age and time—and her accent was, to Safi's surprise, lowborn. This was *not* a typical courtesan and *not* a domna who traded favors for an emperor's time.

And thirty-five years? This woman and Henrick had been meeting for *thirty-five years?*

"How are the boys?" Henrick asked. "Did Dietrik get the money?"

"He did." Paskella laughed, an indulgent sound. A loving sound, and in tones filled with maternal pride, she described how Dietrik had repaired the roof and used leftover funds to make improvements in her kitchen. "He will be a fine builder," she said. "No witchery needed."

"He already is," Henrick replied.

Safi gulped. Almost dropped the belt, for just as maternal pride had thickened the woman's voice, *paternal* pride shone in Henrick's. No falseness in his words—no lies to shudder within her Truth-lens.

As he and Paskella continued their updates and questions, Safi realized three things. First, Paskella was indeed a commoner. Second, she and Henrick were Heart-Threads—true, *real* Heart-Threads like the children's rhyme. *Robins and magpies on branches above. Money for marriage, and Heart-Threads for love.*

And third, Henrick had not one, but *three* sons. Sons who didn't know he existed, sons who would never know he existed, yet sons whom he loved all the same. This was the reason he had never married. Here, in this room, was the reason he had consummated nothing with Safi. And the reason he had groomed Leopold so carefully to succeed his throne.

I am not so awful as you think me, he'd told her two days ago. *You will come to see that in time.* And then in the carriage he had said, *We are not all so lucky, you know,* in reference to building families with the ones we loved.

No, no, *no.* It was too much for Safi's brain to digest. She was not supposed to pity Henrick fon Cartorra. She was not supposed to respect his lifelong devotion to the family he could never have. She was not supposed to appreciate how the woman laughed, throaty and warm, or be impressed that she made no attempts to polish her words or put on airs.

Henrick fon Cartorra was a bad man. He treated his Hell-Bards like cannon fodder. He abused them, he broke them—all in the name of power. He had imprisoned Safi with a golden chain, he had imprisoned her uncle in poison, and he had trampled on smaller nations in the pursuit of dominance and war.

There are degrees of everything, Caden had once told Safi. *Which I know doesn't fit well into your true-or-false view of the world.*

No, it didn't fit, and Safi wished she'd never ever heard this conversation. She was *not* supposed to feel sympathetic toward her enemy. She was *not* supposed to feel this tiny niggling of guilt.

Her freedom mattered. Iseult's safety mattered. And just because Henrick had more sides, more dimensions, more depth, did not erase what he had done or why Safi had to flee.

With a slow, silent breath, she eased the belt—the paste now dried—onto the heap of shadowy clothes. She had what she'd come for.

Fortunately, the sounds of kissing soon filled the room, and when Safi inched her gaze around the chair, she found the curtains were starting to move.

It was definitely time to exit.

After confirming the gold chain and Threadstones were safely in her pocket, she rolled to her feet and tiptoed away. Moments later, Safi was back in the study and returning her noose to her neck. Then, with her breathing and heart only slightly elevated, she settled into the chair before Henrick's desk to wait for a final good-bye.

Iseult found her mother outside the prisoner tent, her two hunter escorts near but out of earshot.

"He is not what he seems." Gretchya uttered this as a statement, her eyes fixed on Iseult's face. Waiting for some emotion to cross, no doubt, so she could scold. Or perhaps waiting on the inevitable stammer to take hold of Iseult's tongue.

She would be disappointed, though. Iseult's mouth felt clear. The parasite had tucked back into its hole; stasis wrapped firmly around her bones. "I know." She met Gretchya's gaze, almost half a head below her own. "He is possessed. That is what the shadow birds mean."

"Shadow birds?" Gretchya's head cocked sideways, and Iseult realized in an instant that her mother hadn't seen them. Like the Severed Threads of the Cleaved, those shadows were only for the Void. Yet how had Gretchya known something was wrong with him? What had her Aether-bound Threadwitchery sensed?

"Did you do that to him?" Gretchya asked. "Did you possess him?"

For a fraction of a heartbeat, Iseult had no answer. Then it bubbled up against her will: she laughed. A real laugh with a real smile, and she didn't care if it wasn't very Threadwitch of her. She didn't care if her mother disapproved. "Of course I didn't possess him." She shook her head, eyes sweeping around the collapsing camp and the Threads blending and braiding nearby.

She opened her arms toward them all. "Monster though you think I am, Mother, I do not *possess* people. And I don't hurt them simply to hurt them. But why argue?" Her arms fell. "You will never believe me?"

Gretchya offered no reply. Arrguing was not something Threadwitches did—and certainly not where everyone could see. The two hunters had perked up at Iseult's laugh, and though they hid their interest behind stiff masks, they couldn't hide their curious, listening Threads.

Gretchya noticed the audience too, and with a lift of her chin, she strode away.

Iseult debated following. Part of her itched to keep their conversation going. To force her mother to talk to her—to admit her disgust, her disdain, her disappointment for the first time in her miserable life.

Another part of her wanted to twist around and stalk the other way. Flee while she could, find a quiet corner, and study Eridysi's diary, still hanging heavy in her pocket. She had fought Corlant to get it, and more importantly, she'd meant what she'd said to the false Aeduan: she would free him soon. *Te librahje ma-in.*

Leaving would be the proper thing to do. It would be what her mother expected, what everyone expected. *Stasis, Iseult, stasis in your . . .* The refrain trickled to a stop. She had abandoned stasis two weeks ago; she couldn't let herself fall into it now. Besides, after Gretchya sounded so much more enticing than walking away. This fizzy chop in her chest, like a river churned by storm, wanted an outlet. It was *accustomed* to having an outlet after weeks on the road, weeks as a Voidwitch, weeks as the Puppeteer.

So she gave in, a small smile playing at the edge of her lips as she stalked after Gretchya. This must be how Safi always felt, letting emotions and fire rule.

"The healer's tent is that one." Gretchya pointed at one of the few tents still intact; weak smoke coiled from its heart.

"I don't seek the healer's tent. I seek you." Iseult studied her mother's profile. "How did you know something was wrong with the Bloodwitch?"

"The same way a healer senses rot within a wound. There are some things one simply recognizes as wrong." She didn't add, *Like you*, but the words drifted between them anyway.

And Iseult's hunger for a fight ratcheted higher. "You may hate my magic, Mother, but *you* were the one who made me. I am of your blood, whether you like that truth or not."

Gretchya conveniently did not reply. Instead, she said: "You will travel with us for a time, but because of the heretic's collar, the child cannot stay."

"You would abandon her? What a great hero you are."

The hunters' Threads winked with surprise and revulsion, tropical blue twined with taupe.

"She is only a child," Iseult continued, "yet you would leave her behind to fend for herself?"

"Many people are under my protection, and Dirdra is a liability—"

"She is a *child*." There was the laugh again, bursting free from Iseult's chest. Shrill and hollow. The Threadwitch tent was only a few paces away, and soon her mother would enter. Soon their exchange would end. So Iseult added, loud enough for the hunters to clearly hear, "Fortunately, *Mother*, the child has me to protect her. We've made it this far without any help. We'll continue on alone."

She ground to a halt though her mother moved on. The hunters had heard this exchange; their Threads mashed with disgust and confusion.

This is your hero, Iseult thought at them as they marched past. *Do you respect her still?*

Gretchya paused at the tent's black entrance, forcing the hunters to pause too. She was absolute stasis, no shame to trip up *her* tongue. No guilt to flush on *her* face.

Goddess, what must it be like, to walk through life unfeeling. A true absence of emotion, no Threads that bind or break or build to ever pull her up or pull Gretchya down. A life without pain . . . And a life without love. But people *were* Threads, and every time Gretchya had denied her own, the less human she had become.

"Where will you go?" Gretchya asked without turning.

"Back to Praga. Where I've been planning to go all along."

"You cannot. Hell-Bards block the way. I have seen the map you brought."

"I have evaded Hell-Bards before."

Gretchya peered back. "And what is in Praga?"

"*Who* is in Praga." Iseult lifted her eyebrows, challenging her mother to press on. "Safi."

Gretchya didn't. Instead she said, "In that case, I can be of no help to you." She swept into her tent. The flap swung with brisk finality.

And a laugh crinkled in Iseult's lungs again. A laugh fed by flames because her mother had not changed and never would. It was good to know that—and even better to leave with a certainty there was no reason to stay.

With a sharp nod for the hunters now claiming positions before the tent, Iseult turned on her heel and set off to find Owl.

THIRTY-THREE

✳

Iseult's anger did not last. She wished it would—goddess, she wished it would. It was so much easier with that heat to keep her moving. So much clearer with that burn to sharpen her eyes.

But anger required energy, and Iseult had none left to give. After days on the run, her insides had been scooped out. She was a human-shaped husk. When she finally stumbled into the healer's tent nestled beside a larger expanse of dark stone wall, familiar Earthwitch Threads awaited within, as did the Threads of an Airwitch healer.

Iseult entered at the tent's closed flap. Heat rolled over her. Heat and darkness lit by lanterns. Firewitched, of course, just as other magic items filled the tent, clustered on crude shelves: Painstones, jars of Earthwitch healer salve, bottles of Waterwitch healer draughts, and countless tools she did not recognize.

At the opposite corner beside a smokeless brazier, Owl sat upon a low table. On one side was the healer, young and amply curved within her furs. On the other side was Alma, smiling a false smile at Owl—who smiled right back, her Threads rosy with pleasure, her eyes locked on Alma's face, as if she had never seen anyone more captivating. As if she'd never adored anyone more in her life.

Because of *course* that was how it would happen. Owl had known the Threadwitch apprentice for less than an hour, but already she was enamored. Alma's perfection could be denied by no one, not even an injured child. Or *especially* not by an injured child on whom Alma plied her fake, forced, perfectly performed smile.

Meanwhile Iseult had been with Owl for six weeks, protecting her and feeding her—giving up her own food just so the child could eat—and yet not once had Owl looked at her like that. Not once had she giggled at something Iseult said.

And she certainly had never willingly reached for Iseult's hand as Owl was doing right now with Alma.

Alma laced her fingers in Owl's and smiled even more brightly. The healer worked on in silence. And Iseult stayed rooted beside the tent's flap. She could leave before anyone saw her. She could leave before this thick, oozing heat reawoke.

Leave, came a voice like the weasel. *Leave the tent and leave the child. You do not need her. She slows you and attracts Hell-Bards. Think how much faster you could travel without her. We could be back to Praga in days.*

Iseult didn't deny this. She couldn't. Now that she had the diary, there was nothing to keep her here. She could march right back across Cartorra and face the Hell-Bards, destroy Henrick, finish the plan she and Safi had first set in motion a month ago.

For some reason at that thought—the thought that had sustained Iseult for three weeks—Gretchya's face filled her mind. The way she'd looked, expressionless though she might have been, when she'd spotted Iseult's Void mark. The way she'd declared, cold as the Sleeping Lands, *Threadwitches do not cause pain.*

"No," Iseult whispered. To herself, to the weasel, to Gretchya's frozen face. "I won't leave her." Then she cleared her throat and walked fully into the lanterns' glow.

Three heads turned. The healer's Threads brightened with grassy curiosity. Owl's sank with pale wariness and her adoring smile for Alma frosted into a scowl.

"Iseult," Alma said, the same false happiness to lace her features and her voice. So convincing. Much better than Iseult had ever been at pretending to feel. She released Owl to quickly cross the space. The healer nodded a greeting and resumed slathering salve upon Owl's wrist.

"Dirdra is such a good child," Alma murmured once she was close enough for Iseult—and only Iseult—to hear. "How did you find her?"

A fresh round of bitter laughter burbled. *A good child.* She squashed it down and arched a razor-sharp eyebrow. "How do you know her name? I saw the look you and my mother shared."

"Ah." Alma's fake smile smoothed away. "Corlant sought her. He expected her to be delivered, in fact, when we were in the Sirmayans. But someone killed the raiders who'd taken her. You, I suppose?"

It had not been Iseult, but Aeduan. Back in the Contested Lands, where death had razed like wildfire. Yet there was no point in explaining this—it was too complicated, too tiresome. Fortunately, Alma's attention had already slid back to Owl.

"The child is a witch?" she asked.

"An Earthwitch."

"What type?"

"No type. She is a full Earthwitch."

"Oh?" The faintest twitch hit Alma's eyes. *Surprise*, Iseult recognized—and the young woman hadn't managed to hide it. *Perhaps she is not so perfect after all.*

Iseult's delight was short-lived, for Alma didn't seem to care that she had shown emotion. She seemed to relax into it, her melodic voice shifting to almost conversational. "I didn't know full Earthwitches existed anymore." She tapped a finger against her thigh. "No wonder Corlant wants her."

"Or maybe Corlant wants her because of who she *used* to be." Iseult scrutinized Alma's face as she said this, hoping for some reaction. Hoping for some clue that the Threadwitch might know more than she let on. But Alma offered nothing. She only shook her head and glanced Iseult's way.

"Used to be? What do you mean?"

"Nothing." Iseult pushed away from the flap before Alma might press for more. In five long strides, she'd reached Owl's side. The healer's work was finished, and a tiny Painstone winked against the girl's chest. Gone was any sign of steel pain in her Threads. Now there was only hostility and exhaustion.

Which of course Alma could see. Iseult's molars ground in her ears, and though she *knew* she ought to start with gentle words—perhaps even ask how the child was feeling—all that came out was a curt "We must move on now, Owl."

"Move on?" Stubborn gray wefted up her Threads. "Why? I don't want to." She looked at Alma, and strands of green Threads reached, *reached*. The Threads that build, looking for a connection. Looking for someone to listen and care.

But Alma didn't care. Not really. She would leave Owl behind just as Gretchya would, and pretending otherwise would help no one. Least of all this little girl with a magic everyone hunted and a past that was not her own.

"They do not want us here," Iseult answered simply. "And so it is time we leave." She offered Owl her hand. The child didn't take it. Instead, she stared at Alma, those green tendrils still straining for humanity of any kind.

Iseult hated how familiar it was.

All she had ever wanted in life was a place to call her own. A home, true and steady, where she would never be afraid. Where she would never feel unwelcome. But she did not belong here, with her Severed Threads and her Void magic, any more than she had in the Midenzi settlement, tucked away from the world with a magic that could never be what her mother wanted. She had not belonged in Veñaza City. She had not belonged in Praga.

Either she was too Nomatsi, or she was not Nomatsi enough. Either she showed too few emotions, or she showed too many. And now Owl was facing that same truth, the same knife she could never escape. *You are unwanted.*

Owl must have seen something on Alma's face—something that even Iseult missed—for her Threads abruptly stopped reaching. Abruptly reversed course, shriveling in while grief-stricken blue laid claim.

Her lip wobbled, but she did not cry, and heartbeat by heartbeat, more of that green determination that made Owl who she was assembled around her Threads. Until at last, she took Iseult's hand, a weak grip but an accepting one all the same.

And something warm and new unwound in Iseult's lungs. Something she'd never felt before but had craved every time another person had sent her away. Such a different heat from the Puppeteer rage, such a different heat from the tongue-thickening shame.

Maybe she and Owl were not enemies after all.

"Thank you," Iseult told the healer as she hefted Owl off the table, the child's eyes holding hers. "We are grateful for your help." She didn't wait for a reply before guiding Owl toward the tent's flap.

Neither she nor Owl looked at Alma as they passed.

There was a way out of this prison tent. That much Aeduan knew—that much had ebbed to the surface, knowledge gleaned from the first Aeduan. Knowledge the new Aeduan should have tamped down . . .

But that he also was desperate to use.

The young woman named Iseult had unsettled him. Weakened him for just long enough that the other soul had clawed upward and seen this world, seen this tent . . . Then he'd overwhelmed Aeduan with a certainty that there was an escape here. It had something to do with his magic, something that Iseult should have seen but failed to protect against.

So now the new Aeduan was puzzling his way through what exactly his escape might be.

He was a Bloodwitch, that much he knew. And he had power over blood so vast that people feared him. Called him *demon* when they thought he could not hear. Even the Raider King had looked at him with mild fear during their journey. But Aeduan still had not tapped into all the nuances and corners of this magic. He still, despite relying on it more and more each day, had no fathoming of just how much he might do.

He could move his muscles faster. He could track people by scent. And what else? What more?

Control. The word curled up from the deepest recesses of Aeduan's body, of Aeduan's brain. It was the first soul again, and Aeduan's initial instinct was to punch it back down. Stopper it behind the walls he'd buried it in.

Except the word came again: *Control,* and this time Aeduan knew exactly what it meant: he could control people's blood. Anyone that he could scent, he could command. Which meant that the hunters watching him stood no chance. It meant these chains could be unbound in an instant.

Oh, what power he'd had within him for a month, yet he'd never known. No wonder people feared him. No wonder the Raider King had tensed whenever he was near. Such power was almost godlike.

And such power was truly worthy of the person he had once been.

Aeduan inhaled as much air as his lungs could contain, ribs bowing wide. The guards' bloods coruscating against his senses. From the woman came a scent like a grandmother's wrinkles and the tang of blood on steel. And from the man was wind from the north and bison fur still warm.

Control, the first soul nudged again, and so Aeduan did. Clumsily at first, his fingers shaping into claws behind his back, behind the column. He grabbed at the closest hunter—the woman—and squeezed.

But it felt like pawing at the breeze. He could *feel* her there, could even stretch his magic to reach for her, but he could not grab hold. His magic grasped nothing but empty air.

He tried again, this time focusing on the man. On the bison he had clearly hunted, on the Windswept Plains where he had clearly lived. There were deeper folds to his blood. *A child's laughter. A wine made from berries heated in the sun. A woman's smile, one tooth crooked in front.*

Aeduan inhaled more, all focus on the blood. On each new element rising to the top as he explored. *Dogs barking. Fresh bison milk. The scrape of a knife on wood.*

There. He had enough. *There.* He had finally grabbed hold. And now, as he squeezed, he took control—except that it was so much more. He was slithering inside, moving through veins and feeling the thump of a heart beating strong. He could stop that heart. He could freeze those veins. He could end this man's life in an instant.

Control, the first Aeduan reminded. *Only control.*

It annoyed him, but the first soul was right. Death would serve no purpose here, at least not before Aeduan was free. So with hard, magic-fueled concentration, Aeduan spread his power into the man's limbs. First into his arms, where he unfastened the keys at his waist. Then into his legs, where he sent the man stepping, one foot, then two, toward Aeduan.

Each movement was halting and crude, but the man could not resist—and the second hunter watched with too much confusion to intervene. It wasn't until the man was almost to Aeduan that she finally called out in that language he didn't understand. And it wasn't until the man was behind Aeduan, a key grating into Aeduan's locked chains, that she finally abandoned her post to hurry toward them.

But she was too late, too slow. By the time she was there, the chains had clanked to the ground. Aeduan was free.

He released the man's blood, dumping it so fast the man collapsed. Not dead, but unconscious. Then he grabbed on to the woman. On to her blood and her body, his fingers clutching at her throat. His magic clutching at her veins.

She had just enough time to widen her eyes in horror before her breath choked off. Before she too went limp and hit the floor.

Aeduan smiled. Oh, what power indeed. No one could stop him, no one could contain him. Not even the Old One named Evrane. Not even Corlant with his Purists always around. There was only one person he could not control. A young woman with no blood-scent—a young woman with a power from the Void.

And a young woman who knew exactly what Aeduan could do, yet she'd said nothing and warned no one. Instead, she had taken the silver taler stained in his own blood so he could follow her. So he *would* follow her. Why? As long as she lived, she was a risk to him. She had to know he could not leave her free.

The reason didn't matter, he decided as he reached the tent's flap. He was coming for her, and neither she nor the first Aeduan, still wrestling within, could stop him.

If Iseult was lucky, she would never see Alma or Gretchya again.

It wasn't as if she'd wanted to stop in the Solfatarra, no matter what accusations her mother might have flung at her. Gretchya and this tribe had been an interruption in her path, an inconvenience blocking her way. They had neutralized Aeduan for her; now Iseult didn't need them; she could dismiss them as easily as Gretchya always dismissed her.

Each step away from the healer's tent brought clarity to Iseult's veins. Men had died at her fingertips, and people had whispered her name in fear. For once, on the road, she had been the one making the choices and the one making change.

But Gretchya and Alma didn't see that—and they wouldn't care if they did. They would only hate her more because it would be the final proof that Iseult was bound to the Void. That she would never fit into the tribe's weave and never follow in Gretchya's perfectly placed footsteps.

Iseult half ran, half skipped due west, back the way they'd come. Back toward Praga and Safi. She was exhausted, she was drained, but anger had gotten her this far. It would get her the rest of the way. Owl kept silent and obedient beside her. Dark clouds scudded across the sun as they moved; snow began to fall. A light, fluffy snow that Iseult would have thought beautiful several weeks ago.

Now she knew such snow made tracks easier to follow. Now she knew such snow killed, gentle as a mother's embrace.

Soon conifers and old-growth forests swallowed them, muting the snow, and Iseult sensed hunters approaching. Three sets of hostile Threads—while countless more waited beyond. Then the first hunter reached them: a gray-haired woman, broad shouldered, with a carving knife drawn. "You are not allowed to leave."

"On whose orders?"

"Our Threadwitch. No one leaves without her approval."

"And I have it." Iseult pumped authority into those words and copied her mother's stiff posture. "Is there a trail leading through the fog?"

The woman hesitated. Then shook her head. "No." Fresh aggression crystallized in the hunter's Threads. "You're not allowed to leave anyway. Come with me."

Before Iseult could argue—or fight back—footsteps pounded close. Footsteps without Threads. Then Alma appeared, her face beautifully flushed. Owl's face lit up. Her Threads too.

"They have Gretchya's permission," Alma declared, only slightly breathless. "Leave us."

The hunter frowned. Alma's eyes thinned. And finally the hunter cowed, slinking away into the trees. Alma didn't wait for her Threads to disappear before rounding on Iseult. "Thank Moon Mother you aren't gone yet." Nothing in her face showed relief. "I ran as fast as I could." In one hand she held a small traveling satchel. "Take this. It isn't much, but it will last a few days."

She thrust the satchel at Iseult, without waiting to see if Iseult wanted it. "And these." Alma held up her other hand, revealing wind-spectacles. "They'll let you see without damage to your eyes. Oh, and this." She fumbled something from her pocket. Vellum and worn.

It was the Hell-Bard map.

A sensation Iseult didn't know wrestled to life in her chest. Both heavy and light at the same time. Both cold and warm. *Confusing.*

"Take it." Gripping Iseult's hand, Alma opened the fingers and placed the rolled page upon her palm. "You need it more than we do." Alma released her, but Iseult didn't lower her hand, didn't close her fist around the map.

"Why?" she asked. "Why are you helping me?"

"Because," she said, her gaze dropping to Owl. Kind eyes, thoughtful eyes. "Moon Mother always protects her own."

But I am not one of her own.

"Thank you," Iseult said, and she meant it. After shoving the map into her pocket and slinging the satchel onto her back, she repeated: "Thank you." Then she did something she'd never done to anyone but Safi—and certainly never to Alma. She grabbed her in a quick embrace. Too fast for Alma to pull away. Too fast for Iseult to reconsider.

Then she released the other woman's shoulders, grabbed Owl's hand, and led her toward the Solfatarra. Owl's Threads drooped with disappointment, blue melting off the sage Threads that build. But the child would forget Alma soon enough, just as she'd forgotten Zander and Leopold and even her precious Blueberry. At least this time she had the Painstone to numb her heart to any pain.

Strangely, Iseult wished she had one too.

They did not travel far before Iseult pulled Owl beneath a broad spruce tree, its branches a skeletal frame insulated with sharp, freshly scented needles. Iseult unpacked the satchel from Alma while Owl watched on curiously. With much drama—as if she were Safi opening a birthday present—Iseult withdrew item after item for Owl to see.

First, she found a roll of fresh linens and a small jar, which turned out to be a willow-bark salve. "This will help your wrist," she told Owl in what she hoped was a cheerful voice.

Next, she withdrew a wheel of cheese (goat, judging by the smell) and bundle of smoked meat strips (also goat). She gave one to Owl for gnawing, even as the girl made a face and her Threads fluttered with disappointment. Two weeks ago, Iseult had discovered the child hated goat. One week ago, Owl had realized that sometimes it was all she got.

Next came a water bag, empty but still useful. And last, Iseult withdrew a wool blanket, thin and cream-colored. She draped it over Owl. "Tell me a story," Iseult whispered while she opened the jar of healing salve and set to carefully slathering it on her neck, her hands, her collarbone. All the places the Solfatarra had bitten.

Owl obeyed, her words muffled by tough goat meat. "Long ago, when the gods walked among us, Trickster took pity on a little witch and her pet hedgehog."

When she'd finished the tale and was singing the final refrain once more—*Save the bones, save the bones!*—she seemed to have forgotten the cold. Her little breaths still fogged, but the rich gray of discomfort was gone from her Threads.

So Iseult took her chance to steal away and fill their water bag. There'd been a small stream nearby, frozen over and possibly acidic, but worth examining. She reached it in minutes, the icy surface covered in fresh snow, and after crouching on the shore, she tapped gently at the ice. It reminded her of the Aether Well. *Threads that break, Threads that die.*

A single punch, and the ice cracked. Then Iseult swept it away, savoring the cold and the black waters now peering up at her. They did not burn her skin, nor stink of sulfur. Snow fell, vanishing on the water's gentle roll. Iseult's reflection was twisted, a shivering shadow that carved the world in two. She looked as she had two weeks ago in Praga . . . yet somehow completely different.

I look like Esme. Not in features—Esme had been one of the most beautiful young women Iseult had ever seen—but in energy. The softness of Esme's face and body had been hardened by a frantic edge.

Iseult had that edge. Maybe because, like Esme, she had been run out of her tribe. Or maybe because, like Esme, her magic was an abomination of gray, gray, gray.

We are just alike, she used to tell Iseult. *We must weave Threads when we can—and break them when we have to.* Iseult had always shied away from those words. She had denied them and fought them and pretended they were not true. She was not like Esme; she was not a Puppeteer.

Until the day when there had been no more running. Esme had been right all along: Iseult did have the need to change things, and she did have the hate to do it.

She also had the tools.

She pulled away from her reflection and eased Eridysi's diary into the afternoon's light. The entire tome, hers for the reading. Hers for the learning. After a glance in Owl's direction and finding the child safe and calm, she peeled back the diary's cover. New leather creaked. Snow landed on the first page.

And Iseult began to read. It was like being handed a key to the universe—except better. This was a key to her own magic. A key to what she could become.

She began where the ripped-out pages ended: raising the dead. It was not true life such magic could create. Void magic had its limits; Portia had only created a *semblance* of returned life. A reanimation with Threads that could not last.

But Eridysi had scribbled notes about what might be done if an Aether-witch attempted the same spell. Her theories and speculations, her diagrams and details filled page after page. Not just on reanimation either, but on cleaving and death. On ghosts and the afterlife, and even on a young shadow wyrm Portia had found a way to kill.

She also had an entire eight pages dedicated to Threadstones. She had apparently worked directly with one of the most famous Threadwitches who'd ever lived, named Vergedi. And where Vergedi had made stones, Portia had cleaved them for power.

Iseult hadn't known you could sever a stone's Threads.

The diary went beyond mere spells too—beyond manipulating Threads and recording Portia's experiments. Eridysi wrote of her life in the Sight-witch Sister Convent. Of the days when she was dragged, all the way across the Witchlands, to live in Portia's decadent court and watch the world descend into chaos.

For that was what had happened in those days. The Paladins had been the only witches in the land, and that power had corrupted them. Instead of supporting rulers chosen by the people, they had become the rulers themselves. Tyrannical. All powerful. Unstoppable.

And Eridysi had watched it, helpless to intervene—and helpless to stop her own fascination with the power Portia had wielded. With the power they all had wielded.

> Theirs is so different from the raw magic inside the mountain, and yet the source is the same: Sirmaya. Midne tells me, in her soft tones, that when she and the other Six enter the mountain, she feels as if she is coming home.

That was the name Corlant had used. *Midne*. Lev had used it too, all those days ago, claiming Midne had been the first Hell-Bard, the first to have her magic expunged . . . And it was true. Iseult found that page within the diary too: the creation of the first Loom. Eridysi had recorded every step with scientific detachment. A stasis Iseult recognized; a stasis she appreciated. Horrible things had happened. All Eridysi had been able to do was bear witness.

And when Portia had cleaved her fellow Paladin, Midne, to build the first Loom, Eridysi had borne meticulous, detailed witness. Here was how she'd cleaved the other Voidwitch. Here was how she'd kept Midne alive—stopping the cleaving before it could fully consume—and here was how she'd used that raw power to build her Loom, binding it to a basin beneath the earth, where Sirmaya's Threads were closest to the surface.

The first Hell-Bard. The first Loom, and all of it laid out step by step upon the page. If Iseult wanted to, she could make one too.

Her mind teemed. Her thoughts skipped from one to the next, unable to settle. Unable to slow. *Building a Loom. Reanimation. The Dreaming.* So much to absorb. Too much for a few minutes of reading. *Midne. Portia. The Sightwitch Sisters.* What could Iseult do with this knowledge? What could she become? *Threads beneath a mountain. Aetherwitches. Sirmaya.*

Other thoughts slipped into her skull too. The words Owl had just sung. *Save the bones, save the bones, lost without them, have no home.* And all the stories she'd told in the past two weeks. *Long ago, when the gods walked among us.*

Iseult's breath slid out, and she ran her thumbs along the diary's cover. Somehow, this book had lasted a thousand years. And somehow, simple paper held more power, more potential than she'd ever known possible.

This diary was her destiny. This diary was her path. All she lacked were two things. Then she and Owl could brave the Solfatarra once more.

"Esme?" she whispered to the forest.

It took a moment for a response to come. But when it did, it was strong—overwhelming in its power. A warm sunset inside Iseult's mind. If Esme had still been herself, she would have been smiling, one dimple carving in deep.

There was something else there, though. Something deep and anxious.

Where are you? Iseult thought. *We won't leave without you.*

Another quaver of sunset warmth, and then branches rustled on the other side of the stream. Moments later, a streak of white slithered from the shadows.

Iseult shot to her feet, delight sparking in her muscles. The weasel reached her and scuttled up her leg with a familiar scratch of claws. "Where have you been?" she asked as Esme wound around her neck.

Hiding, the weasel replied, sharing an image of forest, forest, and more forest steeped in white.

Then came the image of Aeduan, his eyes ablaze and nose sniffing. Snow gathered on his shoulders and hair. *Near,* Esme said. *He is coming.*

THIRTY-FOUR

✳

The shadow birds reached Iseult and Owl first, carried on Threads of green determination. What Iseult didn't know was what Aeduan might be determined to do. His face offered no hint as he pushed beneath the spruce branches, carrying snow and winter air with him. He moved as he always did, feral and caged. Not so different from the true Aeduan, yet marked by just enough discomfort that Iseult would never mistake them.

Iseult sat beside Owl, and to her relief, the Painstone's power thrummed on. Owl was neither surprised nor scared nor even particularly interested that Aeduan had arrived. The weasel was tucked out of sight on a branch.

A single step and he reached them. Red whorled over his eyes and his nostrils widened, a sign he used his magic.

"You figured it out." Iseult patted at the taler once more twined around her neck. Her breath puffed.

He did not answer. Instead he drew a small Nomatsi hunting knife and aimed it toward Iseult. Owl's Threads flickered with gray fear, but only momentarily before the Painstone's power cleaned them away. "You wanted me free. Why?"

"Help me."

"I think not."

Iseult's gaze flitted to the blade. Then back to him. He wouldn't use it. "You owe me, Old One."

A sniff. The knife held steady. Amusement and curiosity wove across his Threads. "Do I?"

"I need to find Corlant."

"And I need to deliver you to him."

"You don't trust him, though," Iseult replied. "He says he'll give you my body, but you know that isn't true."

"And will you give it to me?"

She shook her head. "You don't want it."

"Oh, but I think I do." Purple flashed across his Threads, except it was not the purple of hunger—not quite. It was too pale for that, yet too dark to be desire. "I spent a thousand years in death, Dark-Giver. I have no plans to return."

"And my body is the only means to keep you from it?"

"Your body is the only means to send me to it. Unless I control it."

Iseult's brain instantly sharpened at those words—and Aeduan instantly tensed. His Threads paled with panic. He hadn't meant to say such words. Hadn't meant to give her such power.

The weasel chittered in Iseult's mind. Esme had heard him too, and she also marveled at the words' significance. Iseult's body could send Old Ones back to death. Was that why Corlant so desperately wanted her? *But then where do the Threadstones fit in?*

"Do not play games." Aeduan stood taller. "You were a fool to leave me in that tent with a magic unfettered, and you are a fool for thinking I might help you."

He lifted the knife toward her neck.

And Iseult curled back her lips. A false snarl came with surprising ease. After all, she hadn't expected him to join her right away. "You *are* the weakest of them. You bow to Corlant. You *fear* him—he who was the first Hell-Bard. But I am more powerful than Corlant. I will be the one who destroys him in the end. And I will destroy you too, if you do not choose well."

With each word Iseult spoke, Aeduan's head tipped back more. Until he stared at her from the very bottoms of his eyes. His Threads melted between green concentration and rosy amusement. "You would never harm the monk's body."

"You have no idea what I would do."

His head tipped even further. "You have already failed once against Corlant. Why would you succeed this time?"

"Is removing his eye a failure?"

Again, he sniffed. Again, the amusement winked over his Threads. And Iseult set her jaw. She was stasis. She was power. She was the dark-giver, and this Old One needed to see that *she* was the winning side as long as she kept her own body.

It was at that moment that Owl finally showed interest in Aeduan. Her Threads melted into the sunset shade of family as she scrabbled to her feet. The collar scraped against the tree. "You're not like the first Aeduan," she said in Nomatsi. "But you could be." Then she smiled. A brilliant thing made all the more brilliant by her burning, loving Threads.

And though Aeduan couldn't see such magic, he clearly sensed it. He swallowed. His nostrils flared, and Iseult knew instantly that the real Aeduan was listening. That he understood Owl's Nomatsi words.

Iseult pounced. "Will you help us go west? To Praga?"

"What . . . is there?" He stared at Owl, whose little fingers clutched at his clothes. His knife still hovered, though it had dropped several inches.

Iseult reached into her cloak, ready to remove the diary and explain that she needed to reach Praga, that she could help him become what he wanted to be, but at that moment, a screech filled the afternoon. It scraped down Iseult's spine. It slashed into her eardrums.

Aeduan's head snapped toward the sound. It had come from the Nomatsi camp, and though Iseult couldn't actually sense the Threads at this distance, she had no doubt what they would be: silver Threads.

"Mother." It was the first word to hit Iseult's mind and cross her lips.

The monster from the forest had finally caught up. Which made Gretchya right: she had saved the Nomatsis while Iseult had condemned them.

Iseult rounded on Owl. "You must hide." She hefted the girl into her arms. Owl didn't resist, although it wasn't fear that made her malleable so much as the Painstone, still thrumming and bright.

A blessing, that thing. With it, Owl was unbothered by the distant shrieking. With it, she was content to be shoved onto the lowest branches of the spruce, where Esme hid in silence. Even when Iseult stuffed the diary into their new sack and shoved the sack into her tiny arms, her Threads showed only calm.

To her surprise, Aeduan didn't interfere.

"You must stay here," Iseult told the child. "No matter what you hear, you must stay until I come back for you. Do you understand?"

"What if you don't come back?" Owl's face winked down from above, eyes huge as her namesake's. So much trust in that stare. So much trust in those Threads.

Iseult wondered if she'd ever looked at Gretchya that way.

"I *will* come back," Iseult promised, a fierceness in her voice that sent cyan surprise showering up Owl's Threads. It surprised Iseult too. But she meant what she'd said: "I'll come back for you. But you must stay safe, all right? And hidden. The weasel will watch out for you."

Owl tucked back against the trunk, nodding, Still, no fear tainted her Threads and even her usual distaste for Esme, now curling onto her tiny lap, was nowhere to be seen. It was only a matter of time, though, before fear and hate took hold. The Painstone wouldn't last forever.

Iseult would simply have to return before that happened.

She gave Owl's hand a single squeeze before releasing her. "I'll be back soon." Then she latched on to Aeduan's sleeve and pulled him into a sprint out of the spruce's branches. Her last glimpse of Owl was of hazel eyes unfaltering and of a child's Threads, reaching and green.

When at last Henrick appeared in the study, he wore no masks—and almost no clothes. A dressing robe covered his body, sapphire blue and actually flattering.

He drew up short at the sight of Safi. His eyes bulged, his lips curled back, and if he'd been wearing his belt, she had no doubt he would have grabbed for the chain.

"Who let you in?"

"I let myself in." The Threadstones and chain felt like beacons in her pocket. She itched to touch them. Instead, she cracked her knuckles on the chair's padded arm. "As your empress, I do not see why I cannot enter your quarters—though don't worry, I have no interest in entering your bedchamber. Particularly when it's, um . . . *occupied*."

There was danger in goading Henrick. Safi knew that. But she also knew that *not* goading him came with other risks—namely, his own suspicions. The Safi-who-had-not-just-stolen-from-him would have been flippant, so the Safi-who-*had*-just-stolen-from-him had to be flippant as well.

Her calculation was successful. Henrick stomped toward her and glowered down. "Why are you here?"

"I want to know something."

"And?" His snaggletooth jutted outward. His posture sank inward. He was, before Safi's eyes, reassembling his usual mask.

"It is about my uncle," Safi said.

"I will not tell you where he is."

"And I didn't think you would." She sat taller in her chair. "But I have one question for you. If you'll answer it, then I promise I will never ask you about Uncle Eron again."

"Indeed," he replied, and there was still no change. Only his usual scowl and foul demeanor. It didn't have quite the same effect, though, in a sapphire-blue dressing gown with his hair mussed and cheeks still red from lovemaking.

"Is that a yes?"

"Ask the question and we shall see."

"Why did you arrest him?" Safi enunciated each word carefully. Crisply. Authoritatively. "Why did you decide Uncle Eron was a traitor?"

Henrick did not answer. Instead, he hooded his eyes with calculated disinterest. Safi didn't look away, she didn't relax. She simply stared back and waited. *The Empress card to take the Emperor. The Sun to quash all the Kings.*

Her patience—and her gamble—paid off. Eventually Henrick inhaled, hairy chest widening, and said, "When I ordered your uncle to kill your parents, he refused. When I ordered him to kill you, he removed his own noose."

It was not what Safi had expected. She'd assumed Henrick had discovered Eron's plan for peace. Or at least realized Eron had helped her escape Veñaza City after the engagement announcement. She'd even speculated that Henrick had jailed Eron simply for bait to lure Safi home.

But her uncle disobeying an order to kill her, an order to kill her parents . . . A feather could have knocked her over, she was so stunned. And so hollow too. As if someone had just scraped out all her memories but then failed to fill in the empty space again.

"Did . . . did you kill my parents then?" she asked.

Henrick shook his head. He was done answering questions, he was done with this conversation, and Safi knew it was time to fold.

"Thank you, my Emperor. As promised, I shall never ask about my uncle again." She bowed her head once, wearing a bitter smile. Henrick truly was the villain she'd always believed him to be. Degrees of everything or not, his monstrous side was the one that mattered. The one that left hellfires and destruction wherever his armies spread.

She would ruin him.

After pushing to her feet, Safi strode like the empress she was toward the door. Everything had gone according to her morning's haphazard plan. She had the stones, she had the chain, and she even had an answer for the question that had haunted her for almost two decades.

Now all she had to do was to leave.

Fourteen Days After the Earth Well Healed

on't touch me," Safi screams. "Don't touch me!"

Iseult screams it too. Words that shred her throat. "Don't touch her, don't touch her." There are threats in those words—promises she will kill them. Promises she will cleave them.

But the Emperor of Cartorra, his Threads dull with boredom, does not listen, and the Hell-Bards who do his bidding cannot.

Iseult yanks against her iron restraints. She pulls, she fights, and her chains clatter in time to her growing shrieks. "Don't touch her, don't touch her!"

They hold Safi pinned against the marble table while they strap her in iron. Safi had told Iseult this room was beautiful, but Iseult sees nothing beautiful now. White marble walls, veined with gold and draped in chains—and in spells too, meant to induce calm. Faint Threads of power that are useless against such violence.

The Emperor says something that Iseult cannot hear, and one of the Hell-Bards slaps Safi. A crack of gauntlets against her face. It silences her long enough for them to stuff scarlet cloth inside her mouth.

So Iseult screams even louder, screams for the both of them. "Don't touch her! Don't touch her!"

Before her, Safi's Threads are changing fast, moving from crimson rage to pure white fear. A saturation of terror that makes Iseult strain that much harder against her bindings. She knows what is coming; Safi knows what is coming too.

Again, Henrick speaks, this time glaring in Iseult's direction, as if he wants her dealt with. His Threads flare with red impatience.

And two Hell-Bards turn on Iseult. They reach her in three strides, and she cannot evade. Cannot fight when they slap her too—a bright ignition of pain. It sparks in her left cheek, then erupts through her whole skull. Briefly, the world goes dark, before they stuff her mouth with scarlet and yank a sack over her head.

Now the world is truly dark.

She chokes, she fights, she writhes, but she can do nothing against the re-

straints on her wrists. The Emperor and his Hell-Bards have won. Through the sack, though, she can still sense Safi's Threads, still hear Safi's gagged pleas.

But she cannot see what the Emperor does to her, and she certainly cannot stop it.

One moment, Safi's Threads are white to their very core. Then Iseult hears a muffled shriek, high-pitched and pure, before Safi's Threads turn to shadow.

It is done.

She is a Hell-Bard.

And now it is Iseult's turn. They drag her toward the marble table. Safi's Threads pulse in more closely. It is all Iseult can see: Threads. Safi's, Henrick's, and the Hell-Bards' with shadows at their core.

Safi's has a shadow now too, and muffled sobs slither into Iseult's ears. It is enough to make her weep. Enough to make her scream inside the sack: "I will kill you, I will kill you, I will KILL YOU."

Now Safi's Threads are moving away. A body being dragged, as Iseult is bent onto the table. They do not sprawl her out as they did with Safi. She is simply forced down, her face and chest smashed against stone while shaded Threads crowd in.

In front of her is the Emperor. He must be the one whose hands now reach around her neck while cold stabs into her. It is pain she has never known that steals everything. She feels sucked dry yet stuffed full of frostbite. She is going to explode, to erupt, to collapse inward like broken ice on a stream.

Yet somehow, through the agony, a distant part of her still reigns. A cold, logical, Threadwitch part with a cold, logical voice that says, "You are cleaving."

It is not cleaving like she does—of that much, she is certain. That cleaving is hot, that cleaving is fire. But the principle is the same, which means the mechanics are the same . . .

Which means she can control this.

The Witchmark on her hand is not mere adornment. She is a Weaverwitch with the power of the Void inside her and just enough of Eridysi's old knowledge to guide her. Iseult has cleaved a man before, and she will cleave again because though they bind her and shroud her eyes, they cannot hide their Threads.

They cannot stop her magic.

Before the chain has finished closing, Iseult's fingers claw behind her. She grabs at the closest Threads, Hell-Bard and corrupted. They are lightning made of winter, but she holds on and pulls.

Pulls, pulls, pulls, claiming the man's very will as her own. She doesn't cleave him—she needs her teeth for that—but she squeezes until there is pain. She squeezes as she can only guess the noose must do.

The Hell-Bard releases her, and she hears his legs collapse and armor clank. She feels his body thud down as his Threads bend in ways they were not meant to bend. And for half a moment, shock ripples across the other Threads in the room.

It is the moment Iseult needs. She mule-kicks, straight back until her bootheel connects with Hell-Bard flesh. Then she jerks upright, too hard to stop. Too quick to evade. Her skull hits the Emperor's chin where he'd leaned over.

The wintry pain releases, and clarity charges in. She is standing tall now, and the room has devolved into chaos. Two Hell-Bards lurch for her, two lurch for the Emperor. But Iseult recognizes one of the Threads, so she doesn't resist when Caden grabs her. Nor when she feels steel slice the bindings at her wrist. It is subtle, invisible, and quickly followed by a fake attempt to grab her biceps and control her.

Darkness veils her sight, cloth dulls her hearing. But she has never needed those senses. Moon Mother gave her the ability to see Threads, and she has spent years honing that awareness.

She controls this room. She controls these souls.

A woman lurches in, Threads burning with focused violence, and Iseult ducks. A blade whistles over her head, then Iseult is upright again with her arms outstretched.

She has only cleaved a man once, but it was second nature then and it is second nature now. Her fingers close on the Threads, slippery and frozen like the first Hell-Bard's.

Then she brings them to her teeth and bites.

The strands of Aether snap. The soul that bound this woman as a Hell-Bard finishes the cleaving it had begun so many years ago. And the woman's shrieks rip loose, tainted by oil and power. A Stonewitch, Iseult realizes as Earthwitch-green power rattles the marble pillars and crumbles the table.

She is cleaving. Her magic is exploding. In moments, the room will collapse. Iseult releases the Stonewitch, but before she can turn on another Hell-Bard, Caden is beside her again. He hauls her toward the exit, and Iseult doesn't resist. Safi is no longer in the room. Her broken Threads are somewhere outside, and Henrick is with her.

Iseult will kill him.

They reach the hall. A crack thunders behind them—the first pillar to break. Then a heartbeat later, a second snaps in two and a wall collapses inward. The woman's Threads are shrinking fast, shadowy lines that will soon end in death.

The first Hell-Bard is still trapped inside. The one Iseult had controlled and kicked. His death and the Stonewitch's will be marked on Iseult's conscience, branded on her heart for the rest of her days. She should care, but right now, she doesn't.

All she wants is to get to Safi. All she wants is to destroy the Emperor who would dare hurt her family.

But Safi is nowhere near—her Threads are streaking away, fast, fast, and surrounded by shadows. As if the Hell-Bards carry her.

Worse, more shadows approach. Storm clouds rolling in, and Iseult knows Caden cannot help her. Not without losing his own life, and that is too far. Even for her tainted soul. So she does the only thing she can think of to help him: she grabs his Threads too.

A clasp, a tug, a burst of heat in her palms and elbows. He falls to his knees. Iseult tears off her black bag and takes his longsword. Then she finally bolts after Safi and the Emperor. There are Hell-Bards ahead. Six people Iseult must cleave. They chose the wrong person to try to control. She knows how everyone imagines her: the quiet one, the hidden one, the one who blends and melts away.

No more. She is done with scarves and shadows. Why must she hide while Safi displays? Why must she feel nothing while Safi feels it all? Stasis has taken Iseult nowhere. Stasis has held her back, kept her separate from the world. But rage . . . Oh, it will carry her far.

Esme was right all along.

She is done being the left hand. It is time to become the right hand too. It is time to become the fangs.

The rear guards notice Iseult's clattering approach. A barked command from their emperor, and two break off to face her. But Iseult has no interest in them. She dodges the first attack, then slices into the second. Swords have never been her best weapon, but she does not need finesse here. She has magic, and these poor, indentured Hell-Bards have no idea what is coming.

Like with Caden and the others, Iseult grabs their Threads. It is messy, but the result is instant. They drop.

The result is instant for Iseult too. So much heat, so many flames. They scorch up her bones and into her skull, and suddenly, it's too much to hold on to. Her vision turns to fire. Her knees weaken beneath her.

Cleave them! she screams inwardly, trying to pull the Threads to her mouth. Cleave them, you fool!

Before she can collapse from the force of it all, their Threads wink out. One moment, they are in her grasp and alive. Molten whips she can barely contain.

Then suddenly they are dust. Vanishing twirls of Aether. No heat, no pain, no power. Their bodies fall, and a third set of Threads hits her senses.

"Leopold," she croaks, taking in the prince and the bloodied scene at his feet: two dead Hell-Bards, spines severed. He holds two short sabers, his Threads a cacophony of rage, focus, disgust, pain. And, of course, the wild core that never seems to fade. A crown of silver to pour into the sky.

He drops the two swords and strides toward Iseult, stepping lightly to avoid blood. She doesn't realize she is about to fall until he is there to catch her.

"We have to go," he tells her.

"But Safi," she begins.

He only shakes his head. "It is too late for her, Iseult, but it is not too late for you." And without another word, he slides a bracing arm behind her back and hauls her into a run.

THIRTY-FIVE

✳

There was only one place Vivia knew to go: her final Fox ship, *Baile's Bless-ing*, still waiting in the Hundred Isles. It was the last hole this little fox had to run to. The final place she might find safety.

She and Vaness had sprinted for the first mile, the sun rising before them as the Well's power and the magic in their blood fueled them east along a worn coastal road. Vivia couldn't maintain the curtain of water forever, though, and eventually, the hunters would wrest themselves free of Vaness's restraints. But they had a lead—a large one—and they used it. Even when they were both barely sucking in air and Vivia's vision was starting to spin, she didn't let them slow. She insisted they half jog, half walk, each step thudding after the other.

Every rasping breath, Vivia expected Yoris's hunters to appear. Every heartbeat clashing in her ears, she expected to hear Dalmotti fire. But no one and nothing came.

At some point, she and Vaness released hands. At some point, where a limestone cliff came close enough to the sea to reveal the Dalmottis, they abandoned the road and flew into the wild, breathing forest. Vivia led the way. She was not a hunter; she was not trained for stealth. But at least moving within the trees offered shelter against Dalmotti weapons or mounted hunters on the prowl.

Eventually, they reached a stream heading east. Its burbling waters calmed Vivia's muscles and pacified her frantic mind. Though logic told her there would be no undergrowth, no minnows darting in the sunlight if this water were poison, she couldn't bring herself to drink it.

Vaness did, even as Vivia barked a warning. "The waters in Nubrevna aren't safe."

"Just a sip," Vaness pleaded through panting breaths. Then one iron bracelet melted into a cup, and she scooped up stream water and drank. Nothing happened. No jolt of pain or sudden wrenching. No choking or screams.

Still, Vivia could do nothing but watch her. So many years of fear could not be counteracted in a single moment, no matter how pure the water might seem.

Once Vaness had drunk her fill, she sank onto a flat stone. Ferns sighed against her, green and sparkling beneath the morning sun.

"We cannot stay," Vivia warned.

"I know." Vaness stared into her iron cup. "Just a few moments. I am not as fit as you."

Vivia huffed a tired laugh. She felt anything but fit right now. "You should see my first mate. *She* is fit." Vivia settled into a squat beside the stream. Though she couldn't bring herself to drink, she did let her hand slip into the water. Cold despite the warm air.

"Vizer Sotar's daughter?"

"Hye." Vivia nodded. Her reflection wavered up at her, indistinct and unsteady.

"Where is she?"

"I don't know."

"I am sorry then." Vaness's voice softened, as if her thoughts had turned inward. "I lost my Adder High when I fled Marstok. Rokesh was the closest thing I had to a friend."

"Oh." Vivia didn't know what to say, and judging by the taut line of Vaness's shoulders, there was nothing *to* say.

She pushed back to her feet. Her leg muscles screamed, but she was used to pain. Used to ignoring it and finishing what needed doing. "Come." She offered Vaness a hand.

The Empress didn't take it. Instead, she stared at Vivia's fingers, wet from the stream. "I am sorry about your father. I cannot imagine it is easy to learn that he betrayed you."

"Oh," Vivia repeated, and her hand fell like a hammer. Suddenly the pain seemed impossible to ignore. Suddenly she was tired and thirsty and the horror she'd avoided since fleeing Yoris—it was punching in too fast to escape.

"It . . . is not the first time," she squeezed out.

"But this is the worst," Vaness replied.

Indeed, it was the worst. Before, her father had simply wanted the crown Vivia was meant to inherit. He'd wanted the title he'd had before Jana's death. He'd wanted the power he'd wielded for so many years. And though deep down, past the final shelf of her own being, Vivia believed he'd cared for her . . .

His need for power, for adoration, had won out against any love he had for his own child. And no doubt, he'd expected Vivia to fall in line. When she hadn't, he'd pursued.

That was what she'd told herself for the past month. *That* was the story she'd made herself believe. But where did this new truth fit into it? How could a father sell his child to the enemy? How, how, *how* could he love her at all yet so willingly give her away?

"I am sorry." Vaness shot to her feet, abrupt. Graceless. "I did not intend to cause pain."

"Then why did you say anything?" Vivia snapped. It was getting harder by the moment to form words and sneak them past the heat in her chest.

"I simply . . ." Vaness wet her lips. "I wish I could make it better."

"There's nothing *to* make better."

"I need not be a Truthwitch to spot that lie."

No. Vivia would not have this conversation. She would not give in to the tightening around her chest. She needed to move. *They* needed to move—there were hunters behind them, after all, and sitting still was a quick path to madness. She stepped into the stream to cross it. It kicked and kissed at her, so gentle.

She only made it two steps before Vaness said, "Wait, Vivia . . . Your Majesty. Please wait."

And against her better judgment, Vivia paused, right in the middle of the stream. Behind her, Vaness took her own first step into the running waters.

"My parents died when I was young," she said. "I have been Empress for as long as I can remember." A second step. Then a third. "Like you, I have had to hide everything I feel lest the world use it against me." Three more steps and she was at Vivia's side.

But Vivia did not look toward her. She simply stared at the water and willed the storm clouds inside her to pass. *No regrets, no regrets.*

"I have never had anyone to whom I could show myself," Vaness went on. "But I . . . but *you* . . . We're alike, you see?"

Vivia did not see. The Empress had grown up in a world with wealth beyond imagining. Vivia had been born to a nation poisoned and dead. Before Vivia could stop her, though, Vaness reached out and grabbed Vivia's wrist. "You do not have to hide in front of me, Your Majesty." Her fingers tightened. "Vivia, you do not have to hide."

Vivia frowned at Vaness's fine-boned fingers, curled against her skin. The Empress's Witchmark was sharp and black, even in this dappled light.

As if she had it regularly dyed anew. The hairs on her arms glistened with sweat. Her iron bracelet rested gently against a delicate wrist.

She was beautiful. She was regal. And she and Vivia were nothing alike, no matter how much Vivia might wish that they could be. She'd grown up hating this woman. Like her fear of the waters once poisoned around her, she could not change her hatred overnight.

But that was not why she had to hide from the Empress. It was not why she needed her masks or her little fox den. It was because right now, she needed the bear inside her to keep going. The only reason she was still afloat upon this stream—the only reason the bludgeoning in her lungs had not claimed her—was because she had masks to protect her from a world too bleak to face.

She tugged back her hand, and Vaness released her instantly, though the Empress's arm stayed long, her fingers outstretched as if about to plead. But when Vivia said, "We must keep walking," Vaness did not tell her again to wait.

For some reason, Vivia wished she had.

The Hammer came for Stix and Ryber at the hottest part of the day, when the sun had begun its descent, but the roads and rooftops had soaked up enough heat to emanate their own. The inn bedroom had become an oven, and even the six-fingered tabby had melted away in favor of cooler arenas. Compounded with the voices' endless bellows, it was enough to make Stix consider leaving Saldonica and never coming back.

When the Hammer arrived, Stix practically pounced on him. She didn't care that they were traveling back toward Kahina, nor that the burn mark seemed to itch the closer they got. She didn't care that she might have to fight today. She was *moving*, and Noden bless her, it felt good. The carriage swept in a breeze to cool the sweat on her skin, and the voices quelled with each creaking spin of the wheels over swampy road.

"What is today's fight?" Ryber asked with a suave trainer smile. She shuffled her cards absently, flipping one every few moments. Though Ryber never looked at them, Stix caught glimpses of the corners.

Six of Hawks. Eight of Hawks. Three of Hawks. Queen of Hawks.

"No fight," the Hammer said, and for once he looked at Stix with something other than vague irritation. "Kahina says the prisoners are yours now. To do with as you please."

Stix stiffened upon her seat. She met Ryber's surprised eyes across the bench.

"That was fast," Ryber said. *Shuffle, shuffle.*

"When Kahina wants something," the Hammer replied, "she gets it done." He stared at Stix as he said this, and his fingers tapped a curt rhythm against his knee. Clearly he expected her to explain this enormous gift. And clearly, when she offered nothing up but a blank stare, his usual irritation was returning.

"Draw a card for you?" Ryber's voice trilled through the breeze as she offered her deck to the Hammer.

His nose wrinkled. "I do not play games."

"Not a game." Ryber feigned offense. Her braid sprang free. "I dabble in fortune-telling from time to time. Look." She flipped over a card: the Moon. "You come from the Fareastern continent."

Somehow, the Hammer's nose wrinkled even more. "You could tell that by looking at my face and hair tails."

Ryber cracked a smile and dealt another card. The nine of foxes. "You come from the southwesternmost tip, from an island that has mostly managed to evade the wars of the mainland."

Now the Hammer looked impressed—and even Stix was impressed too. She knew Ryber and the cards were clever, but she'd never seen Ryber play this sort of trick before.

The Hammer's fingers tapped faster against his knee. Outside, the wheels' refrain shifted from a soil-soft creak to a stone-echoed clack. Then shadows fell, the breeze vanished, and they were moving beneath the Ring.

Ryber flipped over two more cards. "Lady Fate's Knife, and . . . Ah, the Lovers." She held them up for Stix and the Hammer to see. "You came to Saldonica by sea because your Heart-Thread came here. They were . . ." She drew a third card, but she didn't show it. Instead, her eyebrows slanted first into confusion. Then a deeper slope of sadness. "Oh," she sighed. "I'm sorry. I see your Heart-Thread was—"

"Enough." The Hammer's fingers went still, and for the first time since meeting him, Stix spotted a blistering mark around his own thumb. "That is enough." He shoved from the carriage before it had fully stopped. In seconds, he was gone, vanished into the limestone labyrinth of the Ring.

"What happened to his Heart-Thread?" Stix asked once she and Ryber were out of the carriage as well. "He has a mark on his thumb like mine."

"Hye," Ryber sighed as she offered Stix the final card. It was the Paladin of Hawks: a spiral of flames encircling a sword. "His Heart-Thread was taken by raiders, and then Kahina sold them into the Ring. I fear he's only fighting so he can earn their freedom."

Stix's fingers tightened around the card. She scarcely noticed when Ryber pried it from her grasp. "But now I'm going to free them. He should be happy, no?"

Ryber's lips pursed. "Or maybe you just made it harder for him to fulfill his own bargain, whatever that might be."

Vivia and the Empress returned to the road sooner than Vivia had intended. She'd gotten turned around in the forest and veered a little too sharply south. She would have returned immediately to the safety of the trees, if not for the cannons.

"Do you hear that?" she asked, venturing onto the road. Midday sun washed over the coastline, making everything overbright. Even with the new growth here, there were still too many bone-bleached trees, too many stretches of dead shoreline.

"The Dalmottis attack," Vaness said simply.

Vivia withdrew her spyglass and squinted north, toward the Well and Noden's Gift. But they were too far; she saw nothing beyond gray ocean and white chop. She kept searching anyway. She had to know if she had done this. If, by running, she had consigned all the people of Noden's Gift to vicious death.

"It might not be an attack," Vaness murmured. "Perhaps the Nubrevnan navy engages—"

"They wouldn't." Vivia snapped down the glass. "As much as my father wishes to destroy the empires, even he is not so foolish as to face them head-on. He boasts, but he doesn't act."

A pause. Then Vaness said, "You cannot go back, Vivia."

Vivia squeezed the spyglass like a breaking spine. It was easy for Vaness to stay away, because these were not her people. Noden's Gift and the Well were not *her* home. There were no words to describe the rightness she'd felt at the sight of the forest. No words to explain her ancient, visceral connection to the river that flowed through.

She should never have left. How could she have left? No queen deserted her people.

She gripped the spyglass tighter. Below, the incoming tide kicked higher, and in the distance, cannon fire still boomed.

"You cannot go back," Vaness repeated, and this time she reached for Vivia.

Vivia jerked aside. "I have to." She shoved the spyglass into her pocket and turned north. She would follow the road directly. She would run the entire way if she had to.

"And what will you do?" Vaness called, striding after. Loud, angry footsteps that gritted on the sand.

"I will turn myself in to the Doge."

"Do not be absurd!" Vaness kicked into a jog. "What good would such a sacrifice do?"

Vivia rounded on her. "My *sacrifice* will save hundreds of innocent lives." She bore down on Vaness. Tiny. Feminine. Everything Vivia could never be. Vaness's black hair whipped across her face; her red lips were pressed into pale displeasure.

And at Vivia's approach, she thrust out her chin. "If you give yourself to the Doge, you will lose far more than Noden's Gift. Do you not *see?* We are important. So important that it was worth sending a navy after us."

"We don't know why the Doge hunts us."

"Because we are royalty! That is reason enough."

"And so, because of that, our lives are worth more than the people of the Gift?"

"Exactly."

For half a crashing wave, Vivia thought she'd misheard. But the Empress's eyes said everything: she *did* believe her life worth more.

Vivia's fingers curled into knuckle-breaking fists. The wild ocean called to her for use. "You," she said, "are a disappointment."

"And you," Vaness replied, "are naive." She shoved up her arms, bringing her wrists between them. Her iron shackles gleamed in Vivia's face. "Do you think I wanted to leave Marstok? Do you think I fled with glee? *No.*" She rattled the iron. "I was forced to leave everyone I cared about—forced to run like a coward from the people who needed me most because in the end, I am the only one who can protect them. I am the Well Chosen, Vivia. Has it never occurred to you that you are too?"

Vivia's nose wrinkled. "What does that phrase even mean, Empress? *Well Chosen.*" She thickened the title with disgust. "It's nonsense. A label old rulers used so no one would question their right. But anyone who thinks they deserve a crown does not, in fact, deserve it. Just look at my father—look at what he has done."

"I never said I deserved it." Vaness matched Vivia, her arms casting wide. "Hye, the world has told me I was Well Chosen since the day I was born, but I have also questioned it every moment since. Why was *I* born with a crown? Why was *I* given so much power?

"But the answer does not matter in the end. What matters is that I *was* given a title, a throne, and an empire. What matters is that I choose to use them to help Marstok. That is all I care about: giving myself to the people." She thrust her shackled wrists in Vivia's face. "You are the same. I see it in you every day, and *that* is what makes you special. *That* is what makes you Well Chosen. I am certain of it."

Vivia sucked in a breath, ready to laugh. Ready to sneer at the Empress for such absurdity. Except as the cannons echoed in time to her heart, her mother's voice whispered at the back of her brain: *This is the source of our power, Little Fox. The reason our family rules Nubrevna and others do not.* Her mother had always believed in the Void Well beneath Lovats, and that ancient lake had always welcomed Vivia, had always loved her. It had been a mother's embrace long after Jana had been taken by the Hagfishes.

"You are like me," Vaness said, and she laced her fingers within Vivia's. Her hands were warm, her grip firm. "We have spent years serving our people because we are the only ones willing to give them everything. And we *still* can. If you want to help the people of Noden's Gift—if you want to help all of Nubrevna—then you have to stay alive. You have to stay free."

Vivia didn't answer. Her mask had fallen and there could be no reclaiming it. Not now, not with Vaness so near and a guilt the size of the Jadansi growing inside her. She would do anything to protect the people of Nubrevna. Even give herself up to a Doge.

But Vaness was right, no matter how sour it tasted: she could help more people alive and free than she could imprisoned by an empire.

"Cam," she said on a sigh, her gaze drifting past Vaness's head, toward an invisible battle waged against a village unprepared. "And Sotar and Ginna and all those people."

"We will come back for them."

"You can't know that."

"I can because I know you." Vaness placed her second hand on Vivia's jaw. Her brown eyes glowed in the sun. "I will not fail Marstok, and you will not fail Nubrevna. Trust me, my Queen. Trust me. We are Well Chosen because we choose to be."

Vivia swallowed. The waves still sang to her, but with a different cadence now. A hot, confused one, scalded by an empress's gentle touch. She had nurtured a hatred for Vaness her whole life, and all her instincts screamed at her to travel north. Yet despite that, she found that she did trust the Empress of Marstok. She did trust Vaness, her friend.

"Hye," she breathed after several dragging moments. "We will not fail." Then she pulled away from Vaness and they set off again southeast.

THIRTY-SIX

✳

In her panic-fueled rush back to the tribe, Iseult had forgotten one thing: this was no ordinary tribe. When she broke from the forest to the remainders of camp, Aeduan just behind, heat gusted against her—a dry heat off a fire now raging across the barren earth and stony ruins. Four witches held their arms high as they guided flames toward . . .

She couldn't see, not with the fire. Nor could she hear anything beyond shouts and footsteps as people gathered. As *witches* gathered.

Windwitches, Tidewitches, Firewitches, and an Icewitch. Plantwitches and Herdwitches and Stonewitches too. At least thirty people, their Threads alight with power, were connected by a single goal: stop the monster with silver Threads.

But even bound as they were, they lacked coordination. These were not soldiers trained to fight, and with no leadership to guide them, they fumbled and flailed. Where was Gretchya?

"Where is my mother?" she asked Aeduan, knowing he could sniff her out. But he only shook his head as if he couldn't hear.

The creature's screams ripped louder, its Threads so bright they hurt Iseult's eyes. Briefly seared them shut, hiding the chaos of flames and revealing more Threads. Familiar Threads, muted though they were.

Corlant and his Purists had arrived.

My fault, my fault. Iseult forced her eyes open again. *My fault, my fault.* She had done this; she had to fix it. If she were Safi, she would run right into the flames, no plan, and somehow the world would right again.

But Iseult wasn't Safi. She wasn't light and sunshine and instinct and ideas. Iseult needed someone to lead her, somewhere to aim.

Safi initiated, Iseult completed.

Ruins ahead. Single stone wall, curved at the edge. Flames engulfing it, and keeping the monster on one side. It also keeps the Nomatsis trapped with the monster—and with Corlant and his Purists too.

Iseult's first priority had to be getting those people to safety. To do so, she would need to distract the silver-Threaded monster, then distract Cor-lant. Fortunately, they had come here for her. She was the Cahr Awen, the dark-giver, and if she could be the distracting right hand, then maybe all of these witches could cut the purse.

But first she turned to Aeduan. "If you try to stop me, I will cleave you." She launched into a run.

Initiate.

Her feet picked up speed, her footfalls hammering in time to a single thought: *My fault, my fault.* Her mother had been more than right, and now her mother—and others—were paying the price. *My fault, my fault.*

Distantly, she sensed Aeduan following her, a host of shadow birds in her periphery. Then she reached the stone wall where the flames billowed highest and the stones dipped lowest. She vaulted upward. The fire parted. She tumbled onto the other side, and a new scene met her eyes: Threads. They were terror-ridden and woven with violence, while keening over them all were the monster's burning silver.

And there was the beast itself. A shadow wyrm, unlike anything Iseult had imagined, made of pure shadow. Her eyes couldn't land on it. Each glance made the creature waver and morph, as if it had no solid shape. As if it were all a trick that would vanish on the next blink.

Its Threads shone too brightly, and only when she let it move in her periphery did it finally seem to gain a solid shape with hundreds of cen-tipedal legs off a body serpentine and glassy. Wherever it moved, hoarfrost crackled.

And right now, it scuttled Iseult's way. It had spotted her. It was scream-ing, and unlike all those hours it had lurked out of sight in the forest, *now* it was ready to come for her. *Now* it was ready to claim.

"Move," Aeduan roared beside her, and she did, pumping instantly back into a run. There were no tents now, no campfires to block her way. It was a straight shot aiming for the fighting, frantic Threads clumped fifty paces away. Too far for Iseult to make out Gretchya's or Alma's faces within the mass.

She charged the Purists closing in around the Nomatsis—not with her body, but with her magic. With her fangs.

At the nearest man, Iseult grabbed his Threads. *Yank and bite.* He cleaved in an instant. So easily, his Threads already weakened by a Curse-witch's control. But just as she'd done with the Cartorran soldiers, Is-eult didn't release him. She simply wound his Threads, electric and alive, around her hand and commanded.

He attacked another Purist, giving the Nomatsis the moment they needed. Hunters charged against their captors while the untrained ran. Blades clashed and bows loosed. Fletching of all shades ripped atop Threads of violence and pain.

No time to watch, no time to celebrate. Iseult latched on to a second Purist. Then a third, yanking and biting, yanking and biting. Where she commanded them, they moved, and all while more Nomatsis escaped for the trees.

But not her mother, not Alma. They were nowhere to be seen, and already Iseult was losing her poise. So many Threads were leashed to her, but she had no staff or tree to lean against.

Worse, the silver Threads cycloned toward her. Pummeling and cold. She released all the Cleaved Purists. Her body swayed. She was going to fall before it even reached her.

Hands caught her. Strong arms steadied her. And birds floated across her vision. "Aeduan," she said, trying and failing to pull free. Cold beat against her. Cleaved oil sprayed and bodies fell.

"This way." His voice was near her ear, his grip firm as he hauled her back the way she'd come.

She resisted. Now that she had released the Severed Threads, dregs of power pulsed through her. Bolstered her muscles, sharpened her eyes, and sent her instincts charging back to life. "Not yet."

Mother, Mother—she needed to find her mother. As she dug her feet into the ground, hoarfrost gathered around her. Threads blared. The ground trembled. "Mother!" she shouted at Aeduan. *Where is she?*

This time Aeduan heard her question. "There." He pointed.

Iseult spun right as purple Threads coagulated into her senses. They pooled with scarlet rage and exuded Cursewitch power. Most shocking of all, they glimmered with sunset family and the warmth of amaranth Threads that bind.

The wyrm paused its advance at Corlant's arrival. Then it skittered sideways, like a dog obeying its master. And the Purists—what few remained—also drew back, revealing their priest. The top half of his face was bandaged, his eyes covered by blood-soaked cloths. His Purist robe whipped around him on an unnatural breeze.

He clearly couldn't see, yet he also didn't need to. Just as Iseult had escaped the Pragan palace without her sight, Corlant could navigate the world by feeling Threads.

At his side, her head bowed, stood Gretchya.

"Mother," Iseult repeated, and had Aeduan not held her back, she would have bolted forward. It was good Aeduan was there. Good she had that half-second pause for logic to serrate in.

Gretchya, unbound and demure. Mother, head bent and willing. It was a pose Iseult had seen her mother wear most of her life, whenever Corlant was near. Whenever he'd come around and forced her to unbolt the rusted lock above the door. Iseult never understood why she'd done it, or fully understood why Corlant had always been there.

Even now, as an answer cemented in her belly—in that secret corner beneath her left lung—she couldn't look at it. She couldn't face it.

"Mother?" Iseult said again, but this time it was a question. And this time, it was so, so loud. A single word to split a newly silenced world. Iseult's Cleaved were dead, the remaining Nomatsis subdued, and the Purists kneeling upon the hard earth. The monster had retreated into darkness cast by ruined stone, and were it not for its silver Threads—dampened once more—Iseult would never have seen it there.

There were no footsteps, no jangling belts or weaponry. It was as if the day itself held its breath. Everyone, everything was transfixed by Corlant. His Threads shone above all others, the purple hunger practically lighting up the sky.

Iseult reached for her sword. Then patted empty air because of course there was no sword. She was a *fool*. Always a fool.

But she still had her fangs and her magic. She would kill Corlant—and kill his monster too, if she had to. They could not have Gretchya, not now that Iseult *was* a Weaverwitch who could fight back.

Threadwitches might not harm, but Puppeteers did.

Iseult sank into her stance. Stretched out one hand, fingers clawed and ready to grab, to yank. Her teeth were ready too, her jaw creaking wide.

Corlant must have sensed her plan, though, for he smiled. The cloths on his face wrinkled, made the bloodstains shrink like red eyes. Meanwhile pink joy spread across his Threads, a disturbing contrast against the muted gray weave of death and shadow.

Iseult had been here before. She had watched as Corlant had pinned her with that same ravenous attention. Then watched as he had lifted his hands with deliberate slowness and crossed his thumbs in the sign to ward off evil.

Except this time, he did not make that symbol. This time, he opened his hands as if in welcome. "My daughter," he said, so softly she almost did not hear. Then again, his smile widening: "My daughter, come join your mother and father."

Daughter. A meaningless word that clunked around in Iseult's skull. That hardened her muscles, holding them still when they ought to move, and wormed through her gut, cold and vicious and impossible.

Daughter. My daughter.

She must have misheard. It was the only possible explanation. Because of course she was not his daughter, even if that answer inside her was now scratching higher.

She didn't want to examine it—and couldn't while Corlant watched her, while Aeduan still gripped her arm and her mother stared at the dirt refusing to lift her gaze.

This wasn't right, this wasn't happening. Iseult's hand fell to her thigh. Her stance weakened and balance wavered. Only her jaw held, open and with teeth bared. But there was no power there anymore, no desire to chomp down and kill.

Daughter. My daughter.

The pleasure in Corlant's Threads had shifted to the sunset gleam of family. Tendrils that reached for Iseult and Gretchya. He smiled so widely, his face had almost folded in on itself, and the stained linens drooped to one side. For once, no trenches marred his forehead, no eyebrows lifted high. There was only delight suffusing his body and his Threads.

Iseult wanted to flee, to run, to fold into a ball and disappear inside herself. But there was nowhere to go, and there was—as she knew, knew, *knew*—no outrunning who she really was.

My fault, my fault. With no one to save her. No weasel, no Alma. She was trapped, faced by a Cursewitch whose Threads gleamed with family. *Daughter, my daughter.*

For two seemingly endless breaths, as the breeze swept up mist off thawing hoarfrost and as Threads danced around her, Iseult was paralyzed by guilt. By how much she hated herself and her magic. *Sever, sever, twist and sever.*

But then she considered one important thing: if Corlant was her father, then she'd been cursed from the day she'd been born. Tainted by evil blood and the Void. Moon Mother's glow had never reached her and never would. Yet like the monster hidden in shadows nearby, there was freedom in darkness. There was power where light never reached.

It was as if, in that moment, time punched forward. No space for thought, no space for logic or concern or the stasis that had never helped her before. There was only action, only instinct, only rage.

Her spine straightened, her arms flung high, and Iseult stretched her fingers long. Aeduan's grip released, and her fingers closed around Corlant's Threads. Lightning seared up her arm. Shock waves to pummel her elbow, her shoulder, her ribs. Even her vision ignited with cold and light—freezing it away. She saw nothing but Corlant's Threads. Nothing but throbbing purple pleasure and that sick sunset love.

But also a dark, icy core she'd never noticed before. One that her fingers closed around. That crackled outward in arcs of power.

Too much power. More than she could control, more than her small, human mind could comprehend.

Cold and light burrowed past her eyeballs and into her brain. Past her lungs, all the way to her heart. She was pure winter. She froze from the inside out; her muscles and bones became fuel for a Cursewitch.

Distantly, Iseult felt her knees give out beneath her. Distantly, she heard screams she knew must be her own. But she was powerless to stop them. She could not even release Corlant's Threads. The dark current at the heart of them would not let her go. It swelled inside her, glaciating every cell it touched and every drop of her Aether too.

I thought you would be stronger, a voice whispered atop the ice. *But there is still time for you to become the dark-giver you were meant to be. The shadow-ender the Witchlands needs. The daughter I thought had been taken from me.*

"No," Iseult tried to say. Or maybe she did say it, though no sound reached her ears. No voice shook in her chest. The crackling core of Corlant's power still consumed, still froze.

Until at last he released her. Laughter briefly filled her skull, pink Threads briefly claimed her vision. Then darkness—blessed and pure—shoved in to drag her down.

Iseult collapsed.

Fourteen Days After the Earth Well Healed

*L*ater, *Iseult will wonder how no one saw her and Leopold. Later, she will have strange memories of gray and snow and walls that open wide. But it will all be so dreamlike that she will not be able to fathom what it means.*

And she certainly cannot fathom what it means while it is happening. She loses track of the turns and passages, of the countless people they pass who never seem to see. Every time she says, "Safi," Leopold ignores her. Or quiets her, a bloodied hand to cover her mouth, as if people might be near to overhear.

She sees no one, though, and Threads are hazy.

Worse, a voice is beginning to speak to her again. Just a tickle at the base of her brain, but Iseult recognizes it. She has been here before. You did this to me. You killed me. I will never let you go. *It is the Hell-Bard's voice. The Stonewitch's ghost.*

But then the voice pulls back. The gray seems to clear, and suddenly Iseult finds herself in a part of the palace she has never seen before, in a round room of dark, ancient stone and blazing hearth.

Owl is here, dressed in a plain traveling cloak and clasped in Zander's patient arms. She gives a soft cry at the sight of Iseult, and relief swells across her Threads. A cleansing wave against the fear that paled them before. "Bad things are happening," she says as Zander eases her to the carpet, red as blood and so much thicker. "We were worried."

"I'm fine," Iseult says, but it's a lie. She is anything but fine. Her Threadsister has been broken and carried away, she has killed two people, and now another ghost of the Cleaved is awakening in her mind.

She glances at Zander and in Cartorran adds, "Thank you for keeping her safe."

"Yes," Leopold inserts. His Threads blaze with a hunter's green of focus. "But now you must leave."

The Hell-Bard bows. "Of course, Your Imperial Highness." He steps softly to the exit, graceful and silent despite his enormity. Leopold trails after, and once the dark wooden door shuts behind him, he taps several lock-spells into place.

"What if he tells someone we're here?" Iseult asks.

Leopold shakes his head. "He won't be able to." Before Iseult can ask what that means, he rushes past her and scoops up Owl. Exactly as Zander had held her, letting her stretch long and brace on his hips.

"Follow me," he orders. "We must be quick." Then he strides right up to the wall and knocks three times.

Iseult briefly sways against the armchair. Because she has been here before, she has seen this glamour magic before. At the Monastery, with Leopold at her side. Except that then, she was the one to solve the mystery of the Rook King's secret wall—and then she was the one to do the tapping.

Leopold does not wait to see if she follows. He simply strides into the darkness, Owl held tight, and Iseult has no choice but to scurry after. It is a stone stairwell, and she traces quickly down until all light vanishes and she is moving solely by the feel of her hand against the wall.

Cold creeps higher with each step; Iseult still wears her flimsy silk gown, though it is torn at the hem and one sleeve is half ripped away. She has no memory of when that might have happened. One moment she was on the balcony, the next she was swarmed by Hell-Bards and carried across the palace.

Now she is here, reaching the end of a secret stairwell cloaked in the magic of the Rook King—and she has no doubt this was the Rook King's work. At least partially, for as light filters onto the final steps and a cave opens up before her, Iseult glimpses a worn carving in the stone: two birds, side by side.

But are they owls, Esme had once asked, referring to ancient statues in the Contested Lands, or are they rooks? Iseult hadn't understood the significance of those animals then, and she doesn't understand it now.

All she knows is that the Rook King had been a Paladin—a real flesh-and-blood man. And somehow he must be bound to these stones just as he is bound to the Monastery. Except Iseult doesn't think it is merely a ghost that haunts here.

After a short drop-off, Leopold sets down Owl and takes her hand in his. She is, to Iseult's surprise, unafraid of this strange place. In fact, her Threads are blue calm tinged with rosy joy, as if the cave is familiar.

But are they owls or are they rooks? Iseult thinks again, and another piece of the puzzle sinks into place.

The cave unfolds ahead, its high ceiling rounded and lit by Firewitched torches. A gentle, sulfur-scented mist hovers, bringing moisture to Iseult's skin. Warmth increases, welcome at first. Then too hot. And eventually, the winding cave gives way to a carved space, lined with columns.

It is a bath, the waters frothing and steaming. Leopold offers no explanation *for the room, but simply strides through. With the steam floating around him, he looks like a ghost from centuries past.*

Beyond is more cave, winding and twisting in a complex labyrinth of stalag-mites and sulfur. The ground ascends slightly, until at last, they reach a wide set of stairs. No one speaks as they climb. Only when they hit the final landing does Leopold break the silence.

"I have no supplies for you. Only a cloak." He moves to a wooden trunk hiding between two torches. In quick, practiced movements, he has it open and a thick gray cape in hand. "Beyond this wall"—he motions to the stone before them—"is the River Praga. You can follow it east, until you reach the wharves. I have someone there who will meet you."

"Who?"

"You will know her," he says simply, and he offers Iseult the cloak.

She wraps her fingers around the rough wool. It will blend in well with the night. "Thank you," Iseult says, and she means it. She would be dead by Hell-Bard blade right now, if not for him. "Please look after Safi."

"You know that I will, Dark-Giver." He bows his head. There is no mockery in his tone or in his Threads—only the grief. The loss. The tears Iseult saw be-fore, a lifetime ago upon the balcony.

And Iseult grasps for some message she can give Safi. Some final departing words that say, "Everything will be all right because I'll make them so." But she can think of nothing, so all she says is "Owl, are you ready?"

She turns away from Leopold and kneels before the child. Owl remains calm, unfazed by the strange night or the strange cave. And as Iseult pulls up her hood and tucks her hair out of sight, she even bares a smile. "Zander says we are to play fox and hen tonight."

"Yes," Iseult agrees. "That is exactly what we are doing."

A musty scent rolls over her, and when Iseult rises, she finds a dark river sloshing against reeds where a wall had just been.

"You will get wet," Leopold says from behind her. He has moved to the stairs again. "But the time in the water is short."

Iseult nods. Water doesn't bother her. It is the thought of leaving Safi that bothers her.

That, and the gaping question that has nagged ever since she saw Leopold tap three times at a stone wall. Ever since they fled a Monastery together in the Sirmayans. Ever since she saw him and thought he was the dappled god she called Trickster.

And ever since Esme asked her, Are they owls or are they rooks?

Yes, Iseult knows she should walk away now. She knows that if she asks, he will not give her a straight answer. Honesty defies the Trickster heart of who he is. But she cannot resist. She must know before she leaves forever.

"Leopold," she murmurs.

His head lifts.

"What happened to your silver crown?"

A beat of tan confusion. Then understanding flushes it away, followed by turquoise surprise—none of which reaches his carefully controlled face.

His eyes bore into hers, green against gold, and heartbeats thump past. Three. Six. Then at last: "How did you know?"

"I suspected at the Monastery," she answers honestly. "But only here could I finally believe it true. How?"

He laughs, a familiar sound with no amusement. A self-loathing laugh that says, I am a fool for letting you catch me. Then comes the languid shrug Iseult knows so well. "I truly can hide nothing from you, can I?"

"How?" she repeats, and this time, her voice is sharp. Owl waits several paces away, and time is running out if she wishes to flee. He knows that; he is hoping to use it against her.

But she is tired of being played, tired of his games. "Leopold, explain how."

Another shrug, this time with a bored twirl of his wrists. "It is the nature of our spirits. We are destined to die and be reborn for all eternity, watching the follies of humanity yet unable to prevent them."

"And she is like you?" Iseult dips her head toward Owl.

Leopold nods. "She is like me, though the collar seems to dampen that part of her. A good thing, I think. It is hard to adjust when the past lives come, and the younger one is when it happens . . . well . . ." His cheeks twitch. "The harder it is."

Iseult nods. She has always known Owl is different, though a Paladin is never something she'd imagined. Never something she'd believed could be real. So she simply repeats "Thank you," before turning to leave.

She only makes it two steps before Leopold's Threads flash with lilac, with sapphire and a desperation bordering on panic. "I love you." His voice cracks.

Her footsteps stop.

"I love you," he says again, and she curses herself. For she should have seen this coming. His Threads have not been subtle, even if she refused to look at them. He is wrong, though, in his interpretation.

And it is wrong for her to leave him without a reply. So Iseult twists back to face him, dappled once again in shadow and dressed in Trickster's favorite silvery gray. Three long strides and she closes the distance between them. He stands one step below her, so their faces are the same height.

He swallows. "Please, Iseult—"

"No." She shakes her head. "You don't love me." She cups his face, a gentle gesture. One she is not accustomed to making, but that, in this moment, feels right.

After all, a thousand years is such a long time to be alone.

"You love me no more than I love you."

"But I do, Iseult—"

"No, Rook King." She drops her hands. "You've simply forgotten what it feels like to be seen."

Then, before he can protest any further, Iseult turns away, gathers Owl to her, and steps into the cold Pragan night.

PART II

Witch Shadows

THIRTY-SEVEN

✳

The dark-giver lay upon a pallet before Aeduan. A small stove warmed the tent, and Evrane, who had first undressed Iseult and cleaned her various wounds, had not come in hours. She'd had duties elsewhere, duties assigned by Corlant.

None dared disobey him—though it was not fear that compelled them. Quite the opposite. The Purists wanted his approval, his nods of pleasure, his promises that Midne would bless them.

It reminded Aeduan of someone who had died all those centuries ago. And sometimes he wondered if perhaps Corlant was not the one he said he was . . . Aeduan had no proof, though, and when he had told Evrane, she had only laughed at him. *Impossible*, she'd declared. *Portia was the first of us to go. We saw her die inside that mountain.*

Aeduan did not remember, but he also saw no reason to argue—just as there was no reason to pursue his suspicions. Corlant had, at the time, wanted what Aeduan and Evrane had wanted. Now, Aeduan was not so sure that held true. He had helped Iseult, even if Corlant and Evrane had not yet realized.

And even if he himself had not fully accepted it.

No, he could not deny the first Aeduan still lived inside him, prodding and hinting and rising to the surface whenever he let down his guard. That soul was proving stronger than he'd anticipated.

It was not entirely unwelcome, though. There were angles and depths in this body that only the first soul understood. And there were angles and depths in the dark-giver too. Ones he did not hate as he ought to. Ones he found himself drawn to, just as he'd once been drawn to Her.

You always were the weakest of us. Maybe that was true.

Outside the tent, Purists mobilized and organized, gathering to serve their master. At a horse's whinny, the girl stirred on her pallet. She did not look good, her neck striped with red and faded black. Her face haggard and ashen. Aeduan could not smell her blood—a fact that confused him.

Her golden eyes opened as he watched her. Then, half hooded, those eyes found his. "Aeduan," she said.

"No," he replied, though he did not know why. He *was* this Bloodwitch Aeduan now.

"Ah," she breathed, and her eyelids sank shut once more. "Who are you, then?"

"I do not know," he answered, truthful again even as he ought to stay silent. He had scolded Evrane for talking too much. "'Six turned on six and made themselves kings. One turned on five and stole everything.'"

"'Eridysi's Lament,'" she said, surprising him. And surprising herself too, for her eyes popped back open. "What does it mean?"

"It means that long ago, I died. Then one day this body came to me and I took it."

Her nose twitched slightly. "And Evrane did the same?"

"Yes."

She nodded, as if this made sense to her—though he knew it made no sense at all. Even he, who'd had centuries to ponder it, could not fully comprehend what had happened on that day a thousand years ago. Or why this body had appeared before him and allowed him to so easily step inside.

"And Corlant? He is like you?"

"No. He is permanent, while we are merely occupants in a house that once belonged to someone else." And unlike Aeduan and Evrane, Corlant had never felt the blade in his heart. He had never had the Threads that bound him to the goddess sliced away.

"But I am the only one to kill him." As Iseult said this, something hardened in the backs of her eyes. "And the only one to kill you."

Aeduan stiffened. He should never have let that piece of information slip. Fortunately, she did not press. "Is Owl safe?" She shifted as if to rise. A grunt fell from her lips, and Aeduan bent forward to help. Instinctive. Foolish.

She flinched at his touch . . . but then allowed him to grip her shoulders and slide a hand fully behind her. Not that she had much choice—she was too weak to rise without assistance.

Whatever she had done to Corlant, it had almost killed her.

"I do not know," Aeduan answered honestly. "I have not looked for her."

"But you will?"

He paused. Then nodded.

"To give her to Corlant or to help her flee?"

Aeduan did not answer. Iseult's eyes were so close to his; the stove's flames guttered within. *Too close, too much.* He released her and tried to withdraw.

Her hands snaked out. She gripped him, knuckles whitening round his biceps. Then her eyes bored into his. Her teardrop scar glimmered. "*Te varuje, Aeduan,*" she said. "*Te varuje.*" She murmured other foreign words to him that the soul swimming inside him understood.

And that soul was trying to surface, trying to rise before Iseult turned away. *Te varuje, te varuje.* She squeezed tighter, her gaze unwavering, and Aeduan found it hard to look away. Impossible even.

"I do not understand you," he finally said, breaking free from her grasp. "Your words are meaningless." Then he straightened to his full height and stared down at her. The change in angle made her look smaller, weaker. Less like Her.

But Iseult merely smiled at Aeduan then. A slow thing. Feral in a way he had never seen her wear—as if she had some secret. Or as if this had been a game between them and she had come out the victor.

He did not like that smile. He wished she would stop.

And when he turned to leave, his movements quick, frustrated, a laugh chased after him. All the way out of the tent and into the dark night.

Iseult had always told Safi that there were some truths one did not need magic to recognize. The truths one always knew but kept hidden away. The truths one never stared at directly. *But they always show up eventually,* she'd said. *And when they do, you just* know.

Corlant's words had been one of those moments. One of those truths hiding in plain sight that Iseult had refused to see or consider.

The daughter I thought had been taken from me.

She'd always wondered about her father. There were few choices within the Midenzi tribe, yet she'd never considered him an option . . . because she'd never *wanted* it to be him. He was the only one, though. He had always been the only one.

The monster inside her had to come from somewhere.

It was good to have an explanation, she decided as she stared at a shadowy tent ceiling. She had no idea where she was, but she was neither bound nor gagged. Outside, a camp clattered and clinked and breathed. Threads drifted past, oblivious in their own goals, existence. Iseult could take them if she wanted to.

She didn't want to.

But she could.

She was the dark-giver, the Puppeteer. She was shadows through and through, and it was not her fault. She had been born this way. She had been *made* this way. Cursewitch blood ran in her veins, and the very Void itself lived inside her.

She had hovered in and out of consciousness for countless hours; Aeduan had been the first to fully rouse her. The usurper Aeduan. Not the *true* Aeduan. He was gone, but not out of reach. One more soul she supposed she ought to save.

Her hands were wrapped in fresh gauze, her fingers stiff and raw. Pain suffused upward in jagged spikes flooding cold across her body. Frostbite from Corlant's Threads.

Pain didn't bother her, though. Stasis had claimed her so completely, she felt no urgency, no impatience, no fear.

She had been wrong before, when she'd thought life without emotion was no life at all. This was still life—she still *lived* and *breathed* and *moved* where her mind conveyed. But it was easier now, without obstacles or frustrations or Threads she could not control.

And if that was who she was—who she was meant to be—then she could stop fighting it. She could give in to this power that she loved. This control, this rage. She could stop trying to be something she hated.

If only Gretchya had told Iseult about Corlant all those years ago, then Iseult would have given up on Threadwitchery and saved herself a lifetime of agony. For so long, she'd had an arsenal of weapons at her disposal she'd never known about. She could have fought against those who had hissed, and those who had hated.

Now she knew, though, that she was the daughter of a monster—that *she* was a monster, and monsters could do whatever they pleased.

Oh yes, it was good to have an explanation. To have absolution and finally know what stasis felt like. No feeling, no worries, no shame. Just existence and a path to tread that led where it had always led: to Safi.

She didn't know how long she sat there, gazing at canvas and tasting the smooth folds of true stasis. She didn't know how long it took her to realize she wasn't alone, but eventually the awareness of eyes—of breath— prickled against her skin.

She swiveled her head, disinterested. There was only one person it could be tucked out of sight like that.

"You should have told me," Iseult told the corner where her mother watched. "Why didn't you?"

"I hoped you would never have to know." Gretchya's voice rasped, as if she'd been crying. Which was impossible, of course. She eased a step toward Iseult, shifting into the stove's weak light. Her ankles were bound by a stretch of rope. Her wrists too. She could move, but she could not run. "Corlant is not the same man that I first knew."

"And I am not the same daughter." With creaking bones and flimsy muscles, Iseult lugged herself upright. A woolen blanket fell from her torso. Fire-warmed air brushed against her, and she realized someone had dressed her in a new gown while she was unconscious. Threadwitch black, with gray dashes, sage circles, and magenta lines sewn into the hems. Even the new velvet pantaloons had been dyed black and marked with Threads.

She yanked the covers over herself again. She didn't want to see those colors, didn't want to see this gown that must have belonged to her mother. "People change," she said. "It's no reason to hide the truth."

Gretchya offered no reaction, but she was close enough now for Iseult to spot splotchy skin and swollen eyes.

She *had* been crying. How strange. How laughable. How much, much too late.

"Corlant did not simply change, Iseult. He went from a simple Nomatsi man to a Cursewitch overnight. From a man who would have loved you—whom I would have told you of with pride—to a demon who hurt others for pleasure."

"Oh?" Iseult asked without interest. She didn't care, and she didn't believe anything her mother said anyway.

She lifted her hands and stared at her bandages. Pain dissolved downward as blood drained. "Where are we?" she asked.

"Where we were before. In the Solfatarra." Gretchya glanced toward the tent's lone flap. No light pilfered in. "Some of the Nomatsis got away. Most did not."

Iseult supposed she should blame herself for that. She didn't.

"Alma?"

A headshake. "She is imprisoned with the others. But she is a good leader. She will keep them calm and give them guidance."

Of course she would. Even now, Alma was the perfect apprentice. Even now, with a confession the size of the Sleeping Giant to scowl between them, Gretchya couldn't help but compliment the other girl.

Though Iseult supposed it was only fair. After all, Alma's father wasn't a monster.

"Hundreds of Purists gather outside," Gretchya went on. "And more come from across the Witchlands. There are settlements everywhere, tucked away where no one else wants to reside. And there are always new converts too. Corlant has always been . . . persuasive."

"Persuasive" was not the word Iseult would have chosen, but if it made her mother hate herself less, then she could have it. Iseult truly did not care.

She looked again at her bound hands. They ached. She'd left the diary with Owl. Her salvation. Her right as the new Puppeteer.

As if reading her mind, Gretchya said, "Do not go to Praga."

"Why? The soldiers cannot hurt me."

"I know why you go there. What you intend to do. But you will regret it."

Iseult's lips pursed. "Regret saving my Threadsister?"

"Regret the lives you take to do so."

Iseult snorted, a harsh un-Threadwitch sound. If her mother truly cared for her soul, then she should never have joined with Corlant. Should never have had a child by him.

She sucked in a long breath and let her eyes shutter. Blessed darkness took hold. *Inhale, exhale. Inhale, exhale.* She sent her mind outward, searching for Owl. She sensed nothing and opened her eyes. "Have you seen Owl? Or Dirdra, as you know her?"

"Corlant just sent the Bloodwitch to find her."

Iseult's eyebrows lifted ever so slightly. If Aeduan had agreed to search for Owl, then that meant he had not admitted to already seeing the child. It also meant Corlant hadn't noticed Aeduan helping Iseult in the fight. He was truly her ally now, and that made her smile. Inwardly, though, only inwardly. Outside, she was stasis forever.

Purple Threads skittered into Iseult's awareness. Corlant approached, new magic writhing within his Threads. Yellow for a Windwitch, orange for Fire. He swept inside the tent, no warning—and no more stiff, blinded movements either. Only one eye was covered now. The one Iseult had removed.

"What a beautiful family." He crossed the small tent in two long strides and stared down at Iseult. His remaining eye was a mess, the iris almost invisible in all the bloodshot red. The bruising around it was as dark as his Threads. He could clearly see, though, for the eye roved across Iseult.

Then it leaped to Gretchya. "Your mother has done well, standing guard."

Gretchya bowed her head. "Thank you, Priest Corlant."

"Leave us." He flipped a hand toward the exit. "I wish to speak to my daughter alone."

Daughter, my daughter.

"She is not dressed," Gretchya replied. "If you would give us a moment of privacy, I will help her."

The lines on Corlant's forehead sliced inward; mild surprise washed in turquoise. But he strode back outside, leaving winter air to kick in behind him. The flap shut, and as Gretchya scooted in close to Iseult, it was all so familiar. A different lie in a different settlement—*It's my moon cycle. I need new blood wrappings*—told to keep Corlant away. For, of course, Iseult *was* dressed. All she lacked were her boots and acid-eaten cloak.

"You must not do as he says," Gretchya whispered, dropping to a kneel beside Iseult. She towed out boots from under the cot and without waiting for Iseult to acknowledge, she tore off Iseult's covers and grabbed Iseult's ankle. "He needs you. Whatever this . . . this magic you can do is, he needs it."

"For what?" Iseult watched her mother lace up the boots just as she had watched her mother chop off all her hair two months ago. Back then, Gretchya had warned her that people might mistake her for the Puppeteer.

Now she warned her not to be one.

"I do not know." Gretchya tugged the other boot onto Iseult's foot. Outside the tent, Corlant's Threads hovered and waited, impatience to mingle with the endless hunger.

"It is something to do with the Threadstones. You must not do as he asks, Iseult. You must not give in to him."

"And how do you propose I do that, Mother? You were not a good teacher."

A quick upward glance, almost ashamed, almost scolding, then Gretchya's attention was on the boot once more. She laced it too tightly; leather creaked. "I did not give in to him. I fought him every day by enduring." She tied off a knot with far too much force. "By being what he wanted so he would never look your way. There is no greater fight than that, and one day—when you have a daughter of your own—maybe you will understand."

She shoved to her feet, a panic in her movements Iseult also recognized from two months ago. The failure of stasis. The punching through of emotions Gretchya was not supposed to have.

But it was too late. Iseult felt nothing; she was nothing. If Gretchya had thought her story would evoke pity, she had been wrong. Iseult had no pity left for anyone nor emotions left at all.

"Thank you," she said, and though it made her muscles scream, she pushed to her feet unaided. The tent wavered; a roar filled her ears.

"I'm dressed," she called. "You can come in now."

THIRTY-EIGHT

✳

Safi had never performed more in her life. If she'd thought the last two days of foul submission to Henrick had been a challenge, they paled in comparison to a day of pretending she was not about to leave.

An eternity passed before the day finally ended, and another eternity passed before the evening's festivities—dancing and smiling and feasting—ended too. Leopold secured Safi's hand for two dances, smiling the entire way. He looked as carefree as he always did. Which meant he must not know about her earlier excursions. Thank the gods.

"Come to my quarters," he told her at the end of their second dance. "Bring only yourself."

So Safi did. She went dressed in the midnight-blue gown she'd worn that night to the dancing celebrations, with only herself, her Truth-lens, the stolen golden chain, and her Threadstones. She still wore her noose too.

Leopold greeted her with his usual kiss, and they followed the same steps they had each night. Only when the lights were low and the wall revealed did he finally speak. "Remove your noose."

Safi obeyed. Then their silence resumed. A chilly silence, for it would seem that Leopold had abandoned his usual masks. Safi was glad. She and Leopold had days alone ahead of them, and she didn't want to wade through every smirk or casual shrug, fretting over what they might mean. Cold and lethal as his true self might be, it was at least easier to understand.

They traced the same path they'd taken before. Leopold's stride was long, and Safi moved to match it. When they reached the chest and stone wall, two large packs and two piles of traveling clothes awaited.

"Change," Leopold commanded, so Safi did—with her back to him and his back to her. The garments were well made, but simple enough to avoid drawing attention on the road. The dark browns and darker grays would blend easily into shadows, forests, or fields.

Once the packs were upon their backs, heavy but not unstable, Leopold asked, "How do you feel?"

"Like last night," Safi answered honestly. "I feel that half of me is gone, but as long as I have this"—she patted her Truth-lens—"the cold and the pain are easy to ignore."

A nod. "I will trust you to tell me if it worsens." He twisted toward the wall, knocked three times, and the outside world rushed in.

Safi smiled. A small, private thing. The Loom might pull at her, the Emperor might discover what she'd done, and this whole plan might be thoroughly stupid, but she was moving. She was initiating. She was free.

Besides, as she'd always told Iseult, *Stupid as it might seem, stupid is also something they never see coming.*

Leopold tromped into the water and Safi followed. The door disappeared, stones returned, and Safi spotted something she hadn't seen the night before: a rook and an owl carved at eye level.

Thank you, Safi thought to those lovers long dead. She owed them so much. Then she splashed after Leopold, through the reeds and into the night.

Safi and Leopold walked for hours. Through Praga and out the same gate they'd approached the night before, then through city after suburb after village. Cold ramped higher in Safi's bones the farther they traveled. A tightening, a thinning, as if her skeleton might snap if she wasn't gentle.

But she ignored it. Just as she ignored the faint lines forming across her hands. Leopold never noticed, and he made no comment when she pulled on gloves. The night was frigid; she had an excuse.

It was at a crossroads outside a farming village that three figures on horseback trotted Safi's and Leopold's way. There were no other people on the road, and no lamps burned here. These were laborers' homes; at night, they slept. And in winter, only silence and snow reigned.

Leopold's breath snagged audibly when it was clear the horses approached. He grabbed Safi's arm, ready to tow her into a run. But she yanked him back.

"They're here to help."

His eyes widened. Then understanding settled, hard and furious, across his face. "What have you done?"

Before she could answer, Lev's voice trilled, "We thought you might prefer to ride. It's faster than walking, you know." Her horse slowed beside Safi, and she dismounted.

Caden and Zander, meanwhile, drew up their horses to Leopold. After dropping to the winter-hardened road, they both popped matching bows. "Your Imperial Highness," Caden said. Then to Safi, "Your Imperial Majesty." He wore well-padded plain clothes, as did Lev and Zander.

Leopold ignored them all. His eyes, still latched onto Safi, were dark with rage. "What," he repeated, "have you done?"

"I told them we were leaving."

"And when Henrick realizes?" He stepped in close, nostrils flared. Jaw set. "You have consigned us to death, Safiya."

"No." She lifted her right wrist and peeled back her sleeve. "I have the chain he uses to control them."

Leopold's focus shifted. His ire did not. For several long breaths, he stared at the chain, glittering and pale in the darkness. His left cheek bounced. "He will have others like it."

"And we will be far away before he gets them."

"He will still know where we've gone, and he will still control these Hell-Bards like the puppets they are."

Lev shifted uneasily. Caden stood stiff as stone. Zander stared at his toes.

"And I"—Safi dipped her chin to stare at Leopold from the tops of her eyes—"will control the Hell-Bards right back." Her wrist remained high; the chain remained shining. "I tested it earlier," she lied. "I can use the chain exactly as Henrick does. If he tries to hurt them, I will stop it."

"But he will still know *where we are!*" Leopold roared.

Safi recoiled. She had never heard him shout before.

"Henrick will be able to follow us every step of the way! I just gave up my entire future as imperial heir, and for what? So you could help three Hell-Bards who can *never be saved*. As soon as Henrick realizes what has happened, he will send every resource after us. He will take control of these Hell-Bards, *and*"—he pitched his voice higher, smashing down on Safi's attempted protests—"who do you think will use the chain better? You, who stole it today, or he, who has been wielding it for decades?

"This is not a battle we can win, which is why we fled without fighting it. Or why we were *supposed* to flee, until you ruined everything."

He spun toward Caden before Safi could reply. Not that she had any suitable words. She'd never seen Leopold's temper fray. Even the cold, lethal prince still possessed poise. *This* Leopold was wild with anger.

"We will take your horses, Captain, and part ways immediately. Return to the palace. Lie for as long as you can." Leopold hefted his pack onto the back of the nearest horse, a dappled gelding.

Caden, however, stood unmoving. He looked at Safi. Then at Leopold. Then back to Safi, his expression pinched and pale. And in that moment, Safi realized that *she* was the person with the highest rank here. *She* was Empress; Leopold was only the heir.

She was also the one with the golden chain. Though she would never use it against the Hell-Bards, in this moment, she had all the power. Her words were law. Her orders could not be disobeyed.

A fresh surge of defiance pulsed through her. She had *not* ruined everything; she had a plan, and for once she felt certain it would work. More importantly, she trusted the Hell-Bards with her life. Even bound as they were to the Emperor, she *trusted* them more than she had ever trusted Leopold. If there was any chance of reaching Iseult and saving Uncle Eron, she needed these people at her side.

All clear, all clear.

Safi puffed out her chest and declared to Leopold's back, "We will not be splitting up, Polly." There was no space for argument, no space for complaint. She imitated Henrick in that moment. "We will indeed take the horses, but the Hell-Bards will remain. And if you disagree, then you—and you alone—may leave."

Leopold's grip on the gelding's saddle tightened. The Hell-Bards, all in varying postures of humility and horror, did not move. Even the horses, their breaths fogging against the cold night, did not move.

Seconds slid past. Snow began to fall, light and ethereal.

Then Leopold's posture finally changed. His hands finally fell. "As you wish," he said, without turning. Without lifting his voice. "We will ride together for as long as we can, and we will pray, Safiya, that your plan succeeds."

THIRTY-NINE

✳

A scarred woman studied Stix up and down, her eyes half-squinted in suspicion. "So you own us now."

"No." Stix spoke Dalmotti as the sailor before her did. "The exact opposite: I'm freeing you."

"But that's not how it works in Saldonica." The woman's four cellmates grunted their agreement.

"Well, that's how it works now." Stix fought off a glare. "Do you want to go free or not?"

"Where am I going to go?" The woman patted her chest. "I don't have a ship, I don't have money, I don't have a place to live. None of us do." More grunts from the others, and for several moments, Stix's glare deepened.

Thirty-six cells she and Ryber had emptied, filled with Nubrevnans and Marstoks and Cartorrans and beyond. Not a one had complained about being set free. In fact, two people had wept, one had embraced her, and three had promised her riches beyond her imagining.

"You can stay in here if you want," Stix began. "I'll leave the door open. No one will stop you if you try to leave. Then you can . . ." She paused, the words *walk outside* dying on her tongue. Because what *would* happen once all of these prisoners walked outside? She had assumed that Kahina's bargain meant they were untouchable, but the pirate Admiral had never actually said those words.

So although Stix might have freed them, she had not truly *saved* them.

She cast a bespectacled glance at the four cellmates. Any one of them could leave and be captured all over again. And though she had plenty of coin left over from her Ring winnings, it wasn't here and it wasn't enough for every prisoner.

"You can walk outside," Stix finally finished, but the words were breathy and defeated. "I'm sorry. That's the best I can do. I . . . I'm sorry."

The woman's posture eased ever so slightly. "All right," she murmured.

"Guess we'll just have to manage." And with that, she jerked a thumb toward her cellmates, and they all shambled out the iron door.

Stix followed more slowly, a frown etched between her brows. Voices echoed off rough stone. Keys and locks clanked; throats coughed; rats scurried and squeaked; and a trundling line of tired souls shambled past her toward the Ring's exits. Freed, but not saved.

We understand, the voices whispered. *We have felt the same, but there is sometimes a limit to what we can do. To whom we can save.* Strangely, Stix found these words a comfort. The voices had been quiet all day, although not in their usual withholding way. They'd held the satisfied silence of an orange tabby purring in a moonbeam. And even now, with Stix's disappointment to flicker against them, they still offered her gentle grace.

Stix watched the guards, who in turn observed the prisoners from a shadow. The Hammer made sure none interfered, and if his Heart-Thread was in the prisoners' parade, he gave no indication, showed no emotion beyond a vague disinterest at the procession.

"I opened the last cell," Ryber said, joining Stix. "It had twelve sailors who cried when they heard me speak their native Kritian." She didn't look happy as she said this.

Stix didn't feel happy as she answered, "Was this the right thing to do?"

Ryber blinked. Then nodded. "Of course it was the right thing to do."

"But should we be doing more? This . . ." She waved to the limestone tunnel; water dripped on her arm. "It isn't enough, is it?"

For half a moment, Ryber held Stix's eyes. Then her own frown deepened. "I know I was angry yesterday, Stix, but I'm not anymore. This *was* a good thing. No one can argue with that."

Except one prisoner did. Before Stix could say this, Ryber leaned in close and slipped her arms around Stix's shoulders. It was a stiff, awkward embrace because Ryber wasn't one for affection, but Stix found herself squeezing the other girl back with a ferocity that startled her.

Because Ryber had stayed. For a month now, she had stayed by Stix's side, unwavering and true. That made her Stix's Threadsister. That made her family.

"Thank you," Stix told her, pulling away.

"Hye," Ryber replied, an embarrassed scrunch on her face. Then, a cough. Then a nod toward the quickly emptying hall. "Shall we leave?"

"You go on." Stix bobbed her chin. "There's still one more prisoner I need to free."

Ryber's ribs expanded—an argument clearly on its way. But then the edges of her face smoothed away. "All right. I'll meet you outside. Be careful."

"I always am," Stix agreed, a vague phrase and a vague wave to join it. Her focus was already on what waited ahead, at the end of the cells, down a narrow tunnel of its own. She navigated there quickly, footsteps half jogging while puddles splashed beneath her heels and condensation dripped on her head.

A lone lantern hung beside an iron door with no lock. Stix crept toward it. All was silent. She pressed her palm against the iron, expecting heat, but it was cold to the touch. Water dripped off the limestone ceiling, pooling at her feet.

"Anything to say?" Stix asked the voices, sliding her fingers over a single rusted latch. She waited, wondering if the voices would resist. If anything, though, they purred more insistently.

This, Stix knew, was the right thing to do.

She gripped the iron latch and yanked it down. The door swung wide. Shadows spread. She sensed water, dripping as it did everywhere ... But also something faster ahead, something thicker, like an underground stream.

Stix unhooked the lantern beside the door and ventured in. She had expected the hawk to be desperate for escape. That, like most caged animals, it would be waiting for an opportunity to spring. But as she swung the lantern around the cavernous space, she found nothing.

The hawk wasn't there. Nor were there signs it was *ever* there beyond a nest-like arrangement of stones in one corner. No charred carcasses littered the floor, no droppings from an animal the size of a galleon. It was as if the creature didn't even live here.

Come this way. Stix flinched at the voices—mere murmurs at the back of her skull. They weren't displeased, but they were insistent she listen. *This way, this way.*

"I hear you," Stix muttered, and with her lantern high, she hurried toward a darkened corner behind the nest. Water swelled inside her, like an orchestra building, and the sense of movement, of clean water swelled too. Until sure enough, she found a wide hole dipped into the ground. Cold air drifted upward, carrying the brackish scent of a tidal river. The waves wanted Stix to play, to explore, to see how far she could ride them. It came from inland and stretched all the way to the sea, splashing against a wide tunnel as it moved.

A tunnel that led to freedom. Which meant the flame hawk was not a prisoner.

Stix went still as this realization sieved through her. The flame hawk was *not* a prisoner. It could leave at any time—and clearly did. Which meant the creature was exactly as Kahina had described, exactly as Lovats had too: a pet.

At that moment, as the shards of an image fitted together to form a whole, the water below gave a hiss of interruption. *Intruder*, it seemed to say. *Unwelcome*. Then came heat. Then came a crackling that built toward a roar.

The flame hawk was returning, and if it was home, then what if its master had returned too?

A scream ripped out behind Stix, distant but unmistakable. *Ryber*.

Something had changed between Vivia and the Empress. Vivia couldn't say what precisely, except that it was more than a wall falling, more than her mask—their masks—finally crumbling away. It was something warm, and she let it come. Welcomed it, even, for it soothed away the cannon fire still echoing behind. It kept her feet moving southward even as her heart beckoned north.

Eventually, the forest vanished. Desert and death reclaimed the soil and shore—though not before Vivia caught them a fish in the shallow waves. She even coaxed a tiny fire to light, but she was so worried about undercooking the mullet, she burned it to a foul crisp. One more reason among the thousands that she wished Stix were there: Stix was an even worse cook than Vivia, and it always made her laugh when Vivia messed up.

Not that the Empress complained about the fish. She had not complained at all since fleeing the Well, and the one time Vivia asked if her feet hurt, she replied, "I've experienced worse."

It was well past midnight when they finally found a better mode of travel: a dinghy wrecked upon the shore. Vaness spotted it; Vivia confirmed it through her spyglass.

"Can you sail it?"

"Hye," Vivia replied, and she grinned. Her first grin in over a day. One that built up from her belly and spread across her lips. "Though we're both going to get wet."

Vaness smiled back, a sight Vivia wasn't sure she'd ever seen before. So rich, so real, with her forehead smoothed and the barest glimpse of teeth.

Vivia clacked shut her spyglass. Then cleared her throat, and without waiting to see if Vaness followed, she hurried down a runoff groove in the cliff. Scree loosed beneath her feet; she almost fell twice in her haste; but soon, she was on the rocky shore and peering down at the dinghy. The heat that had built within her moments before was now replaced by the heat of exertion.

Broken, half decayed, sodden, this boat wouldn't stay afloat for long—unless you were a Tidewitch. "I hope you trust me," she said as the Empress finally caught up. Vaness offered a grimace in reply, and to Vivia's surprise, she found herself laughing. As real as the smile on the cliff top, it loosed from her chest and softened in her muscles. She would find the Fox ship. She would find a way to protect her people.

She squared her shoulders to the sea, arms opening and magic reaching. The sparkle of the Well had worn off, but now she had the sparkle of the sea. Always flowing, always alive, always ready to be what Vivia needed.

Come, she summoned, and her fingers and toes curled in. *Come and take us.* Then she hopped into the half-buried boat, her feet squelching on damp sand, and offered a hand to the Empress.

Vaness took it, though her gaze was on the water. It rivered upward, following creases and seams worn into stone. Then covering sand and seaweed it had already abandoned until the next tide. By the time it reached the dinghy, Vaness was seated on the crooked remains of a bench and Vivia stood at what little remained of a stern.

Take us, Vivia said, half request, half command, and as always, the water obeyed. It licked around the boat's skeleton, careful to remain outside even when holes welcomed it in. Then it tugged, it lifted, it lurched the vessel to sea.

Vaness yelped at the first jerk. Vivia only smiled. Two more jerks as the water forced the wreck from its longtime home. Then they were sailing. Up, over the shore, and finally into the dark, lapping waves.

A few kicks from the tide, but otherwise, the ride was smooth. Like attendants carrying a litter, the water aimed to please Vivia. It aimed to keep her safe and comfortable—and fast. Within moments of clearing the last breaker, the dinghy accelerated to a wild speed. Spindrift sprayed. Waves snuck in through cracks. But never did the boat falter, and never did Vivia's magic. These past days, she had felt more connected to her power than she had in her entire lifetime. These waters were hers. These waters were home.

Time became meaningless as the boat sailed on. Her Tidewitchery was one with the sea. It navigated by instinct. It set course by timeless truth. Coral reefs older than humanity, shipwrecks ancient but new, and creatures that lived so very briefly but that the water intimately knew—each piece told Vivia where she was. Each piece guided her true.

It was midmorning when they reached the Hundred Isles. A record time, Vivia thought in that vague part of her mind that was still human. Now if she could just find where the Fox ship was meant to be.

The water knew, though—of course it knew, and it guided her with ease toward the heart of the Isles, where only the cleverest of ships could sail. Where only Nubrevnans dared risk the fickle seas and shallow shoals.

When she finally spotted *Baile's Blessing* anchored in the hidden harbor of a crescent-shaped isle, the sun was just beginning its ascent. Golden light flickered against Vivia's right side, and a warm figure leaned against her left: the Empress of Marstok, soaked by sea spray yet stiff and strong. She had her arms looped around Vivia, as if propping her for support. As if Vivia might have collapsed at any moment, and only Vaness's iron spine kept her in place upon the dinghy.

It was as Vivia finally allowed the waters to slow—as the dinghy took a sudden lurching dip into the sea—that she realized she *was* about to collapse. Vaness *was* the only thing holding her upright.

"Thank you," she tried to say, but words would not come. It was as if she had become the sea, and all she could do was bubble and froth.

Vaness seemed to understand, though, for she gripped Vivia more tightly and said, "Do not sink us just yet." She lifted her voice next and shouted at the *Blessing*, at sailors now scurrying to the railing, "I have brought you your queen, Vivia Nihar. Help us. Please, help!"

Stix had never sprinted so fast in her life. Ryber was in danger, Ryber was in pain.

And Ryber was right. Kahina had returned after one day away, and now she was already back to claim what Stix had hidden from her.

Stix pounded through stone hallways, following the screams, always just out of sight, just out of reach. Until at last, she reached the wooden stall that led into the arena. She stumbled through, where she found the Ring had been drained, leaving a muddied basin that dipped down.

Kahina stood at the heart, watching Stix through half-lidded eyes, her pipe clutched between her teeth. No tobacco burned, no smoke puffed. Her hair was looser than usual, the tight curls free around her face, and her skin shimmering with sweat as if she too had just been running.

Though she was fifty paces away, Stix's spectacles sharpened her, revealing a furious edge Stix had never seen before. This was not the Admiral who controlled the Ring. This was a Paladin thwarted.

"Where is Ryber?" Stix panted, stalking nearer. Mud squelched beneath her feet.

"Where are the blade and glass?" The jade around Kahina's thumb flashed.

"I don't know."

"Wrong answer."

The pain began.

Once, as a girl, Stix had been swimming on the beach when fire had suddenly wrapped around her arm. It had moved down her torso and onto her leg, a spiraling line that had quickly flamed throughout her body from a jellyfish tentacle tangled across her skin. The jellyfish itself was gone, but the danger of its tentacle had lived on. A tiny, autonomous weapon that had needed no master to ensure pain.

The blister on Stix's thumb was the same. A fire so sudden, so pronged, Stix didn't react at first. Even when it spread across her body, too fast for her mind to follow, she was locked in place by shock.

Until suddenly, exactly as had happened on that day paddling through the waves, she was screaming and clawing and crumpling in on herself. And this was worse—so, so much worse—for no amount of wriggling or scratching could remove it.

She fell to the earth, vision blurring beneath pain. She thought she was screaming, but she couldn't be sure. All she knew was agony.

When at last the magic flames receded, Stix found herself supine across the mud with Kahina gazing down. "My pet and I went all the way to that damnable mountain, Water Brawler, and all the way into that room of which you spoke, so imagine my consternation when there was no broken blade nor broken glass upon a pedestal. There were only the ghosts from our past, still whispering of treachery. A new treachery. *Your* treachery.

"Now I will give you a second try to do this properly: where are the blade and glass?"

"No," Stix rasped.

Kahina's face twitched at that word—a movement Stix would never have detected without her spectacles. As it was though, she saw the creasing around Kahina's eyes. Awkward lines that she didn't use often because she was not a woman used to disappointment.

The expression departed as quickly as it had come, and with it came a false calm. A loosening in her limbs as she emptied her pipe onto the mud. *Tap-tap-tap.* Ash floated down near Stix's head. "I had hoped we would not come to this, Water Brawler. I had also hoped you would be the one I thought you were, but . . ." A brittle smile. "I should have realized the truth of you. Baile would never forget the tide comes at midnight. Bring her out!"

It took Stix a moment to realize Kahina didn't shout her final words at Stix. That they were instead directed toward the wooden stall, to where a figure with broad shoulders now formed in the shadows.

The Hammer emerged a moment later, and stumbling behind him, her mouth and hands gagged by stone, was Ryber.

Stix instantly grabbed for her waters, even as Ryber shook her head. Even as Stix felt Kahina touch the jade ring and fresh flames awaken in her muscles, her veins, her soul. But then flames ignited around Ryber—real flames from a Firewitch—and she vanished in an instant. The entire wooden stall did.

Stix screamed, *Douse!*, with her throat and her mind, but her magic couldn't answer. Not while Kahina's pain stabbed though her.

"Enough." Kahina's voice bent into Stix's ear, crackling like a fire's heartbeat. "I have your friend, Water Brawler, leaving you only one choice: tell me where the blade and glass are." At this command, the pain in Stix's body receded enough for her to see Kahina's eyes, blazing with reflected flame.

And enough for her to frantically scour her mind for some other lie. Some other trick of words to fool Kahina and her blighted ring. Perhaps if she said the tools were somewhere in Saldonica. Or that she didn't know precisely where they were. Or maybe if she said they'd been broken . . .

Stix never got to speak. Not before the Hammer lifted his arms, revealing a shattered blade and a shattered glass. "The girl was carrying them with her. They were right beside you all along."

Somewhere in the flames that imprisoned Ryber, Stix thought she heard a muffled scream, thought she felt a wordless apology vibrate through what little water still remained in the arena. Which was wrong, all wrong. None of this was Ryber's fault. It was Stix's and Stix's all alone.

Now Kahina had the tools that would destroy her. The tools Eridysi had made so Paladins like Kahina would never rule the land, while Paladins like Stix would always remain to protect it.

Kahina had the blade and glass. Kahina had won.

FORTY

✳

The night was cold, the wind sharp. But the woolen cloaks Leopold had chosen for himself and Safi were thick, and Zander at Safi's back blocked the brunt of the wind's bite.

The only words exchanged in the past two hours had come from Leopold. "How do you feel?" he would ask. "Fine," Safi would answer, hoping no lines snaked up her neck or across her face. Leopold always accepted her answer, though, and the Hell-Bards never noticed anything.

A good sign, so long as she continued to feel herself—and she did, even with the frost snapping at her organs. Digging into her bones. So long as she kept moving closer to Iseult, closer to Uncle, she could ignore this strain.

Snow fell all night. Soon, a thick dusting had replaced all melt from the day before and managed to wriggle into any exposed spots on Safi's body. The tops of her boots, the edge of her collar, the tips of her sleeves. Until eventually, she was too cold to keep going.

"I need a fire," she called to Leopold on the gelding. Her first words in hours.

"We're almost there," Leopold replied.

"Almost where?"

He twisted in his saddle to look at her—and to her shock, a smile played on his lips. A *real* smile with familiar mischief to sparkle in his eyes. "To the transportation that will get us over the Ohrins." He bounced his eyebrows. "You did not think we would ride the entire way, did you?"

Safi hesitated. Leopold's declaration—the flash of humor that accompanied it—made her uneasy, even if her Truth-lens did not buzz. Hours ago, he had hated her. Now, he was charm and boyish wiles.

"Continue on then," she told him, and on the chestnut behind, Lev said, "Thank the gods. My ass hurts."

Leopold led them up a winding, poorly tended path. When it grew too steep for the horses, they dismounted, gathered their packs, and sent the noble steeds back to Praga. It was nearing dawn before they finally reached their destination on foot: a decrepit, half-collapsed barn.

"That," Zander said dubiously, "will get us across the Ohrins?" He had insisted on carrying Safi's pack, while Caden carried Leopold's.

"Ah, but Hell-Bard." Leopold twirled his arms like a maestro. "Wait until you see what's *inside*. Though first . . ." His attention shot to Safi. His eyes thinned. "How do you feel?"

"Fine," she lied. "Nothing's changed." Then she waited until he'd spun away to adjust her collar and quickly peek beneath her gloves.

The lines were worse. Ropier, darker. *But you feel the same*, she told herself. *So there is no need to worry.*

"The rest of you?" Leopold's gaze slid over the Hell-Bards. "No tugs from the Emperor?"

Murmurs of no and headshakes, but it was clear no one considered this much comfort, and the words "not yet" floated with the snowflakes around them.

Leopold led Safi and the Hell-Bards around the back of the structure, where a door sagged on its hinges and boards hung over three windows. The hinges bore no rust.

"Someone has been here recently," Caden observed as Leopold began tapping out a complicated rhythm on the door.

The prince didn't answer. All his attention was on the beats and pauses, on the eventual soft *click!* that whispered out. Three more clicks sounded, as if bolts all the way around the door were sliding free. Then the lock-spell finished its work, the door swung wide, and snow-reflected moonlight spilled over a massive ship-like device.

Safi had no idea what it was. A white canvas spiraled around a single mast, like a sail that had been twisted and coiled into a nautilus. Rather than attach to a boat, though, the mast attached to a circular platform surrounded by a wooden railing. There was nowhere to sit, only a place to steer—or that was what Safi *guessed* the central lever must be for.

"Behold," Leopold declared, gazing at the wood and canvas with the adoration of a parent, "the flying machine that will get us across the Ohrins."

"A . . . flying machine," Caden repeated at the same moment Lev blurted, "A what now?"

"It is perfectly safe." Leopold hurried into the barn's shadow. "The sails are imbued with Windwitch power, and I have tested it myself several times. We can cross the entire mountain range in hours."

While all three Hell-Bards followed Leopold inside, Safi lingered back, snow gathering on her shoulders. "Where did it come from, Polly?"

"I made it."

Her eyebrows shot high. "And did you design it too?"

"Not entirely." He circled away from his machine; impatience glinted in his eye. He didn't like questions. He expected Safi and everyone else to board without argument.

And Safi *would* board. Eventually. "Whose design was it then?"

"A friend," he snipped. "This was her idea, but I expanded upon it."

That *friend*, Safi thought, was a lie. Her Truth-lens told her as much. And for the thousandth time, she wished she had her full magic back. Despite its failings, it at least let her see more deeply into a person's heart. It let her sense both lies and truth—and in instances like these, truth was so much more important than lies. Who was Leopold the Fourth? Who *was* this person she'd always called Polly and considered a childhood friend?

She was trusting him with her life. She was trusting a machine she hadn't known he was capable of building, and it wasn't only her own neck on the line. It was the Hell-Bards', it was her uncle's, it was Iseult's.

Then again, he had tricked her throughout their lives, playing a part she'd always believed and her magic had never questioned. Two months ago Safi had told Merik that her magic was not as powerful as people assumed. That she was easily confused by strong faith. So long as a speaker believed their words to be true, her magic could detect no falsehood.

She was beginning to realize it was not merely strong faith that fooled her, but masks that ran so deep they'd become inseparable from the truth.

Safi reached for the Threadstones in her pocket. Her fingers brushed against the warm rubies. *I'm coming, Iz.*

"How do we get it aloft?" Zander asked.

"It will roll." Leopold knocked a wheel with his boot. "And once we are on board, it will lift off its wheels and take flight."

"What about landing?" This came from Lev.

Leopold's smile cracked slightly. "Yes, well, landing is never particularly *pretty*, but as long as we find a large enough space, we should have no trouble."

Caden and Lev exchanged grimaces.

"Eridysi?" Zander asked. He pointed at a small name painted on the tiller.

"Yes." Leopold plastered on a fake smile. "The machine's name."

"After the Lament?" Caden asked.

"After the old Sightwitch for whom the Lament was named." Leopold spoke in a manner that allowed no more questions, and now his gaze had settled on Safi. It razed over her as if he saw something he hated.

She quickly whirled away, pulling again at her collar and sleeves. "Let's go," she called. "There's no time to waste."

With the Hell-Bards' help, Safi and Leopold rolled the flying machine into the final dregs of night. Their breath fogged; they had to fight drifts to get the wheels through; snow fell around them. But after much heaving and groaning, they had the *Eridysi* fully outside and far from any trees.

The deck on the *Eridysi*, if it could even be called that, was no larger than a river raft. And the balustrade around its edges was entirely too short to do much good.

"You will want to sit," Leopold said after hopping on board with the Hell-Bards. He handed Safi a pair of flying spectacles like the ones Windwitches wore. He did not offer any to the Hell-Bards. He also did not wait for Safi to pull on the lenses before clasping the tiller and shouting, "*Fly!*"

The machine obeyed immediately. One moment, the *Eridysi* was on the ground, surrounded by snow. The next, a great gust of wind barreled into it. The machine jolted. Safi caught herself on her hands. The machine jerked. Safi landed on her back.

The machine *flew*. A great eruption of air and power that punched through the spiral sail and set it to spinning. Fast as a pinwheel, fast as a tornado. Treetops blurred past and the world expanded around them. Higher, higher. Safi's ears popped. Cold sliced into her. But the wind never calmed, and the sail never stopped spinning. Snowflakes clattered and clawed.

Safi fumbled on her spectacles. Already, her fingers were going numb.

Despite the snow, the flying machine ascended smoothly. The earth shrank into a white-draped miniature, then vanished from view entirely as gray storm light clotted below. By the time the machine had stopped rising, Safi was upright. Zander too, and she staggered to his side at the balustrade. Steps away, Caden and Lev were huddled close, cheeks red and eyes wide.

"He's afraid of heights," Lev blurted at the same moment Caden also said, "She's afraid of heights."

"Praga," Zander called, pointing west, and sure enough, when Safi squinted that way, she could see the faintest darkness sprawled across hills of white. To the east, the Ohrins rose. Craggy, snowcapped, and impossibly high—yet not too high for the *Eridysi*.

"Hold on!" Leopold ordered. His curls ran wild in the wind. His cloak flapped and billowed about him. When he pushed the tiller to his left, the machine lurched east. No more vertical gains, only a sideways flight that tipped the wooden raft and sent Safi and Zander leaning.

Her pack fell. She and Zander both grabbed for it. "*Slow down!*" she shrieked, but either Leopold didn't hear or Leopold didn't care. She had no choice but to cling to the balustrade with one arm while her other arm clung tightly to her pack.

Leopold's pack, she realized, had been tied down. How very convenient that he had forgotten to mention such precautions to her.

And hell-pits, if she'd thought it was cold being in the snow below, it was nothing to the cold of the storm. Wind and ice clawed into everything. Up her nose, down her throat, into her clothes and through her skin. For a time, she forgot the doom. For a time, her muscles were wholly consumed with the strength needed to stay on board. Shadowed lines of cleaving seemed a thousand miles away.

The Hell-Bards fared no better. Only Leopold seemed at ease with a preternatural grace to stay on his feet.

Eventually, the *Eridysi* leveled out. Safi didn't release the balustrade. The Hell-Bards, she noticed, did not either. Leopold, however, bared a smile and abandoned the tiller to stroll toward them. "How is everyone?" he asked in a way that suggested he hoped they were terrible.

"Shouldn't you be steering?" Safi asked through chattering teeth.

"No." He bobbed a bored shoulder. "The *Eridysi* can fly herself now. We are headed in one direction for quite a while."

"Still." She glared at him. "I'd feel much better if you kept your hand on the tiller."

He snorted and crooked forward to pat her head. "Don't you worry your pretty little—"

Safi grabbed his hand, flipped it up, and twisted his wrist toward his rib cage. "Hold," she snarled at him, "the tiller."

Leopold grunted, but if it was in pain or surprise, Safi couldn't say. He kept his fake smile glued to his face the entire time. "Of course, my *Empress*," he murmured. "Anything you wish, my *Empress*."

The Truth-lens scratched against her chest. She released him. Let him be a petty child. Let him be a foppish prince. She was in charge here, whether he liked it or not.

He gave her a mocking bow when he reached the tiller, and in that moment, Safi decided she hated him. She was tired of masks. She was tired of games.

So she moved toward the Hell-Bards. Zander had pried himself free of the railing and turned his attention to Caden and Lev. Though none of them stood, they were at least upright and slightly more relaxed. After finding an empty patch of balustrade and grabbing hold with a white-knuckled grip, she gazed down, into the gray, storm-swept expanse.

She had never flown this high before. In fact, the one time she *had* been in the air had been with Merik Nihar. They'd coasted over a lucent sea, so close to the water she had seen individual waves and the moon's glow upon each.

Now, the *Eridysi* flew so high that what few landmarks Safi glimpsed within the storm—rivers like silver thread and lakes like shadowy mirrors—were too far, too small. They didn't feel real.

With a sigh, Safi pushed away thoughts of Merik. He was alive somewhere, and one day she would find him again. When the world was no longer a shitstorm clogging a storm drain. When Iseult was safe. When Uncle Eron was safe. When her Hell-Bard friends were safe and she was safe too.

Gazing down at a brief stretch of logging camps layered in white, Safi dug deep inside herself. The remnants of the Loom were still in there, its hold still cinched around her bones. The altitude's cold might make the doom harder to tease out, but it lurked all the same. The dark magic, the vast power of control—they remained clamped around her heart.

Another peek beneath her gloves. Like a patch of untreated frostbite still exposed to the blizzard air, the darkness had grown across her skin. Shadows wriggled, and eventually there would be no stopping this. But she had not reached that point yet. She would not stop. She *could* not stop.

Her fingers moved to her pocket, where she gripped the Threadstones tight. She could almost pretend they were warm to the touch. She could almost pretend they made the Hell-Bard Loom weaken, her own heart and colors booming strong.

I'm coming, Iz, she told the horizon. *I'm coming.*

FORTY-ONE

✳

"You have lost the diary and the Threadstones." Corlant peered down at Iseult. So tall, his head almost reached the tent's domed ceiling. And so near, Iseult had to crane her neck to meet his lopsided gaze.

Her mother had returned to her shadow, head bent, and a third person had joined them: Evrane, her Threads alight with smokelike birds and cruel curiosity. But there was fear in there too, rooted at the heart of every other feeling. Fear of Corlant, Iseult assumed. The false monk certainly shot wary glances his way every few moments while she, like Gretchya, tucked herself into a shadow.

Corlant scratched at his bindings. Fresher now, no longer stained with blood—though a patch of yellow did ooze outward. Slick in the weak firelight.

"It would seem you are an agent of chaos, Iseult. Years I held both stones and diary, then you ruined it in an instant, like one of Trickster's own."

Iseult blinked slowly. "I belong to no gods."

He chuckled. "If only you knew how true that was, Dark-Giver." His Threads flared with familiar amusement, and a chill slid down Iseult's spine. It had been strange enough to have Aeduan call her that title. It was worse when Corlant said it. For him, it was a crooned endearment. Something that meant more than the sum of its two words.

She angled away from him. Her hands hurt. She wanted to sit, wanted to stop straining her neck. And above all, she wanted Corlant to see she wasn't afraid of him. At her cot, she sank down. Corlant followed, but did not sit—this man who had so easily defeated her magic. So easily frozen her alive from the inside out and who was somehow related to her by blood.

She supposed she did have his nose.

"Why do you want the Threadstones?" she asked, staring at the bandages on her hands. She had taken his sight; he had taken her touch.

"You stole the diary but did not read it?" His Threads shimmered with incredulity. Iseult knew if she glanced up, the trenches on his forehead would be deep.

"I didn't have time. Not with your monster hunting me."

"Ah. Then just think of what the Nubrevnans say: *Why do you hold a razor in one hand? So men know that I am sharp as any edge. And why do you hold broken glass in the other? So men remember that I am always watching.*" Another chuckle, but this time his Threads glinted with amusement turned inward. As if he'd made a joke only he could understand. "The Fury spent so long searching for the old tools, Iseult, but he had no idea what the Rook King had done. And the Rook King has no idea what I have done."

"And what is that?"

"We take power as we need it, and no one can resist." He directed those words toward Gretchya's corner. Iseult did not look back. "It is the power of Midne."

"It sounds more like the power of Portia."

Now full-throated surprise flashed over Corlant's Threads, and before Iseult could pull away, he had dropped to a seat beside her. He smelled of old blood and pine trees. "So you did read the diary. Where is it now?"

"Lost in the Solfatarra," she lied. He was so close. Cloying in his closeness, overwhelming in his Threads. The yellow stain where his eye had been now stank. Fetid, rotting—it was not healing well.

"Luckily for you," he said, "I recall most of it. There is much you can learn from me."

"From you," Iseult countered, using the moment to launch back to her feet. "Or from Eridysi, who actually wrote it?" She stared down at him, briefly taller.

And he smiled, though it did not reach his eye. "Your mother used to have a sharp tongue too, Iseult. It did not last."

"And I am not my mother."

"A good thing, for she was too weak to serve my purpose in the end." Still sitting, he waved to Evrane. While the monk approached, Iseult finally glanced at her mother's shadow.

Gretchya did not lift her head. She was made of stone. A stasis statue, as she'd always been.

Evrane reached Corlant and offered him a small white cloth, folded

over something that Corlant quickly withdrew: the noose off a Hell-Bard.
The one that had first connected Iseult to Corlant several days before. He
could touch it without being sucked in. He could hold it to the light and
watch it glitter, no fear of its frozen grasp.

"You will take this," he said, lone eye pinned to Iseult's face. "And together we will enter the Loom."

"Why?"

"Because there is work to be done and Threadstones to be found."

Before Iseult could react, before she could back away and try to flee,
Corlant's fingers lashed out and gripped her wrist. Then he shoved the gold
against her hand, warm from Evrane's pocket, and the world of the living
fell away.

It started with Caden. They were an hour into their flight when he floundered away from the railing, a choke garbling from his throat. Then he was
on all fours and gasping for air. Black lines crawled across his face.

Safi dropped to his side in an instant. "Caden." She tried to haul him
upright. "Caden, Caden."

He pawed her away, head shaking. "He . . . wants you." His eyes screwed
shut. "He wants me to bring—"

Lev screamed. She fell to the deck, and when Safi whipped toward
her, she found veins of shadow crawling beneath the woman's skin. They
were like Safi's, but wilder. More deadly and spreading fast. Only Zander
seemed untouched as he scrabbled toward Lev.

He yanked off his belt. "Between the teeth," he barked at Safi, and she
quickly moved to do the same with Caden.

But Caden grabbed her wrist. Stopped her from shoving the leather in.
"Dump us. Run."

"Never."

"You have to," he begged. His eyes blackened, pupils claiming everything. "Please, Safi—"

"No." Leopold's voice sliced out, calm and commanding. He stalked
toward them from the tiller. "Safiya claimed she could stop Henrick's
command, so . . ." He pinned her with a hooded stare. "Stop the command, please."

Safi stared right back. Caden's grip tightened on her wrist; nails dug in.
But she didn't withdraw—and she didn't recoil from Leopold's challenge.
She had known this moment would come, and if Leopold sought to make

an example, to teach her a lesson, to catch her in her earlier lie and force her to watch as her friends were doomed before her eyes . . .

Well, Leopold fon Cartorra—and Henrick fon Cartorra too—could eat goat shit.

She pulled her wrist free from Caden. He was convulsing now. His nails had drawn blood on the sliver of space between cuff and glove. She welcomed the pain, the welling heat. It brought her clarity as she forced her belt between his teeth. Then she sank onto her haunches and grabbed the gold chain still looped about her wrist.

Instantly, Caden and Lev stopped seizing.

At first, Safi thought she'd done it. That just by touching the chain and willing her friends to be better, she had stopped the doom and interfered with Henrick's command. Leopold seemed to think the same, for his posture softened as if on the cusp of an apology.

But then Lev's voice croaked out. "He has a message."

"Yes," Caden wheezed, a broken beat later. "He says you will not . . . get far. He will find you."

And Safi realized in that moment that she had done nothing; Henrick had simply released them and finished his punishment.

Leopold realized the same. His sneer returned, hard eyes sweeping over the Hell-Bards before settling at last on Safi. "Do you still believe they should have joined us?"

"Yes." No hesitation. Safi clambered to her feet and met Leopold's gaze. "And the Hell-Bards are with us now, so our course is set no matter what."

"Oh yes," he answered softly, and his eyes lingered on her neck, keen as a hawk's. *No, as a crow's.* Two breaths passed. *He knows,* Safi realized, watching as he smiled. *He sees my own doom.*

Yet the prince made no comment on the lines that must be tracing there. He simply said, "Our course *is* set, Safiya, so let us hope you chose the right one." Then he returned to the tiller, graceful as a prince crossing a ballroom. Graceful as a crow taking flight.

It was like before. As soon as the golden chain touched Iseult's skin, she was inside the Dreaming. Gray waves undulated around her. The sense of endless expanse somehow condensed to muffled containment.

Beside her, Corlant stood, his Threads twice as bright—and twice as wrong too, for the icy core shone silvery here.

"The souls," Iseult began, lifting a hand to the wave of shadows speeding their way. She'd once read of tidal waves, massive and destructive. How people could do nothing but watch as the deadly waters charged in.

She felt like that now. Helpless to escape the voices and ghost hands that wanted to drag her down.

Except they did not reach her like before. This time, as the broken Threads and vague shapes barreled close, Corlant lifted a single hand, and the Hell-Bard ghosts parted. Splitting left and right, they streamed around Iseult and Corlant like a river glides around stone.

Cold heaved against Iseult, shouts, screams, pleas from the damned. But she simply watched them pass. It was like the image from the diary, the one Esme had shown Iseult, of a single leader at the Loom's heart

But that person couldn't be Corlant. He was the first bound to it, not the Loom's creator. Which meant if he could move here, then so could she. "How do you do that?"

Corlant turned to her. Here, his one eye was golden and unhurt. Iseult glanced down. She too was healed, her fingers unmarred.

"You can do it too, Iseult. All you need is more power." Corlant seemed only to whisper, yet the words cut directly into Iseult's ears. As if his lips were against her, each breath made of ice. "But first you must find the Threadstones. Use your magic to locate them in the Loom."

Iseult shuddered—and Corlant smiled. "I don't know how to find them." She pulled her gaze from him to stare at the Hell-Bards, still closing in.

So many lost lives. And one of them, somewhere, was Safi.

"Imagine what it felt like to use the stones. Imagine what it feels like to be bound to your Threadsister."

"Maybe if you told me what the stones were, I could find them—"

"You will learn soon." Annoyed red whipped up his Threads. "Once I possess the stones again, I will show you. First, though, we must *find* them. Now imagine." He reached for Iseult, his palm flat as if to touch her forehead—as if to steal her magic like he'd taken the Herdwitch's. She reeled back. Her heel hit the current of shadows.

And the ghosts swept her away. So fast, she had no time to cry out. So hard, she had no strength to fight. The dead carried her, and it was worse than before. This time, the souls claimed her before she had a goal. All she could do was be punched along, carried by a thousand cold hands and screamed at by a thousand lost throats. She became their fury, she became their need.

Living, living, they seemed to shriek at her. *Breath and living.* But there was a second refrain too, from new souls—younger and sharper, with Severed Threads still pulsing with hope. *Threads that heal, Threads that thrive.*

"I can't help you," she wanted to say, but all that came out was choking and ice. Claws stabbed and her spine cracked. *Living, living, breath and living. Threads that heal, Threads that thrive.* On and on they carried her. Over and over they broke her. Punishment for all her sins. For the Void that lived inside her.

But then she heard something—a voice she knew. A voice she loved. "Weasels piss on you. You're not supposed to be here."

Instantly, Iseult's mind sharpened, homing in on that sound. On the certainty that filled her as soon as she heard it. And like anchors dropping overboard, Iseult's limbs solidified. Her body, her soul—they stopped their free-fall tumble through the tidal wave of souls.

She found her feet. "Safi?" She imagined the timbre of what she'd just heard. The emotion behind it—*Weasels piss on you!*—and the sideways grin attached. She imagined how it sounded when Safi spoke in real life, cavalier and crass; she imagined how it felt when Safi spoke across the Threadstones, more reticent, more exposed.

Then Safi was there. Before Iseult with Threads so familiar that dream-tears ached in Iseult's throat. So much depth, so much dimension. Even the Hell-Bard Loom could not replace all those folds and filaments, all those colors and smiles. Shadows might course in her severed soul, but it was still *her.* Right here, close enough to touch.

"Safi," Iseult said to the Threads, and she reached out to stroke them. They were frozen to the touch.

"Good," Corlant crooned, words oozing into Iseult's ears.

She jerked. Her hand fell, and Corlant laughed. He was right beside her, face creased with pleasure and Threads skittering with want. "You are a natural, it would seem."

Iseult stepped in front of Safi's Threads. Futile but instinctive. "I found Safi, not the Threadstones." Her voice slithered out, strong. Plumed by fog. She no longer drowned in the Dreaming, she controlled it.

At least so long as her Threadsister was beside her.

"Oh, but the light-bringer has the Threadstones, Iseult. She stole them, you see." He flicked a hand toward Safi, and her Threads briefly parted like tassels on a gown, revealing two bright pinpricks of red. They glimmered and flared, embers of power Iseult instantly recognized.

But how had Corlant known they would be there? How could he have possibly known Safi had stolen them? Before Iseult could ask, Corlant's hand dropped. The Threadstones disappeared, and the false priest fastened his attention on Iseult once more.

"We must figure out where she is, Iseult. *You* must learn by connecting with her. By seeing through her eyes."

Iseult swallowed, dream-lips so cold, so dry. Part of her desperately wanted to connect to Safi, to see where she was to promise that everything would be better because she, Iseult, was going to fix it. But another part of her—the smarter, logical part of her—prickled with warning. Corlant did not want to know Safi's whereabouts to help her, and Iseult was in no position to fight him again.

She was also in no position to resist him. He manipulated this space, he manipulated the ghosts and the Dreaming that contained them. If he wanted Iseult to see through Safi's eyes, then he would make it happen.

She might as well do it on her own terms.

"Yes," she said with a nod. "I will try to see through her eyes." Without another word or even a glance for Corlant, Iseult grabbed Safi's Threads again. She had no idea what she was doing, but she'd found her Threadsister without assistance. Surely she could figure this out too.

Cold speared up Iseult's dream-hands. She flinched, squeezing instinctively.

And Safi screamed. A real scream from a real throat in the real world. And just like that, Iseult became one with Safi's mind.

It was wrong, so wrong. A violation she'd never imagined herself committing. A step too far as the Puppeteer, and no matter how much she told herself it was to protect Safi, she couldn't stop the guilt from sludging through her.

"I'm sorry," Iseult whispered. "I'm so, so sorry." She tugged at the Threads and moved Safi's head. A swivel left, a swivel right. *Wind and clouds, cold and creaking wood. Hell-Bards made of shadow. A man with wild violent Threads. Spinning cloth, glowing Airwitch power, and mountains slipping by.*

"I'm sorry," Iseult said again, and this time, she released Safi. Heat stifled through her, despite the eternal cold of the Loom. Wrong, wrong— she had done something irredeemably wrong. *Because you are a monster and it is all you can do.*

"What did you see?" Corlant asked, his head crooking down to Iseult's like a vulture sizing up its prey. "What did you find, Iseult?"

"A flying machine." Her voice scraped out, raw with inner heat and inner hate. "Safi is with three Hell-Bards, and they are coming this way."

Iseult did not mention the fifth person, angry and brooding and powerful in his own way. She didn't know why, but the words stayed stuffed in her throat. *The Fool card still to be played.*

"Excellent," Corlant said. His long fingers laced into a triumphant fist. "You truly were born to do this. Now let us leave the Loom and find a way to bring them to us, shall we?" His fingers unwound. He offered her a hand.

And she swallowed. The last thing she wanted was to touch him, in the Loom or in real life. But she also needed him to believe her a willing student and willing daughter.

She took his hand, corpse-like and foul.

It was only as the world of the Dreaming melted away and warmth—real, living warmth—caressed in that Iseult wondered if perhaps Corlant had already known about Leopold on the machine. If perhaps *Leopold* was the one who'd told Corlant about the stolen Threadstones.

Wicked Cousin and Trickster. Old Ones forgotten, Paladins returned.

FORTY-TWO

✳

Kahina possessed the blade and glass. Exactly what Ryber had feared would happen, exactly what Stix had believed, in all her overconfidence, would not.

The Hammer handed Kahina the broken blade, and she held it toward the light that roiled off Ryber's cage of flames. Orange and white glittered on the steel. Kahina smiled. It was not a gloating smile, nor even a delighted one, but rather a smile of relief.

"*Death, death, the final end,*" she said, finding Stix's eyes over the fast-drying mud. "It sings to you too, does it not?" She thrust out the blade as if preparing to attack. "I could kill you permanently with it. No more Paladin souls. No more Water Brawlers. But I will spare you, Stacia Sotar, because even Exalted Ones can still be saved." She snapped down the blade and handed it to the Hammer, who quickly wrapped it in cloth. The same cloth Ryber had hidden it within for so many days.

Then, with nothing more than an over-the-shoulder wave—as if she were departing from a casual meeting between friends—Kahina strode into the wooden stall. The fire parted to allow the Hammer to follow and for Ryber to come crawling out.

As soon as Stix rushed to Ryber's side, the entirety of the Ring ignited.

It was like a thousand firepots going off at once. One moment, there were flames on the stall; the next moment, everything burned. Blue heat rumbled over Stix. No time to think, no time to assess or do anything but haul Ryber close and run. *Freeze,* she commanded. *Freeze, douse, freeze.* What little water still survived here fought to obey, elated to be useful, and in two fire-choked breaths, the flames nearest to Stix and Ryber snuffed out.

"I'm sorry," Ryber said from smoke-rasped lungs. Over and over again. "I'm sorry, he . . . the Hammer . . . he surprised me. I'm sorry, Stix."

But it wasn't Ryber's fault that this had happened. Stix couldn't even blame the Hammer. He'd had a bargain with Kahina—Stix knew what that meant now.

No, all of this chaos, every flame now streaming toward the sky, was Stix's fault and her fault alone. Noden save her, if she ever saw her father again, she'd tell him he was right. That her natural power *had* made her overconfident, that one day she *had* met someone she couldn't match. And that hye, a magic as strong as hers did need honing, and she should never have taken it for granted.

Even the voices had abandoned her to her mistakes. No more satisfied quiet. Only cold, resentful silence.

Stix floundered for any water in the air or in the soil, but there was too much heat for her to fight against. Worse—because of course it could somehow get worse—a new roar was filling the Ring. A rattling, shuddering sound that shook the water and shook Stix's bones with a thousand tiny feet.

She turned right as the first of the rats entered the ruined arena, streaming from the burning, collapsing scaffolding. They aimed for the only place absent of flames. They aimed for Stix and Ryber.

The captain's room on the *Blessing* was almost identical to Vivia's on the *Iris*. A slight rearrangement of furniture, slightly rougher floors, and slightly brighter lighting. Otherwise, all was the same—for which Vivia was grateful. She had been asleep in the captain's bed for several hours, and there was a comfort in waking to familiarity.

"This is becoming a most inconvenient habit." Vaness shifted in a chair and leaned out of a shadow. Lantern light warmed her face. "I thought I was the one with a sickness."

Vivia offered a weak laugh and pushed herself upright. Vaness leaped forward to help, but Vivia was already sitting by the time the Empress reached her. So she stared down at Vivia, and Vivia stared at up at her.

"This isn't normal." "Vivia rubbed at her eyes, crusted with sea salt. "I've never passed out from my magic before. And certainly not twice in two days."

"Hmmm." Vaness eased onto the bed's edge. She sat primly, hands folded upon her lap. Like Vivia, salt had caked against her skin.

"All magic has a price," Vaness said after several moments. "And the more powerful the witchery, the steeper the toll. Although . . ." A tightening of her face. Then a full frown. "I have noticed my own sickness getting worse. As if the magic I'm tapping into has a limit. As if—"

"You are becoming the iron you need to use."

Vaness blinked. "Hye. That is exactly it." Her head tipped sideways, gaze roaming over Vivia's face. "It happens to you then?"

"Hye." Vivia's cheeks warmed at the scrutiny. "And because of it, I lose sight of my own limits. I lose sight of—"

"Who I am."

Vivia swallowed. Vaness wet her lips. And for several long seconds, they stared at each other. An open, unmasked stare that made Vivia's neck warm. And her chest and hands too.

A knock thumped at the door. Vivia's heart jumped; Vaness startled to her feet. And a moment later, the *Blessing*'s captain shoved in. A stocky woman, shorter even than Vaness, she had been several years ahead of Vivia in training—but like Stix, her family was nobility. And like Vivia, she could control the tides.

Shanna Quintay. She nodded at Vivia and her swagger across the room paused just long enough for a bow, fist over heart. Then she directed her attention to Vaness. "We could not reach Ginna, Your Imperial Majesty. We tried several times, but the Voicewitch must be drugged as you were."

Vivia's eyebrows lifted, and she turned a surprised eye on Vaness. The Empress had clearly updated Shanna *and* asked her to reach out to Vivia's crew, for which Vivia was . . . grateful. Surprised, impressed, and grateful.

"We did, however," Shanna continued, "contact a Voicewitch from Noden's Gift. She said only that the village was under attack and Lovats would not reply."

Of course they wouldn't. It was so like Serafin to hide himself behind the Sentries of Noden. To lock himself within the city while the rest of the world burned. *Share the glory, share the blame.*

"Then we must help them," Vivia said. She scrubbed at her eyes—so salty—and searched for the right words, the right plan to help a village faced with hundreds of Dalmotti sailors.

Before she could conjure anything or sort through all this spinning and tightening in her gut, Shanna said: "Where Noden's Gift has failed, though, we have succeeded. My Voicewitch is in contact with Lovats right now." She snapped her fingers toward the door, and a lithe man walked into the cabin. His eyes glowed rose, his attention fixed on the middle distance. At his side, a ship's boy cradled his arm and guided him toward the table.

"He's connected right now?" Vivia asked, finally shoving off the cot and crossing to him. Her legs, though weak from lying down, were strong from the boat's tender rocking. "To whom?"

The Voicewitch found Vivia's face. "Daughter."

And Vivia's stomach bottomed out. She hadn't heard her father's voice in over a month—and though this was not truly his voice, it was close enough. The sharpened consonants, the subtle condescension. It was a perfect mimicry. Bile swam upward in Vivia's belly. Her fingers curled into her thighs.

"Your Maj—" She broke off. *No.* "Father," she offered instead. "Nihar burns. You must send in the Royal Navy."

"*I* must do nothing," he replied, and she could just imagine him seated at his desk, cold eyes locked upon his Voicewitch. Gray light filtering through threadbare blue curtains. "*You* must turn yourself in. You and that Marstoki smut must give yourselves up to Dalmotti immediately."

"Our people are dying—"

"Exactly," he barked. "And the longer you wait, the more lives will be lost."

"Ah." The word escaped on a sigh, and for some inexplicable reason, Vivia wanted to laugh. She shouldn't be surprised by his words. She'd told Vaness what he was made of. Yet knowing and *knowing* were not the same thing.

What a silly little fox. What a sad little fox.

"What happened to 'bringing the empires to their knees'?" she asked, head shaking. "What happened to the man who would never surrender, never give in—"

"Says the girl who consorts with the Iron Bitch."

Girl. Vivia had not been a girl in so long. Not since Jana had died. Not since she'd been left with a parent who bragged and boasted and convinced the world with his charm that he was one way . . . while none of his actions spoke the same. He'd fooled all the admirals of the Royal Navy, all the generals of the Royal Soil-Bound. He'd fooled Lovats. He'd fooled Vivia.

She'd always believed his self-flattery worth emulating. That such confidence was something to aspire toward. But tucked within the constant crowing were pointed insults. *Jokes*, he would call them, though Vivia never laughed. *Advice*, he would proclaim, though Vivia never learned. *Concern*, he would insist, though Vivia never felt loved.

She glanced at Vaness, held the Empress's dark, earthen gaze. Vaness wasn't perfect, but at least she was her own person. Her own well-honed blade of steel tempered by herself and those she ruled.

"I am not turning myself in," Vivia said at last. "I am queen, and a queen must be free to help her people."

A beat passed. The faintest curve hit Vaness's lips.

Then Serafin replied: "If only Merik had not been the one to die."

The Voicewitch's magic ended. The man's eyes shuddered, his breath loosed, and the ship's boy gripped him steadily. But already the man's lips were parting in horror as he realized what he'd just said.

Shanna's neck muscles tensed and bulged. The ship's boy stared at anywhere but Vivia. And Vaness . . .

The glint in her eyes had changed from amusement and pride, from approval and admiration, to something made of daggers. She, like the others, clearly expected Vivia to erupt. Or perhaps to cry. *Something* after words as hateful as the King Regent's. But for once, Vivia felt no anger or grief. Gone was the churn in her gut and the sense that she was falling. It was as if some final mooring had been released. Now her ship was free. No anchors, no barricades, no shoals to block her way. Now the little fox *knew*.

Vivia smoothed at her salt-stiffened shirt. Then adjusted her collar. Then finally patted at the edges of her face. No mask now, for she was not a bear and didn't need to be. Foxes had all the cleverness and wiles she could ever wish for.

"Contact the Dalmotti ships," she told the Voicewitch. And then to Vaness, her mouth twisting sideways, "I think it's time we turned ourselves in. But on our terms and as the Well Chosen you think we're meant to be."

Stix held Ryber's hand and ran toward the center of the Ring. She didn't know what else to do. The stall was in flames, the scaffolding and towers were in flames, and high-pitched squeaking filled Stix's ears, lungs, bones.

Safety, she thought with each footfall. *Safety, safety.* She summoned ice to crack up around her and Ryber, but the heat was too strong. Each crackling shard melted almost as soon as it appeared, then puffed into steam and vanished.

So Stix tried freezing the rats instead, but Hagfishes take her, there were too many. For every ten she got, another hundred came rushing over, close enough that she could feel their footsteps vibrating into her teeth.

She and Ryber reached the center of the Ring, where the mud dipped to its lowest. A floor waited there—one Stix hadn't noticed the day before with the lake atop it. Now, there was no missing the ancient flagstones, nor the orange tabby sitting at the heart. Red-furred and ragged, she licked her paw, grooming as if nothing of interest happened around her.

Stix had never minded the six-fingered tabby, but in that moment, she hated her. "Help us!" she shrieked. "Isn't this what you were made for? Here are all the rodents you could ever want to destroy—"

A rat leaped onto Ryber's leg. She yelped and whirled around, leg flinging out. But it wasn't the only rat. Three more had reached her and were climbing up with fangs out.

Stix blasted ice onto the beasts, but they thawed almost as quickly as they froze. Kahina's heat would not be denied. Ryber fell. Stix fell too. Their hands came apart, and Stix thumped back first onto the muddied flagstones. She punched and kicked and wriggled at rats, and she banged against the stone.

Once. Twice. Thrice. On what would have been the fourth bump against the wall—as two more rats leaped toward her face—Stix hit the stones . . . And then sank through.

Darkness swallowed her. Ryber screamed, and the world of the Ring vanished around them. They plummeted for what felt an eternity, her stomach stretching long and her brain crushing inward.

Then Stix hit more stone, and Ryber crashed down beside her. Rats landed atop them, so Stix kept kicking and punching and wriggling. One landed beneath her fist; she felt its skull crunch. Another went flying off her when she finally grabbed its scruff and threw. And the last, still attached, suddenly screamed and fled when a light flared.

Stix screamed too, more burst of sound than actual scream. She expected guards or Kahina and flames and more rats, but in the several moments it took for her vision to adjust, she found neither. It was simply a Firewitched lantern, ancient in style and strangely familiar, revealing a small stone space around them.

Stix and Ryber lay at one end, and at the other was the orange tabby, looking very pleased by the rat now dangling from her mouth. The other rats were nowhere to be seen, save the two Stix had crushed. They rested, bloodied and dead, several paces away.

Ryber groaned, and Stix rolled to her friend's side. "Are you hurt?"

"No." Ryber waved her off, eyes shuttering as she took in the room around them. "What *is* this place?" Without waiting for an answer, she crawled unsteadily to her feet.

"I don't know." Stix rubbed at her eyes. Without her spectacles, Ryber was a vague blur circling the room. "The voices refuse to speak to me anymore."

A sharp huff from Ryber, though Stix couldn't gauge if the frustration was aimed at her or at the voices.

"Listen," she began, "about what just happened. I should never have made that deal with Kahina. You were right, and now the prisoners . . ." Stix trailed off. Ryber wasn't listening, and not because she was angry—though she had every right to be—but because she was absorbed in exploring the room. As if none of the chaos from the Ring had just happened. As if she didn't have a charred shirt or several braids singed at the edges. This was a new realm, new knowledge, and she was a scholar to her core.

"I've heard of these places," Ryber murmured, awe rounding her words. "The Six made them. Secret spots where the Exalted Ones wouldn't find them . . . And oh." She clapped her hands to her mouth. "Come look at this."

Though Stix really didn't want to stand—her breaths were sharp and fast, her heart the dominant sound within her ears—she straggled to Ryber's side, to where a stone relief filled one wall. It looked identical to a relief in the capital of Lovats, in the under-city that had first triggered the wretched voices to rise.

"Lady Baile," Ryber said. "Noden's Right Hand. A saint in Nubrevna. A saint in Saldonica. The Paladin of Water." She swiveled toward Stix. "You."

Stix ran her fingers over the relief, exactly as she had only a month ago, when the voices had first started speaking and the memories had first started rising. This relief was in better condition than the one beneath Lovats. Water had not weathered this limestone, and no fungus called it home.

"Though we cannot always see," Stix murmured, "the blessing in the loss, strength is the gift of our Lady Baile, and she will never abandon us." Those were the words beneath every relief in Lovats, where Baile stood with a trout in one hand and wheat in the other. Her fox-shaped mask speckled with stars, and a moon passed over her.

They were not the words here. "Three rules has she," Ryber read. "Our Lady of the Seas. No whistling when a storm's in sight, six-fingered cats will ward off mice, and always, always stay the night for . . ."

She paused. For here the words were different than what was written elsewhere. "For Baile's slaughtering," she finished.

"Slaughtering," Stix repeated. "Slaughter Ring." She frowned at the relief, but Ryber had read it accurately. It said *slaughtering* instead of *Slaughter Ring*." What does it mean?" She glanced at the tabby, who of course did not reply, and Ryber merely shrugged, a helpless movement. "Still no voices?"

"Of course not." Although Stix wasn't sure she needed them. She could sense, all on her own, that something critical was here—the missing shard to finally give her the full picture.

She'd whistled and summoned a sea fox. Not because she'd known that was what her whistle would do, but because she'd had a hunch guided by Kahina, the woman who kept flame hawks as pets. *The Paladin of Fire.*

And now, though the cat hadn't exactly warded off mice, that six-fingered tabby had helped her escape the rats. Which left only one line in the poem that perhaps was not a poem at all.

"Always, always stay the night for Baile's slaughtering," Stix repeated. "Slaughter Ring. Slaughtering." Her eyes lit on the moon shining above Baile's head. Another difference between this relief and the one in Lovats. "Midnight?"

The tabby nuzzled against Stix's calf with a purr.

"What happens at midnight?" Ryber asked, but Stix only shook her head. The answer was so close. Within reach. She just needed the proper angle. Just needed the proper words. Damn the voices for always going silent . . .

Baile would never forget the tide comes at midnight.

"Oh," Stix breathed to the relief. "Oh." Kahina had already given her the answer—and really, it had been there all along. The tidal river beneath the Ring. The condensation that lived on the stones. The humidity that breathed in the very air of Saldonica. Lady Baile had built her palace here for a reason; Stix had simply been unwilling to see.

Unwilling to accept she didn't know everything already.

With that thought, the memories finally awoke. The stone room disappeared.

"Only in darkness can we understand life, and only in life can we change the world." Stix frowns at the paper, a torn edge from Eridysi's diary. The Sight-witch has gathered a whole stack of young Lisbet's prophecies, and now she is laying them out, one by one, for Stix and Rhian, the Paladin of Fire, to see.

Rhian palms one of the papers, her muscled forearms rippling and her large, round eyes widening. "Six turned on six," Rhian reads. "And made themselves kings. One turned on five and stole everything. It means we will die, doesn't it?"

Eridysi cringes. "I hope not." She rustles through the stack for several moments. She has never been the most organized person—her workshop always makes Stix's fingers itch to move, to rearrange, to label. But eventually Dysi finds the page she needs and thrusts it toward Stix and Rhian. "Lisbet also said this, the next day. I don't know if it's a correction of what she said before or if it's a new prophecy . . ."

Stix takes the page and reads aloud, "Six turned on six and made themselves kings. Five turned on one and stole everything."

Rhian's frown—a constant on her olive face these days—briefly smooths with surprise. "Perhaps there are two possible outcomes?"

"Perhaps." Dysi shrugs. "When I ask Lisbet, all she will say is, 'A good question, Dysi. A good one indeed.'"

Stix sighs. Why the Sleeper chooses to speak through an eight-year-old, she'll never know—and why the goddess can't speak more plainly is an old frustration, rounded at the edges.

"We need to go," Rhian says, her fingers moving to Stix's shoulder. A gentle gesture, for she knows how much Stix despises returning to Lovats's court. The jade ring she always wears rubs against Stix's silken sleeve. "The Exalted Ones will wonder where we are if we do not return soon. Lovats will wonder."

Stix nods and lays the prophecy atop the others. Before she can exit Dysi's workshop, however, the Sightwitch calls, "Wait. There's one more. For you, Baile." She gathers up Stix's hand and curls a large page into her palm. "Like most of Lisbet's declarations, I don't know what it means. But perhaps you will. Perhaps one day it will save you."

Stix bows her head. She will read it later, in privacy. Later when there is time.

It is several days before such a moment comes and she can tuck herself away in her quarters at Paladin's Keep on the edge of Lovats's lush granite city. On the top floor with the door locked and no one but her tabby to see, she unfurls the page—wrinkled from several days tucked within her bodice. Then she reads:

> Three rules has she, our Lady of the Seas.
> No whistling when a storm's in sight.
> Six-fingered cats will ward off mice,
> And always, always stay the night for Baile's slaughtering.

Stix came out of the memory gasping for air. Unlike the violence of other memories, this one had felt so calm. So simple, so *real* with Rhian beside her. One of the Six, Rhian had been a mothering type who had died the same day Baile had, when the Rook King had killed them all. *Six turned on six and made themselves kings. One turned on five and stole everything.*

"I understand," Stix said. Then she pressed her head against the stone and thanked the past lives for finally answering her call. "I understand."

"What happened?" Ryber asked beside her. "Did you see something?"

"Hye," Stix murmured, and taking Ryber's hand into hers, she glanced down at the tabby. "Are you ready?" The cat purred, and Stix smiled. Then she raised her foot and stomped once. Twice. Thrice.

The floor beneath them vanished. They dropped once more into the Ring—into a clashing of sound and humidity and rumbling rodent feet.

The flames of the Ring burst against Stix. So hot her heart compressed beneath them, her ears and skull felt pummeled in two. Or perhaps that was the rats, now surging toward her, climbing over her toes, up her body. But the night's clouds had dispersed, revealing moonlight.

Revealing midnight.

Which meant it was time to follow the rhyme. Time to become the Lady Baile whom Stix was meant to be. Not just the saint's chosen, not just a vessel for memories a thousand years past, but Baile herself. A Paladin. Someone as strong as Kahina, if not stronger. Because this was her palace, and her water-filled home.

Fangs cut into Stix's legs. Bright bursts of pain punctuated by squeals that claimed all hearing. Bodies covered her with warmth and fur and claws to draw blood. She had to ignore it though. Just for a moment, she had to *ignore it* and pray she had interpreted the writing correctly.

Slaughter Ring, slaughtering. Slaughter Ring, slaughtering. Always, always stay the night.

Her arms stretched long. She was done with seeking answers. Done with the timeless existence of the voices. She was done picking at an open sore and wondering what Vivia must think.

Stix *reached*. She knew what her magic felt like. It had been a part of her for almost a decade. An organ, a limb, a piece of soul that not even flames could contain.

Come, Stix told the tide rising in a river below. *We are one, and I need you. Come.* Power wove through her muscles, even as her vision wavered. *Come this way, keep coming.* The Ring and Ryber and all the rats hazed away. Stars sprayed across Stix's eyes, but the water listened. Her oldest, dearest friend.

It slithered as she needed it to slither, wringing from the very air itself and squeezing into the gaps between flames. It obeyed and rejoiced and sank until the flames had no more fuel, no more will to live. And as the conflagration paled, ice rose up from the earth to claim each rat, to freeze them one by one.

Power surged over Stix. All of it, straight from Noden. So vast and full and entirely her own. She saw almost nothing. There was only darkness and flashes of weary light. But for now, while she revelled in the true edges of her magic, she didn't need her vision. The slaughtering was done.

Fingers gripped her shoulder—so much like the memory of a Paladin named Rhian. But it was Ryber's voice who said, "We're safe. You can stop now."

"Hye," Stix answered, a sound both ragged and elated. Then: "I can't see. The magic is . . . everything."

"It will recede," Ryber assured her. "Kullen's lungs always failed him when he used too much power."

"I can't wait for it to return, though, Ry. We need to get to the harbor. Can you lead us there?"

"Why?" Ryber asked, even as she scooped an arm behind Stix. Water rushed around their feet, rivulets melting off the rats. "What's at the harbor?"

"What your cards were pointing us to all along: the Queen of Hawks, the Queen of Foxes, and the Giant."

FORTY-THREE

※

It was a good dream. Yes, Safi was back in the Loom, but this time she wasn't slowly fading while Zander held her aloft. This time, she floated and flitted and followed the sound of Iseult's voice.

Then she found her Threadsister. She was *right there*, flesh and blood, standing before her. "Weasels piss on you!" Safi laughed, a trilling sound that seemed to vanish as soon as it left her lips. "You're not supposed to be here."

"Safi," Iseult said in that special way she had: inflectionless yet somehow carrying a thousand emotions. She reached for Safi, and Safi, formless though she was, tried to reach back.

But a shadow came. It spread behind Iseult, liquid and alive, before solidifying into a man. Gold winked at his throat, and he crooned something in Nomatsi—something Safi couldn't quite hear and wasn't sure she'd understand anyway. Iseult turned away.

"No," Safi tried to say. "Stay." But Iseult didn't hear. She spoke to the shadow man, a cold, detached version of herself. The one that sometimes frightened Safi.

Whoever the shadow was, he was bad. Iseult needed her help. Yet right as Safi brushed forward to speak again, to reach again, Iseult rounded back. Arms outstretched and fingers long, she grabbed for Safi as if to embrace. So Safi swept into it. *Yes, yes, I am here!*

Then the pain began. Safi shattered awake.

Her whole body shook. Her teeth rattled in her ears. And someone was grabbing her, holding her, and shouting her name over and over again. *Caden.* She twisted her stiff neck toward him, but her muscles were not her own. Left, right, she looked where Iseult wanted her to look.

No, not Iseult. This could not be Iseult's doing. It would never be Iseult's doing.

"Safi." Caden gripped her biceps tightly. "Can you hear me?"

She nodded dimly. Still, no words would form; no breath would gather.

She was going to suffocate, and this was going to be the end. *Let go*, she tried to tell Iseult. *Please, please let go.*

"Shit," Caden hissed, and suddenly Safi was being hauled into an upright position. Then dragged over wood and leaned against the railing.

He ripped open her shirt, no ceremony, no gentleness, and exposed her chest to cold and starlight. "The Hell-Bard's doom," he said. "You should have *said* something."

Safi could only shake her head. What was there to say? It wasn't just the doom. It was Iseult, now gone, and the shadow man with gold upon his neck.

The longer she sat there with Caden's fingers upon her chest, the more air seeped into her lungs, blessed and true. "I feel . . . fine," she rasped.

"Liar," he replied.

She shook her head. "Truly."

A frown pinched his brow. His gaze lingered on her bare skin, yet when Safi towed her gaze downward, only the faintest of black lines radiated across her chest. Fewer with each heartbeat. Then after several ragged breaths, no lines wriggled at all.

Caden exhaled roughly and closed her shirt. "I don't understand."

"Nor I," Safi admitted, and for the first time, she looked past him and realized everyone watched with wide eyes. Everyone except Leopold; he watched with bored calculation, like a crow watches carrion. He had done nothing to help her, and he did nothing now.

"We should turn back," Caden said, rising as if to stand.

Safi grabbed his collar and yanked him back down. "*No.* That is exactly what Henrick wants us to do. And it wasn't the doom that hit me. It was . . ." She couldn't say Iseult. They wouldn't understand. *She* didn't understand.

Before she could find a solid argument, Leopold's voice pitched out, "We are almost there anyway."

He spoke so quietly Safi thought she'd imagined it. Except Caden stiffened too. And when she angled toward Leopold, she found him staring calmly their way.

"We are almost there," he repeated. Then he waved to the horizon. "Welcome to the Solfatarra."

Safi dragged herself around to peer through the railing. Night faded in the west, blanketing the world in soft blue light, though it could not hide the stretch of white fog. As if all the clouds in the sky had fallen to the earth and gathered close. For miles and miles, the earth was nothing but white.

"Where will we land? Where is Iseult?"

Leopold didn't answer. He remained bored and statuesque beside the tiller.

"Polly," she barked at him. "Now is not the time for games. Where is Iseult?"

"Near," he replied. "Very near."

She curled back her lips, and with a glare made of glass shards, she drew in her feet and stood. The world bled. Her head spun.

Frozen air gusted against her. Slithered into the cracks of her still un-buttoned blouse. "You will tell me, Polly, or I swear I will—" She made it only two steps toward him before the *Eridysi* lurched. A vicious sideways snap that flung Safi backward against the railing.

"The hells?" Lev barked, as all attention shot to Leopold. But he wasn't looking at Safi or the Hell-Bards. His face had gone white as the sail; his knuckles too against the tiller.

"Windwitches," he said. "In Cartorran colors."

Then the world turned upside down, and the *Eridysi* fell.

"I found them for you," Iseult said once she was back in the real world. Back upon her cot. Corlant stood before her, neck cracking side to side while Gretchya and Evrane watched silently. He had dropped the noose to the floor.

"You did indeed." Corlant's Threads thrummed with pleasure. "And now I shall reward you. Follow." He spun about, his movements pointed and long. Eager as a child going to claim dessert.

Iseult didn't follow. Not right away. First, she gathered the noose with a bandaged hand and dropped it into a pocket on her new gown. Then she searched for her mother's eyes across the tent. But Gretchya wouldn't lift her head. Wouldn't move at all. She was stone, stone, always made of stone.

Well, Iseult was made of stone now too.

She joined Corlant outside the tent, where the edge of night awaited. Fourth chimes, she guessed, though clouds blocked the sinking moon as Corlant led the way through slouching square tents.

Never in her life had she willingly followed Corlant anywhere. Now here she was, trailing behind him through this new Purist encampment. *Daughter, my daughter.*

Iseult saw no sign of the shadow wyrm's silver Threads. Purists, how-ever, were everywhere. Like flies to a corpse, they'd gathered in vast numbers.

Dressed in brown and gray, their Threads muted and muffled by Cursewitchery, they all wore identical focus. Identical fervor. They followed orders from Corlant willingly, desperately, and at the sight of him, they dropped low, a bowing of bodies and chorus of "*Blessed are the pure, blessed are the pure.*"

They also recognized Iseult. Many smiled at her, a few bowed, and one elderly woman even grabbed her bandaged hands and kissed them.

It hurt.

"Bless you, daughter of Midne," the woman said. "We have waited so long."

Iseult observed her and everyone else without emotion, without interest. These people didn't see Corlant for what he truly was, but their blindness was a willing one. Corlant had made no effort to hide his power. Anyone who'd seen him face off against Iseult must've realized what he could do.

"Why don't these people care about your magic?" she asked. No inflection. No stammer. Stasis lived inside her, and if Corlant wouldn't answer her questions about Threadstones, then she would attempt to leach out other information instead.

"What magic?" he countered, the lines on his forehead sinking inward with mock innocence. Then he laughed, a rose-tinted chuckle edged with gray pain. "Oh, naive child. People don't *want* facts. They want feelings. And they don't want truth. They want faith that someone is fighting for them. I"—he splayed his hand on his chest, the fingers chapped with cold—"am fighting for them."

Iseult's breath hiccuped ever so slightly. His words sounded like what Leopold had said only two weeks ago: *How often do people make choices based on truth? Based on facts or what their logic tells them?* Leopold had been right—the Purists alone were proof of that. But Iseult had no feeling; logic and facts had always been her guide.

Which was why she had to keep pressing him for information. "Tell me about Midne. How can you be a woman who lived a thousand years ago?"

"You already know the answer to that." Corlant slowed his steps as they turned down a new stretch of tents. "You have seen parts of the diary. You know that I and the other Twelve are born and reborn for all of time. Well, only six of us now." He smiled. A stretched, unnatural thing.

Yes, Iseult thought. *I do have his nose.* And she had that smile too.

"But I was blessed." He patted the gold draped around his neck, longer than what the Hell-Bards wore but otherwise identical. "One of my fellow Paladins purged me of the unclean power of Sirmaya."

Sirmaya. That name had been in the diary. A goddess whom Eridysi had worshipped.

Ahead, a long tent leaned against a half-fallen wall. "The prisoners' tent," Corlant explained, and sure enough, subdued, grief-swallowed Threads shivered into Iseult's senses.

Purist guards nodded reverently at Corlant's approach, their Threads grassy with curiosity and peach with respect. "Blessed are the pure," they mumbled in unison, while one swept open the tent's flap.

Corlant's spine crooked. He slithered inside.

Iseult slithered in too.

"You will begin training today." Corlant paused just beyond the entrance, and Iseult paused beside him while heartbeat by heartbeat, her eyes adjusted and the prisoners came into view, enclosed in crude cages too low for standing. Their bodies and faces were as subdued as their Threads.

"Your reward." Corlant opened his arms and moved to the nearest cage, where he rapped a knobby knuckle against the wood. The Threads within shook with fear. Against her will, Iseult's stasis faltered. Gooseflesh raked down her arms.

"I will take her now," he ordered a Purist guard. "The Threadwitch."

The Threadwitch. There was only one person it could be, and sure enough, Alma moved to the front of the cage. Her arms were bound, but her chin was high. Her eyes drilled into Iseult's. *Do something,* she seemed to say. *Do it now.*

Iseult turned away.

"Bring her into the moonlight," Corlant commanded, and before Iseult could scuttle away from his touch, he had his fingers on her shoulder. Five icicles digging deep. He pushed her toward the exit and back into the cold.

Alma and the Purist shambled just behind, joining Iseult and Corlant fifteen paces from the tent, beside a pile of old stones. Snow began to fall.

"Place her on the rocks."

The Purist obeyed, shoving Alma chest-first onto the remnants of a wall. Her back and neck were exposed as if execution loomed, and Purists gathered to watch. Some were soldiers, some were guards; most were simply fanatics who smelled blood in the water.

"Now cleave her," Corlant commanded.

Iseult blinked, while all around, Purists sucked in their breaths. Their Threads melted into pink delight. Maybe they'd always enjoyed dominance and pain, or maybe Corlant had brought that out in them. Either way, Iseult was again struck by their willingness to overlook the truth. She was a witch.

Corlant was a witch. But these people didn't care so long as others with magic suffered.

"She has no Threads," Iseult said eventually. She watched Alma's back. Watched the steady movement of the girl's ribs. Alma offered no cries. No begging.

"Of course she has Threads," Corlant countered. "All life has Threads. You simply cannot see them." His Threads simmered with purple. He was a lion eyeing its next meal. "In the Dreaming, though, you can see them. So much more is visible there."

Iseult brushed snow off her lashes and frozen cheeks. "I cannot enter the Dreaming."

Corlant's Threads glistened a deeper purple. "If you are in the right place, then the wall between worlds disappears."

Iseult perked up slightly at that. Esme had once spoken of such a thing: *You must be in one of the old places. Somewhere like my tower, where the wall between this world and the Old Ones' is thinner.*

"So these ruins?" She opened her arms. "Are they an old place? Can I enter here?"

Corlant didn't answer. Instead, he shook his head. "Relying on the Dreaming is an inconvenience. You are unprotected while there, your body exposed. As such, you must learn to find Threads even when you cannot see them." He pointed at Alma with a single spindly finger. "Now find her Threads and cleave her."

Iseult wet her lips and did nothing. Alma still showed no fear. Snow gathered in a white film across her back.

"Feel for her Threads as I do, Iseult. Then take her power for yours."

Iseult wet her lips again. Something wiggled in her chest—something she didn't like. And with a twist of her nose, she stamped it into oblivion. Stasis through and through. As cold as the snow building around her feet. "How can I feel for Threads when my hands are like this?" She lifted her bandages.

"Her Threads will not hurt you. Not as badly as mine did, at least." He grinned. His own bandages oozed.

"In that case, I want someone with more power."

Now his smile stiffened. A flicker of annoyance reached his Threads. "She is all that remains, Iseult." He swiped a hand toward the tent. "I could not allow those traitors to use their magic on me, so I had to purify them. Besides, Iseult, Threadwitches have more power than you can possibly imagine. They—and you—see what people feel. What is more powerful than that?"

Again, his words were like Leopold's. The wiggling returned to that spot beneath her lung. *You see emotions. You are far more powerful than she.* Iseult squashed the memory. "What good is her magic to me, though?" She cocked her head sideways. "I can already see emotions. I want something different. Find me someone different."

Now Corlant's smile fell entirely. "This is your last chance." He grabbed Alma by her hair and yanked up her head. Alma didn't resist.

And she still didn't speak.

The Purists did, though, murmuring excitement while their Threads shivered with anticipation for her pain.

"Take her Threads, Iseult. Now."

Iseult didn't. She wanted to. Of course she wanted to. She was a monster. And it wasn't as if she liked Alma. The girl had always been there, perfect yet untouchable. Everything Iseult could never be.

Alma never failed; Alma always won; Alma was beautiful and talented and stasis through and through.

Corlant snarled. His Threads burned brighter. "Take her magic now or I will."

Iseult's lips widened. She lifted her maimed hands. *Yank and snap.* It was all she had to do. *Yank and snap.* Then she would be the untouchable one. She would be the girl to always win . . .

"Too slow," Corlant snapped, and he slammed his palm against Alma's forehead. "May you become as clean as Midne, as pure as the world when it was born." Alma screamed. Her body arched, her head flew back, eyes huge. A pose to pierce Iseult's skull and jam into her heart.

Her hair streamed toward the ground and her upside-down eyes found Iseult's. No emotion burned within, only pain.

Until suddenly Alma's screams stopped, and a spark of what might have been rage swelled in her pupils. "It didn't have to be this way. *We* didn't have to be this way." She straightened, arms yanking wide and her ropes dropping to the snow.

She attacked Corlant.

FORTY-FOUR

✳

The Nomatsis who'd escaped had returned. Winds barreled out, fires ignited, and stone punched up from the earth.

Iseult didn't know where they'd come from. She hadn't sensed them hiding among the Purists, clothed in matching gray. She hadn't felt their witcheries writhing inside their Threads until suddenly they were using them.

Paces away, Alma swiped at Corlant with a blade that hadn't been there moments before. The steel connected; blood sprayed from a shallow wound across his chest. But he only laughed and grappled for Threads that he—and Iseult—could not see. He was a tick filled with magic and witcheries. Impossible to defeat, and any moment now, he would grab hold and drain. Any moment now, Alma would lose.

It didn't have to be this way.

Iseult wondered if she should do something. She wondered if this niggling beneath her lung meant she should help Alma or help Corlant. The Threadwitch she could never be like or the man who'd given her the Void. The girl who had replaced her at her mother's side or the father whose Threads shone with family.

We didn't have to be this way.

Everything seemed to happen with sluggish confusion, softened by the snow and cusp between night and day. Like a funeral dirge played at half speed. Iseult caught every beat. Every failed attack from Nomatsis and Purists alike. Every shriek of the shadow wyrm as it stampeded onto the scene, shadows and icicles bleeding off it. Silver Threads blaring.

Flames heated Iseult's back and wind battered her side. No one attacked her, though. Purists gave her berth; Nomatsis too. She remained untouched beside the fallen wall, snow piling around her feet.

That was when Iseult saw her mother. Across the way where flames burned and an Icewitch aimed shards at a Purist, Gretchya waited, no longer bound in ropes. In her left hand, a knife dangled. Clean, unused. Even now, she would not join the fight.

Because Threadwitches do not cause pain, Iseult. That is only for the Void. Only for people like you.

But Iseult wasn't causing pain. She'd become as still as the stasis inside her. As still as her mother twenty paces away. Snow trickled between them.

Until pain snapped through Iseult—winds she hadn't sensed coming. A Nomatsi with fury in his heart and a funnel of air to fell her. She stumbled forward, catching herself on the snow with bandaged hands. Without thought—with only cool reaction, cool completion to what this man had initiated—she rounded on him and attacked.

Her fingers, still in their bandages, closed around his Threads. Too far for the old Iseult to have reached, but new Iseult had read the diary, and new Iseult knew how to cover distances. More importantly, new Iseult was stasis through and through. No conscience to get in her way. *Sever, sever, twist and sever.*

Iseult squeezed and the man collapsed in an instant. If he screamed, she didn't hear it. Not with the shadow wyrm feasting nearby. Not with Corlant and Alma still locked, somehow, in combat.

The man's soul slid into her, a subtle drip like blood off the tip of a blade. She didn't need her fangs, yet bit by brutal bit, his Threads cleaved. His power became hers. Her heart swelled. Her belly. Her brain. A warmth instead of the usual heat, and no pain against her ruined hands. If anything, the draining Threads soothed. She could stand here all day and do this.

Except now other Threads were shoving into her awareness. An onslaught of magics, of witches now turning their attention to Iseult as she claimed one of their own. Their Threads pulsed with battle, their eyes fastened on her face—on her bandaged hands still squeezing—and they abandoned their various fights to attack Iseult instead.

Iseult released the Windwitch. He still lived, if weaker, but she had enough power. She would use it to fight the witches now storming her. She would kill and cleave, severing each soul until there was nothing left but shriveled Threads.

And now here was the shadow wyrm, each leg lifting through frozen darkness. Half speed because the funeral dirge slogged on in Iseult's brain. The monster aimed for Purists. It killed with no real goal in its beastly, Void-filled heart, and second by second, it careered nearer to Iseult.

For some reason, though, Iseult didn't move. She *should*. She should fight and cleave and kill because Puppeteers had no conscience. Void-witches did not care.

As a wall of murderous Threads bounded toward her, as a monster thundered her way, Iseult simply swiveled her head and found her mother's eyes again. Green and gold and so familiar. Too far to see clearly, but forever etched in her brain. *Mother.* The woman who'd raised her. The woman Iseult had always believed she wanted to be.

Somehow she felt those eyes more sharply than the billowing flames or clawing winds.

Nearby, Alma shouted at Corlant. With hate and a rage so raw it needled through Iseult's stasis and punctured the tiny corner beneath her lung. "*I will die,*" she roared, "*before I let you take what I am!*" Then Alma lifted her blade and turned it on herself. It moved toward her heart, listless and unreal. Just as Corlant bore down with unnatural height. Stretched out like a rag doll ripping at the seams.

And Iseult's stasis punctured wider. *It didn't have to be this way. We didn't have to be this way.*

That was when the next attacks hit Iseult. Two at once with a punch of winds to break her in two. Hot, sudden, potent with rage. She flew, her spine cracking and the world melting into a blur of snow and smoke and Threads of violent gray.

She hit a wall, the stones ancient and unyielding.

Pain exploded through her chest and shoulder. Her palms shredded anew, and black silted across her vision, briefly erasing the battle—though not the silver Threads arcing her way. They shook with the screams of a monster ready to feast. She would break a thousand ways before it was done.

Iseult drew in her legs to stand, but her muscles wouldn't cooperate. Not fast enough, at least. Each movement took a lifetime, each heartbeat stretched into infinity.

And there were the silver Threads. There was the monster's maw leaking shadows. Ice sizzled over her. And in that moment, time stopped completely.

Later, Iseult would wonder how such a thing was possible. Later, she would assume she'd imagined the whole thing. But as it happened, there was too much time for thought. Too much time to pick apart where everything had gone so terribly wrong. And too much time to realize exactly what would happen the instant time resumed.

Alma would die, and she, Iseult, would die too.

It wasn't her rage that had killed this time, though. It wasn't her power of the Puppeteer breaking the world at its seams. Instead, it was stasis. Indiscriminate in its target. Cold in its indifference. By doing nothing, Iseult had chosen to do something.

And there was no way to logic herself out of that truth. Her numbness had a price, and now there would be no escape from these frozen jaws made of Void. No escape from the vengeful witches waiting just behind.

Iseult had no one to blame but herself. She'd lived with blood on her hands and she would die that way too. Payment for all her mistakes. Punishment for all she'd done wrong.

I'm sorry, Iseult thought. To Alma, dying nearby. To Safi, hundreds of miles away. To her mother, shrouded by smoke and snow. Gretchya had lifted her blade, had raised a single leg.

It would seem she was finally taking action. She was finally making a choice and moving in exactly the way Iseult had failed to do.

Which was good, Iseult thought. She would save Alma, the girl who didn't deserve to die. The girl bound to Aether, who would lead as a Threadwitch ought to lead and whose blood didn't pump with wickedness and wrong.

Iseult closed her eyes. She didn't want to watch her mother choose.

Time resumed. Silver Threads beat down. Ice knifed through her, and screams pummeled her bones. Any moment now, the wyrm would reach her. Any moment, any moment.

I'm sorry, Alma. I'm sorry, Safi. I'm sorry, Mother.

Except the teeth never came.

Instead, a body crashed into her. Threadless and strong and attached to a voice screaming, *"Stay back!"* Then Gretchya roared again, a shriek of indomitable rage. *"No one touches my daughter!"*

Aeduan found the child's collar beneath the spruce. No sign of the strange weasel that had been with her, the one that had smelled of flooded rivers and freedom. The wood had not been sawed or broken. In fact, it lay perfectly intact upon the frozen ground, not even opened. As if she'd slipped it right over her head.

Rosewater and wool-wrapped lullabies. Her scent smelled as it always had, and the first Aeduan responded to it.

With a deep inhale, Aeduan stepped away from the tree and into snowfall lit by the end of night. Magic surged through him. Such power in this body's blood. It sparkled and warmed and set his muscles to itching.

Another breath, deeper. Longer. Reaching wider for some spark of rosewater or lullabies. *There.* A flicker to the north. Not far. Fresh enough that it might be the girl herself, instead of mere traces like this collar had left behind.

He set off. The magic consumed him, eliminating thought. Eliminating questions. There was only moving forward, only tracking this smell wherever it might lead. There was no past, no future, no ancient soul trapped for a thousand years or new soul trapped for several weeks.

There was clarity, there was speed, there was the hunt.

He moved faster, his boots falling lightly across the earth. Unimportant, unimpeding. When the Bloodwitchery coursed high, this body could *fly.*

The scent pulsed closer in Aeduan's veins. The child waited ahead, beyond a clearing filled with forgotten walls like those in the Nomatsi camp and like his old soul had once seen before. Perhaps he had even been here when this fortress still stood.

Those memories could be untangled later, though. For now, there was only Saria. Near, near, so very near.

Then a second scent hit Aeduan's awareness: *Clear lake water and frozen winters.*

He knew that smell. Knew it as well as he knew the child's, as well as he knew Evrane's . . . Except his mind conjured no face, no person, no name. This scent belonged to a specter. This scent belonged to a ghost. It had evaded the first Aeduan for months, leading him across the Witchlands.

And stealing silver coins.

Aeduan drew in steady, heavy breaths. The Bloodwitchery still throbbed inside his veins and muscles. The first Aeduan itched to find this mystery scent, and that first Aeduan was growing stronger and stronger by the hour.

Yes, he told that soul. *We will look and then be on our way.* He angled toward the clear lake waters. Crept toward the frozen winters. A fallen court waited ahead, four walls mostly still standing.

Aeduan slowed his pace to a predatory stalk and with all the silence that only magic-fueled muscles could achieve, he unsheathed a knife from his chest. The world around him was silent. Few plants had taken root here, as if the ruins frightened them away. Even the forest, which clustered close and stared down, offered no sounds of life. Only gentle snowfall.

And *ah,* there was Saria's blood-scent too. The faintest whiff of lullabies and rosewater. She was in this tower.

Aeduan moved more slowly. His toes landed exactly where he wanted; no snow crunched. No leather creaked. After finding a small crack in the rubble that might have once been a door, he peered through. Saria sat upon a pile of broken marble.

No, not a pile—it was a throne. Aeduan remembered it, even if he could not recall where or how. Her feet dangled, and her cold-flushed face had creased into a frown. Her head turned. Her hazel eyes met Aeduan's.

She grinned.

He tried to drop to his knees, tried to turn away and summon any power he could, but he was too late—just as he had been a thousand years ago.

And just as it had happened a thousand years ago, stone erupted against him. Bricks from the tower, pebbles from the ground, boulders and rubble and soil filled with worms. They crashed around him, hard and unyielding, until he was fully encased. Until his legs, his arms, even his head could not move.

Not again. His lungs collapsed. His vision crossed. Not again, not again. He had been held like this before, and then the blade had pierced through. Not again, *not again*.

He wriggled and pried, he shoved and hissed. But his Bloodwitchery—even with the first soul's help—was no match for Saria's magic. She strode into view, walking like a queen. A familiar black bird stood on her shoulder. Its beak clacked, and no, no, no. Aeduan remembered that sound too.

But this was not that moment, and Saria held no Paladin blade. It was only her and the bird and the silence of a wintry forest. She raked her ancient gaze up Aeduan's stone-bound form. "You were never the worst of them, but you still chose wrong in the end."

"Free . . . me," Aeduan gritted out. Stone compressed his throat. Each breath tasted of nightmares. *Not again, not again.*

"I will." She nodded. "Eventually. When I feel certain you've chosen correctly this time. I think you already have, but I prefer to have a guarantee. So consider this a reminder of what I can do to you."

Before Aeduan could ask what that meant, the Rook leaped off Saria's shoulder. Two quick flaps, and the bird thunked onto Aeduan's head. Vaguely, Aeduan's magic sensed forest fog atop freedom. Then the Rook squawked, a sound to rattle in his eardrums and shake the stones that chained him.

It was the sound he'd heard just before his death. Before pain and shadow overwhelmed him. Before the waters of a thousand years had dragged him down. Except this time, there was no Rook King to say, *It was not supposed to be this way.* There was only his bird, gloating and gleeful.

And suddenly understanding notched into place. Why the Rook King had been waiting for Evrane when she'd awoken. Why he had said, *It is good to have you back.*

The power of the Aether. The power to place souls where he willed—*that* was how Aeduan had come into this world again, into this body. The first Monk Evrane had entered the Water Well to heal, and the Rook King had done his work. Then the first Aeduan had stepped into the Aether Well, and the Rook King had acted again. Old souls placed into new homes.

It was not a permanent solution, though, and as easily as the Rook King had given the old soul a body, he could also take it away.

Which meant Corlant's promises of new bodies were hollow. He could no more touch the work of the Rook King than the Rook King could touch the wind. But of course Corlant would lie; that had always been Portia's way.

"So you have figured it out," Saria said with a sly grin. "I knew you would eventually. Still, one cannot be too careful." She raised a single hand. Then a second squawk shattered over Aeduan—and with it came the sound of stone against stone. Of gravel rising, ready to choke and claim and crush and end.

Moments later, Aeduan's mouth was covered. His nose, his eyes. His everything. He could not see, he could not move. And it did not take long before darkness swept in.

She chose me.

She chose me.

Impossible.

Gretchya had entered the fight and chosen to save Iseult. Yet even as Iseult watched her mother fling up her blade, a tiny figure against a monster wreathed in shadow, her mind could not accept it.

She chose me. She chose me. Impossible.

Then her mother bellowed with a voice to shred and to break, "*No one touches my daughter!*" And a tiny sliver of truth cut into Iseult's heart.

Not impossible.

The sliver cut deeper. It curved beneath her left lung and latched on.

And the shadow wyrm seemed as surprised as Iseult. As if the same word—"impossible"—sang through its mind too. Cyan speckled over silver Threads, and it paused its attack. Mouth open and shadows near enough for Gretchya to touch.

Even the winter coiling off its body seemed to pause. There was only Iseult and Gretchya and this monster.

Except it didn't look so monstrous now. Tucked beneath the shadows were two eyes, dark as a new moon and just as fathomless. And tucked within those eyes was understanding. It knew what mothers were; it recognized what Gretchya had dared to do, and perhaps it was even a mother too.

It was all the time Gretchya needed. With hands that had carried Iseult and guided her, had fought for her and endured, she hauled Iseult to her feet. Then she braced an arm behind her daughter's back and together, they limped away.

The shadow wyrm let them. Though whether by choice or by circumstance, Iseult would never know, for now the concerted efforts of the Nomatsi witches had turned on it. Now it had new targets to keep it busy, new people on which to feed.

"Alma," Iseult tried to say, but her throat had rusted and the battle was too loud. New winds, new flames, new screams from a shadow wyrm to drown the world in its pain. Gretchya had already aimed them toward the other girl anyway. To the body, now lying upon the snow while Corlant leered.

Blood, blood, great swaths of red stained the white and stained the crumbled stones.

"Her Threads linger," Corlant said. He turned his bruised eye first on Iseult. Then on Gretchya. Then onto the chaos unraveling around them, as if he'd only just noticed the wind and flame, the stone and ice, the water and fury ripping across the encampment.

Snow still fell.

"Take her Threads." Corlant returned his focus to Iseult. Somehow, he didn't have to yell to be heard. "She cannot resist you now."

Iseult didn't respond. Instead, she slid to the snow beside Alma while Gretchya dropped to Alma's other side. Blood streaked over their clothes, snow seeped into their knees. Alma's knife's hilt, embedded in her chest, shivered and quaked with ragged breaths.

"I'm sorry." Iseult clutched at the edges of the wound with bandaged hands. The blood soaked into them. "I'll find you a healer."

Alma laughed. A sound filled with more emotion than Iseult had ever heard. Alma's eyes, unsteady and half closed, found Iseult's face. "We didn't . . . have to . . ."

"Stop talking," Gretchya said curtly. Her stasis had returned, though tears gathered in her eyes. "We will find help—"

Alma's eyes closed. Her belly shuddered. "Be." A final spurt of blood, and she died. The clouds parted. Moonlight peeked through, small pinpricks on Alma's face. As pale in death as she had been in life.

"A pity," Corlant said, his voice a cold font in Iseult's ear. She hadn't noticed him crooking in, hadn't sensed his Threads throbbing. "Now she is dead, and no one can save her."

Iseult's fingers tightened in her bandages, clutching at the knife hilt. Snow melted into Alma's blood. "Now she is dead," she repeated. "And no one can save her."

With those words, the final dregs of Iseult's stasis toppled to the snow. Dust, ash, swept away on winds and flame, the walls she'd built to hold everything in could no longer contain the truth. Thousands of secrets she'd stuffed away for years.

Years and years and *years*. Everything she'd never wanted to face and never wanted to feel. Even now, her first instinct was to frantically push it back in. *Stasis, stasis! In your fingers and in your toes!*

But there was no more space to hold it. Not now that Gretchya had chosen to save Iseult. Not now that Alma was dead. Iseult had refused to move in time, and worse—so, *so* much worse—Iseult had refused to be the one thing Alma had so clearly always wanted: a friend. A sister.

And in that moment, Iseult realized she had been wrong. For eighteen years, she'd had it so backward. Her mother had feelings. Her mother felt love. And so had Alma. Of course they both had. They were human.

And Iseult was human too.

But just as Iseult had *wanted* to take Owl into her arms and tell her everything would be all right, Gretchya hadn't known how. Her own mother had been a Threadwitch with love buried deep beneath stasis, just as every mother before her had been. An endless, icy cycle because Threadwitches were not meant to feel, were not allowed to display. So Iseult had become exactly the same in turn, alongside Alma. Isolated, cold, alone but always wanting.

Oh, how much Iseult had never seen, had willingly turned her eyes away from. No one had rejected her; she'd simply rejected herself. Now, she was caught in this moment, and just as Gretchya had warned, there could be no coming back from it.

She had done something irredeemably wrong because she was a monster and it was all she could ever do. Where were her gods now? Where was Wicked Cousin to intervene? Where was Trickster to step in and reanimate a little hedgehog? Where was Moon Mother to wash away her pain?

You tell too many stories, Aeduan had said, and it had been true. Iseult had clung to old tales that always ended happily. That always saw the heroine win because it had been easier than feeling. Or looking at the truth. But now there would be no perfect ending. No grand adventures for the rest of Alma's days.

Reanimation. The word slithered into Iseult's mind, sly as an assassin in the night. It might have been Esme's thought, it might have been her own. Either way, the word came again: *Reanimation.* Eridysi had described the magic in her diary—in the pages Iseult had read only a day before. Portia had been so close to true restoration of life. All she'd lacked was the power of an Aetherwitch.

An Aetherwitch who could see Threads instead of simply feel them. Who could assess the nuance needed to reattach life to a corpse growing cold.

Iseult's heart gave a sigh. Perhaps it was simply the familiarity of the logic she'd always relied on, but in that moment, a plan settled into place.

"Reanimation." The word jumped from her tongue, directed at Corlant though her gaze skipped to her mother. Tears had left streaks on Gretchya's cold-flushed cheeks, though still she kept her features blank.

Trust me, Iseult thought at her. *I will fix this.*

She pushed weakly to her feet, her bandages stained entirely to red, and looked square in Corlant's face. "Reanimation was in the diary. How did Portia do it? You told me you remembered everything."

A hint of shock in his Threads, a hint of the lines upon his forehead. Then Corlant tipped back his head and laughed. A full-throated howl at a cloud-clotted sky. No moonlight now. Nor sun nor even flame. Only shadow.

"Reanimation is one thing you and I will never do." Corlant's face thrust in, so close. The rotting bandages, the skin sallow and slick. "That was only ever *his* power, no matter how much Portia tried. The Aether decides where souls rest, Iseult; we simply rule their bodies. *But.*" He leaned in closer, his breath as fetid as his wound. "Why do you care if this girl dies? Why do you want to bring back the reward that could have been yours?

"I gave you a chance to claim power. I gave you a chance to become the dark-giver at my side, yet still you fight it. Why? You are my daughter, and there is only one way you can ever be."

"You're wrong." Iseult spoke so quietly, he had to dip in all the nearer to hear her. And she smiled at him, a real smile borne on real emotion now flooding out fast. "Because you've forgotten one thing, *Father.*" She thrust up a blade. *The* blade she'd pulled from Alma's body and so easily hidden within her bloodied bandages. "I am my mother's daughter too."

Iseult shoved the knife into Corlant's other eye.

Blood sprayed, hot and foul, and Corlant's Threads tore wide as a cyclone. His screams did too. He didn't die because he'd stolen too much power from the Nomatsi prisoners to go that easily.

But he hurt—oh, he *hurt*, his Threads white and frantic. His shrieks beating into her.

Iseult dove for her mother and grabbed Gretchya's arm with her ruined hands. Together, they sprinted for the nearest copse of trees.

FORTY-FIVE

✳

"I'm going to fix this," Iseult panted as she and Gretchya raced through a forest doused in snow. They'd left behind bloody tracks—Alma's blood and so, so much of it. "I swear . . . Mother. I can fix this."

These were words Iseult had uttered a thousand times since Praga. Words that had been an empty vow with no true power behind them because she'd lacked a magic vast enough to do what needed doing. She'd lacked the knowledge too.

Now she had clarity. Now she understood.

Gretchya didn't ask how Iseult would fix everything. Her breaths were labored and already her pace was lagging. Purists had chased them ever since they'd left Corlant, who'd been screeching and bleeding and only temporarily maimed.

Worse, Iseult and Gretchya were closing in on the Solfatarra with no goggles to help them see, no salamander fibers to protect their skin. And no way to cross the lake if they even got there.

Think, Iseult, think. The Nomatsi trail was too far away, as was the spit of land that would lead out of the Solfatarra. They were going to have to run into the fog. They were going to have to ignore the burn and risk the inhalation. And once they reached the lake's shore . . .

Iseult would figure it out then. Channel Safi and think with her feet, with her palms. Her aching, bandaged palms. Because her Threadsister was near, and she *had* to find Safi before Corlant did. She *had* to get her hands on their Threadstones first.

Those rubies were the key. Everything—her safety, her mother's life, and Alma's fading soul—hinged on those stones. If she could only figure out why.

Shouts echoed, layered thick atop hunting Threads. There could be no pauses. Only dragging Gretchya onward. Only stumbling forward, one foot after the next.

They reached the fog, a wall of death that hid the snow, and there, waiting for them upon a pile of ancient stones, was the weasel. Esme darted for Iseult, almost invisible against the snow. As she ran, an image assembled in Iseult's mind: *Heretic's collar, removed beneath the spruce. Owl in a ruined courtyard, seated on an ancient throne. Aeduan bound in stone.*

It made no sense, and before Iseult could try to sort her way through it, shouts clashed against her. Threads too, hungry and hunting. Iseult allowed Esme to curl around her neck before pulling her mother onward toward the wall of fog.

Except Gretchya didn't move. She jerked her arm free, shooting pain up Iseult's arm, and when Iseult rounded on her, she found her mother's eyes fastened on the weasel.

"What," she began, voice weak from running, "is that?"

"The Puppeteer," Iseult answered honestly. "Or what's left of her. But she's our ally, Mother, and right now, we need all the help we can get."

Gretchya didn't move. Her labored breaths stilled, her eyes held fast to Esme. Even the snow seemed to have paused its thick fall.

Which made the approaching Threads that much harder to ignore. An onslaught of fanatics. People willing to hunt Iseult and her mother to the end so long as it meant Corlant would favor them.

"Please, Mother." Iseult offered her bandaged hand. "We have to move."

Gretchya didn't respond, and for a flicker of a heartbeat, the old heat wormed to life in Iseult's chest. It slid up her spine. Fire to melt the cold around her. Rage, defiance, shame, and a thousand regrets still seeping out from that secret corner.

Her face warmed. Her tongue fattened. She offered her hand again. "M-Mother." She swallowed. "You told me yesterday that . . . *magic* was what we made of it. Esme is not the m-monster she used to be, and . . ." Another swallow. Then she let the full breadth of her desperation reach her face. Her nose twitched, her brow pinched tight, and the stutter broke completely free. "I-I . . . I am not either."

And with those words—with that stammer, embraced and unbound— her mother's face relaxed. Her eyes abandoned Esme's and found Iseult's instead. No sharp words about Threadwitches controlling their tongues nor stony silence with lips compressed in withdrawn disapproval.

Instead, she looked sad. So, so sad that Iseult almost imagined grieving blue Threads wisped over her like a crown.

"Go," Gretchya said softly. "Do what you must to fix this, Iseult, and I will lead the Purists away."

Iseult blinked. She was so stunned by the heartbreak on her mother's face, by the gentleness in her tone, that it took her a moment to actually comprehend Gretchya's words.

"No, Mother, that isn't what I meant—"

"*Do it.*" Gretchya's nose wrinkled; authority hardened her eyes. "Corlant will not kill me—even now. And I will gain you the time you need."

"No." Iseult thrust out her bandaged hand again. Purists were so near, she could see their cloaked shapes within the trees. "I don't care if he won't hurt you, Mother. I won't risk anyone—"

"Go." Gretchya lunged at Iseult and shoved. Strong enough to launch her back three steps.

Strong enough to push her into the Solfatarra's grasp. Acid flamed in. No sight, no breath, no touch. Only the sound of her mother whispering, "You were always meant for bigger things than I could give."

Then Gretchya roared at the top of her lungs and her footsteps stomped away, aiming once more toward camp.

Gravity and winds punched in. The forest below zoomed to eye level. White fog too, until that was all Safi could see—white, white, endless white.

She was falling. Dangling like a marionette with only desperate muscles keeping her attached to the *Eridysi*'s railing.

Safi's muscles shrieked and stretched. Her vision crossed and blurred. Even with the goggles, her eyes streamed. Distantly, she felt acid sear her skin, and distantly, she glimpsed scarlet uniforms streaking through the sky.

Instinct told her to squeeze her eyes shut; self-preservation kept them open. The *Eridysi* was going to crash into the Solfatarra. Acid and heat would boil Safi alive—and there was nothing she could do about it except watch death zoom closer.

Then a jolt battered through her. The *Eridysi* changed course, pitched a different way. Someone screamed; it might have been her.

Safi clung more frantically to the balustrade. As tightly as her arms would allow, though gravity clawed.

Fog streamed past. A living, moving thing. But no longer was the *Eridysi* aimed for it. The machine was swerving sideways now, and the Solfatarra's end was so near. If they could just reach the forest beyond before they crashed. *Please*, she prayed. *Noden, Hagfishes, the Twelve—please, let us reach the other side.*

Then the machine was past. The last tendrils of fog whispered out of sight, and Safi spotted individual branches on individual trees. For some inexplicable reason, her brain identified every one rushing her way. There was a silver fir. A spruce over there. And straight ahead, where the *Eridysi* was going to land any moment, was a barren hornbeam.

Perhaps jumping overboard would be the safer option. Better to hit branches than to get tangled in a flying machine—

"*Do not let go!*" Leopold roared over the winds.

So Safi did not let go, and a fraction of a heartbeat later, the *Eridysi* swung in a new direction. Then back again. *Swing, swoop, spin, swing.* A sinking ship with too much speed. Bile rose in Safi's throat. Her vision crossed.

They hit the tree.

Shock rammed through her. Wood crunched and hornbeam snapped, so loud that Safi lost all sense of sight or sound. Pain blasted through her. Blood welled on her tongue—and elsewhere too, deep scrapes on her left forearm, her right calf, the whole back side of her head . . .

As fast as they had hit, the crashing stopped. The *Eridysi* was no longer falling and the wood no longer cracking in two.

"Safiya." Caden's voice fuzzed into her awareness. He was dragging her. Wood scraped under her boots. Splinters snagged on her clothes. She thought she heard something creaking, but her ears weren't working as they ought to be.

"Climb," she heard, and with a confused blink, she realized a rope ladder now hung beneath her. It extended toward a hard earth, half hidden by shadows that would not stay still. Thick branches scraped and spun.

The creaking groaned louder.

"*Climb*," Caden repeated, and suddenly he was on the ladder and trying to pull Safi onto it.

Gods below, why was the earth moving so much? And *what* was that creaking?

Somehow, she got her feet beneath her and her arms onto the rope. Somehow, she descended. Every fiber scraped fresh pain into her left palm. Her right leg trembled and burned. Bare branches scratched at her cheeks, streaked in her vision. Yet Safi moved, slowly, slowly, toward the ground.

Until suddenly the creaking turned to crashing. Until suddenly Caden bellowed, *"Jump!,"* and Safi realized the *Eridysi* was coming down on top of her.

She jumped. A clumsy, painful move from a ladder that offered no traction, no force. Air whizzed past. She was still so high . . .

Her feet hit the ground. Instinct took hold, and she transferred into a roll. Two rolls. Maybe three. Then she landed on her back as the last of the branches holding the *Eridysi* broke in two.

Safi curled into a ball, head protected.

The *Eridysi* hit the ground. The earth trembled. Splinters flew. Then it was over. She was alive and she was safe.

For several moments, Safi stayed tucked in her ball. She waited for the cracking sounds to dissipate from her hearing, for the ground to stop its trembling. When eventually she felt safe enough to breathe and look around, she unfurled. Then patted her pockets: the Threadstones were still safe.

Caden lay sprawled nearby, but no one else. No Lev, no Zander, no Leopold. She jolted upright, gaze spinning. The flying machine was a wreck of wood and branches and shredded sail. "Lev?" she called, towing in her feet. "Zander? Polly?"

"They . . . fell."

Safi spun toward Caden. He looked as bad as Safi felt—a deep gash across his cheek. Twigs and dirt in his hair. "They fell," he repeated.

"No," Safi breathed. "How far back?"

"I don't know, but we'll go after them. We *have* to go after them." *All clear, all clear.*

"Yes," Safi agreed. She moved to help him rise . . . only to get a full view of Caden's leg. Blood oozed outward from his calf, and his pants were stained through. "Can you stand?"

Before he could say this, though—before Safi could get him up to test the leg—footsteps thumped out in the forest. Hope surged in her chest. She spun about, ready to welcome Lev and Zander and Leopold. Ready to laugh and hug them close.

But it was not her friends who charged out from the underbrush. It was two Windwitches, each with Cartorran armor and air spinning around them.

"Surrender," barked the nearest, "or die." Then he and his partner lifted two pistols and aimed them at Safi's and Caden's hearts.

Iseult shambled through the fog. Without sight, she was aimless. Without breath, she was fading fast. And without touch, she was nothing but her insides. Her soul. Her emotions gushing outward: hate, love, frustration.

And regret. So, so much regret. *I will fix this. I will fix this.* She *had* to fix this. Her face seared, her eyes streamed, but at least she sensed no Threads tracking behind.

Except now that she was reaching and stretching, no other senses to interfere, there was something new within her magic. Unfamiliar, tinted yellow, and sparkling with air. *Windwitchery.* It was the power she'd leeched, but with no ghost attached, no voice to shout at her and drag her into nightmares. Just a tiny well, finite and waiting.

Esme squeaked into her ear. *Use it, use it now.* And Iseult didn't need any more prodding. She had stolen that power, but now it would be her salvation.

Go, she told the magic. *Fly.*

The wind burst free. A punch of air that lashed around her, just as it had lashed around the Windwitch. Up it flew, a single magic assigned a single task. Iseult's feet left the earth, and with each inch she lifted—faster, faster—the more true air slipped into her lungs and acid flames pulled away. Her stomach dropped. Her ears and brain swelled, then popped, and Esme clung so tightly her claws pierced skin.

Until at last they were above the fog, above the Solfatarra. Wind thundered, a roar of sound and cold and blessed purity. It was not the first time Iseult had flown, but it was the first time she had been the one to control it.

To the west, the moon hung low upon the sky. Full, glowing, silvery against a still-darkened sky. To the east, sunrise peeked out with golden light.

Mother. Iseult directed the winds south, toward the forest and the camp. She would find Gretchya, fly her away on these winds she should have discovered—*would* have discovered if she weren't always such a fool.

But instead of forest and snow, instead of Purists and tents and ruins forgotten, there were only Threads to the south. A hurricane, swirling and gathering, engorging and darkening as one by one, more Threads were sucked in.

Corlant was coming.

Lightning cracked. A black cloud abruptly formed, and winds that were not Iseult's clawed against her. Powerful enough to tow her down, cold enough to freeze her where she flew.

There would be no finding Gretchya, and as Iseult yanked in her own winds, screaming inwardly and aloud, *Fly, fly, fly*, Esme wedged a vision into her mind.

Northern horizon. White-sailed machine tumbling from the sky.

Iseult flung around, her winds wobbling against Corlant's storm. He must be stealing every magic nearby. He must be stealing magic from the very earth itself. She couldn't see it through the icy tears streaming from her eyes, she trusted Esme. Safi was ahead; the Threadstones were near. Once she had those, she could fix this. She *would* fix this.

They flew toward barren winter forests dotted by evergreens and a castle of white stone rooted atop the only hill for miles: the Emperor's hunting lodge. Safi's flying machine had crashed nearby. Yet with Corlant scratching and pulling from behind, Iseult's winds grew weaker by the second. She hadn't drained the Windwitch fully, and she hated that she wished she had.

She lost all sense of time as she flew, the moon on one side, the sun on the other. She was the winds that roared around her, the winds that sparked within her. She was her mother's words and Alma's. *No one hurts my daughter. We didn't have to be this way.*

So much she hadn't seen. So much she'd gotten wrong. Soon she would be with Safi, though. Soon she would make it all right again.

She reached the Solfatarra's end. Anything that wasn't blanketed in white caught her blurry eyes: a tower, crumbled like the ruins from the camp. A river, snaking and dark. And finally a splintered hole in the forest where a flying machine might have crashed down.

Descend, she told the magic. And it obeyed—but with no finesse and the magic fading fast. Ten feet of careful descent, no faster than the snow falling around her. Then a lurch, a drop, an abandonment of organs somewhere above.

Iseult yelped; Esme squealed. Then they flipped in midair and Iseult caught sight of Corlant's storm anew. Only once had she seen anything like it: two months ago on the Nubrevnan coast when Merik Nihar's

Threadbrother had cleaved. Kullen had been a full Airwitch, and his Threads had stood no chance against the distant severing call of the Puppeteer.

Now, though, it wasn't Corlant who cleaved. It was everyone around him, it was the sky and the forest and the Solfatarra. He sucked them and sapped them, gathering so much power he would be unstoppable.

Yet in the three booming heartbeats while Iseult and Esme hung suspended, Iseult realized there must be a price for what he did. There must be a reason he hadn't used such magic before, and whatever the reason or cost might be, Iseult would find a way to use it.

She flipped again, Esme screeching in her ear, and once more gazed upon a winter-calm forest disrupted only by a fallen machine—and by Threads too.

A hundred of them clustered on a snaking trail nearby, all with shadowy Hell-Bard hearts. They hunted for Safi.

Another plummet, another yelp, and now broken trees crossed Iseult's vision. Then a clearing dotted with Threads—*Safi's* Threads, as beautiful as they had been in the Loom and with Caden's Threads pulsing beside her.

And with two Windwitches in Cartorran red too. Threads of violence spun over Threads of yellow magic.

At that moment, the last of Iseult's stolen power bled away. She plunged straight down. Air beat against her, cold and frostbitten. The winds of gravity pounded, scraping her acid-raw skin.

One hundred feet until she and Esme hit the ground.

Iseult had to do something. Plan, plan—she needed a plan. And time, more time.

Esme shrieked in her ear. Eighty feet until they hit.

They were going to die. Gretchya's choice and Alma's sacrifice would be for nothing.

Seventy feet.

Safi looked up. Her Threads glared with surprise. Then fear. Then recognition and love. It was warm and unabashed. The bolstering Iseult so desperately needed.

Fifty feet.

Iseult's fingers extended, wide within the bandages, and she grabbed two sets of Threads. The lightning she knew so well seared against her scarred hands. She yanked and snapped anyway, clutching at the Threads right as the first tips of trees blurred past.

Then there it was: the power. New winds to surge into her body. Fresh, alive. Stolen too, but she would face that truth another time.

Slow, she commanded the magic, and her speed all but stopped. She became a feather. She became snow, falling in perfect time to the flakes drifting down. Until at last, her feet touched the earth—right between her newly created Cleaved—and she met Safi's blue eyes.

FORTY-SIX

✳

A *vixen never hunts near her den.*

As Vivia swam silently through cool moonlit waters, she couldn't stop thinking that phrase. She'd read it once in a book plucked off her mother's shelf, back before her father had removed all of Jana's things. *A vixen never hunts near her den.*

It made sense that foxes traveled abroad to avoid bringing trouble near their litters. Too bad Vivia hadn't remembered that phrase before leading the Dalmotti navy directly to her home. Then again, she hadn't known people lived in Nihar, hadn't known Noden's Gift and its thrumming cicadas lived again, much less that they would dig so deeply into her heart. She just prayed her newest hunt, once more upon her own den's shores, wouldn't make things worse.

She had learned two things in her communication with Captain Kadossi of the *Lioness*. One, the entirety of Yoris's hunters had been made prisoners of war, along with her crew from the *Iris*. And two, they would all be returned—alive—once Vivia and Vaness turned themselves in.

So Vivia and Vaness had agreed, and *Baile's Blessing* now sailed in the same direction that Vivia swam. Slowly and on natural winds aimed for the Origin Well, it should arrive just in time for Vivia to board as if she'd been there all along.

First, though, she had work to do.

She coasted through the calm waters of a lull between tides. Below her, crepuscular fish awoke for their predawn meals and sharks skated over the ocean floor and sunken ships, dark shadows more interested in bite-size prey than her. She passed anemones unfurling and squid returning to the depths they called home. She glimpsed pelicans diving, crabs scuttling.

Stix had grown up by the sea, northeast of the Hundred Isles; Vivia had always envied her that.

And as Vivia had told Vaness only hours before, she felt more connected to each creature, each fleck of water and salt around her, than she'd ever felt before. Twenty-three years she had been bound to the tides, yet never had she felt as if she *was* the tides. She would have forgone breath entirely if her body hadn't been smarter—hadn't thrust her to the sea's surface when the distant needles in her chest turned to ice picks.

At this hour, the world was nothing but vague shapes smeared in shadow. There was the Origin Well, its fox ears perked high. There was the shoreline, craggy and unwelcoming even with fresh forest to breathe and sigh. And there was the Dalmotti navy, still stationed upon the waves, like lions guarding their prey.

Once her lungs were happy, Vivia dove again, letting the water propel her as it desired, letting her magic glide in harmony alongside it. The water knew where she needed to be, and she trusted it to get her there—faster than any boat and with far more stealth. Soon, she reached the first warship.

Twelve of them floated atop the waves, creaking and swathed in algae. She needed to move quickly. Already, dawn lightened the skies. She'd taken too long swimming, been too engrossed in the reefs and their denizens— too willing to let the water lead and move at its languid, ancient pace.

Focus, she told herself as she swam up to the *Lioness*, its masts repaired and captain satisfied he was about to win. She planted her hands on the hull. Barnacles, crusted thick, fluttered their feathers. Bubbles slipped from her lips and skated toward the sky. She fumbled with the satchel tied at her hip, almost dropped the first corkscrewed iron that was within, then swore at her clumsiness and lost more bubbles to the sea.

Focus. Shanna was depending on Vivia to get this right. All of Noden's Gift, all of Vivia's crew, and even blighted Yoris who didn't deserve her help but was getting it anyway—for as Jana had taught her: *We rule everyone, not just those who agree with us.*

In seconds, Vivia had the drill fastened to the tarred planks. At the right command, it would spin. It would pierce. It would sink.

Breathe, her lungs reminded her once she was done, and though her mind and witchery wanted to continue on her mission, her body had the good sense to obey. She briefly shot to the surface. Briefly let air and gray dawn gulp over her. All around, the Dalmotti navy groaned and listed.

Carry me? Vivia asked the water, and the water obeyed, towing her down once more, away from the warm pink and gold upon the waves and to a second spot, on the opposite side of the *Lioness*. Two drills for that warship, followed by a smile for the water, who was excited at the storm to come.

It was dawn when Stix and Ryber reached Nubrevna, the sun an indigo smile upon their backs as they ascended a narrow switchback that led from the tide and turned the limestone cliff blue. Ryber moved behind Stix, tired and wary and rechecking her cards endlessly.

They never changed. Always she drew the Queen of Hawks, the Queen of Foxes, the Giant.

"I hope you're right," Ryber said as they finally crested the cliff and an empty stretch of rock spread before them. Green forest clutched at a strip of untended road, and morning crickets hummed, vibrating sea mist that beaded on Stix's skin.

A lone figure stood at the cliff's edge a hundred paces away, her red coat billowing on the breeze and her spyglass trained on the horizon. Stix had reclaimed her spectacles from the arena, though now the metal was truly bent and the edge of one lens cracked. It broke Kahina into a hundred tiny pieces.

"I'm definitely right," Stix said, and she patted Ryber's arm. The girl's sleeve was damp, despite Stix's best efforts to keep their small, stolen craft dry. The water had had a mind of its own, and the more Ryber had tried to stay dry, the more spindrift had seemed to find her.

They had sailed all night, Stix's sight returning with each wave. With each influx of new waters and ancient song. *Welcome home*, the sea said. And the Paladin souls within her purred like the orange tabby. Stix's sight returned too, bit by bit, but it was clear that using too much magic came at a price. It was a warning for her and the entirety of the Witchlands.

When at last they reached Kahina, Stix glimpsed what the Admiral studied: a Dalmotti blockade near the Origin Well. With unhurried ease, Kahina closed her spyglass. Face-framing curls had fallen from her bun, and they bounced with the tidal wind.

"You aren't the Exalted One called Lovats," Stix said.

"No." Kahina rubbed at her jade ring. "Which means you are, I suppose, indeed Lady Baile."

"It would seem I am."

Kahina sighed, a dramatic huff. "So much chaos could have been avoided if you had only played nice with me from the start."

"I could say the same to you. Rhian would never have killed so many people."

"Rhian would never have been a pirate either, but we needed a navy for the cause, so I acquired one." Kahina shrugged, baring a sidelong smile.

"Where have you put the blade and glass?" Ryber blurted with none of her usual poise. Her jaw cut a hard slant, her silver eyes had turned to steel.

But Kahina only smiled more widely. "You will forgive me if I do not reveal them quite yet, Sightwitch. We have only just become allies, you know. And as broken as they are, they are all we have against what is coming."

"And what is that?"

"I think you know." She dipped her head toward the diary at Ryber's hip. "What is it your order sings? *When the sky splits and the mountain quakes, make time for goodbyes, for the Sleeper soon breaks.*"

Stix frowned; she really *should* read Ryber's diary, she supposed. "And where are the rest of the Six?" she asked.

This prompted another sigh from Kahina, heavy and frustrated. "The Fury has vanished, Dysi is dead, Saria refuses to pick a side, and the one called Corlant isn't who he seems. But our cause is not lost, Water Brawler. So long as I remain and you remain, we can fight to the splintered end."

Stix's lips pursed at those words. They tickled with familiarity—or maybe it was simply Ryber's gaze locked on her face that tickled. "And what of the one who betrayed us? The king with the silver crown?"

"He is still out there, playing his own game until there is nothing left but chaos." Kahina slid her pipe from her pocket. Overhead, a lone gull cried its *scree, scr-scree*, while in the jungle, cicadas buzzed into wakefulness and welcomed the day. "You want to go after your queen. As do I. But until the Sleeper rests, we are no use to anyone."

"No," Stix said, a small pinch gathering between her brows. "I understand that now. And yet." She rubbed at her chest, an ineffectual movement for the enormity of what swelled inside her. Like a firepot in a birdcage just waiting to go off.

"And yet," Kahina agreed. "Here you are, and here I am, driven by the same need to always keep the Goddess-chosen rulers safe."

"Oh," Ryber murmured, a breathiness to the word, as if she finally understood why Stix had come here. Then her cards began whispering while she flipped them out one by one. "The Queen of Hawks, the Queen of Foxes, and the Giant."

Kahina nodded at that, tapping her bowl against her ring. Ash floated on the breeze. "It is almost time for the battle to begin here. After that, we will have to leave. Sirmaya depends upon us. The entire Witchlands depends upon us."

Stix squinted out over the dawn-bright sea, the cracks in her spectacles distorting each splash and wave. "Your ships are out there, then?"

"Near, and when we are finished aiding our rulers, my Red Sails will pick off any remaining ships. But until that moment . . ."

"We fight," Stix finished.

"We fight," Kahina confirmed. Then she waved her pipe at the Dalmotti navy, floating obliviously upon the waves. "'Tis a fine day for destruction, don't you think?"

A light rain misted the dawn, though sun warmed Vivia's back as she rocked upon the deck of the *Lioness*. She wondered if she'd find a rainbow in the southern sky. She didn't turn to look. Didn't take her eyes off Captain Kadossi before her. To her right, Vaness stood tall and impeccable, dressed once more in her golden gown. Vivia too had donned her finest clothes, red broadcloth as bright as the rising sun, silver buttons winking.

They would turn themselves in looking like the rulers they were.

"Welcome aboard," the captain said, his mustache twitching in time to his nose. A fresh shaving cut marred his otherwise flawless chin. He was a handsome man, young and less weathered by sun than the sailors and witches clustered around him—which meant he was not an opponent Vivia wanted to cross. In Dalmotti, only pure merit earned rank.

Fortunately, if all went according to plan, she wouldn't have to fight him.

"You made a wise choice turning yourself in, Your Highness."

"It's 'Your Majesty,'" Vivia replied. "And I know. That's why I made it."

Beside her, Vaness huffed a sigh that on anyone else would seem dramatic. On her, it was threatening. "Let us dispense with conversation, Captain Kadossi. We are here as your doge desires, now call off your sailors, return the prisoners to shore, and let us make way."

A slight bow, a nod at his second-in-command, then he motioned to the nearest railing, beyond which the Origin Well stood. "You may watch, if you wish."

Vivia did wish. The entirety of her plan relied on all prisoners reaching shore. Only then would she utter the trigger for Vaness's Ironwitched drills: a common Nubrevnan curse, but spoken in Dalmotti so no one would accidentally release the drills too soon. Vivia and Vaness needed to be far from land when that happened.

With Vaness beside her, Vivia strode to the balustrade, chin high. A perfect mimicry of the Empress, who, exactly as she'd done in Veñaza City, moved effortlessly. Boredom hooded her eyes, impatience sharpened her movements. All her life, Vivia had believed this performance was the true Vaness—the only Vaness—just as she'd always believed her father was actually a man of grandeur and accomplishment. The difference between them, she supposed, was that her father's mask hid nothing but emptiness; Vaness's hid iron and heat and sacrifice.

They stood together, Vivia with her hands behind her back and Vaness with hers gracefully at her sides, while they watched eleven dinghies bob toward shore, some Tidewitched, some rowed, all filled with Yoris's hunters. Vivia's crew, meanwhile, sat chained on a nearby warship, their heads bowed while *Baile's Blessing* sailed in close enough to rescue them.

Vivia opened her spyglass. There was Sotar, posture erect and lips pressed tight. Beside him sat a lanky Cam with hair whipping on the breeze. Just seeing them made Vivia's heart pump faster, her grip tighten on the glass. This plan had to work. *No regrets, keep moving.*

"When will you release my sailors?" She clacked shut the spyglass and rounded on the captain.

"After the hunters reach the shore." Like Vivia, Kadossi stood with his hands behind his back. Unlike Vivia, he hadn't watched the dinghies sail, but had instead observed Vivia with inscrutable eyes. "They are my guarantee."

"Guarantee of what?"

"Guarantee that you do not try something. After all, you and a single ship beat us once before." Respect glinted in his eyes as he said this, along with something else—something Vivia recognized from her father. Kadossi *wanted* to fight them again; he wanted a second chance to win. And, as if to prove her estimation of him, he flipped his hand her way, revealing a triangle tattoo.

Revealing he was a Firewitch.

No wonder he had elevated through the ranks so young, and, Vivia realized with a dredging sort of horror, no wonder the *Iris* had escaped. He hadn't used his magic on them. He could have ended them so easily . . . but he hadn't.

We are important, Vaness had said. *So important that it was worth sending a navy after us.* And so important that she and Vivia had to be kept alive. In theory, Vivia had known that, but it wasn't until she saw Kadossi's Witchmark—coupled with that gleam in his eyes—that it hit her viscerally.

She was important. So important it was worth sending a navy after her.

"There is only one prisoner that still remains," Kadossi continued, and he pointed down. Vivia crooked over the railing to find a final dinghy pushing away from the *Lioness*. On it was a man with a cruel scar and crueler scowl. He caught sight of her, and for half a heartbeat, Vivia almost wanted to laugh at the sight of the old huntsman, chained between two sailors twice his size.

"Smut," Yoris snarled, voice thick with spindrift. "Now you choose to do the right thing? After our village is ruined?"

Vaness hissed beside Vivia, and her lips parted. Vivia silenced her with a hand. Not because Yoris didn't deserve a reply—he didn't—but because for once he was right. So right that Vivia's throat closed up and her joints locked tight. Worse, he wasn't finished yet. He had one more thing to roar before his boat tipped away.

"May the Hagfishes claim your soul and may Noden reject it!" he bellowed, and Vivia's breath caught. Her vision shrank down to only him. *Don't say it, don't say it.*

He said it, this time in rough Dalmotti with an accent thick as Nubrevnan sand: "May the Hagfishes claim your soul and may Noden reject it!"

The drills beneath the *Lioness* awoke.

FORTY-SEVEN

✳

Aeduan did not know how long he stayed trapped in stone, neither living nor awake. All he knew was that, when his eyes fluttered open, he was on his back and the sky was thick with storm clouds.

He took his time rising, testing each muscle, each bone. But he had no wounds or pain, and he was alone. Gone was the child named Saria, and gone was the black bird who had laughed at Aeduan's pain.

All that lingered was a scent like rosewater, and a second like forest fog. The clear lake waters and frozen winters were gone entirely.

Now you understand, said the first Aeduan. *The mystery of that smell. The games it likes to play.*

Yes, Aeduan did understand, and he hated it. The Rook King had always enjoyed his mischief, and now Aeduan's existence was beholden to him. As Paladins, they had both been bound to the Aether all those centuries ago, but the Rook King had always been much stronger.

You also understand, first Aeduan continued, *what you must do. I do not care what you do to me, but she must be protected at all costs.*

"Yes," he croaked in reply, a mere whisper choked with soil, and though he told himself he would help the dark-giver simply because Saria's punishment was not worth risking, the truth was murkier. It lay submerged, bound to the very skin and bones of this body in a shade of deepest red.

He would help her because the first Bloodwitch loved her.

And he would help her because he, the Old One, loved *Her.* The goddess who'd made them all. Even in a thousand years of dark water, he had never lost Her memory. How could he? She was the closest to a mother he'd ever had.

Yet that hadn't stopped him from betraying her in the end because, as Evrane had said, he always *had* been the weakest of them all. He had never truly become an Exalted One, yet he'd never joined the Six.

He knew what he had to do now, though. Which side he had to choose, and it was not between bickering Old Ones and Paladins divided. It was

the side of the dark-giver. The girl who looked so much like She once had—
and not by mere coincidence.

Stones in motion,
Tools cleft in two.
The wyrm fell to the daughter made of moonlight long ago,
He just did not know it yet.

Snow beat against Aeduan as he aimed for Corlant's camp. Winds
picked up speed, shifting from a charged breeze to icy gusts. They slanted
against him, slowing his steps. Blasting snow into his vision.

Lightning cracked, and hail pelted down. The evergreens and winter
hardwoods creaked. The ground began to shake. Soon, Corlant's blood
dominated all others. *Wet caves and white-knuckled grips. Rusted locks and*
endless hunger.

Yet mingling within that scent was a second smell—a new smell that
plowed into him so forcefully he slammed to a stop as if it were physical.
Hail beat against him; snow blustered and flew. Yet all of his being, all of
the Bloodwitch's magic had shrunk down to that smell.

A sky singing with snow. Meadows drenched in moonlight. Sun and sand
and auburn leaves falling.

It was Her scent. Corlant was draining Her—again—because that had
always been Portia's aim. The General and the true Six wanted to restore
the goddess; Portia wanted to end her. No more Paladins, no more Sirmaya. Only Portia's soul for all eternity.

How had he *ever* mistaken Corlant for Midne?

Aeduan ran faster, tapping into the deepest parts of his Bloodwitchery.
Letting the first soul surge upward and claim control. There was no reason
to fight now that they wanted the same thing.

The nearer he came to camp, the more scents crashed against him: fresh
blood thick on the air, hundreds of scents to mash and mix. Sounds came
too, carried on winds that flayed. Weapons and breaking stone, screams
upon screams upon screams.

He smelled the shadow wyrm. *Dark crevices and glowing ice. A lost child,*
forever pain. And above it all, brighter than any other blood, was Corlant.
The hunger was larger than before. A scent to dominate, a need so powerful
it had taken almost complete control. And already, the scent of Sirmaya was
fading beneath it.

Aeduan reached the camp and took in the chaos. Purist, Nomatsi—

some locked in combat. Most convulsing upon the snow as Corlant gorged on their magics and drained their souls. Snow still sliced down, hail still fell, and through the wild winds, Aeduan glimpsed no sign of the dark-giver.

He cursed that he couldn't smell her blood. *The mother,* first Aeduan nudged. *Find the mother.* So the Old One did, seeking out the lavender and lullabies, the cold earth and colder gemstones. He found her at the center of the fray, and he set off across the madness of a battle dominated by one.

He had to lean against storm winds, he had to squint and strain against ice and snow. The closer he came to Corlant, the wilder the blizzard. The more lightning cracked and sizzled. He did not stop, though, for each step brought Gretchya's scent closer.

And it also brought glimmers of Sirmaya again. A warmth to fight toward. A calm he missed more with every tilted step he claimed.

Until at last, he'd reached the eye of Corlant's storm, and there was the man himself. The Paladin, the Exalted One he had feared so deeply a thousand years ago—and still feared. He could not help it. Sirmaya's smile might live forever in his heart, but Portia's laugh lived forever in his skull.

Corlant made that laugh now as Aeduan finally mangled free from the storm. A hurricane of white raged around them—and around Gretchya too, who knelt beside a fresh corpse that smelled of missed smiles and aching regret, of humid swamps and a child's laugh.

For some reason, the first Aeduan mourned that blood-scent and the life that had been attached.

"You are just in time," Corlant called, and with another laugh, he lifted from the ground. Snow gusted away from his feet. His robe billowed, and his bandage slid downward, revealing an empty socket. A fresh wound, savage and deep, had claimed the other eye. Yet somehow, Corlant could see. Somehow, he only looked more powerful, more dangerous.

"Keep my Heart-Thread safe," Corlant ordered, flying higher. High enough that Aeduan should not have been able to hear him. "And if she tries to leave, *maim* her."

Then, with the power of stolen magic, he launched away—and where he flew, his storm flew too. Suddenly winds and snow blasted into Aeduan again. He dove for the Threadwitch, who hunched over her dead apprentice.

Even in the whiteout, he could not miss the streaks of blood or the scent of a girl dead too soon. Gone was Sirmaya, though. The autumn leaves and moonlit meadows had trickled away with Corlant's storm.

"Stay back," Gretchya shrieked at Aeduan. She thrust up a blade. "I will kill myself if you come near, and I can promise you, Corlant would not like that."

Aeduan lifted his hands. He could not possibly convince her that he was on her side. She had no reason to believe him, and he had no way to prove. All he could do was nod at her and remain staked in place. "Where is Iseult?" he shouted.

She bared a grin as terrifying as the dark-giver's had been. "Far away where you will never find her." She sheathed her knife and with a grunt that quickly became a moan, she ducked beneath the dead girl and hauled her stiffening body onto her back.

"Do . . . not . . . follow!" she ground out, and Aeduan nodded again, his empty hands still high. Yet as Gretchya set off through the storm, he sensed smells closing in. Purists that would intersect with her at any moment. That would, he had to assume, try to stop her as their master desired.

So Aeduan knew what he had to do: he might not be able to find the dark-giver, but he would keep her mother safe. And he would not fail her as he had failed his own.

FORTY-EIGHT

✳

Safi had never seen Iseult cleave before. She knew her Threadsister could do it, just as she knew what witchery lived inside her and how much Iseult grappled with it. It was bad enough being Nomatsi on a continent that feared them, but her magic linked to the Void had only made people treat her like a demon wherever she went.

She wasn't a demon, though. When Safi had possessed her full magic, she'd seen the truth inside Iseult's heart: a wicked power, but not a wicked girl.

And she'd never been more certain of that than now, with snow falling around her and her ears still ringing from the crash. She saw it in the way Iseult landed in the clearing, imbued with Windwitchery and graceful as a moonrise. And she *felt* it in the way Iseult looked at the newly cleaved witches beside her, relief mingling with something frantic.

Their skin boiled with tar. Their eyes had gone black, though they didn't attack, they didn't move. Iseult controlled their minds, their magics, and their bodies. Two pistols lay useless on the snow before them.

Safi wasn't sure when she'd started crying. Nor when she started running. All she knew was that she was suddenly stumbling over the ground toward her Threadsister. "You're here, you're here. I don't know how, but you're here."

"Stop." Iseult rocked back a step. The Windwitches rocked back too. Her golden eyes latched on to Safi, panic spinning brighter. "If I release them, they'll die. I-I . . . don't want to kill." A pause. "Them or you."

"So don't release them." Safi slowed, feet unwilling but brain understanding. "Why must you?"

Behind her, Caden rasped, "I've seen you control Cleaved before." He attempted to rise. Then toppled back to the snow, his injured leg crumpling beneath him. Yet when Safi tried to help him, he waved her off. "Can you do what you did in the palace?"

"I don't . . . w-want to. Besides." She gave a dry, familiar Iseult laugh. "I-it hurts." She lifted her hands, wrapped in bloodied bandages.

Safi gasped. "You're wounded."

"It's not my blood."

"Thank the gods for that. Whose is it though?"

Iseult never answered. Not before the white collar at her neck burst into movement. It raced down her body and hit the snow.

It was an ermine. A weasel with its winter coat. And somehow, though it didn't speak with actual words, it uttered a sentient chatter that reminded Safi of another creature—except that the weasel was the old crow's opposite: white fur with black upon the tail versus black feathers with white around the beak.

The weasel squeaked, a frustrated sound that seemed to say, *Just let them die and be done with it.*

Iseult shook her head. Her bandaged hands trembled. "Not again. Not this time."

The weasel's tail flicked. She chattered and ran toward the nearest Windwitch. She twirled twice around his legs, but Iseult only shook her head harder. Her hands quaked. "I *know* I need a Loom, Esme, but there's no time."

Safi eyed the weasel with a frown. She knew the name Esme, and though her Truth-lens said nothing, her gut told her plenty: that animal had once been human. That animal had once been the Puppeteer. "Iseult," she started to say at the same moment Iseult jerked her chin toward the sky.

"Corlant is coming."

Safi looked south—Caden too, still kneeling with his face pinched tight. It pinched all the tighter once he spotted what Safi saw: a storm gusted their way. No snowstorm either, but a hurricane with black clouds and lightning.

Safi's heel started bouncing. "The Cursewitch made that?" Iseult had told her of the priest who'd hunted her, but Safi didn't understand how he could be here. Or for that matter, how he could be controlling such a storm.

"There's more." Iseult flexed and fisted her shaking hands. "Hell-Bards approach from the north. They march this way from the hunting lodge, and will be here any moment. We need to move."

"Shit." Caden towed in his legs again. "The Windwitches must have come from there. How close are they? I can walk."

"Lie," Safi spat as her lens murmured the same. And this time when she dropped to Caden's side, he didn't resist. He was much too cold to the touch, though sweat shone on his brow. She looped an arm behind him and helped him clumsily to his feet. "You're . . . heavy," she said, trying for a distraction.

"All muscle," he wheezed. Then he leaned upon her, his chest billowing. The crash must've damaged a vital muscle. Possibly even broken a bone.

"Caden." Iseult swallowed, a sign that her stutter was taking control. A sign that she was losing her Threadwitch calm. "We're going to have to run. Their Th-Threads are . . . *near*."

"I can manage," he said, and though he believed his words and the Truthlens stayed silent, Safi shook her head at Iseult. He definitely couldn't make it.

Iseult winced. "Y-you two go first. I'll . . . hold on to these witches as long as I can."

"Iseult," Safi said, as lightly as the snow still falling. As gentle as the truth she saw inside her Threadsister. "Release them."

Iseult's knees trembled. "Then they will attack us."

The weasel squeaked loudly at this, but Iseult only winced more deeply. "I . . . d-don't want to," she squeezed at the creature. "I've already k-killed too many. I've already ruined . . . and lost . . ." Iseult's voice choked off. Her eyes screwed shut. Whatever had happened to her hands, it hurt her as much as Caden's leg pained him.

The Cleaved started to groan; and Iseult's eyes squinted tighter, tighter. Meanwhile, stamping feet of Cartorrans now reached Safi's hearing. The Hell-Bards would soon arrive.

And Iseult's shoulders drooped. "Forgive me," she whispered to the dawn. "I do not want to do this." Then her eyes burst wide, her arms leaped above her head, and as one, the Cleaved collapsed beside her.

They convulsed upon the snow. Tar erupted across their bodies, and two streaks splattered Iseult. Not that she seemed to notice. With each passing heartbeat, as the men cleaved and died, her spine straightened. Her chin lifted. Until at last her eyes opened and she nodded.

"Let's go," she said. "Let's fly."

The tower remnants Iseult had seen from the sky were an old place. Iseult felt it as soon as she landed. *Where the walls between this world and the Old Ones' are thinner.*

The *real* walls were thinner too, the forest visible through cracks and a gaping hole that might have been a door. Curving stairs led to nowhere in one corner, and the edges of two more stories clung to stones high above.

No roof, but what remained of the walls blocked the wind. Snow slanted down now.

Safi landed less gracefully beside Iseult, Caden still clasped against her, and though Iseult tried to make his landing soft, his leg collapsed beneath him the instant his feet touched down. His face was red with pain and cold; Safi's teeth chattered every few moments.

It was only going to get colder as Corlant's storm approached.

The Cartorrans approached too, for the tower wasn't far from the crash, and an old, snow-strewn trail led right to it. But Iseult needed access to the Dreaming, and this was the only place she could think of.

Esme squeaked in Iseult's ear, offering the image of a stone table at the tower's heart. Almost altar-like, it had collapsed on one side. After hastily wiping off the snow with a sleeved forearm, Iseult nodded. It would have to do.

She turned to Safi, who crouched beside Caden trying to get the Hell-Bard into a more comfortable position. The gash in his leg glistened; his pale skin did too. It was the sort of wound that would kill slowly, festering and seeping and plucking away at life bit by bit—assuming the snow didn't get him first.

His Threads verged on unconsciousness, though red dwelled there too. Yet from frustration at his weakness or frustration with the situation, Iseult couldn't gauge. And Safi's Threads held their own mystery: a beige worry Iseult didn't recognize. A faint horror she'd never seen her Thread-sister wear before.

One she prayed was not aimed at her.

But there was no time to worry about Threads or winter's breath, just as there was no time to listen to the voices gathering in her brain: two Wind-witches, freshly dead. Freshly trapped inside her veins. No time to worry over Gretchya either, dependent on Corlant's obsession to keep her alive, and no time to dwell on Alma, cloaked in blood and dead upon the snow. There was only moving forward. Only following what had to be done so Iseult could finally, *finally* make things right.

"The Threadstones," she said, crossing the small space to Safi. "I need the Threadstones."

Safi blinked up, clearly startled by the request—though she didn't argue and didn't question. She simply plucked them from a pocket and dropped them onto Iseult's bandaged palms.

Two drops of pressure. Two sparks of pain. Iseult swallowed at the sight of them, a hunger opening wide inside her belly. The rubies seemed to glow, dim light bouncing off them. An eternal flame, eternal sunshine. The bright half of the Cahr Awen to Iseult's eternal frost and midnight.

But then she caught sight of Safi's wrist. "You're cleaving." She grabbed for her Threadsister with her other hand, clumsy and aching.

Safi withdrew. "It's fine."

"It isn't fine."

"I'm not cleaving. It's the Hell-Bard's doom."

"Same thing. You'll die if those lines keep spreading, Safi. Show me your neck. Has it reached your chest?" She pawed again for Safi.

Again, Safi retreated. "Iseult, there's no time. I made it this far without the doom claiming me. I'll make it the rest of the way."

And how far is that? Iseult wanted to demand, but logic held her tongue. Safi was right; like everything else, the doom would have to wait.

"I must enter the Dreaming," she said. "The place I told you about, where I first saw Esme. It's the only way I can stop what's coming. But I'll be exposed when I do. I know you can't protect us from a hundred soldiers or Corlant's storm, but—"

"Oh?" Safi interrupted, eyebrows bouncing. "I'm offended you would doubt me, Iz."

Iseult's nose twitched. She tried for a smile. Safi might be performing, but Iseult appreciated the gesture all the same. "I'll be as fast as I can. Stay safe." Then before Iseult could second-guess or check either horizon for the enemy, she darted back to the stone table.

A clumsy rip with her teeth, and the bandages came free. Cold cut across her brutalized skin. She hadn't seen the full damage until now, and in the dim light of dawn's edge, she could only make out wrinkled, puffy palms.

They throbbed. She ignored them, homing in on the Threadstones. She couldn't see the Threads bound to them. That power belonged to the Aether; her soul was chained to the Void.

"You should move," she told Esme, and the weasel needed no urging. With animal grace, she leaped to the snow and aimed for the door. *I will keep watch,* she seemed to say. *I'll return if I see anything.*

Iseult nodded absently. No time, no time. Snow dotted the rubies now. Soon they would be covered. She draped her ruined palms over the cold stones and closed her eyes exactly as Eridysi had described. Exactly as she had tried so many times to do.

In and out, in and out. Each breath froze her lungs. Each moment brought a storm and Hell-Bards nearer. If only the tower had been farther away. If only she'd found another old place.

No, she snapped at herself. She had to focus. The Dreaming was so near. All she had to do was enter it.

Inhale, exhale. *Safi, Safi, Safi*. Inhale, exhale. *Alma*. Inhale, exhale. *Gretchya*.

Then it happened: the sounds around Iseult changed. Gone were Caden's wheezing breaths and the creak of wind through winter trees. Gone was the wet cold of snow, replaced instead by the dry cold of the Dreaming. She'd done it. She had crossed the wall between worlds.

And this was not the gray, shifting, living world of the Hell-Bard Loom, but rather the Dreaming that overlaid reality. That allowed her to move around within, to see people and Threads exactly as they truly were.

Iseult's dream-self smiled. Then laughed—loud and full, a wild frizzing in her chest that had wanted freedom ever since she'd first spotted Safi on the snow. She was finally in the Dreaming. After two weeks of trying and failing, all it had taken was finding the right location. She glanced at Safi and Caden, their Threads undampened by the Loom's control. They were luminous and alive.

Next, she turned her attention to the horizon, a mere glimpse above the tower's fallen walls. Threads blazed like beacons to the north, green as pine trees with a single focused goal: pursuit. And worse—far worse—was Corlant's storm. It seethed to the south, silver Threads spun from stolen power. Brighter than the shadow wyrm's had ever been and convulsing with countless shades, countless magics. He would be unstoppable when he arrived.

Iseult just prayed that she would be too.

FORTY-NINE

✳

Safi paced the stone tower in a loose perimeter. Each squint through a crack or a hole revealed only forest, wind and snow.

Darkness coiled off Iseult at the tower's heart, tendrils thick as river eels. Safi kept her distance—not merely because of the hoarfrost crackling around her Threadsister, but because those shadows and ice reached for Safi whenever she got too near. Like a hundred little vines to drag her down.

She rubbed her hands together as she strode and tried to remember what gloves felt like. She had no weapons, no shield. Her fists and fingers were all she possessed if the Cartorrans arrived.

When the Cartorrans arrived.

She also tried to recall what life had been like before she'd become a Hell-Bard. Before she'd had this strain tugging inside her chest. Iseult had been right: the doom was coming. And quickly. Compounded by the blizzard or simply a result of traveling too far from her chain, she couldn't say. And it didn't matter. The result was the same in the end.

"There's . . . something," Caden said, slouched against the only spot where snow didn't reach. A corner tucked beneath all that remained of the second floor. "Something we need to discuss."

"Now?" Safi asked. She tried for a smile. "Could we save the chat for when death isn't right outside—"

"*Now*." His head lolled back against the stone wall.

And Safi frowned, veering away from her circular path to join the Hell-Bard in his darkness.

"I will fight as best I can, but . . ." He swallowed. Tried to sit up, face tightening, but he'd lost too much blood and he couldn't resist when Safi knelt and pushed him back down. His wound spurted. "Please find Zander and Lev. If you can. Even if it's just bodies, I'll die easier knowing—"

"*No one* is dying." Safi shot back to her feet, head wagging. "That's not an option. It's *never* an option. Plus, Iseult will be done in the Dreaming soon, and she'll be able to track their Threads—"

A squeak broke through the tower. Safi's gaze lurched toward the weasel, racing toward her. It clawed up her body with ease, and just like with the old crow, a sensation of words, of meaning cut through Safi's mind.

Person. Here.

Then the weasel shared an image of Henrick fon Cartorra. He wore simple hunting clothes, forest green draped in snow, and were it not for the crown still clutching his brow, he might have been no more than a weary soldier. He moved with a comfortable stealth Safi had suspected, but never seen.

And he was right outside the tower.

"Is he alone?" Safi asked the weasel, but she knew the answer well before the creature shoved her frozen nose into Safi's cheek.

More soldiers, she showed. *Dressed like Henrick, circling through the trees. Approaching without noise and with swords clasped tightly.*

"Cow piss and goat shit," she snarled. "Henrick is here."

"I am," said a voice behind her, and when she spun about, hands rising, she found him stepping lightly through the tower's ancient door.

There was a logic to Iseult's plan—haphazard though its assembly had been. And as wrong, wrong, *wrong* as the final impetus was. But it was as if the last two days had slowly contributed a scaffolding of ideas and knowledge.

First, she knew that Corlant wanted the Threadstones more than anything. So badly, in fact, he'd been willing to trek all the way across Cartorra to claim them from a capital filled with soldiers.

Second, she knew that Threadstones possessed power, and as a Weaverwitch, Iseult could take that power. She could cleave the Threads bound to stones and absorb them as her own.

Third, she knew that Corlant was not what he pretended to be. He was not a Purist, he was not a priest, and he was not even truly human. He was a Paladin reborn with the raw power of the Void coursing through him. Iseult could never defeat him on her own.

Nor could she fix what she had done by unraveling her mistakes and weaving anew. Not without power. Not without whatever rested inside the Threadstones she and Safi shared.

They rested now on the ruins, exactly as they were in life, except that here they glowed with such brilliance, Iseult had to shield her eyes. In fact, they shone brighter than Corlant's Threads, thickening behind her.

And it was like stepping into daylight. The longer Iseult stared at the stones, the more she saw within and around. Hundreds of Threads—thousands even—climbing and flying, coiling and connecting toward the cloudy sky. Unlike Corlant's storm these Threads wore only a single shade: the sunset of friendship. The sunset of family.

And the last nail in her scaffolding hammered down. No wonder Corlant wanted these stones. The bonds of love were powerful. It was why Esme had always cleaved the Threads that bind. And now such power was contained in two uncut rubies wrapped in string.

This was more magic than Corlant could gather in a morning. More magic than he could gather in a lifetime, and now all Iseult had to do was take it.

Her nose wiggled, skin stretching with cold. All she had wanted these past weeks was more power. All she needed *right now* was more power, and it rested before her. Yet something pricked at the back of her mind. Not her conscience, but her logic. As if there might still be one nail missing.

Thunder rolled from Corlant's storm, audible even in the Dreaming. So without another thought, Iseult grabbed the first stone's Threads and chomped down. Hard. And as her teeth cut in, she felt no resistance. No fiery pain like cleaving a person, no frozen ice like hurting a Hell-Bard.

These were ocean shallows on a hot day, tender and soothing. Welcoming and warm. Sheer pleasure to touch. Then the power washed over Iseult, a wave of strength to buoy her toward some nearby shore she hadn't known she'd been swimming toward. Her chest swelled with a feeling she didn't recognize. Her muscles and blood relaxed.

She had never felt so good in her entire life. It was as if there was nowhere else to be. As if past, present, and future all rested inside this moment and these Threads.

So content was she, she almost missed the chanting, cascading upward, carried on currents of power directly from the stones. *Finally,* they seemed to say, swelling in Iseult's veins and in her eardrums. *Finally, finally we are saved.*

"What are you?" Iseult tried to ask, but the Threads had no answer. The stones had no real voice. All they could say was *Finally, finally we are saved.* Then they rushed against the Windwitch souls, not simply swallowing them but rubbing them away. Smoothing them down like waves to a stone.

And for a fraction of a moment, the clouds parted—in the Dreaming and in life. Both sun and moon beamed down, sharpening the endless gray and revealing faces within the Threads. They smiled at Iseult, as familiar as her own pulse even though they were unknown.

Use us well, they seemed to sing. Then the last of the Threads, the last of these lost and forgotten dark-givers, fused into Iseult's being. A vast piece of her soul she'd never known she was missing.

Ah. So that was the nail she'd lacked. That was why Corlant wanted these stones and why he'd kept Iseult so near. That was why no Cahr Awen had been seen in so many years and why Aeduan had declared the Water Well only half healed. Corlant had killed and bound their souls—many of them only children—leaving each reincarnation weaker. Smaller.

Until now.

Iseult smiled at the altar. At Safi's stone still shining. She would release those Threads too, let them flow into the light-bringer. Then she would leave the Dreaming and use her new power, ancient as the ruins around her, keen as a blade honed by moonlight.

Safi raked her gaze over Henrick's storm-shadowed figure. A single sword, unadorned, hung at his hip.

"Surrender," he said. "There is no escape." He didn't smile as he spoke, didn't gloat. There was only the hardened, perhaps even tired frown of a soldier too long in the snow.

Safi fought the urge to glance at Caden. As doused in darkness as he was, she hoped Henrick hadn't noticed him. He had, of course, noticed Iseult, but he offered her only a cursory glance, as if he recognized she was no threat to him in her current state. "You are surrounded, Safiya, and more forces approach from all sides."

She flashed him a smile. The same smile she'd been wearing for the last two weeks. "But it was never escape I sought, Your Imperial Majesty." *Keep him talking, keep him busy.* "I sought to protect my family, you see. My uncle. My Threadsister and all the Hell-Bards"—she motioned vaguely toward the forest outside—"bound to me in a way we didn't ask for."

Henrick said nothing. Snow gathered on his shoulders, glistened on his crown.

So Safi pushed on, sliding into a saunter around the tower, hands behind her back. The perfect distraction, and as hoped, his eyes remained on her. "I know you have a family. Sons you've never seen and a nephew you love. I *know* you understand what I feel for my own family, but—"

"Enough," he barked, and Safi expected his sneer to return at any moment or for his hand to grab at the chain on his belt. Instead, he raised his chin and said, "We all have our burdens to bear. I will not shirk mine." He grasped for the blade at his hip. "The fon Cartorran line will continue, and you will continue it. I am sorry, though, that it had to come to this."

He unsheathed his sword.

And in that moment, as steel breathed free from its sheath, the full picture finally locked into place. Safi paused her amble. Her hands fell loose to her sides.

The Emperor's crown *was* too tight. Not by choice, but by the confines of family—a different family than the one he kept tucked away in Praga. This burden came from his parents, his ancestors, his title passed down from mother to son in a cold castle wreathed in scarlet.

Which was not so different from Safi in the end. She'd tried to outrun her uncle and her Hasstrel blood, yet here she was, running right back to it.

"Surrender now," he said, no cruelty in his tone, "and I guarantee neither you nor your Threadsister will be harmed." He advanced a single step.

And Safi softened her stance. "No." She offered him a sad smile—a real one. "You have your duties, Henrick, and I have mine."

It was the first time she'd addressed him by his given name. The first time she hadn't called him by his title, and he tensed at the sound of it. Then something almost like grief crossed his eyes.

She'd seen that look before, in his study when she'd called him poison.

Two heartbeats passed; the snow briefly lightened. Then Henrick sighed. "I am sorry," he said, and he brushed softly at the chain glistening upon his belt.

Blades swiped free, a great clash of noise from outside the tower. Loud enough to sing above the blizzard winds, near enough to flash glimmers of movement through cracks in the ruined tower.

Safi lifted her hands. Cleaved lines crawled over them now, blending into her Witchmark. Warning of a doom so near. But that didn't make her fists any less effective, thanks to the family who had trained her. The family she would fight for until the end.

"I will not go easily," she told him honestly.

"And," began a new voice, cutting through the snow as sharp as a north wind, "she will not go alone." Then Iseult moved into position beside Safi. No more smoke around her, no more ice. Awake and glowing in this tower surrounded by storm.

Initiate, complete.

The Old One had never fought in a storm before—had never fought without sight to guide him. The first Bloodwitch, however, knew exactly what to do as Purists closed in on Gretchya.

There was memory in his muscles if he was willing to listen and let them move free.

A woman with sallow skin loose upon her bones charged Gretchya with a hatchet. A young man with a black beard lunged in with two blades. Behind them, more bodies—mindless husks—coalesced within the snow. Aeduan knew not why they attacked their master's Heart-Thread. It was as if they were cleaved, no longer in control of their minds. He could only guess that the storm and Sirmaya's sapped power had driven them to this chaotic thirst for blood.

Aeduan dealt with all of them. He ducked, he spun, he grabbed arms and levered bodies. He kicked at any knees near enough to reach and hammer-fisted at noses or throats or ears. Duck, spin, lever, kick. Elbows, feet, knees, and flat-palmed hands. His body moved in a blur of magic-fueled speed through an unnatural storm that chomped with ice teeth.

One by one the Purists fell, yet not a one of them died.

Distantly, as bodies poured in with the snow and sleet and winds, and as Aeduan's muscles moved with a forgotten harmony, he noticed that each defense the first Bloodwitch called on was only meant to disable. Each attack was only meant to gain time.

The first Bloodwitch was merciful. He had a power to dominate men, yet he'd never used it that way.

What a waste, Aeduan thought as he flipped a man to the cold earth. These Purists would all rise again, driven by Corlant's command. Their deaths would be so much better for the dark-giver's safety—and so much better for Aeduan's own. Already, he smelled that the first woman had risen again. Already she'd resumed her steady hunt for Gretchya. But Aeduan could not go after her. There were too many. Purists of every age, every gender, every race.

He should be angry at the first Aeduan. He should hate this weakness and curse these muscles that betrayed. There was no order in mercy;

only chaos in an already turbulent storm. And yet, with each twirl and kick, each grab and bend, Aeduan let the muscles' memories rise higher. A strange warmth had settled over him. A foreign certainty that cemented around his bones and pumped his magic harder, faster.

More and more bodies fell. More and more bodies got up again. Until eventually he realized the storm had fallen away. He was no longer in the camp, but back at the spruce tree where he'd found Iseult and the child. There was the icy stream, snow vanishing into its dark waters, and on the bank Gretchya had dropped the young Threadwitch's corpse.

She held her knife aloft again, except it was not aimed at Aeduan but at a figure in white stalking from the trees on the stream's other side.

And it was only then that Aeduan caught the new scent against his magic. *Crisp spring water and salt-lined cliffs.* He did not think but simply moved, sprinting with heightened muscles past Gretchya, past the corpse stiff as stone, and then over the stream in a bounding leap.

He sank to the snow on the other side, catching himself on one knee, and pinned his gaze on the woman who had once been his mentor but was now as tormented as he.

Evrane smiled. A foreign thing that clashed with her blood-scent and grated against the memories pumping in Aeduan's limbs. "I see you have changed sides."

"I see you have not."

Evrane sniffed and lifted her sword slightly. She had paused ten paces away, but now she advanced again, circling left. Aiming for a fallen tree that would give her higher ground.

Aeduan let her have it and did not rise.

She frowned, almost disappointed. "You will not fight me?"

"I do not need to." It was true: he could control her blood. Choke off her heart, her brain. But just as the first Aeduan had let his mentor remain untouched, months ago on a Nubrevnan cliff, this Aeduan let the Old One be.

And though he told himself it was because the first Aeduan pushed through, whispering to him of mercy, he knew it was not true. Not entirely, at least, for there was only silence in his brain, save for a conscience newly grown.

Evrane's frown deepened to a sneer. "Still you are the weakest." She stomped her boots. Two blades sliced free at the toes. Then she leaped at Aeduan.

He swept sideways. Her blade sang past his ears—fast enough to carve him in two. But not fast enough to beat his Bloodwitchery. He shot up the log in a single leap, legs scissoring as he passed her. His foot hit her spine. She stumbled forward, hitting the snow on one knee, toe blade dragging.

He could have ended her then. But he didn't, and that truth made her scream as she thrust back to her feet. "Fight me." She brandished her blade. "Quit being a coward and *fight me*." She charged, sword swiping.

Aeduan skipped backward again. Once, twice. Each attack he avoided, and each moment for retaliation he let slip by. "We are not enemies."

"We are since you betrayed us."

"Portia is the enemy."

"He is not Portia."

"Of course he is."

A strangled snarl. More arcs of silver steel. More snow to settle on her hair and shining cloak. Aeduan had thought Evrane Moon Mother when she had saved him as a boy. The first Aeduan, that was.

Ah, the Old One thought. *There you are to join me.*

I never left, Aeduan replied, and the Old One found himself smiling.

"Stop that," Evrane barked, following Aeduan over roots and into the trees. "Stop smiling and fight me."

"Why?" He bounded around a hemlock and opened his empty hands, briefly whirling about to face her.

She lashed out with her sword, aiming for his calves. But he easily slipped behind her and grabbed her in a choke hold.

"You can still change your mind, Evrane. Now that you know he is not truly Midne."

"It changes . . . nothing," she forced out. "So what if Corlant is an Exalted One? We are too, in case you have forgotten."

"I have not." He squeezed his forearm against her throat. "And I no longer like what I remember."

She dropped her sword. It thumped, a sound muffled by snow.

"Why do you want to die?" he asked. She was so sturdy against him, her browned Nubrevnan skin a sharp contrast to his half-Nomatsi pallor. "You know that if I truly fight you, you will not win."

She did not answer right away, though she could have. Blood might drain from her brain, but her lungs and throat, tongue and mouth still functioned. He felt them shivering like she had words she wanted to say. Then at last: "I see . . . why everyone loves the dark-giver." Her neck wobbled against his forearm. "She looks like Her when She came out of the

Sleeping Lands. I never loved Her, though. Not like everyone else did, so I do not want to bring Her back. I do not want our power to end or to be *weak* like you."

"Mercy," Aeduan said, "is not a weakness. You taught me that, Monk Evrane. And now I will teach it to you." He squeezed more tightly with the forearm against her throat, waiting for her blood to stop its ascent. A careful, patient choke, for the careful, patient soul that he hoped still lived within.

Then she slipped into unconsciousness; her body slumped against his. And with the utmost care for a woman who had raised him, he eased her to the snow.

FIFTY

✳

Safi made her move. She lunged for Henrick right as he lifted his sword. Except he didn't attack. Instead he gave Iseult a single glance and turned away, bolting into the storm. As soon as his figure faded, Hell-Bards charged in.

"Go after him," Iseult said. She spread her arms and splayed her fingers. Then she grinned at Safi, a vicious thing that Safi hadn't seen in so long—hadn't realized she'd missed so badly until right now. It made her heart rise and her own lips twist upward.

"I will handle the Hell-Bards."

Safi believed her. She had no idea what Iseult had done in the Dreaming, but it didn't matter. If her Threadsister said she could manage them, then she could.

She flung a look toward Caden, still veiled in shadow, but his eyes were closed, his breaths ragged. "Stay alive," she hissed at him. Then she kicked into a run. Out of the tower, into the cloud-filtered dawn.

And though it made no sense with the snow now spraying around her and the Loom still fastened tight against her bones, a warmth was coursing through her. A strength that hadn't been there moments before, like she could face a thousand Henricks and come out the victor every time.

"Arrest them!" he commanded as he sprinted past Hell-Bards. "*Arrest them!*"

"Lost control of your soldiers?" Safi called.

Henrick glanced back at the edge of the trees. A single glare to split the snow, then he bolted between a haggard ash and a broken oak. His footfalls were light and fast, and Safi could almost imagine how her magic would respond to this version of him. *True, true, true.*

She stalked after him. No soldiers advanced on her; none even glanced her way. They were dominated by a Weaverwitch. They were controlled by a Puppeteer.

Henrick left tracks, though snow slashed harder now and wind sheared. Safi pumped her arms and squinted through the storm, through waving, creaking trees. Henrick was healthier than she'd realized and adept at moving over such ground.

But it made no difference. She would catch him, and she would finally end this. This warmth in her gut told her it was true.

In what felt like mere seconds, she caught sight of him dipping between trees. A flash of dark green in a world growing whiter by the heartbeat. Then she was to him. He'd reached a thicket of holly, its berries red as the Cartorran sigil.

"You cannot defeat me." Henrick had to shout over the storm, but no fatigue strained his voice. No rapid breaths shook his chest.

"Funny." Safi marched up to him, snow cutting into her cheeks. "I was going to say the same to you." She ducked as soon as she was near, as soon as the inevitable swing arced in.

Her hands swooped to the snow, her fingers closed around a branch. Sturdy silver fir. Perfect for warding off nightmares. Then she rolled sideways. Her muscles thrummed with energy, her vision sharpened, and her mind was alight. Though she didn't understand why, the gray misery of the Loom felt almost negated. Almost erased.

Initiate, complete.

Safi swung at Henrick's knee, but he dodged. His sword hissed down. Steel scraped her shoulder, hot and sudden, yet nothing compared to the pain of the Loom. And nothing compared to the shared agony of a thousand Hell-Bards.

Plus, she was ready for it. As his sword hissed near, Safi looped her branch over his wrist. Exactly as Caden had done to her. She yanked down.

Henrick dropped the sword.

She kicked him in the belly. Once. He flopped backward. Twice, he hit the holly. A third time, and he doubled over. His crown sprang off and landed on the blustering snow.

Safi aimed her branch at his head. Angry red lines circled the skin there, but to her surprise, when she found his brown eyes, there was no fury. Nor cruelty nor pain. There was only resignation.

"Be quick about it." He didn't yell over the winds, but Safi was near enough to hear.

She punted his sword out of reach and glared down. "Why me, Henrick? Why did you marry me?"

Again, his face tightened at his name, but for once he didn't dodge her question. He didn't look away. "For the same reason I nudged your uncle into the Hell-Bards." His eyes shuttered. "For the same reason Eron worked in secret for all those years to depose me. The Well, Safiya. It has always been about the Well."

"The Well?" It was easily the last answer she'd expected. In fact, it was a reply that had never occurred to her. She inched the branch nearer. "Explain."

"Did you never wonder why your family's lands were near the Earth Well?" His eyes opened. Though his crown had fallen, the weight of it had not. "It is your bloodline, Safiya. Your family was chosen, and mine..." A tired laugh. A single shrug. "We were not. But my ancestor took your family's throne a thousand years ago, and ever since I have learned of it, I have tried to restore it."

"Restore the throne without giving it up." Safi barked a laugh of her own. It was thick with cold and hate.

Another defeated shrug. "I cannot deny it. My family worked centuries to improve Cartorra. Our borders are safe, our people are fed. Why would I give all of that up? Better to blend our bloodlines into one."

"So that was why you wanted me to bear Leopold's child. Our heir would be..." She searched her memory for the title Vaness had always used. A title she'd thought absurd, and yet clearly Henrick took it seriously. "Well Chosen," she finished.

"Well Chosen," he repeated.

"But why not betroth me to Leopold from the start?" Safi had to yell now. The wind whistled with speed, bending trees and covering the world in white. "Why did *you* marry me?"

"Because I... wanted Leopold to marry for love." He looked strangely pained as he admitted this. Embarrassed even. "I did not know he loved you, or I would have done things differently."

Snow gathered on Henrick's shoulders, on the holly, on Safi's arms still stretched long. And strangely, thunder rolled. A false, unnatural thunder that set her Truth-lens to frizzing. None of this made sense. Well Chosen and forgotten rulers—so many lives had been sacrificed for *that?*

"Why do you care about the Earth Well?" She waved the branch at him. Snow swept off. "No one remembers whom it chose to rule—if that ever truly happened."

"So I thought too, until I met your mother. Laia remembered. Laia *believed*, and she'd spent years gathering proof. Old Sightwitch Sister records, old stories the rest of us had relegated to myth."

"So you killed her."

"I am not proud of what I did, but in the end, you are correct: I under-stand the bonds of family, Safiya, and I I did what I had to do to protect my own."

Safi's fingers, numb and stiff upon the branch, squeezed until she felt splinters. Wind battered against her, and the thunder pulsed *wrong, wrong, wrong* against her chest. There was so much Uncle Eron hadn't told her, and for what? Secrets hadn't helped anyone; they'd only cursed himself, his sister, and now her too in the end.

Ever so slowly, Henrick lifted his hands. Not in supplication but in surrender. "Please tell Paskella I love her."

Safi glared. "You can tell her yourself." She swung the branch at his head, not hard enough to kill. Only hard enough to neutralize. It cracked against his skull, jolting shock waves up her arms. He slumped, a heap of flesh quickly vanishing beneath the snow. She would come back for him. Eventually.

After claiming his crown and then his newest golden chain to control Hell-Bards, Safi turned away from this powerless man who could do no more harm. And away from the holly berries now hidden beneath a storm's vengeful snow.

It had never been so easy. All Iseult had to do was flick her hand toward a soldier, toward a Hell-Bard, and their Threads twined into her body. She didn't have to hold on; their souls didn't scorch or scream. She simply ges-tured and the world obeyed.

And part of her laughed at that. Finally, she and Safi were completing their plan—completing Eron's plan. Finally, they were eliminating Hen-rick and taking control of Hell-Bards who didn't deserve their eternal pain.

More soldiers advanced from the north, but as soon as they hit Iseult's magical range, she claimed them. Like plucking berries off a tree, she added them one by one. When Iseult said, "Stay," to the Cartorrans, the Cartor-rans stayed. And when she told a nearby woman, "Give me your sword," the woman did exactly that, unfastening it from her belt and handing it off with blank eyes.

So it was that no one followed Safi or Henrick, and no one advanced on Iseult or Caden. No one but Corlant. His storm still came, building by the second. But Iseult wasn't afraid of him. He had power vast and stolen, but in the end, he was only a Paladin. *She* was the Cahr Awen. So many dark-givers now pumped through Iseult. Vibrant, sparkling, elated to be set free. They wouldn't last forever, but they would take her far.

With the sword fastened at her hip, Iseult returned to the tower, to Caden hunched within the shadows. The wind now reached him, the snow now pelted. He had stopped shivering and lay limp.

He did not have much time left.

Iseult sank to her knees beside the Hell-Bard. Snow soaked her pants, spreading Alma's blood anew. "I will send a Hell-Bard to find a healer," Iseult said, hoping she radiated the same calm Gretchya always wore. "Surely, there's someone to tend your wounds."

But Caden only shook his head. One eye cracked open. "Only the Hell-Bard Loom can heal me."

"I can access the Loom if you tell me what to do."

Again, he wagged his head. "It . . . doesn't work that way." His eyelids fell shut, though he beckoned her near.

So Iseult leaned in, and his breath, weak and frozen, reached her ear. "We . . . are not your tools." His chest shuddered; his body slouched; his leg gave an oozing spurt. Unconsciousness claimed his Threads.

And Iseult swallowed, tongue suddenly fat. Hot guilt suddenly rising. "It is . . . *not* forever," she told his limp form. "It is o-only to keep us safe." Her argument sounded flimsy, though, even to her own ears.

It was as she pushed back to her feet that the storm faded. The snow paused, the thunder silenced, and the winds whimpered into a false calm. The eye of the storm had arrived. Corlant was here.

His Threads descended behind Iseult, twining lazily toward the tower as their owner eased from the sky. Purple hunger, amaranth laughter, and the eternally spinning silver.

The hairs on Iseult's skin pricked high. Her spine tingled and crawled, but she took her time prying Esme off her neck and easing her to the snow. She took her time removing her cloak and draping it over Caden's body. Little protection against the cold, but better than nothing.

And she no longer needed it. Not with freed souls to keep her warm. And not when she wore Threadwitch black that she wanted Corlant to see.

He landed in the tower, a soft brush of winds to flip at her hair. His storm pummeled and spun outside, but not here. Not inside these ancient walls.

Iseult turned to face him. *Father, my father.*

He had pulled the knife from his eye, leaving a bloodied abyss still leaking, the hole from his first eye was no longer bandaged, but exposed and crusted yellow with pus. Shadows twisted off him and frost hissed.

Iseult lifted her new sword at him. "I have a weapon. Come no closer."

"Oh, I can see that." He smiled. "Though not in this world. I see you in the Dreaming with perfect clarity." He opened his arms. "A clever spot you chose, my daughter. It used to be mine, you know. So very, *very* long ago."

He advanced a step, smooth as a snake over water or a wyrm over snow. "I see your sword, and your Hell-Bards too. And all the little souls you sapped from the Threadstone."

Iseult held her stance. "I *will* kill you."

His hurricane of Threads gleamed with delight. "Your own father?"

"I am the only one who can."

The amusement creaked brighter. His eyebrows leaped, squeezing fresh blood from his eye. "So you figured that out, did you? Clever, though ultimately useless in the end." He flipped up his arms, robe falling back to reveal skeletal limbs oozing shadows.

Ice lanced out from his feet, hardening the snow and shooting toward Iseult. She dove sideways, where a stone crunched up to block her way. Another dive and she was at the exit. She didn't flee, though. Not this time.

She rounded back and launched full speed at Corlant. He flung more ice at her, then flames, but she could see each attack coming. His Threads—his stolen, engorged Threads—gave him away. A flare of green meant stones barraging. A burst of yellow meant winds to slay. Red pulses meant flames, and the sudden shadows meant he grappled to claim her Threads.

He wanted to drain her as he'd drained so many others and as he'd tried to do to Alma, though she'd been too strong to relent and too good. Not an enemy for Iseult to envy, but a goal to aspire toward.

And a girl she still had to save.

Iseult reached Corlant, her blade stretched and ready. She would end him quickly. Finish the nightmare that had entrapped her mother for so long. Except that when she reached Corlant, when her sword hit the place where his skin should have been . . .

It pierced right through.

Magic hissed over her, and with yawning horror, she realized she'd fought a glamour. He'd taken that power too, off a Nomatsi from the camp. Corlant's laughter slid into her ear. Cold as he always was. "Find me, Iseult. If you want to kill me, you have to find me."

She spun about, but there was no one in the tower. No Corlant—and no Caden either. Shit, shit, *shit*.

In moments, she was outside. Snow blasted, and storm winds hurled, but Iseult was ready. Six Hell-Bards immediately fell into position around her, exactly like her guards had at the Pragan palace. Their faces were veiled in snow, their Threads unfeeling thanks to Iseult's control.

And as she'd hoped, the storm silenced as soon as the Hell-Bards moved around her. No winds, no snow, no threat—for Corlant's storm was magical, and the Hell-Bards were immune.

It wasn't a permanent solution against Corlant, but all she needed was time to find him.

She sent out her senses, reaching with the power and connection of a hundred Hell-Bards. Of fifty dark-givers finally freed from stone. But Corlants's Threads swelled so far now; there was no telling where he ended and the rest of the world began. It was as if he'd sprouted roots, the Threads shooting out and down, digging into the soil.

Or as if the soil feeds him. When she'd seen his storm forming, she'd thought he had claimed his power from the very earth itself. Just as Portia had once done to build her Loom, where the Threads of Sirmaya were closest to the surface.

"Aren't you coming?" Corlant whispered. "Or is your Hell-Bard friend not enough to entice? I can take the light-bringer too. She is so near—"

"*Don't touch her,*" Iseult snarled, and immediately she sent out a new command: *Protect Safi.* Six Hell-Bards shot off toward the forest. Toward the brilliant colors of her Threadsister—now beside a fallen emperor. And as the Hell-Bards ran, Iseult ran too.

"Closer," Corlant purred. "Closer, closer."

She hopped roots and ducked under branches, her Hell-Bard guardians moving in perfect synchrony around her—and the rest of her army moving too. Corlant would not touch Safi. She would crush him with Hell-Bard bodies he could not maim. She would break and bend him as he had tried to do to her. And as he had succeeded with so many others.

Safi canted against the storm, crossing a small clearing where fallen trees had opened up the sky.

Wrong, wrong, her lens warned with each step. *False, false.*

Safi pushed all the harder. Whatever waited ahead, she wouldn't leave Iseult to face it alone. Yet as soon as she pushed back into trees, a fir briefly blocking her from hail as large as her fists, the world went silent and still.

No lightning, no winds, and no hail—only the holes they had pocked into the snowfall. And her Truth-lens practically screaming against her skin.

She scanned the forest, holding Henrick's sword with the gentle grip Habim had taught her. *Not too tight, not too loose. Simply ready.* The storm continued unabated in the trees beyond. She saw it, a wall of gray and white. She heard it, a thousand angry sighs.

A laugh trilled behind her. She tore around. *Wrong, wrong, wrong.* But there was no one within the trees.

"Come out!" she shouted. "And maybe I'll go easy on you."

Another laugh, so close she felt it on her skin like a winter draft leaking through a window. She spun again, now facing the clearing she'd just abandoned. But still, no one. And still, her Truth-lens screamed of wrong.

Then something fell into the snow, straight out of the sky. So fast, she almost missed it—and so hard, the earth trembled beneath her feet. A body, human and limp.

"Caden." Safi rushed for him, all thoughts of the laughter gone. All thoughts of the storm or danger gone. She only made it three steps, though, before wind surged against her.

A man descended into the clearing. Snow billowed away from him as he landed beside Caden. Safi's vision crossed. Dizziness wheeled over her, and for half a frozen breath, she saw only the man's face—except that there were so many. Face after face smeared and melted and formed, as if he were the pages of a book being rapidly flipped.

And her Truth-lens shrieked so intensely, it practically bounced against her skin.

Then the book settled, a single page unfurling. A single face for her to blink at, blood oozing from an eye that would never see again.

"What a clever light-bringer," he said in Cartorran. "Using your device like that to negate the Loom. Useless, but clever all the same." He advanced a step. No eyes, yet he could clearly see.

And Safi lifted her sword. "Who are you?"

"Your Threadsister did not tell you?" He fanned his fingers at his face. "You do not see the family resemblance?"

Safi didn't know what that meant and didn't care. There was only one person he could possibly be. "The Cursewitch," she said, and his cheeks bunched with a smile. It squeezed blood from the eye that still remained.

"*Do not touch them,*" Iseult shouted, fierce and right and good. Then a breath later, she stalked into the clearing, her cheeks bright, hair wild, and body covered in snow. Marching on either side were Hell-Bards, moving wherever she bade.

She briefly met Safi's eyes, and there was that vicious smile again. "You can steal all the power you want," Iseult called, striding to Safi's side, "but your magic can't touch a Hell-Bard." Then, a flip of her hands and the Hell-Bards around her shot into guarding positions around Safi and Iseult. Six bodies to block Corlant.

Another flip and more Hell-Bards shoved out from the trees. They too encircled Safi and Iseult, more and more of them by the second. Row upon row, until Safi lost sight of Caden and Corlant. All she saw were forest-camouflaged uniforms and empty, controlled eyes.

She didn't like those eyes. Didn't like how her Truth-lens reacted to Iseult now, saying *wrong, wrong, wrong.* And suddenly, she remembered that Iseult had controlled *her* too. On the flying machine, Iseult had taken over her muscles and her eyes and it had been as wicked as Corlant, as foul as the cleaving lines that wormed over her hands.

Yet before she could plead with Iseult to find a different way, Corlant spoke. A frostbitten whisper that filled the entire clearing.

"Oh but my daughter," he said, "I *can* hurt a Hell-Bard. I can hurt them very badly indeed."

As one, the Hell-Bards collapsed to the snow. As one, black lines of the doom laid claim to their bodies, to their faces, to their eyes. And beside Corlant, Caden screamed.

"Do something," Safi begged Iseult, but Iseult only shook her head and grappled at the air. As if reaching for Threads she could no longer see.

So Safi dropped her sword and grabbed for her belt. *The tongue, protect the tongue.* Her frozen fingers fumbled. Her brain tried to remember what Zander had told her to do. She couldn't save them all, but she could at least try to reach Caden.

Yet as she twisted toward him, she found Iseult had grabbed the fallen sword and was now sprinting toward Corlant. No grace, no control, only erratic desperation like Safi had never seen her stoic Threadsister wear.

Corlant's laughter came again. "Nice try, Dark-Giver." He tossed out his hand. Wind hit her, a funnel to smash ribs and lift Iseult high. Then he turned his focus toward Safi. With long steps with spider-like legs over each fallen Hell-Bard, he walked. And as she moved, he killed them. A snap of fingers, a widening smile, and they stilled upon the snow-thick earth.

Safi could do nothing but watch. Her muscles were no longer her own.

"I told you it was useless," he said. "Now I believe I will take back all these souls I worked so hard to claim." He snapped again.

Pain shattered through Safi. A cold pain borne on knives made of ice—
and with it was a laughter to fill her, to crush her, to end her. The snowy
clearing faded. The doom closed in.

Iseult flew. Her back hit the tree. Her skull too, and stars flashed over her
vision. But Corlant wasn't done. A gust of winds laced with fire lashed
out, catapulting her up, up, through snow and Threads and frozen shadows. Then she was above the trees and sucked into Corlant's spinning
storm.

Winds hit her, collapsing her lungs, and erasing all sight. There was only
snow and wind and unconsciousness clawing in. She could do nothing.
She had no army. She had no stolen power, and the lives of the Cahr Awen
couldn't help her here.

Then as quickly as she'd been siphoned upward, she was tossed back
down. A sack of organs and bone, she hit the ground with such force she
couldn't even feel the pain. There was only death rushing in.

And cold. A distant, numbing cold from a Void Paladin's Threads.

Laughter trickled into Iseult's hazy, spinning awareness. *You have no
idea what I can do, daughter, and this is not a fight you can win.* As if to prove
his point, the earth began to shake. First a lurch beneath Iseult's back.
Then a quivering that rattled her teeth and kicked up snow. Winds roared
in her ears, yet the earth roared louder.

With each fraction of a heartbeat that passed, more shadows coiled up
around her. As if the earth itself were cleaving—as if Corlant had taken
too much power, and now the soil died. Ropes sliced over her and held her
down. More, more, hundreds of them, then thousands. She couldn't move,
couldn't see, couldn't feel. There were only shadows and snow. Lightning
and pain.

She would die here. One more dark-giver fallen to Corlant's power.

And so much power it was. Too much power. She'd been a fool to think
she could ever beat him. Fool, fool, always a stupid fool.

I'm sorry, Alma. I'm sorry, Mother. I'm sorry, Safi.

As the last of consciousness faded and the last of her senses rubbed
away, Threads punctured in. They replaced the earth's shadows. Silver and
hungry and burning with eternal rage. Corlant, she thought, come to end
her once and for all.

Except that instead of destroying her, the Threads only closed in. Instead of laughing at her, they softened into understanding.

The shadow wyrm, she realized distantly. It had found her, and rather than devour, it was protecting. A shield against the storm with no cold to pitch off it, nor even Void darkness. It was simply a monster who had lived too long, beholden to a master it feared.

Slowly, Iseult's senses returned. The twisted world of snow and storm was replaced by a billowing chest covered in onyx scales. Its heart beat, bound in silver Threads.

And in the sunset bond of family.

It *was* a mother. It *did* understand, and unlike Gretchya, it hadn't been there to save its child when death had come closing in. Now it wanted to protect Iseult.

And spooling atop the sunset was another shade—one she'd seen on Owl. One she hadn't appreciated, though that color was the source of everything.

Three lines upon her Threadwitch gown. Three lines to represent the world of Threads: Threads that break, Threads that bind, and Threads that build. Iseult had lived so long with the gray, lived so long craving pink, she had forgotten entirely about the green.

Forever reaching, forever trying to forge and grow and become the bond this wyrm now offered her simply because it understood what it meant to love. Simply because even a monster could feel empathy and pain.

Iseult began to cry. Unbidden and unstoppable, the tears swelled in her chest. Her mouth hinged wide, and a hiccuping, sobbing scream tore free. It broke her more than Corlant's storm had, and she welcomed it.

Because she had lived so long without seeing.

Even after she'd crossed a continent to save her Threadsister, even after Gretchya had chosen her, and even after Alma had died because of her inaction, Iseult still had not *seen* that true power had never been in death or in control. Cleaving was something she could do, but just as Alma had told her: it didn't have to be that way.

She wasn't merely the dark-giver. She was the shadow-ender too, and the Hell-Bards were *not* her tools.

"Thank you," she said to the wyrm. A sound lost to the earth's shaking and the storm still punching around them. "Thank you."

At those words, the shadow wyrm gave a rumbling purr—more feeling than sound—and slithered its shielding body away. The storm instantly pummeled in. The earth's shadows instantly grasped for Iseult again. But she was prepared; she already had exactly what she needed clutched in her hand.

The noose she'd taken a lifetime ago off a man she should never have slain.

She opened the cloth around it and placed her bare palm atop it. Then the world around her disappeared.

FIFTY-ONE

✳

ivia could not stop the drills. Vaness had crafted them for speed, and even she with her Ironwitchery could not stop the spell before the damage was done. *No,* Vivia wanted to scream. This warship wasn't supposed to sink here. The *Iris* crew wasn't supposed to still be in chains. The hunters weren't supposed to still be in dinghies bouncing toward shore.

Now the plan was ruined. There was nothing for Vivia to do but fight and try to save as many Nubrevnans as she could.

Kadossi leaped into action. He opened his mouth, and pure fire poured forth, a stream targeted directly at Vivia. And this was exactly what she *hadn't* wanted to do: face him directly.

At that moment, right as her muscles prepared to evade, the second drill ripped loose. The *Lioness* rolled sharply to port, flinging Vivia and Vaness out of Kadossi's path—and instead toward all the sailors who'd realized an attack was underway.

"*Free my crew!*" she shouted at Vaness. And, for once in her imperial life, the Empress obeyed. She ducked beneath a sailor and flung her hands toward the warship holding the *Iris* crew.

More sailors stampeded, and Kadossi aimed his flames at Vivia once again. She summoned water from the hungry sea right as flame spewed across her vision. She dove sideways, launching her waters at the captain, but the water hit nothing.

He really was the best.

Vivia pummeled sailors instead. Strong as a shark beneath the sea, she slammed them one by one. No dexterity, no subtlety. Pure force that made the water laugh as it plunged bodies overboard.

Vivia didn't laugh with it. Already the tides threatened to overwhelm her. Already, they saturated her with power and urged her into chaos. She needed her wits, though for such close combat and a Firewitch on the loose. Nubrevnans were depending on her.

As she leaped up the listing ladder to the half deck, she scoured the battle for Vaness, only to find that the Empress had one arm looped around the balustrade and one arm stretched high. When Vivia squinted toward her crew, she found chains melting off Cam, off Sotar, off everyone from the *Iris*. Then the iron flew toward Vaness, ready to be used and morphing as it crossed the churning sea.

She plucked the iron—now shaped like a flail—from the air, and with a wild spin, the spiked head swung outward and hammered into a sailor's chest.

Vivia lost sight of Vaness then. Flames rushed toward her, up the ladder, forcing her to splash up a wall of water. Steam hissed. Then Kadossi lunged through. He moved easily despite the ship's lean. His shaving scar oozed fresh blood. His cheeks were flushed from heat.

Vivia propelled more water, two ropes to splash his face and veil his eyes. But he ducked easily and blasted rounds of fire—a pounding of them, one after the other that her waters couldn't stop. Each blast created more steam, scalding, blinding. And in the time it took Vivia to rush across the half deck, its angle increasing by the second, her world turned to fog.

The chaotic fight disappeared. The captain disappeared. *Baile's Blessing*, the crew from the *Iris*, and even the groaning masts of the *Lioness* were all hidden within a realm of steam.

If only Vivia were like Stix, then she'd have been able to control it. Able to sense where, in all that mist, the captain lurked. But she was only Vivia. Only a Tidewitch. Only a little fox who'd hunted exactly where she shouldn't have.

Vivia reached the railing. A pistol fired behind her, cracking loud. Impossible to avoid. Yet somehow, she had the time to turn her head back and look. Somehow, she had the time to think, *I am too far from the Origin Well to survive this time.* And somehow, she had the time to watch as the round bullet from the captain's Firewitched pistol cut through steam and careered her way.

Except it was barely moving. As the bullet reached her, as it came close enough for her to grab from the air, the iron spliced into countless smaller shots that sprayed sideways. Then Vaness coalesced in the fog, her nose bloody and gown shredded. Behind her, more shots fired and orange light seared Vivia's way.

Vaness reached Vivia first, arms flinging wide as she tackled Vivia overboard. They fell toward the sea. Fire ripped out above them, singeing the edges of Vaness's hair and gown and blasting Vivia with heat. But it was too slow, and now Vivia and Vaness were beneath the fog. Beneath the *Lioness*'s decks.

They hit the waves. Vivia's breath burst from her as the sea enveloped them. Vaness still held on, though, and when Vivia opened her eyes, she found blood trailing behind them, a stringing silhouette upon a sea gone mad.

She yanked water to her, though she didn't carry them to the surface. Instead, Vivia let them sink, let the water cradle her and feed her power.

It foamed and roiled as the *Lioness* sank, displacing the water—angering the water. *Use us*, it told Vivia. *Use us and attack.*

How? Vivia wanted to ask it. *How can I use you to protect my crew? To protect Noden's Gift?* She could try to sink more ships, but those hulls would simply become more skeletons upon the seafloor while the sailors would live on. They would swim ashore, Kadossi at the lead, and they would destroy the Gift anew. *How can I use you? Tell me what to do.*

As Vivia and Vaness sank, the Empress's fingers clutched at Vivia's biceps and bubbles roared from her mouth. The *Lioness* bore down, a massive shadow from above. They were deep enough now that the waves had calmed. No more currents to spin and dunk. They would hit coral soon or one of the many skeletal ships filling the sea.

Here, Vivia sensed a deep bass thrum within the water. One she'd never sensed before. An undertow that quavered in her belly and trickled up from beyond the farthest shelf. Perhaps all the way from Noden's court. *Become us*, it urged. *Become us and attack.*

The Empress clawed at Vivia, a vague, distant sensation compared to the water's command. *Become us*, the water said. *Join us and attack.* There was no malice in the undertow. Only welcome. Only an element accustomed to being ignored until someone entered its realm.

The Empress shouted, a water-filled burble that hit Vivia's skin. Blood still streamed from her nose as she shook her head, eyes bulging. Then a hundred tiny pricks pierced Vivia's biceps. Painful, sudden, and jolting. Vivia blinked, and *this* time, she focused fully on Vaness.

The Empress was drowning. She didn't have the lung capacity Vivia did. She hadn't spent half her life surrounded by waves or riding rivers to their falls.

Vivia glanced up, at the wild silhouette of the *Lioness* descending. Even if they could make it to the surface, only pistols and flames would await. Never had she wished for Stix more, to help her, to lift her, to guide her because Stix always knew what to do. How to make everything better. But Stix wasn't here, and Vivia had only herself to do what needed doing.

So she did the one thing she could think of that would keep the Empress alive in this tiny cocoon of safety: she pulled Vaness to her and kissed her.

As the Queen of Hawks and the Queen of Foxes vanished beneath the roiling sea, Stix, Ryber, and Kahina watched in silence from a stretch of gravel beside the Origin Well.

"Are you ready?" Kahina asked. Smoke curled from her pipe, mingling with the acrid stench the battle. She had shed her admiral's coat and boots.

"Yes," Stix answered, and she turned to Ryber. "Safe harbors. We'll return soon."

"Safe harbors," the Sightwitch replied, and her lips twitched with a rare grin. Then she held out the Giant card for Stix to see. Its gold back winked in the morning's coral light. "Do not take too much magic from Her."

"No." Stix wagged her head. "We'll only take what we need." She walked to Kahina's side, her own bare feet rolling over tide-worn gravel, and together, the Paladin of Hawks and the Paladin of Foxes walked into the sea to help their queens as the Sleeping Giant—the goddess at the heart of everything—wished for them to do.

It wasn't a true kiss. Or Vivia didn't think it was. Later, she would agonize over that distinction, but during the panicked moments while it happened, while she pressed her lips to Vaness's and shared every remnant of breath in her lungs, while the Empress crushed her lips back and drew in air like the drowning woman she was, Vivia saw it only as a way to save the Empress and buy them more time beneath the waves.

Because the undertow's song wasn't finished with Vivia yet—*Become us, become us and attack.* It sounded like Stix. Vivia didn't know how, she didn't know why, but it was as if her Threadsister were right beside her, pumping her fists and urging her on.

Vivia had wished Stix were near to save her only moments ago, and now it felt as if she really were. Become us, become us and attack. Go, Vivia, go.

The iron needles on Vivia's arm pulled back, leaving only the Empress's fingers, stronger by the heartbeat. Then the Empress herself pulled back, nothing more than a shadowy shape swept in gold. Vivia's sinking feet brushed a long-forgotten hull. Kelp reached for her ankles. *Become us, become us and attack.*

Yes, she replied, and in that moment, she sensed Vaness do the same. Like a scale glinting in a tide pool, something flashed in the Empress's eyes. Something that Vivia spotted despite the shadows, despite the crude light of a rising dawn. Iron had summoned Vaness, and she too was answering the call.

It was like the Origin Well all over again, but a hundred times stronger. As if the very Threads between Vivia and the Empress had thickened into roots that could not be broken. They no longer belonged to themselves, but to the elements they commanded.

Vivia lifted her arms; Vaness raised hers. The sea obeyed, the iron obeyed, and the sunken ship obeyed.

Whirlpools formed around Vivia and Vaness as water was displaced. As sand that hadn't moved in decades sloughed off a keel long dead. Iron creaked, a higher-pitched descant to the groan of wooden ribs—just as Vaness's magic seemed to sing atop Vivia's undertow. Water lifted and moved, hands to raise a ghost ship while iron reassembled into the ghost cannons it had once been.

A galleon, Vivia recognized. Perhaps even Dalmotti all those years ago.

Now it was Nubrevnan. Now it belonged to the seas that had always lived here, to the undertow that had outlived nations. It remembered more than Vivia's human mind could conceive, though her tiny brain tried to stretch and warp and absorb as the water flushed into her, flooded through. It had seen continents grow and shorelines fall. It had tended corals large as cities and fed every life that had ever flickered. It had caressed and nurtured and killed and destroyed.

As the galleon lifted, it carried Vivia and Vaness higher and higher, eventually angling to avoid the *Lioness* as that ship sank lower and lower.

She lost all sense of her body. Like her brain, she became a vessel for the water. She *became* the water, exactly as it desired. And she would swear, again, that Stix was somehow right beside her. *Go, Vivia, go.*

The galleon rose, lifting Vivia's head above the water's surface, then her neck, her chest, her legs. Water sluiced off of her, dawn air crashed in. Distantly she sensed other ships rising, carried by the water. Two, three, fourteen, the undertow lifted fallen galleys and half-galleys, sunken carracks and longships shed here by different empires over decades of a war that had never claimed Nubrevna.

And would not claim it now, for the undertow protected its own. Nubrevnans respected the sea; the empires did not. Vivia respected the sea; these intruders did not.

Cannons fired, sopping and rusted yet propelled by iron that begged to be used, and somehow—though she didn't understand it—propelled by fire too. Vivia heard their eruptions, a vibrant call that shivered through Vaness and laughed atop the sea. Yet the cannons didn't aim for the Dalmotti ships, but rather sent their iron right past. Warnings of what might happen if the Dalmottis did not flee. Promises of violence and death the flaming iron would gleefully claim. That it *wanted* to claim, but that somehow Vaness kept leashed.

Or did she? As Vivia forced her own eyes to see, not as an undertow but as a human, she found Vaness before her on planks slick with algae and gray with time. Her nose gushed blood, her head slumped. How she still stood, how her arms still reached, Vivia had no idea.

And she discovered with a drooping wrench of horror that she was faring no better. Her own posture had crumpled, her own arms shook like the deck beneath her, and the longer her eyes clung to Vaness's face, the more darkness swept across them. She couldn't do this forever. If she did, then the water would take her completely. She would lose herself entirely to the undertow—and rather than allow the Dalmottis to leave, it would drag and drown and feed. It didn't care that *Baile's Blessing* would be caught too, that the Nubrevnans it respected would sink and die. What was one life compared to the civilizations it had lived beside?

No, Vivia thought. Then harder, a word to rip up from her stomach: "*No*." She loved the tides, she loved the sea, and she loved this echo of Stix that seemed to live within them, but they could not have her. They could not have these people, Nubrevnan or Dalmotti.

Vivia released her magic. Like blocking a waterfall, one moment she was filled with rapids she could not swim against. The next, she was empty and still. A riverbed drained dry. Her heart boomed and rain still drizzled. The ghost galleon still thundered beneath her feet. And when Vivia twisted her focus left, right, her muscles protesting as if she were made of the same decayed wood as this galleon, she found the rest of the undertow's navy. Already, those ships capsized anew, though their ancient cannons still fired—and kept on firing even as the waves swallowed them plank by plank.

But the Dalmottis were leaving. Not the *Lioness*, for the sea had eaten her, bones and all, yet the rest of the fleet now sped toward the horizon, where a rainbow did indeed split the misty sky.

So as Vivia and Vaness once more sank into water that was quickly rising above their knees, Vivia pulled the Empress to her. "Come back," she said, pumping her words with the same authority she'd heard in the undertow, the same bass line the iron had responded to so well. "Come back to me, Vaness. Come back."

FIFTY-TWO

✳

Iseult was in the Hell-Bard Loom again. It looked as it always had. Gray, gray, endless heaving gray. And there were the ghosts. There were the Hell-Bards she'd so foolishly thought she could control—and so wickedly thought she *should* control. They swarmed her exactly as they always had, singing the same refrain they'd always sung.

Except that this time, when they came, she did not fight them. Their voices clawed, their ghost hands pierced. And she let them. No trying to fight what crashed against her. No trying to rule what should not be ruled.

Yet no letting them rule her either. They would crush her if she listened too closely. If she gave them the notice they so desperately craved. Just like her own rage, just like all those feelings she'd kept shuttered away for a lifetime: too much and you would drown. But too little, and you would shrivel away.

I see you, she told each face that grappled in. *I understand. But I am* not *you. I am me, and I must be set free.*

And that was all it took. Acknowledgment. Acceptance. Then every shadow face reared away. Hundreds of them, thousands, all crowding in and wanting to be seen. Yet none tore her away—not when she looked them in the face and repeated, *I see you, I understand.*

Iseult wasn't sure when her dream-self began crying. They weren't the stunned tears of too much emotion from a secret corner broken wide, nor the bereft tears from a daughter wrapped in the Threads that build. These were tears of relief, tears of joy.

Because she really, truly understood now. *This* was stasis. *This* was what Threadwitches were meant to do. All the emotions of the world around them, yet never seeing their own—of course they had to keep themselves apart. Otherwise the weave of the world would overwhelm them. But somewhere over the generations, simple separation had become denial. Pale-knuckled, viciously fisted denial in a way that no human could ever sustain.

People were meant to feel.

And people were meant to dance, as Iseult had danced with a prince on a balcony unseen.

I see you, she told the ghosts over and over. *I understand you, but I am not you.* She lost all sense of time, of ghosts, of tears. Yet with each acknowledgment, she was carried farther through the Loom. A current of ghosts to take her where she wanted to go. A raft atop waves she could neither swim with nor swim against.

Until at last, she reached the person at the center of it all.

He wasn't expecting her. That much was clear. His spirit stood unguarded at the center of a simple basin. The edges of this space—the only *real* space in the Loom—blurred into gray nothing beyond. The ghosts couldn't enter here; they clustered and clawed on all sides like faces pressed against glass.

"Father," Iseult said. "I have come for you."

Indeed, Corlant crooned, and instantly, his ghost form solidified. When he lurched around, she found—as before—that his one remaining eye was healed here.

He grinned at the sight of her, an expression that had become so familiar in her childhood. One she now understood was filled with centuries of hate and with, tucked deep inside his own secret corner, centuries of fear.

She wondered what his old smile might have looked like. The one before his Paladin memories had awoken. The smile of a man who'd loved a Threadwitch.

"I thought you would be wiser." He twirled open his hands. "This is *my* space. I made it."

"Yes." She nodded. "I guessed you were Portia a long time ago. Though I do wonder why you lied."

"Because if I had not, the Six would have killed me. I died that day, but not forever like the Exalted Ones. And so I have lived a thousand years, growing stronger with each incarnation. And oh, Iseult." He clucked his tongue, his forehead trenches sinking deep. "It will hurt you so much more to die here than it would have in the real world."

"Yes," she agreed. "I'm afraid it will."

Then, before he could react or guess what she might do, she opened her hands. Unlike before, they were not healed in the Dreaming. Instead her palms were rough with scars—scars she had earned. An eternal reminder of the choices she hadn't made.

Living, living, she thought, *breath and living.* She turned toward the ghosts, clustered and desperate outside the basin. *Threads that heal, Threads that thrive.* Then again, though this time she sang it aloud. *"Living, living, breath and living. Threads that heal, Threads that thrive."*

Each soul required its own caress, its own reminder of life. So many Hell-Bards had been dead a hundred years. A thousand. But she gave each soul the magic it had lost, the Threads that had been erased.

And there was nothing Corlant could do. When he sent his Hell-Bards to attack, nothing happened. When he tried to flee the basin, he was swarmed by the lives he had claimed—ghosts now set free and ready to exact their vengeance.

It was slow work. It was exhausting, and the power of the dark-givers that Iseult had taken from the Threadstones now seeped away with each soul Iseult saved. But the dark-givers had wanted freedom, and these Hell-Bards did too.

Green Threads that build spiraled upward, a thousand thousand blades of new life to replace the ash wasteland of the Hell-Bard Loom. And it was like the old rhyme Iseult had once sung to Aeduan:

Dead grass is awakened by fire,
Dead earth is awakened by rain.
One life will give way to another,
The cycle will begin again.

No more Threads that break. Only Threads that build, on and on for as far as Iseult could see, as far as she could feel. And with each Hell-Bard she healed, Corlant grew weaker.

Living, living, breath and living. Iseult didn't stop until she saw only a realm of green. *Threads that heal, Threads that thrive.* Until she had healed Caden and Lev and Zander. Until she had healed Eron and every guard she'd ever met. Until they had all been healed and there was only one spirit left.

"Safi." Iseult smiled at her other half, bright and beautiful and golden. "Be free, Light-Bringer. Be free." Then she carefully unbound her Thread-sister from the Loom. Here was Safi's Truthwitchery, if only half, and here were the colors and brilliance of her being. The bursts of laughter. The crass swears. The eternal loyalty and moral compass always aimed true.

Initiate, complete.

Safi and all the other Hell-Bards were finally free.

And Iseult finally turned to face Corlant. Like a corpse left to deflate in the rain, he had shrunk in on himself, an empty, desperate body huddled within the basin. She could cleave him with just a thought. He was too weak to fight her. The daughter with a Void power he'd passed on.

But Iseult did not want to cleave him. He would be the last life she would willingly claim, and she would not twist it or sever it. Not the man who was her father.

She closed her eyes, inhaled deeply, and imagined the forest and the snow she had left behind. No other thought, no distraction to keep her from doing what she had struggled so long to do. True stasis guided her, grounded her. All the way into her fingers, all the way into her toes.

The Loom disappeared.

She found her father curled in on himself upon the snow. He was inside the tower. No more storm, no more stolen Threads. Simply a man drained to his true essence.

And she'd been right: it contained only fear—and fear had so easily become hate. Hate for oneself, hate for the world that had rejected you. She had lived a lifetime with it; she understood that concept well.

Corlant unfurled from beside the altar as she approached. Then dragged himself to his feet. He couldn't escape; he knew that, and his Threads wore weary resignation.

Hell-Bards, newly freed, flared like fireflies at the edges of her magic. The shadow wyrm was nowhere she could feel. With its master weakened, it had returned to the darkness in which it thrived.

Iseult reached Corlant. Huddled in as he was, his head was at her level. He clutched his damaged face in his hands. "I don't want to kill you," she told him.

"Coward." He didn't remove his hands. She wondered if he could still see her through the Dreaming. "I will simply be reborn again."

"All the more reason to let you live."

His Threads glistened with sky blue. Relief perhaps. Or maybe sadness. Then he lunged at her, arm extended. Hand flat. And suddenly his palm was on her, his crusted, oozing face only inches away.

Cold stabbed through everything, sucking Iseult dry yet stuffing her full. It was like Praga all over again, when Henrick had almost claimed her for the Loom. She was going to explode, to erupt, to collapse inward like broken ice upon a stream. Yet just like in Praga, a distant part of her still reigned. The cold, logical, Threadwitch part her mother had taught her so well. *Lift up your sword*, it said. So Iseult did. *And kill him.*

"May Moon Mother," she gritted out, forcing her eyes to meet the bloodied crevices where his had been, "light your path, and may—"

Steel burst through Corlant's heart, the tip piercing toward Iseult from a saber thrust into his back. A saber she had not wielded and had not seen coming. Blood spewed. Corlant gasped. His palm fell from her forehead, his magic failed.

And warmth rushed over Iseult as her own power roared in.

Corlant collapsed to the snow.

"And may Trickster never find you," said Leopold the Fourth of Cartorra.

The Fool card finally played.

He looked just as he had in the palace when he'd helped Iseult escape: his sword dripped blood and his Threads were a cacophony of color with a wild core that would never fade. The only difference was that now Iseult knew who he was. Knew *what* he was.

"Why?" she asked him.

"Because no one should have to kill their own parent." He sheathed the saber with practiced ease, his Threads briefly shrinking with an inward contemplation. Then he added, "Trust me, I would know."

Corlant's Threads gave a final shivering twist between them, and when Iseult looked down, she found that the lines on her father's forehead had smoothed away. She could almost imagine the man he might have been. Could almost imagine the childhood she might have had if he hadn't been cursed with Portia's soul.

"Let's go." Her gaze lifted to Leopold once more. "There is one more person I must still try to save."

FIFTY-THREE

✳

Safi and Iseult parted ways. Not because Safi wanted to leave her Thread-sister so soon, but because Iseult still had work to do . . . and Safi did too. They would find each other after—Safi made Iseult swear that a thousand times over, and she waited until Iseult was nothing more than a fading silhouette within the trees before she set off too. Then with Caden slumped on a black mare before her, a hundred Hell-Bards trailing behind, she rode to the Emperor's hunting lodge.

And as she rode, Safi surveyed a new world.

Before life as a Hell-Bard, she would have thought it bleak and barren. A wasteland where death crept in on silent, frozen feet. Winter's breath cut into her. Snow blanched everything, and gray forest bled into gray sky.

After life as a Hell-Bard, Safi saw only potential. This winter, like all winters, would end eventually; green would return; the cycle would start anew. In the meantime, life harbored in countless pockets she'd never noticed before. Glimpses of evergreen thick with snow. Paw prints tracing between trees. Birds startling into flight. Holly berries beating red.

So much she had missed. So much she was grateful to see now—and to feel too, with her magic and soul fully returned. Both truth and lie, she sensed with stark clarity. Not merely half of her magic, but somehow the full entirety had been restored. Louder too, like an exuberant chorus living inside her.

True, true, true, it sang. *Free, free, free.*

The hunting lodge soon loomed ahead, perched on a craggy ledge above the Solfatarra. It reminded Safi of a different castle exposed to cold. A different life a hundred miles away. But where her childhood home had fallen into disrepair, the lodge had windows and walls intact, roofs without holes, and life—so much life.

Hasstrel would look that way again soon.

People crawled over the ramparts, moved within windows, and circled the various paths through the forest. Their scarlet uniforms flashed like fires, but no one interfered with Safi's approach on horseback. She was in charge for now. Shambling along at the end of this imperial procession was the Emperor. *Former* Emperor. She was glad she hadn't killed him. The Hell-Bards could decide his fate.

After crossing a wide bridge over a dark-watered moat, Safi's mare reached a wide yard where soldiers and stable hands scurried about. No one argued when she bellowed for a healer. Instead, Hell-Bards rushed to help her. *Freed* Hell-Bards, who could do as they pleased, who wanted to aid her and *wanted* to follow a woman who had once been one of their own.

After ensuring Caden would be properly tended and after ordering a search for Leopold, Zander, and Lev, still somewhere out there, Safi followed a guard to a corner tower where stairs descended into the frozen earth. Each step into candlelit darkness tingled against her skin. So mild at first, she thought she imagined it. Then hotter, itchier, until it burned in her eyes and scratched in her throat.

This was the acid of the Solfatarra. Poison on the skin, poison in the lungs. Safi coughed. Her magic frizzed inside her, and the Truth-lens frizzed against her chest too, as if this whole place was wrong, wrong, *wrong.*

Slivers of panic set in as she walked. No one should have to come here, no prisoner should have to endure. She passed several doors with haggard eyes behind rusted slots. Most of these people, she suspected, were innocents she could free. Anyone else would be moved and healed.

When at last her guard reached a door so narrow, so dark that she saw nothing through the slot, she snatched a weak lantern off the wall and ventured in. Orange light filtered over a long, rectangular space, like two coffins lined toe to head—and over a mound of rags at the back of the room.

The mound coughed, a vicious, solid sound from a throat that had coughed so long, it now had nothing but blood and phlegm to give. She slung the lantern onto a hook and darted forward.

"Uncle." She grabbed hold of the rags. Here was a hand. Here was an arm. Here was a head, covered in matted hair. If not for the sulfur, his unwashed stench would be unbearable. "*Uncle.*" She dug her arms beneath his frail shoulders and tugged him upright.

He groaned, but did not resist. Could not resist, actually, and now fresh coughs laid claim to his broken lungs. Something warm hit Safi's cheek. Spit, she hoped. Blood, she feared.

Eron's face was hidden behind a beard; his eyes were crusted and fathomless. His clothes shimmered ever so slightly, as if they had once been clean velvet—finery worn at court before Henrick had turned on him.

"Laia," he croaked.

Safi's muscles locked. Paused in midlift at her mother's name. Not once—not *once*—in Safi's life had she heard her uncle say his sister's name.

"Laia," he repeated, and his fingers clawed into Safi's forearms. "Why are you here?"

"I'm not . . ." Safi braced him into a seated position on damp stone. "It's me, Safi. Your niece."

He coughed, and more heat splattered Safi's skin. Then he squinted and leaned in. Three inches he moved before he seemed to see. "No," he exhaled. "You cannot be here." With shocking strength, he tore free from Safi's grip and scuttled backward against the wall. "Go away." His voice was a splintered snarl. "*Go away.*"

"I'm here to free you." Safi reached for him again.

He swatted her. Cold, callused hands in the dark. "You cannot help me."

At first, Safi thought he meant it was too late for him. That he had lived here too long, so only death waited ahead. But then he added, "You ruin everything you touch, Safi. Leave this place. Go."

She inhaled slowly, sulfur harsh in her nose and Eron's words harsh in her ears. A familiar knife slid into a familiar hole above her heart, but for once, it did not hurt her. For once, the knife sliced in . . . then sliced right through. Because all these years, she'd misread him. All these years, her magic had fed her lies.

Only with her powers removed had she finally seen the truth.

"No," she said quietly. Then stronger, harder: "No. You don't mean that, Uncle, and you never have. It was all an act. I see that now. A stupid act designed to make me hate you—and I *do* hate you. You succeeded in that.

"But I also know you did it and are still doing it to protect me. All those years, you were the distracting right hand to an emperor who wanted me dead. And all those years, it worked. He never looked my way while you assembled your plan—a vast plan that might have started out pure, but has grown so terrible and wrong along the way.

"Which is why I've done it *my* way, Uncle. Do you hear me?" Safi pushed to her feet and grabbed him. Rough, intractable, she gripped him as if he were a child and heaved him to his feet. "I completed your plan with no bloodshed and no pain. The Hell-Bards are free—*you* are free— and Henrick is deposed. But if you think I'll rule as an Empress, then you're going to be disappointed."

Eron didn't resist her pull—not that he could have. His muscles had atrophied in the month here, and the instant he was on his feet, coughing overtook him. It *was* blood spraying from his mouth. Splattering to the stones as he tried to curve away from her.

Safi was stronger, though, and she hauled him toward the exit. Toward the light. When at last his coughing had subsided, they were almost to the stairs. Clean air brushed down, cold and crisp and alive. "Can you manage these steps or will I have to carry you the entire way?"

Eron growled, a sound Safi had once loathed but now found thoroughly delightful. He would heal in time.

"What do you mean," he rasped, squinting against the natural light. "What do you mean you will not rule?"

She laughed, a harsh sound but not a bitter one. "Just because I was born with the proper bloodline doesn't mean I deserve a throne, Uncle. Besides, you once told me I wasn't cut out for leadership, and since Leopold has worked with you this long, I have no doubt he would be amenable to finishing your plan—"

"Leopold?" Eron coughed. "He . . ." Another cough. "Was not part of our plan." Again, the brutal hacking overtook his lungs, his ribs, his throat. But this time, Safi did not lean in to help him. Instead, she simply held her uncle upright and stared with unseeing eyes at dark weathered steps that led into daylight.

She had been played then. *True, true, true.* And quite neatly too. *True, true, true.* Leopold had not been a part of Eron's plan; he'd had nothing to do with peace in the Witchlands or Mathew or Habim.

"Oh," she said on an acid exhale, and something angry settled across the tops of her bones. She was quite certain now that the Hell-Bards would find no sign of the prince in the Solfatarra.

Wherever he was, he would be very safe. And very alone. But had she completed his plan or ruined it? Likely she would never know, so she dismissed it from her mind.

Then, one step at a time into a rising day, Safi helped her uncle ascend. Toward life with wide eyes. All clear, all clear.

FIFTY-FOUR

＊

The Rook King came for Aeduan, as Aeduan knew he would, materializing from snow-shod trees, his gray clothes blending into shadow. Likely, he had been there some time, watching Aeduan. Perhaps throughout the fight with Evrane, perhaps while Aeduan had stood sentry and sheltered her body against the cursed storm.

He always had been a silent observer—he and that bird of his.

The bird now roosted on his shoulder, button eyes leveled on Aeduan as the Rook King crossed the clearing on sure, determined feet. Snow crunched with each step. His cloak billowed and curls shone. He wore a different face, a different body than one thousand years ago, but the same energy filled him. The sense of someone larger than the frame in which he'd been housed. He could have been an Exalted One a thousand years. They'd certainly courted him instead of Aeduan, but the Rook King had been indomitable in the end.

Aeduan had not. He really had been the weakest.

No more, though. He was ready to give back what should never have been his. Like before, it would not be death, just a return to the dark waters he had endured for so long. He dreaded returning to them. Dreaded the way they bore down, weighted and lightless and eternal. But he had made his choice, exactly as Saria had commanded him.

Evrane, he knew, would not agree. Yet as the Rook King paused before Aeduan with all the poise of a prince inside a palace, Aeduan also knew Evrane would have no choice. The Rook King had allowed their souls to return; now he would send them away.

His blood sang with a choir of scents—*new leather and smoky hearths. Hot springs and empty halls. Hunger and loneliness and musty tomes stacked high.* Dominating them all, though, was the smell that the first Bloodwitch had so fixated on: *clear lake water and frozen winters.* And deep within Aeduan, that first soul sighed. He had the answer that had eluded him for two months. He understood that the scents were not two people, but a Paladin's spirit inside a prince's body.

The Rook King smiled at Aeduan then, a real thing. Sad in a way that only the Old Ones could be. "It will not be the end, Nadje. The Lament is not yet finished with you."

Nadje. So that had been his name. "I will reawaken?" He was ashamed at how much relief wept through him at those words.

"*In light, twelve will meet on lands long contested, while in darkness, the shadow-ender will topple nightmares and the world-starter will build us anew.*"

Now Aeduan was the one to smile, though his smile was not a sad one. He would live again, and in his own body. "When?" he asked.

"Soon." The bird ruffled his feathers upon the Rook King's shoulder, and the Rook King patted him with absentminded affection. "She will awaken too." He dipped his head toward Evrane, still and half frozen upon the snow. "I had hoped that, like you, she would change her mind. Change her course. Then again, I always did have too much faith in people." He sighed through his nose. "Or too little, if you were to ask Her."

"Is She gone forever?" Aeduan asked as the Rook King crossed the final ten paces between them.

"No." He extended a hand, winglike beneath his draping cloak. "Not if we win." Cold fingers grazed Aeduan's forehead. The Rook King's eyes glowed silver, a light Aeduan remembered, as if he too had once possessed such power. "Find me when you wake up, Nadje. We have a great deal of work to do."

The waters swept in. Nadje heard them first, sloshing and soughing like a waterfall awakening. Then he smelled them, crystalline and pure, glacier-formed and snow-fed. Finally, he felt them, as frozen as death but far more eternal. They sapped life and movement, breath and blood. Each of his organs iced over, each of his senses frosted away until there was nothing left but water. Until he was once more drowning and alone.

Yet only in death could he understand life, and only in life would he change the world.

The Bloodwitch named Aeduan returned to his body cold and supine. As the tides of possession receded, his senses expanded. Sunlight warmed his face. Snow melted against his arms. He shivered, and nearby, someone moaned. *Crisp spring water and salt-lined cliffs.*

In a heartbeat he had rolled to his feet. Two more heartbeats and he was over the shallow snow to Evrane's side. Her eyelids cracked apart, squinting against a midday sun. Her teeth chattered.

"Aeduan," she croaked, reaching for him with cold-chapped fingers. He hastily scooped his arms beneath her. She needed warmth—they both did—and a memory unfurled in his mind of this silver-haired monk doing the same to him all those years ago in a tent burned to ember and ash.

"Why," she asked as he hauled her to him, "do I feel like I was eaten by a sea fox?" She leaned heavily on his shoulder. Her Carawen cloak was soaked and torn.

"It's a long story, Monk Evrane." He inhaled deeply, letting his magic pummel to the surface. Strong and alive and entirely his own. *Mountain ranges and cliffsides. Meadows laced with dandelions and truth hidden beneath snow.* The Truthwitch was near. And alongside her was a flicker of his own scent. A flash of blood upon a silver taler that Iseult had had the foresight to reclaim.

It made him smile.

The older monk frowned, and her dark eyes, the lashes snow-flecked, ran over Aeduan's face as if he were only just coming into focus—or as if she were only just realizing they were in a snow-draped forest clasped in cold. "We are not at the Monastery, are we?"

"No." He withdrew slightly and helped her rise. "But the Cahr Awen are near, and we should find them."

She smiled, amused and slightly vicious—but wholly her own and untainted by dark waters. Unsullied by an Old One returned. And as Aeduan guided her toward the trees, toward the truth hidden beneath snow and a silver taler draped in blood, he couldn't help but match her grin.

Evrane was herself again, and as ruthless as ever.

With that truth to warm him, he braced himself firmly against her. Then two rolls of his wrists, a crack of his neck, and together with his mentor, the Bloodwitch named Aeduan set off into the winter's light.

FIFTY-FIVE

※

Vivia stood at the edge of the Origin Well and watched the Dalmotti fleet, mere specks on an ocean bright with sunshine. Any moment now, they would sail past the horizon. Any moment now, and she could finally breathe.

Beside her was Vaness, also watching the Jadansi. Her gown had finally stopped dripping, though her hair still hung in long, damp hanks. Since ascending the rough stairs to the Well, Vivia had said nothing. Vaness had said nothing. They had simply marched across the plateau and taken up sentry above the Nihar coastline.

Somewhere behind them, below them, Shanna negotiated with Yoris so that Vivia and her Foxes might remain here. And though Yoris still hated Vivia, he now also feared her. She had raised a ghost navy; she had scared off a fleet of twelve warships; she had won what Serafin had avoided entirely.

Such stories would cross the Witchlands. Vivia and Vaness could earn enemies from it—but also gain many more allies to their cause.

When at last there were no more ships upon the waves—when even her spyglass could discern nothing—Vivia's lungs unwound. Though only slightly, for there was still so much to do. A village that needed repairing, a shoreline that needed fortifying, and a future that needed planning.

She turned away from the sea. Vaness, however, did not. Her gaze had turned glassy, her focus somewhere on the middle distance.

"We strike," the Empress said softly, "which justifies that they strike, which justifies that we strike. And it goes back and forth for all eternity. Echoes bouncing across a cavern, except that in a cavern, the sounds eventually fade. With war . . ."

"It only grows." Vivia ran her fingers over her spyglass, the brass warm and reflecting the sun. "Justice, we called it here, but in truth, it was just a reason to fight. I would have killed you and all of Marstok, Empress, because it's what I was taught to do."

Vaness swallowed. Her eyes, dark and sunlit, dragged to Vivia's face. "I do not blame you. I was the one who let Nubrevna become a wasteland, all in the name of protecting my people. I never questioned if my methods were right. I simply believed they had to be done." She squared her body to Vivia, her fingers reaching for Vivia's hands.

And rather than withdraw like she always did, Vivia slid her glass into her pocket and allowed Vaness to clasp them. The Empress's touch was cool. The salt wind wefted through her hair. "How do we change that echo? If we try to reclaim our thrones, people will die. How do we keep that from escalating into war?"

"I don't know," Vivia answered honestly. "But I do know that I don't want to kill you anymore, Empress. It's . . . well, it's hard to truly hate someone you know."

The Empress laughed, a wry rush of air over lips reddened from the sun. "So the solution to continental war is getting to know each other?"

And now Vivia laughed too. The idea sounded absurd when Vaness put it that way. "Well, it certainly can't make things worse."

"No." The Empress squeezed Vivia's hands, a brief burst of pressure before she withdrew. Strangely, Vivia wished she hadn't.

"Why the questions?" Vivia scrubbed the back of her head. "Why the doubt? Yesterday you were proclaiming us Well Chosen and convincing me to gallivant into open rebellion."

"Ah, but doubt is *good*." Vaness arched her spine, face cresting toward the sky. "It means we question our choices. It means we look for better solutions. In Marstok, we have a saying: They who see only one way forward are they who step off the cliff." She glided forward as if to do just that, and without thinking—without pausing to realize that *of course* Vaness wasn't going to stride off the plateau and into the sea—Vivia slung her arms around the Empress.

She whirled Vaness toward her and clutched her close. Chest-to-chest, clothes wet and faces flushed. And though Vivia ought to pull away now that she realized it had been a joke, she didn't.

Vaness didn't either. Her eyes moved to Vivia's lips, and Vivia realized in a vague, incredulous sort of way that the Empress wanted to kiss her.

An earnest voice shouted from across the Well: "Your Majesty, Your Majesty!"

Vivia jolted; Vaness flinched, and as they lurched apart, heat billowed up from Vivia's ribs, from a firepot that had gone off inside her chest and was now burning, burning, boiling through her.

"Your Majesty," Cam called again, oblivious to the scene he'd interrupted as his booted feet slapped over flagstones and around cypress trees. He came to a panting stop before Vivia and Vaness. "We've . . . had word," he gasped, "from the Red . . . Sails. They're attacking the Dalmotti ships and want to know . . . if we'd like to take Captain Kadossi into our custody."

Vivia and Vaness locked eyes—Vivia's wide, the Empress's razor thin. "Well, this is unexpected," Vivia murmured. Her thoughts were flustered, her skin aflame from a kiss she'd seen in Vaness's eyes.

"That is a vast understatement," the Empress replied, while the iron at her wrists shivered restlessly. If she was flustered, she didn't show it. "He could be useful to us."

"He could also be dangerous," Vivia countered. "And we shouldn't accept gifts from pirates."

"Says the woman who was a pirate."

Vivia shook her head. Then shook it more emphatically when Vaness's expression remained unchanged. "You cannot possibly think we should take him, Empress. The Red Sails have no reason to aid us. This is clearly a trap."

"Or perhaps they simply know which side will win the war." Vaness turned to Cam. "Tell the Red Sails we will take Captain Kadossi into our custody immediately—"

"Cam," Vivia snapped, "tell the Red Sails we will *not* take Captain Kadossi."

"—and then contact the Doge," the Empress finished. "We will want to ransom the man."

"No, we absolutely will not." A new heat brewed in Vivia's chest. "I will not have Red Sails or Dalmotti captains on Nubrevnan soil, Empress. This is my homeland, and we will do things *my* way. I believe I've warned you about disobedience before . . ." She trailed off at the sight of Cam, his face green with horror.

Clearly the poor boy didn't want to risk disobeying either of his majesties.

And Vivia couldn't help it: she started laughing. First it was just a bark of air, but then it quickly burgeoned and bloomed into something so full and rich, she couldn't contain it. And the more she laughed, the more furious and tense the Empress became—which only made Vivia laugh harder. It just toppled out of her, as relentless as a burst dam.

She couldn't remember when she'd laughed this hard. Months ago. Years. Maybe never.

Eventually, even Cam was chuckling too, albeit nervously. Vaness, however, remained wrathful. "What," she said in a voice made of ice chips, "is so funny?"

"Us," Vivia squeezed out between laughs. "You . . . and I. The world might be a mess, Empress, but . . ." Noden save her, were there *tears* in her eyes? "But you and I are still just two bitches in an alley who think we own the street outside."

"I have no idea what you mean."

"And you don't need to know." Vivia wiped her eyes and towed the Empress toward her—a familiar movement with her arm slinging around Vaness's shoulders. And though she could tell Vaness really didn't want to smile, the Empress also couldn't quite hold one at bay. "Lead us to Noden's Gift, Cam," Vivia said, tugging the Empress into a saunter. "And as we walk, Her Majesty and I will discuss calmly—like the logical, *thoughtful* Well Chosen that we are—why she is for and I am opposed to working with the Red Sails. I shall go first."

"No." Vaness bristled against her. "I will go first."

Vivia only laughed all over again.

On the beach below the Origin Well, Stix stared up at the woman who was her Threadsister and her queen. Vivia had just abandoned the cliff's edge, her arm around an empress while the wind tangled her hair and toyed with her coat. One step, two steps, three, and she was gone.

A knot clenched in Stix's belly as the lens-shattered image of Vivia, the Empress, and Cam disappeared. It wasn't indigestion, it wasn't hunger, and it wasn't her moon cycle either. Yet it hurt as much as all of them combined, and she kneaded uselessly at her belly. Ryber had been right when she had warned Stix not to come back to say goodbye.

With a harsh puff of air, she launched herself for the nearest cluster of jungle. Hunters and sailors and civilians prowled within the trees, but Ryber had traced a path separate from prying eyes. Stix ducked around a cypress and found Kahina waiting for her, leaning against the edge of the Origin Well's plateau. White streaks of limestone marked her red coat.

"You will come here again one day."

"I know," Stix said, even if her gut wasn't so sure.

"We are here to protect the people, nothing more. That was always the mistake of the Exalted Ones—pushing the levers of the land where all could see, and then growing bitter when the people did not appreciate. Praise is not ours to claim, though, Water Brawler. Paladins were not meant to rule."

"I don't want praise. I don't want to rule."

"If not that, then . . . Ah." Kahina's face relaxed, and Stix hated the pity in her eyes. "You are not the first Paladin to fall for their charge."

"I don't know what you mean." Stix strode past Kahina; pipe smoke wafted up her nostrils.

"Of course you do." Kahina trailed behind, unhurried. "I loved my ruler once too, and I have never loved anyone as much as I loved them. But they could not love me in return, for that was not what they were put here to do."

Stix walked faster, noisier than she ought to have been, desperate to end this conversation. Ferns lashed against her knees. Nettle pricked against her forearms.

"*Wait*." Kahina's hand grabbed Stix's forearm, and though Stix wanted to bark at the other woman to *leave her be*, she allowed Kahina to tow her to a stop. She couldn't help it. Rhian had once been a comfort to Baile; their souls still sang to each other. "You will see your queen in her golden crown," Kahina told her, "just as I will see mine wearing a crown of iron. But it will not be two crowns, so much as one woven together."

Stix gritted her teeth, wishing those words didn't have such pointed fangs. "You mean they will rule as one."

"I do." Kahina sucked a long drag from her pipe. Smoke hissed out between her teeth. "That is what our great maker wants, and it is best to accept such reality now. It will save you from heartache in the end."

Stix's teeth gnashed all the harder, but she could no more deny Kahina's words than she could the sea always inside her veins. And Ryber's cards *had* warned her, even if she hadn't wanted to see.

The Queen of Hawks, the Queen of Foxes, and the Giant.

"Come." Kahina released her hold on Stix and pushed through the jungle. Stix followed more slowly, her fingers scraping over limestone while the jungle clicked and wheezed around her. She had come here a month ago, following the voices. *Come this way, keep coming.* It had been so easy back then, when she had thought she would soon return to

Vivia's side. And despite what Kahina might say, Stix wasn't abandoning that hope yet.

She missed Vivia. She missed her father. She missed the Cleaved Man and she missed home.

Soon, Stix caught up to Kahina, now standing before a jagged doorway sliced into the limestone. It was one of only a few passages remaining into the Sightwitch mountain, though it was half destroyed. Blue light hummed around it. Nearby, Ryber shuffled her cards absently, watching Stix approach with a sympathetic slant to her brow. She never missed anything; Stix sometimes wished she would.

Fortunately, Ryber said nothing as she tucked away her cards. "Ready?" she asked, and at Stix's and Kahina's nods, she dipped low and stepped through. Static frizzed over Stix's skin. Ryber disappeared.

Kahina went next, pipe still puffing even as she ducked through and her smoke winked away. Then it was only Stix who remained, Stix still lingering. All she wanted to do was run—sprint right back to Vivia and say, *I'm so sorry I left. I'll never go again.* But that wasn't her path. Not yet, at least.

There was work to be done. The rest of the Six were waiting for her, and strange as it was, she missed these people she didn't really know. They were old family with Threads still bound to hers..

Yet before Stix could scrabble through the canted doorway, a familiar purr crooned over the jungle's choir. Moments later, a furry cat rubbed against her calf.

And Stix laughed as she peered down at the six-fingered tabby. "I don't know how you always find me." She hefted up the creature. "But I'll admit I'm glad to see you." Then she hugged the tabby close, and murmured: "Though we cannot always see the blessing in the loss, strength is the gift of our Lady Baile, and she will never abandon us."

Together, Stix and the familiar six-fingered tabby entered the Sightwitch mountain.

FIFTY-SIX

✳

The prince awoke to a dog howling. He couldn't say how he recognized the sound; he'd never had a dog, and they had been rare in the Nihar lands. With so many human mouths to feed, the only animals worth keeping had been livestock.

Yet somehow Merik *knew* as soon as he came into blurry consciousness that a tiny hound called for him. The sound scratched against his eardrums, part whimper, part wail. Sharp and hungry and alone. He wanted it to end as soon as he heard it.

With monumental effort, Merik forced open his eyelids. Cold scraped against the flesh. Ice whispered against his pupils. Then they were wide. Then he could *see*. Blue, blue, brilliant, glowing blue. No end, no beginning . . .

Except for that shadow.

No, three shadows, he realized the longer he stared. Two that were vaguely human, though small and lithe. And the final shadow that was the source of all that whining—a massive mound, far too large to be a puppy, yet keening like one all the same.

"She needs a master," the taller of the humanlike shadows declared. She had to yell to be heard, and her voice was high and melodic. *A child*, Merik thought at the same time he realized the language she used: old Arithuanian. He'd never actually heard it spoken aloud before.

"She needs a master," the girl repeated. Then the second shadow piped up: "And Sirmaya says that for now, it'll have to be you." She laughed, the delighted sound of a child feeling genuine pleasure, and for the first time since Merik's awakening, the puppy's cries faded to silence. Its shadowy form shifted. Then unfurled, stretching into a creature far larger than the two girls—and larger than Merik too.

"You'll have to hurry," the first girl said. "Because the ice is hungry, and if you don't break free, it will eat the baby. But you can do it, Wind King. I saw it, and so it will be."

"However," the second girl inserted, "there's one thing you have to do once you're free: you have to find our father. Right, Lizzie?"

A shadowy nod. "Sirmaya tells me he's in Poznin right now. He calls himself the Raider King, though I don't believe it's a name he gave himself. Find him and help him," she added, no begging in her childish voice. Only command. "His goal is a noble one, if misguided in the end. Now come along, Cora. We have work to do." She grasped at the smaller girl. Then together they turned, and together they left, vanishing shadows soon absorbed by blue.

Which left only the puppy still waiting nearby. It was whining again and beneath its shrill cries, a crunching, crackling sound tore out. It vibrated through the ice, juddered Merik's whole body, and through the blue that clouded his eyes, he glimpsed frozen shards bursting up from the floor.

The child had been right: if he didn't hurry, the ice would eat the puppy just as it had eaten him.

The puppy's whines turned to screams, and without thought, Merik found himself fighting. Punching and kicking and calling to winds in a tomb made of ice. With each howl of canine pain, he clawed. With each wail, he slashed with tiny razors of wind. Until he too was howling and wailing and screaming, like the puppy being ripped apart.

Then abruptly he and his magic were free. One moment, the ice still imprisoned Merik. The next, he was erupting forth on a thousand vicious winds. Each of the winds was so small it was insignificant, but when corralled together, they had become a cyclone.

He toppled forward, his winds razing outward to crush any ice that chained the puppy down. Yet as he collapsed to the frozen floor, he saw it was no puppy at all—at least not in the traditional sense.

It was a storm hound.

And now, free of the ice, she stumbled toward him on long, loping legs. Floppy and golden-furred, her wings dragging and her tail wagging hesitantly. Then she was to Merik and nuzzling against him, bleating like a babe who'd lost her mom.

She needs a master, the strange girl had said. And then the second girl had added, *And Sirmaya says that for now, it will have to be you.*

"All right," Merik rasped, his first words in what might have been only hours or might have been centuries. "Let's leave this tomb and return to life." As he clambered to unsteady feet, the storm hound helped him rise with all the enthusiasm of a puppy excited to play. And as he shuffled toward the tomb's narrow exit, she galloped ahead, all memories of her near death forgotten. All fear of the ice erased.

Merik glanced back only once before trudging after her. Three empty holes now rested, gouged into the ice. One had been Merik's. The other two, he presumed, had belonged to the strange little girls. The fourth and final hole remained filled with shadow.

"I'll be back for you, Kull," Merik said. "Come floods or hell-waters, I'll be back for you." Then he turned away, tugged at his ice-shredded cuffs, and followed the storm hound into a nautilus-shaped hallway beyond.

Aurora, he decided. He would call her Aurora.

FIFTY-SEVEN

✳

Aeduan found her at the Purist camp. It belonged to the Nomatsis again, and to his initial shock and wariness, Cartorran soldiers were there too. But no one paid him or Evrane any mind. There was too much carnage to clean up, too many wounds to heal for anyone to notice two monks wandering through. So Aeduan and Evrane ignored the Nomatsis and Cartorrans in kind.

After leaving Evrane with a Nomatsi healer to ensure she had no permanent wounds, Aeduan traced through the encampment. Each step made his fingers flex, and for some reason, he couldn't seem to draw full breaths. It felt as if a fist was closing around his lungs the deeper he entered the camp—and the nearer he came to the silver taler.

Its scent was muddied by other bloods that oozed from wounds or coagulated on corpses. Laced faintly beneath it all was a sky that sang with snow and meadows drenched in moonlight. He knew what that scent was now.

The Sleeping Giant. The goddess at the heart of everything. Iseult called her Moon Mother; Evrane called her Noden; but she was both of them—and more—in the end.

When at last Aeduan found the silver taler, its owner was tucked behind a ruin wall. Alone with her palms outstretched into a sunbeam. Even from here, he could see the skin was puckered and raw. These were the sort of scars that even salves would never erase.

Her fingers were stretched long, making branch-like shadows dance across the snow. She didn't notice him, and he hovered ten paces away, trapped in indecision. Should he speak, should he approach, should he walk away?

He settled on clearing his throat.

She startled, whipping toward him with wide, golden eyes. They were bloodshot from exhaustion, but when they found his face, they didn't waver.

They never did.

Her nose twitched. She lowered her hands. "It . . . is you."

He nodded. Words suddenly seemed impossible. Both because his throat had stopped working and because he couldn't think of anything to say. He wished he had his Carawen cloak still. He wished he had armor.

She moved first, taking a cautious step. Then two. Her gaze, unabashed, scanned over him, and he found himself doing the same. She was not the girl he had met two months ago on a dusty road beside Veñaza City. Nor was she the Threadwitch who had broken his spine and stabbed him in the heart. She was not even the Weaverwitch who had dragged him into an Origin Well because her resolve was stronger than death's.

He didn't know who she was now, and he could see from the faint pinching on her brow that she felt the same. It took her four steps to reach him. "You found me," she said.

"Always," he replied, his voice strained. Having her so near was . . . not painful, but something close to it, and he had no idea how to proceed. For a month, all he'd wanted was to be with her again. Now that he had found her, he found himself lost.

He had forgotten how big she was. Not physically, but the general essence of her. She filled the entirety of this snowy space, somehow sharpening the edges of it like a lens clears sight. The sun shone brighter. The air bit colder. The scar beside her eye flickered like a real tear.

He could not stop staring at it—that scar. Or her eyes. Or her lips. They were pinker than he remembered, as were her cheeks, flushed with winter cold. And maybe with something more, although he could not find a word for it.

Her hand lifted. She reached for his face, but he caught her wrist before she could touch him, break him, shatter him like ice atop a stream. His eyes moved to the damage on her palms. Frostbite. Or burns. Or both. "You're hurt."

"It will heal," she replied, but now it was her voice that was strained. Her cheeks flushed brighter. Her nose wiggled.

Then she leaned in, a quick, almost frightened movement, and pressed her lips to his jaw.

No, she *almost* pressed her lips to his jaw. Instead, she paused just below the ear, where her breath could whisper against his skin. Where he could pull back in case he did not want her there. But he didn't pull back, and so her lips grazed over his skin. So lightly, he feared he might be imagining it.

Too much! his instincts screamed at him. *Too much! Retreat!* But Aeduan didn't retreat because inexplicably, the too much was also not enough.

She kissed him a second time, her lips more firm, more sure, and he definitely was not imagining it. His body told him that—the way his lungs constricted and his stomach dropped low. The way his magic charged to life and his fingers, still clasped around her wrist, tightened until he could feel her pulse thrumming against them.

He wanted to turn into it. He wanted to find the same spot on her jaw and try to kiss her too, but he found he could not move.

It was too much, too much. The feel of her lips, both hesitant and sure. The feel of her breath, warm in this wintry world of stone and forgotten time. He had faced armies and monsters. He had died and been brought back to life. Yet somehow, Iseult was more daunting than all of them.

Eventually, she pulled away and she smiled at him—a sly, subtle movement only visible if you knew what you were looking for.

He always knew what he was looking for.

"I am glad you're back," she said, and he nodded faintly, letting his fingers release so she could withdraw her pattering pulse.

He had no words to offer as she turned away, nor even breath to sustain them. Not that he needed to speak. The words that mattered most had already raveled between them on a Thread he could not see.

Mhe varujta. Te varuje.

Iseult didn't know if her plan would work. After all, it was just a story. But all stories had roots in truth, and the specifics had been so similar to what Eridysi had written that she had to at least try.

The moon gleamed down, no longer full but bright enough to see by. A perfect hour for Threadwitching. A perfect hour for a Voidwitch with sparkles of Aether in her blood.

Alma's body lay shrouded beneath a pale sheet upon the ground. Iseult had brushed away the previous night's snow. Nearby, the spring Iseult had once gazed into burbled into the quiet winter night.

On a bare stone, Eridysi's diary lay open to the page about reanimation. Owl had left the diary for her beneath their spruce tree, along with a single mountain-bat claw. The length of her old moon-scythe blade and just as sharp, it now rested atop the weathered page. Iseult had already imagined ways to fasten it to a handle. Crude but deadly, just like Owl.

Iseult walked in a slow circle, unwinding a strip of gray thread her mother had given her. First a circle around her, then zigzags across Alma's still form. And as she walked, she tugged at the broken Threads within herself. Little severed beacons meant to draw Alma's soul into life.

All the mistakes Iseult had made—so many—and all the relationships she'd lost. *It didn't have to be this way. We didn't have to be this way.* Like drawing poison from a wound, she pulled out each splinter that had festered too long beneath her left lung. Round and round she walked until the entirety of the gray thread was gone.

Then she began anew, except this time with magenta thread. This time with thoughts of love and memories of affection. The times she and Alma had played with dolls made of straw, had climbed an oak tree and gotten stuck in its branches, had discovered eggs hatching and tens of tiny turtles waddling toward a marsh. Every instance in which they had acted not as rivals but as the sisters they could have been.

And finally, Iseult draped sage-green thread over Alma's body, envisioning what she wanted for Alma's future. The friendship and connection they could share—and *would* share once Alma's Threads had returned.

Because this would work; it had to work. Where Portia had only ever used gray, had only ever tapped into the Threads that break, Iseult was drawing on all three Threads. Life contained love, loss, and growth, each powerful in its own unique way.

When at last all the threads were unfurled, and all the Threads poured forth from Iseult's being, she whispered the words all Threadwitches used when focusing their magic: "Bind and bend. Build and blossom. Family fills the heart." She'd never gotten those words to work before, but this time . . .

This time was different.

Iseult smiled up at her goddess. The night smiled down, washing her in silver light. She might not be like Safi, golden and gleaming and good, but that didn't mean she was only destined for darkness. It didn't mean she had to live in shadow.

After all, the moon shone light too.

Iseult turned away from Alma's body. There was nothing more to do but wait for the Threads to work.

"Come," Gretchya said, stepping from the trees. A tension hugged her muscles, a tautness in her arms as if she wanted to offer Iseult her hand or an embrace, but, as was the curse of all Threadwitches, still did not know how.

And if Iseult was being honest with herself, she didn't mind. It wasn't as if she had become an expert at this new stasis overnight. If anything, she felt more awkward and unsure than she had before. But maybe one day, she and her mother would figure out some way to show they cared. Maybe one day, this stiffness between them would grow into something comfortable.

Maybe.

"Your Threadsister claims to know a good spiced-wine recipe." Gretchya rubbed the cold off her arms. "It will be ready soon, back at camp."

Iseult grimaced. "S-Safi's idea of good is relative, Mother." She paused. Swallowed. "Yes, it's better than what Habim used to make, but that isn't saying much."

Now Gretchya grimaced. A stiff and awkward expression, but an attempt all the same. "Then perhaps I should make it."

Iseult nodded. "And we'll save a mug for Alma." She gave the Thread-wrapped sheet a final glance and offered a final prayer to Moon Mother, who had been watching over Iseult all along. Not Trickster, not Wicked Cousin, but the goddess who did indeed look out for her own, just as Alma had told her.

Iseult joined her mother at the edge of a silver fir, and side by side, they entered the night. Stasis through and through, in their fingers and in their toes.

TRICKSTER

✳

The Rook King gazes down at the body, covered in so many threads and Threads. It has been a long time since he has returned a soul permanently to its body, and even longer since he has returned it to a body dead this long. He hasn't attempted such magic since Sirmaya became the Sleeper. He isn't sure it will work without Her there. But he also knows he would do anything to see the shadow-ender happy, and so he will at least try.

Not that she will ever know. Or see him again as an ally. His work is done, his plan set in motion. There will be no stopping the Lament now.

The weasel squeaks at him as she curls tightly around his neck. She is pleased with her work, and he nods. "I am pleased with your work too. You guided her well."

Preening on a branch nearby, the Rook huffs. So needy, he seems to say, but the Rook King only sends him a sideways smile. "You were once the same."

He pets the weasel, enjoying how she purrs. Enjoying the sensation of reciprocated love. Perhaps he should bind dying souls into animals more often. After all, it is the closest he will ever have to friends. Am-lejatu, she had called him. The life-sleeper. He wishes it were less true.

He kneels and rests a hand over the dead girl's forehead. A cold cloth and threads hardened to ice pierce against his palm. Portia has always used this pose to claim Threads. He uses it to give them back.

His eyes close. "Save the bones," he murmurs, exactly as he'd done once a thousand years ago. "Save the bones. Lost without them, have no home. Wrapped in twine to keep them grounded, trapped in time and moonlight crown'd them."

Nothing happens.

And he sighs. It was worth trying, but now he feels foolish. A grown man trying to raise the dead with a song from a child's tale. Yet as he pushes to his feet, the clouds part. Sirmaya's silver sheen flickers down, and one by one, the Threads offered up from the shadow-ender slide first into the physical threads. Then those threads dissolve into the sheet, into the body.

The girl stirs. Another little hedgehog saved, and the Rook King glances at the moon. *Although She is gone from this world, Her help still comes at a price. "How else do we keep balance?" She used to say. "For every light, there is a shadow, and for every shadow, a light."*

It is all too painfully true, and he is still paying for a shadow he'd cast a thousand years ago. An accident, a misstep, a misunderstanding that ultimately ruined the goddess they all loved so dearly, even the Exalted Ones.

He doesn't make it back to the cover of trees before Little Sister materializes before him, stepping around a silver fir and into the clearing. She has her mountain bat with her, though the beast hides within the forest, silent despite his size. The bat cannot hide his silvery, immortal Threads, though—or his stench.

"I remember you now," she says in her child's voice. "You made me very sad."

"Which one?"

"All of them."

He watches her glide over the snow toward him. She has always moved with an animal grace; it is especially strange in this child's body. She pauses before him, on the opposite side of the stream. Cold, midnight waters trickle between them. "'Stones in motion,'" she quotes. "'Tools cleft in two. The wyrm fell to the daughter made of moonlight long ago. He just did not know it yet.' Well, he certainly knows now, though I wonder why you killed him in the end."

He sniffs. "I had to ensure the job was done."

"Liar." She laughs, a sound that echoes with who she'd been a thousand years ago. It makes his heart hurt to hear. "But that has always been your problem, hasn't it? Keeping secrets. Playing a game without sharing the rules. Tell me, Trickster—"

"Do not call me that."

"—is it hubris that makes you this way? Or is it that deep down, you are so lonely you want to be caught. That you have always wanted to be caught, just so someone would notice you are still here."

His teeth grind in his ears. "So you have come to gloat, have you?"

"Not entirely." She sighs and extends an open palm, watching as the snow lands upon her skin. "I have come to persuade. You have always controlled people sideways. Manipulating and guiding, but never directly confronting."

"Spoken like an Earthwitch."

"But in the end, no human can truly be another's puppet—and no human can truly be a puppeteer. You would have been better served telling them the truth, just as you would have a thousand years ago with the Six. With me."

He glares at her now, unable to maintain his careful cool. She has always had this effect on him. "I was not the one to betray you, Saria. The Lament was wrong. The one who turned on five was never me."

"No," she says with a sad smile. "I don't think it was." Her hand finally falls, and she turns away from the Rook King, away from the dark, whispering stream between them.

"I tried to give the Cahr Awen an army," he calls after her, more bitter than he wants to be—and certainly more bitter than he wants Saria to hear. "I tried to give them soldiers that would keep them safe, but they rejected my plans in the end."

"You mean they rejected you." She glances back with her glittering teardrop eyes. "Just as She once did. Because you love no one but yourself and you will always be alone." Then, as she strides away once more, leaving tiny footprints in her wake, a soft song ripples across the clearing:

"Never trust what you see in the shadows,
for Trickster he hides in darkness and dapples.
High in a tree, deep underground,
never trust when Trickster's around."

ACKNOWLEDGMENTS

There are always so many people to thank at the end of a book. This book in particular was a beast—the ultimate craft challenge of my life while I was going through a lot of personal upheaval too. It took me far more time than any other book to finish, and I owe so many thanks to the *incredible* team at Tor Teen for supporting me the entire way. And I also have to shout-out to my editors, Diana Gill and Lindsey Hall. This book finally found its shape because of you.

To my friends Alex Bracken, Erin Bowman, Leigh Bardugo, Victoria Aveyard, and Shanna Hughes: I leaned on you all so *hard* throughout this book, creatively and emotionally. Thank you for always being there.

To Melody Simpson, Samantha Tan, Sanya Macadam, Melissa Lee, Cait Listro: thank you for being early readers who helped me both fix the gaping story holes and find the problematic plot points—all while cheering me on when I needed it most.

To Joanna Volpe, Jordan Hill, Abigail Donoghue, and the entire team at New Leaf: we've been together a decade—can you believe it?—and you're still the best advocates and friends a gal could ever ask for.

To Mom and Dad, David and Jen, I hope you enjoy this story that is all about family. Know that I love you, even if I'm not the best at saying it or showing it. It's written here, so that makes it true.

To the Frenchman: the last two years of our life were one heck of a *journey*. We logged hundreds of IVF needles and more loss than I want to look back on, but we made it. Together. And now we have a beautiful, perfect human to show for it. I have never loved you more.

And to that beautiful, perfect human: I started drafting this book when you were just an embryo being formed for IVF, and I finished writing it shortly after you were born. Becoming your mom was the best choice I ever made, Cricket, and the best battle I ever fought. It wasn't until you existed in this world that I could finally understand Gretchya's character. This story is for you.

Finally, to the Witchlanders (or are you DenNerds now?), *thank you!!!!* I cannot say it enough or add enough exclamation points to fully encompass how grateful I am. This series exists because of you and for you, and our cozy community has been my safe spot for the past three years. I truly hope you've enjoyed *Witchshadow*.